MESSINA

CRIME

FAMILY

BOOK FO

Savage WOUNDS

LILIAN HARRIS

Editing/Interior Formatting: CPR Editing

Proofreader: Judy's Proofreading

Cover Design: Kate Decided to Design

*This one is for all the girls who love a broken boy.
Of course, the boy also wears a mask and stalks
you, because what's a story without that?*

One

KAYLA

The world is full of monsters. Some show their faces, while others hide in plain sight, waiting for their chance to take you alive.

I've met my share. Watched as they shed their skins until all that was left was the savagery beneath.

And once they show you who they are, there's no reason for them to hide any longer. They'll make you beg and bleed until all you have are tears. But see, they're useless against monsters. Your tears only strengthen them.

I should know.

My monsters took everything from me.

Tore the soul from my bleeding body while I lay there on the ground, wishing for it to be over.

I was theirs for nine and a half brutal years. Raped, sold, tortured until I begged to die. But I had my friend Elsie to live for.

We kept each other alive somehow.

I often think back on the day that started it all. The day we were taken, all three of us. And I regret it instantly. I'd go back in time and tell us not to go.

Just stay. Fuck the road trip.

We were young, only nineteen. Just children. But we stopped being little girls as soon as they took us.

Jade's mom didn't want us to go.

Neither did my parents, but they wanted me to make my own choices.

If it's what you want, honey, then we won't stop you.

I wish they had.

Though they don't like to bring up what happened, I know my parents wish the same. Wish they had forced me to stay home. Locked me up in my room and thrown away the key.

Instead, we left—Elsie, Jade, and I. We decided to have one last adventure together before college started. But things took an ugly turn when our car broke down in the middle of an empty highway. And that was when we met our first monsters. Men who worked for our captors.

They shot us and took us away to be sold like property, stripped of our dignity and pride. Jade was separated from us, but Elsie and I endured together all those years.

We were nothing but toys for the ones who owned us.

Faro Bianchi and his brothers ran the Palermo crime family. Dirty and vicious, they took everything from us.

They ran a members-only sex club, where men wore those fancy masquerade masks that covered everything but their eyes. They did whatever they wanted to us…for the right price, of course.

We were nothing but dollar signs.

Elsie and I were forced to work at the club more times than I can remember. Other times, we were shipped off to fancy hotels where rich, powerful men pretended we were theirs for a night or two.

Often, I envisioned my death. Or theirs. Or both, if I'm honest. I wanted to kill them all. I wanted to pick up a knife and stab them in their throat. Over and over until they stopped breathing. Stopped touching me. Touching us.

My heart beats fast as thoughts of the past run rampant.

When they were inside me, I'd smile as I pictured their blood dripping from their throats. Once they were done, I'd realize it was just me and my imagination making me think I had power. But I had nothing but skin and bones.

And even that wasn't mine anymore.

If I hadn't been weak and pathetic, I could've done it. I could've killed them. So what if I'd ended up dead in the process? I was already dead anyway.

But then I'd think of Elsie and cry into the stained pillow. I couldn't leave her. I was all she had, and vice versa. So I let the pain consume me until all I had were tears.

But monsters don't care about tears. They're hungry for pain to satisfy their pleasure.

And night after night, I gave them that.

I gave them everything I had. And now I'm left with eternal emptiness.

Once upon a time, I dreamed of becoming an oncologist. I wanted to help people get rid of cancer. But instead, I fed the cancer that was my torment. I gave the men power. I gave them everything they wanted. Because I had no choice.

Girls like me had no other options but to submit.

It's been four months since I was freed by people who hated the Bianchis as much as we did. Jade's boyfriend, Enzo Cavaleri, and his brothers destroyed that family. Killed them all.

But recently…

My heart lurches.

Recently, someone started trafficking again in their name. I try not to think about it. Because between that and the murders, I'll lose my mind.

There's been a serial killer on the loose. The Midnight Murderer is what they call him, and every day I wonder when they'll catch him. *If* they'll catch him.

But I have to focus on the good things, like reuniting with both Elsie and Jade again. It's a miracle none of us thought we'd ever get.

I was without Elsie for about a month, and I hated that I no longer had her with me, but I stayed strong. I didn't tell anyone where she was. Even when they tortured me.

I was happy she managed to get away. Happy that she found the perfect opportunity to escape, running off into a strange man's car who happened to show up at the house we were kept in.

She begged me to come with her, tried to refuse to leave without me, but I made her go, knowing that my cowardice would only consume her. She didn't need to pay the price for my weakness. So she left, vowing to come back for me.

And she tried. But once those bastards realized she was gone, they moved me and the other girls. Elsie looked for me, but it was Jade who found me. And a few days later, we all found each other.

Now we're free. We have a second chance. Something to live for.

But me? I'm still there, trapped in a timeless loop of hell. I want them all to suffer. I want them all to pay. But I know that'll never happen now.

Because most of them are dead, while the others are rotting in prison.

That should've brought me some peace.

But it hasn't.

That's not enough. It'll never be enough.

I began seeing a therapist at Helping Hand, a center for trafficked women that Jade recently started. Can't say it's doing much, though.

I go every week. Talk about my feelings. Some of what happened to me. But it doesn't do a thing.

Maybe I'm just broken. And some broken things can't be fixed, no matter how badly you wish they could.

I started boxing and taking self-defense classes recently as a way to release all this rage. But instead, it just reminds me why I'm still so angry, still pounding on the bars that kept me caged.

When my fists connect with the punching bag, I imagine it's *their* faces. Their grins, their laughs. And I destroy them. I let their blood fuel my rage, even for a moment. Even if it isn't real.

I won't be weak again. I won't be the girl I used to be. It's different now.

I'm different.

I have to be.

It's the only way I can survive this world where bad men roam free, preying on the next weak woman they can find.

"Did you hear me, Kayla?" Doctor Eric Collins calls, his smile as soft as his crystal-blue eyes. "Do you need a minute?"

No. I need a new fucking life. Think you can help with that?

But of course, I don't say that. Kayla is nice to people. She doesn't talk like that. Doesn't let anyone see what's truly behind her pretty mask.

A flush creeps across my cheeks, for losing myself for a moment and forgetting where I am: in his office at Helping Hand.

"It's a lot to process," he goes on. "The things that are happening are bound to be triggering for you, and you need to be able to talk about them."

I give him a tight-lipped smile, but I snicker to myself.

Yeah, murders are definitely triggering for people like me, especially when there's a damn serial killer on the loose, raping and killing women.

"I can understand if speaking to me about this is hard. So if you prefer a female therapist, I can refer you to someone else."

Helping Hand has a bunch of them on staff, but he's the one I connected with. I don't know why. Maybe because he didn't push like the other two I tried out did. He gave me space to talk as much or as little as I wanted. He has a kindness to him, and I almost forgot men can be kind. It's been so long since I met one like that, so when I was in his office and felt this ease, I chose him.

My eyes find his, and I let out a deep sigh. "It's not about who I talk to. It's talking about it at all that's the problem."

He nods and lifts his black frames up the bridge of his nose. Dr. Collins has been as helpful as he possibly can be. Providing me with techniques to deal with my anxiety and panic attacks, giving me a safe space where I can tell him my worst thoughts. And he's heard them all—the things I wish I could do to those men if I had the chance. He just listens and writes his notes on that yellow notepad he carries with him. But I don't let him know all my thoughts. Those are mine, and no one has a claim to them.

Maybe that's why therapy sucks for me. I can't really open up. I can't be myself. Not with anyone. Not even with my friends, which is odd since they know exactly what I went through. They went through it too. But unlike me, they're managing. They're living their lives. Sure, they're hurting in their own way, but not like me. I'm glad about that, though. They should be happy.

But when will *I* be happy?

Elsie's with Michael Marino, the man whose car she escaped into after she ran away from our traffickers. He's also the head of the Messina crime family. Yeah, I know. Why would she ever want to get involved with the Mafia after what they did to us?

But it wasn't them. They're nothing like the Bianchis. Everyone hated those bastards. They were rotten fruit, and no one mourned their deaths.

Michael, for all his flaws, is good to her, and together with his six-year-old daughter, Sophia, they're a family.

I envy that.

What kind of person envies her friends for falling in love? But I do. I wonder how it feels to even trust a man. To let him touch you and do all the things those men did to us without it being ugly and cruel.

Tears sting my eyes, and I grind my molars to stop the aching.

But I'm not dead. I feel things. I want things. And some of them, I don't even understand. Like how I want to be subdued. Thrown on the ground and fucked like an animal.

Disgust curls in my gut even as arousal grows between my thighs.

Maybe I'm a monster too. Maybe that's what I've become.

"How about we start at the beginning again?" the doctor says.

My attention zeroes in on him because I know what he's going to ask. What he always asks.

"Tell me about the first time you were taken."

As soon as those words leave his mouth, my stomach heaves, because I don't want to think about it. I don't want to remember the time I was ripped from my family and thrown into a world far uglier than I ever realized.

"Isn't she pretty, boss?" The man with the yellow-stained teeth grins at Agnelo Bianchi, the older man beside him. The one I know to be in charge of the girls and the children.

"Why is she still dressed?" He pops a brow, his brown eyes dark and dirty.

Simultaneously, his mouth curls and I start to tremble and whimper, tears aching behind my eyes.

Please don't touch me. Please let me go.

My arms are curled tight around my body while I stand in a cold warehouse, nothing but crates and thick pipes all around me.

Two other girls stand on each side of me. Elsie and Jade, though? They aren't here. They separated us, and the very thought causes me to burst out crying.

The pain stings as I sob and collapse to the floor. But I don't stop, even as the men scream at me. Even as one drags me up by my hair and slaps my face.

Because my friends could be dead right now.

"Where—" I sniffle. "Wh-where are my friends?"

With eyes born from death, Agnelo paces up to me slowly. My body shudders as he comes closer. As he does, his palm snatches my throat, fingers boring deeper until I find it hard to breathe.

"You don't ask questions here." His glare is strong enough to crack glass. He grinds his teeth as he moves his face so close his nose touches mine.

My insides gnaw.

"Now, you're gonna take off your clothes and show us what you're hiding. Because I have a feeling you're gonna make us a lot of money..."

And I did. I made those bastards tons. But I never saw a dime. All we got was moldy pancakes and a stained mattress on the floor.

We lived worse than the rats that scurried past the grass on the lawn. I have no desire to relive those days with anyone. Not my therapist, not my friends, not even myself.

But the truth is, I can't seem to forget. I can't seem to let go. Of any of it.

Clearing my throat, I whisper to Dr. Collins. "I don't want to talk about that."

Sweat beads across my brow…

I can't stop seeing Agnelo's face. He's there in my mind as though he's in the room with us.

What they did to me once Elsie ran off… I don't want to remember any of it.

"Tell me where Elsie is, you stupid whore, or I'll whip you until your bones break."

My chest is heavy, as though someone's sitting on it. I try to keep it together. To pretend. My hands shake, and I curl both into fists and tuck them under my thighs to stop the tremors.

It doesn't work.

"That's your choice, of course," Dr. Collins says, oblivious to my inner turmoil. "But my hope is that at every session we can explore more of that. Make you comfortable enough to talk about it. So that over time, it doesn't hold power over you."

"Is that even possible? Do people like me ever truly heal?"

My pulse pounds in my neck as I wait for his answer. Not even sure why I asked in the first place. He'll just tell me what he thinks I need to hear.

"Healing is a process. It's work. And even when we think we're done, there's still more work to do."

I scoff. "That's such a Dr. Collins answer."

He laughs and shakes his head as he jots something else down on his pad.

I glance at it, my brows gathering. "What are you writing? How hopeless I am?"

He lowers his pen onto his lap. "Do you think you're hopeless?"

I huff and drop my head to the back of the chair. "Don't shrink me for just one moment, okay?"

I register his harsh intake of breath before he says, "I never once thought of you as hopeless, Kayla. You're strong. Resilient. So, if you're using a word like hopeless to describe yourself, it's because you may be seeing yourself that way."

He pauses as I look back at him.

"Are you still having those dreams about hurting your captors?"

I nod.

"Have they become more frequent since the murders began?"

No, they became more frequent when I found out about the traffickers coming back. Maybe even coming for me.

I nod.

"I thought so. It's not uncommon for similar events to trigger you and cause the nightmares to increase."

"They're not nightmares," I clarify. "They're more like fantasies."

His eyes narrow thoughtfully. "Yes, I can see that. Nevertheless, I think it's imperative you're aware of the impact the murders have had on you. I also think it would be good if we increased our sessions to twice a week."

"Okay." I shrug. "I can do that as long as it's on Fridays. Other than today, my schedule is busy with school."

"That's right. How is that going?"

"As okay as it can be."

When I decided to go to college, something those monsters took from me, everyone supported me. Though my parents worried about how I would do on my own, especially with having my own place now, they allowed me space.

I couldn't live with them anymore. They hovered too much. Watched me every moment as though I'd disappear.

I get it. If I were them, I'd probably do the same.

When I first began to live with my parents, I entered a dark place. I barely ate. Barely showered. I could hardly get out of bed. I'd stay awake all night remembering everything.

And I cried. I cried so much my tears would drench the pillow.

My mother knew. She cried too when she thought I wasn't listening. But I heard. I was breaking her heart all over again.

I wanted to die. Imagined how I'd kill myself. It'd have been easy. Take a bunch of my mother's pills and drown in them.

The pain would have gone away then. I'd have been…empty. Numb.

There'd have been no more tears.

No more memories of what was.

I'd have been gone. And good riddance.

I couldn't tell anyone about my thoughts. They'd have institutionalized me. Called me crazy and thrown me in some solitary room for God knew how long.

I'd never allow that.

But one day, when I was with Elsie and Jade, I let it slip, thinking I was talking inside my head. And that was all it took for me to start therapy. To start caring for myself the way I should've. Because those monsters? They want me to suffer. They want to take all the good and strip me bare until I have nothing but my demons.

So I ripped those demons from my soul, and I watched their flesh burn until all that was left of me was who I am today.

But their remnants still linger, still corrupt and enrage me.

Once I got a little better, I moved out. My parents weren't thrilled with the idea. Who could blame them? They moved to New York from our home state so that I could be near Elsie and Jade. If they hadn't, I'd probably have had to leave here.

I was staying with Jade and Enzo for a bit after I was rescued, then Elsie and Michael. But I didn't want to continue to impose on any of them, and I didn't have money for a place of my own. Once my parents got here and found a place, I moved in with them.

But I wanted freedom. I needed to prove to myself that I could do this alone.

When I told my friends about my desire to get my own place, that I was thinking of renting an apartment in a run-down area in the city, Michael found out and nixed that idea real fast. He bought me a home instead, under an hour from my parents. Which, of course, thrilled them and is why they absolutely adore that man.

I'm grateful to both Elsie and Michael for what they did for me, and I intend to pay them back every penny, even though Michael vows to give it right back to me.

I'm where I'm supposed to be in my life right now. I've come to accept that, thanks to my therapist. More or less…

"They found another body last night," I say in almost a whisper, my heart racing right out of my chest.

This killer needs to be stopped. Someone has to put an end to him. Too many innocent women have been killed by his hand.

The newest victim was only twenty-three, bright future as a lawyer, engaged to be married, when she was taken while running in Central Park. She was found three days later—face mutilated, raped, with something carved into her body. The killer does that to all his victims. Slices his signature into them like they're his property.

The police won't tell the public exactly what he carves, probably afraid of a copycat. But that's how they've connected the murders.

"They'll find him." Dr. Collins's comforting voice does nothing to soothe me. "Just stay vigilant, and maybe think about going back to your parents' for the time being."

"No." I shake my head. "I'm tired of having my life implode because of these people. I'm gonna stay exactly where I am."

He purses his mouth and lets out a deep exhale. "I got my wife one of those watches that can call the police and alerts me of her location. Maybe get one of those and some pepper spray too."

"Don't worry, Doctor. I've got lots of pepper spray."

Pretty sure that would be useless against people like that.

But I don't say that to him. What's the point? He'll never get it.

My mind goes back to that poor girl, the madman's fourth victim.

There'll be more.

There always is.

Whoever this killer is, he's vicious. Cruel. And he won't stop.

Because monsters don't know how to.

Not until someone does it for them.

Two

ADRIEL

He struck again. The Midnight Murderer. That's what the news calls him because the time of death is always around twelve.

But me? I call him a coward.

Who else would kill young women? They can't defend themselves against him. He overpowers them, violates them, takes their lives slowly and painfully.

He butchers them while they're still alive. Cuts a star onto their abdomen, like some kind of branding. I have no idea why, but I intend to find out. I will know everything about him.

I bet he enjoys every moment of his sick game. Likes to watch them as he cuts into them.

I know the type of animal he is. Sick. Depraved. A devil in human flesh. And when I find him, I will take his rotting soul and I will feed it to the devil.

In the multi-room basement of my two-story home, I stare at one of my large computer screens in the security room, which I keep locked. Can never be too careful. The other rooms down here look like regular bedrooms, plus a living room. No one would even suspect what I have here.

Hacking into some police files, I attempt to find more evidence the cops may be too blind to decipher.

When I find the killer, I'll enjoy taking his life. I'll do to him what he's done to them.

An eye for an eye. Of sorts. Except what I do to him will be far worse.

He won't be my first, nor my last, but at least I have a method to my madness. I choose them wisely. Methodically. Or they choose themselves, if I'm honest.

There's no sense of guilt or shame for my actions, for the lives I cut short, for the demons I eradicate. I kill them because I want to. Because they *need* to die.

There's a hunger embedded inside me, a thirst I need to quench, and this is how I do it: ridding the world of the cancer spreading through its streets. I'm the doctor who contains it, ridding them of a disease that exudes a putridness like no other. That's what they all are. I'm doing the world a favor.

But in the same token, I'm doing myself one too. There is a deep sense of loathing and rage behind my actions, this need to extinguish. It fuels me, like oil to a flame, like heat energy strengthening a storm strong enough to wipe out cities.

But harming innocents? No. There's no honor in that. I kill those like *him*, and that's as far as it ever goes. And I will kill him too. I just have to find him first.

I've hacked cameras in the areas where he's dumped the bodies. Searched every inch for clues. He's good. Too good.

But I'm better.

He doesn't leave the women in the same places. And he never shows his face on camera.

Of course not. Because, like me, he knows where every one of them is. Every street. Every corner. He studied it until he knew the city like the back of his hand.

But unlike me, he doesn't run an underground tech company. One that creates surveillance equipment for those who can afford it, among many other things. Not all of it legal, of course.

Eventually he'll get sloppy, and that'll be my chance to take him out and clean up my mess.

I'm good at that. The nuns at the orphanage where Mommy Dearest abandoned me made sure I learned how important cleanliness was. And those bitches loved to show us what happened when we didn't obey.

At sixteen, after I escaped that place, I freed the children and burned it to the ground. Some of the nuns I knew from the time I was a little boy still worked there. I tied them up and made them beg before I burned them.

Hearing their screams fed my depravity. I *wanted* it. Knowing they were suffering was the best revenge I could've asked for.

The police never did find who did it. The kids described a man with a scary mask. Because that's what I wore. A frightening Halloween mask made to terrify little children. I was their boogeyman *and* their savior.

One good thing came out of it, though. I met a kid at that shithole about my age who taught me about computers. It was the one thing we had at the orphanage. Once he was adopted, I continued to teach myself. Got myself a job after I ran and saved enough for a crappy computer. Then I slowly built what I have today.

My work keeps me sane and focused. As sane and focused as

a man like me can be. Everything I've grown in my business is my work alone. I don't employ anyone. I prefer it that way. It's a necessity, really.

This is where sinners come to die.

This is their purgatory.

Where they burn for their crimes.

And when I say burn, I mean it. The room adjacent is installed with a cremation furnace. Except when I torch them, they're very much alive. And here, they are forgotten. Their ashes never to be traced.

I've killed twenty, and I'm still here to tell the tale. And I'll kill twenty more if I have to.

Turning to another computer screen, I watch her—the woman who gave me life, with a little girl I know to be my niece, Sophia, skipping around beside her as they get ice cream at my mother's favorite shop.

The nuns never kept it a secret. That I was left as a newborn, still wailing for a mother who didn't want him. I grew up hating her, not knowing who she was at first. Not until I found my birth certificate that the nuns kept hidden.

I wanted to ask her why.

Why did she keep my twin, Raphael, but abandon me? What made him special? What was it about me that made me unlovable? Did she sense my depravity? Was it there from the time I climbed out of her womb? Did she hate me instantly?

I wanted to ask her all these things. When I infiltrated my brother Gio's wedding a month ago, I was gonna take her and ask her everything, but instead, I left her a little note to remember me by. Cut off the hand of one of the guards and pinned it to the fence, along with the note, where my whole family would find it.

I still recall every detail from that day. The words I wrote are etched into my memory. It's too bad I didn't get to see her face as she read it.

Dear Mother,

I hope this letter finds you well. I'm so glad to see the beautiful life you've built for yourself. But I must admit, I am a little hurt that life didn't include me. I see you kept my twin, Raphael, but I guess I was disposable. Thrown away like trash.

But don't worry. I know where you live. I've known for a long time. Waiting in the shadows. But I'm done waiting. And I'm coming for you. For all of you.

—A

I meant every word in that letter. I want her dead. And whether my father dies too depends heavily on whether he knew about me.

I look like him, Patrick Quinn. Have his green eyes, while Raphael has the eyes of the man she married before my father. The one she spent her whole life with until he died. At first, I thought he was my father, but the more I watched the family, the more I stared into the eyes of Patrick…I knew. He was my father.

I didn't discover I had a fraternal twin until I saw the birth certificates of all three of her sons. And Raphael? He had my birthday. She kept him. And the day I was born, she left me.

She didn't even bother to make sure I had a loving home to go to. No. Not Mommy. She threw me into the hands of monsters. Tortured and bruised with every passing year.

While they lived as one happy fucking family.

Fisting my hands, I slow my breathing, needing to control myself before I get too entwined in my fury. But it's what she did to me, and it's what she'll have to deal with when I show her my face.

I've imagined her death over and over. Want to take a garrote to her throat and watch her bleed across the plastic in my basement.

My heart drums with thrill. She'll deserve it. Worse was done to me, and it's all her fault. I want to take everything from her, from my father. But I have to be sure he knew about me. It would be like her to lie.

When I'm through, though, they'll all pay the price for her mistakes.

I watch her again, examining her laugh.

Did she even care? Did she watch me wail for her while she held my twin in her arms? Was he enough? Did she even think about me? Look for me?

I doubt it. She'd have found me if she wanted to, but she didn't.

She was glad to see me gone.

Unwanted. Abandoned.

It's what I'm used to. Being alone. I'm comfortable here in this house. I've never needed companionship. Sure, I feed my need for pleasure, but it's never been anything more.

Love is a concept I fail to comprehend. It's an emotion I don't know how to decipher. It's a good thing, too. It'd be worse if I craved it.

But rage, I know. Rage, I feel. And soon, Mommy Dearest will know just what became of her darling boy.

If I ever felt an ounce of love, my upbringing ripped it out of me. They starved me of the need for affection until I didn't know what it felt like to have it. To want it. Whips and chains are what I know. What I need. What I desire. The pain, it's my only friend.

And when I'm through with the Marinos, that's all they'll ever know too.

Sophia's dark brows crease as she looks up at the exact spot where the camera sits, right in the corner of the ice cream shop.

Her chocolate cone drips past her little fingers as she slants her head thoughtfully, staring right at me. A moment later, she grins and looks back at her grandmother.

My mother takes her by the hand, while my finger draws an X over her face. My niece doesn't deserve to be with that cruel woman. She'd give her up too if it served a purpose. She's not a good person. Never was.

Sophia gives the camera one last look before they head out. And I start to wonder if that little girl would recognize me. She saw me at my mother's wedding not too long ago. Asked me if I was her father's friend.

I smile at the memory. I like her. I don't know why, but I do. It's not affection, not really. But it's something…

I scrub the thought from my head. No need for that clouding my intentions for tonight.

My mind must remain sharp.

The next one on my list is someone I'll enjoy killing.

Slowly.

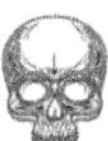

Hours later, I'm in the city, a smile plastered on my face, three men in suits laughing at a joke the other said. Something about a stripper and a horse. I stopped paying attention. Even my drink isn't much of a drink. It's all for show. There's no alcohol in it. I don't drink when I'm working. And this is work.

Casius chuckles as he tosses his third bourbon.

My eyes slowly take him in, from the hint of gray around his temples to his pale blue eyes, the same ones he uses to stare at the women he forces against their will. Dozens of them. He even brags about it. Not in so many words, but he says enough to know what he means.

I met him through my business. An owner of a hedge fund. Someone who's used many of the products I offer my clientele. He's special. Or he thinks he is.

But I don't discriminate. Tonight, I will do what must be done. I will rid the world of his evil.

"You're awfully quiet, Andy." His attention lines with mine, his irises doused in a red hue from all the alcohol he's consumed. "I wanted to hear about the new tech you developed. Cameras in pens?"

Of course, I don't tell them the name my mother gave me. Andy is how everyone knows me. How I stay discreet.

I nod. "Completely undetectable. And the smallest of its kind. Without sacrificing sound or image quality."

He grins. "I want five hundred."

"Done." I toss the rest of my water so they think I'm actually drinking. That I'm one of them.

But I never will be.

He inclines his chin and jerks it toward his right. "Look at that hot piece of ass."

My jaw tightens, but I turn to face the direction he's looking and find a woman sitting at a bar, drinking something. Her eyes are absent, and her long, light brown hair lies in waves across her shoulders.

She doesn't notice us. Doesn't notice anyone, really. I return my gaze to Casius, seeing the sinister objective in his expression, knowing exactly what he wants to do to her.

"I think she wants to be left alone," I tell him.

But he continues to ogle her, and I know just what he plans to do to her anyway.

"Be right back." He rises to his feet as the other two men chuckle, giving each other knowing looks.

They're aware of what he does. How he doesn't take no for an answer. He just tosses money at the problem afterward and pays off the women and the cops.

I should kill his friends too. Since they find his actions so amusing.

My hand clamps across my thigh as I watch him rush over to her, almost tripping on his own feet with how inebriated he is.

Unable to peel my gaze from him and the woman, I glare as he smiles, flashing a set of white teeth that does nothing for her except make her face tighten. She shakes her head and tries to look away, but he grabs her arm instead and laughs.

In a flash, she rushes to her feet, flips his arm against his back, and presses herself into him from behind. She leans her mouth close to his ear, her eyes carrying a hint of danger.

I don't hear a word she says, but if looks could kill…

A cold grin curls around my mouth.

As she lets him go, she snarls and turns on her heels before strutting away.

I watch her go as he returns, still grinning like a motherfucker.

Shaking his head, he drops back onto his chair. "She's fire. My God…" A whoosh of a breath tramples out of his thin mouth. "I want her. I bet she fights just like that in bed."

"Pretty sure she didn't want what you were dishing out." One of the men shakes his head, laughing as he does. Like this is some big joke.

He chuckles low, like a predator calculating his next attack. "Women don't know what they want, man. It's our job to show them."

My heart pounds, adrenaline bursting inside me, needing to take him right here, right now. My eyes remain glued to him while I grind my teeth, unable to stop the vengeance that pierces through my molecules. He's gonna die tonight, and I'll take great pleasure in it.

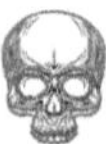

Hours pass, and it's just me and him now. The others went home a while ago.

When I got this invitation from Casius, I was pleased. I know how drunk he gets, how easy it'll be to take him back to my house. I do own a penthouse in the city, but I don't do *this* there. That would be a lot less discreet.

He starts to get up, grabbing the edge of the chair as he steadies himself.

"Heading out?" I clasp him on the shoulder.

"Mmm," he grumbles. "Gonna catch a…uh, you know." He chuckles, gait tottering.

"A taxi?" My chuckle is low, almost breathy. This is gonna be so easy.

"That's right." He scoffs. "I need some s-sleep."

I nod as we stride out together onto a bustling city street. "How about I take you home?"

Of course I offer my dear friend a ride. How else will I manage to kill him?

He glances with watery eyes, unsure of my proposition. "Yeah?"

"Of course. I have nothing to do anyway." I grin as he hums a response. "My car is just over there."

I point left, but before we start toward that direction, I spot the woman from the bar, sitting inside her sedan, her hands gripping the steering wheel.

If I was the kind of man who cared, I'd probably knock and ask her if she's okay. Maybe apologize for his dickish behavior. But I don't do a thing except take note of her license plate so I can look her up later.

She remains behind us, growing distant, while together we make it down two blocks until we're in front of my black SUV. Nothing special about it. I prefer not to draw unnecessary attention to myself. I don't flaunt my money—except the penthouse, of course. That's mine. I earned it. Put everything into my work to be where I am. My mother may have left me in the hands of evil, but I rose to the top by clawing my way out.

I open the backseat for him, because that's where he belongs. As he starts to climb up, I reach inside my pocket and retrieve a syringe.

He doesn't register my breaths lingering around his nape, the way my hand moves up slowly, while the other curls around his front before it fastens around his neck.

"What the—"

But it's too late. The needle punctures the side of his throat, and his words die as quickly as he will.

People dart past us, but no one cares as I subtly shove his body across the seats and shut the door behind him.

I enter the driver's side and start the car, rolling it onto the street.

Can't wait until he wakes up so the fun can begin.

Three

KAYLA

My blood boils, my pulse battering as I slam my knuckles over and over against my steering wheel. That man from the bar… His breath reeking of liquor, his leery gaze running down my body like he was picturing himself in places others have invaded.

I couldn't help the emotions he brought out in me. The desire to end him, to take a bottle to his throat, overwhelmed me until I forced myself to leave.

He laughed as I flipped him around and subdued him. Like I'm some big joke.

Thinks he can touch me without my permission? Not anymore. No one will get to do that again.

As soon as I walked out of the bar, I wanted to return and find him. I wanted to do bad things.

Would I have done it, though, if I'd had the chance? Would I have taken his life? Could I be pushed far enough?

My phone rings and I look down at it to find Elsie's name. Taking a deep breath, I fix a smile and answer it.

"Hey!" I hope she doesn't catch the nervous skittering in my voice.

"Where are you?" Her question is lined with worry as I shut my eyes and steady my breathing. "Your mother called looking for you. Said your phone was going to voicemail and she started to panic."

I blow air into my cheeks and shake my head. "I'm fine. I was just out on a drive. It helps clear my mind. I saw she called. I just didn't want to deal with her constant worry. It drains me."

Staring at the ceiling, I wonder how different my life would be if I wasn't who I am.

"Oh, Kayla. I'm sorry." Her pity is reflected in each syllable. "I wish you'd talk to me about what happened after I escaped. I should never have left you."

"Don't you dare say that!" My throat snaps with a raw ache. "You had to go. You couldn't stay when you had a chance at freedom." Tears line my eyes. "Sometimes…"

"Yeah?"

"Sometimes I just wish I'd left with you." The words leave in a quiet whisper, the scars on my back stinging as though the wounds are still fresh.

Through the phone, I hear her cry. "I sometimes wish I hadn't left. That I'd stayed with you."

"No you don't, Elsie. Believe me, you don't." I close my eyes and remember the things those men did to me to make me talk.

The Bianchis thought I was weak. That I'd rat on my best friend.

I guess they didn't realize how strong they truly made me.

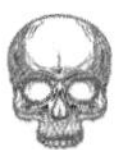

"Tell me where she is, you little bitch!" Agnelo snaps the whip across my back while I hang in the middle of a room at the club they use for shows.

Not the kind you think. The ones where they force us to perform on each other for the viewing pleasure of their paying customers.

But now the place is empty except for him, his brother, Faro, who's the don of the Palermo crime family, and other men who came to watch what he's doing to me. All of them cackling like my pain feeds their madness.

Because of course it does. They're beasts in three-piece suits. Kissing their children goodbye as they send them off to school while they do vicious things.

Another strike lands hard against my throbbing flesh while I whimper, sobbing as the agonizing pain overtakes me.

But I won't give Elsie up. I won't tell him where she went. And hopefully, the man with the scar on his cheek, the one whose car she escaped into, won't find her and bring her back.

I want her out of this place. Someone has to come out alive. So many of us have been killed, either for running or trying to get help. Others were disposed of for trying to hurt the men who hurt us.

It's debilitating to be powerless this way. Knowing in the end, nothing will stop the monsters from eating you alive.

Palms clamp my hips, Agnelo's hand lowering between my thighs as he touches me there, groaning with sadistic pleasure as he enters me with two fingers. I fight it, trying to tighten my legs, but two men come to hold them apart while he continues to invade me.

The blood from my back drips across the floor while he tortures me. It's as though I'm burning at the stake. Cast into the flames that char through my veins. I don't even want to see what my back looks like. What he did to it.

"If you don't talk, we're all gonna take turns."

He uses his other hand to trap my throat, the whip tangling between my bare breasts. There is promise in his words, and I know he means it. Not as though it hasn't happened before. Many times. Why should it scare me now? What else can they take from me that they haven't already?

"G-g-go ahead." I let a small laugh spit through my teeth.

He growls sadistically before he tells the men, "Do it. Make it hurt."

They sneer, and that's when one of them starts to unbuckle his belt, the clinking resonating as he lets himself free from his slacks. And when he grabs both of my thighs and enters me, I close my eyes and I dream.

And in it, I'm free.

While they're dead.

Every last one of them.

"Kayla?" Elsie calls from the other side of the speaker. "Are you still there?"

"Yeah." I shake my head and pinch the bridge of my nose. "I've gotta get some sleep. I'll text my mom."

"Before you go, I wanted to talk to you about having a bodyguard. I know you dismissed it last time, but—"

I groan, throwing my head back against the seat. "Not this again."

"Please? It'll help me not worry. With this killer on the loose and someone trafficking again, I don't like you out there without protection. Between you going to college in the city and then driving an hour home, I want you to be safe."

"I'm safe. I swear."

I don't want to feel like I'm caged again.

"Just think about it, okay? Michael insists, and so do I. Jade and I have one, and we can still do whatever we want. It's not prison, Kayla."

Then why does it feel like it?

I don't want someone following me around, keeping tabs on me and what I do.

He's going to report to Michael and tell him about the bars I go to. Tell him about the other stuff… I can't let anyone find out.

"I'll think about it," I lie right through my teeth. "Get some rest. Love you."

"Love—"

But I drop the call before she can say any more. I know she loves me too. But I can't be a prisoner again.

ADRIEL

"What the hell are you doing?!" Casius roars, standing on the plastic that covers the span of one large room in my basement.

His hands are free. The drunken fog no longer coats his vision. There's nothing stopping him from attempting to overtake me and run. I like a good chase.

I'm glad I get to do this while he's conscious.

Unspooling the garrote, I clutch it in both hands as I take slow, menacing steps. He moves back, his eyes wide as he takes in my movement, the wire that will soon trap his throat.

But it won't kill him. No, it will spill enough blood to make him wish for death. And once it comes, it'll be in the form of flames.

He will know true suffering, and he will deserve it.

"You're insane," he whispers. "You need help. You…you can't do this."

He trips against the chair behind him and clutches the back of it with both hands, as though a measly chair will save him. He lifts it in the air and throws it at me with a roar, but I merely smile and shove it away.

"It's always the insane ones who think everyone else is crazy." Dry laughter escapes my lungs, while his eyes only grow with fear. So much of it, I rejoice in it.

It's what his victims felt. The way he didn't care when they did. I don't care either. There is this detached feeling I can't explain in words, but it helps not to have it. Makes it much easier to stomach.

As he tries to rush around me, I grab his hair and throw him on the floor, his body beneath mine. Before he can do a thing, the wire cuts into his throat, blood beading around it. I push it further into his skin, sinking it with gradual power, hard enough for him to know this is it.

His hands fight me, but it's too late. When his movements slow, I drag him up with me and bring him to the far end of the room where an electric furnace waits.

By all appearances, it looks like a regular wall, a painting of sunrise hiding the opening. And even then, when the artwork is removed, it's as though it's a white wall. Nothing there at all. But with the press of a button on my keychain, a rectangular section of it opens to reveal Casius's new home.

He groans while I hold him up with the wire still cutting into him.

"You will die today. You will see what hell is like. It's what you did to those women, didn't you?" I taunt.

It gives me pleasure. I want his agony.

"Confess." I pulse the cord around his throat. "Tell me how many."

"F-fuck you," he grumbles, choking on his words.

"If you don't tell me what I want to know, I'll cut every limb from your body and burn you after. There's a saw I like to use. Take my time with it too." I chuckle menacingly.

"P-p-please…" he cries, and from the sound of it, I know he believes me.

"Tell me." I crush my molars, needing this to be over.

"T-twelve," he stammers, choking out the words. "There… there were t-twelve."

"And what did you do with them?" I hiss.

He cries. How fucking pathetic.

"What did you do?!" My scream makes him shiver.

"I—I—I r-raped them, then…"

More fucking tears. My God, I just wanna kill him.

I tighten the wire.

"Th-then I—I paid off the cops and the g-girls," he pants.

"You disgust me." I press another button, and the flames roar to life.

His chest climbs with small breaths.

I chuckle victoriously. It's what I wanted. His confession.

"I will savor your screams."

The cord cuts into him as he fights me while I bring him closer to his end. Lifting his smaller frame up by his hips doesn't take much effort, even while he tries to get back down.

But as soon as the flames lick his face, it's over.

He roars as I push the rest of him inside and lock the door.

If I had my way, I'd record this moment so I could play it over and over.

With a fucking smile on my face.

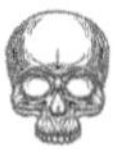

The next day, I'm back in the city, having had a few meetings with some clients, one of whom has forced me to talk shop at a strip club.

Now, I don't normally like to frequent these places. They reek of sin and seduction, and not the kind of sins I desire to partake in.

I enjoy women, sure, but on my own terms, and only when I need them to satiate the hunger inside me. Which is never that often.

I don't need them for affection, nor for some convoluted idea of love. They know exactly where I stand. It's the sexual gratification I'm after—theirs and mine. And once that's served, we go on our merry fucking ways.

"You've gotta live a little, man!" my new client, Matthew, hollers into my ear.

The music blasts as he stares at a woman with olive skin, her breasts bigger than her head. But he doesn't seem to mind.

Her lips curl as she takes me in, giving me a wink as she squats and whispers in my ear. "Want a private, handsome? I'll make it extra special for you."

She tries to make herself sound enticing. I can respect that. It's her job, after all. To make every sucker here feel like he's the most important man in the room.

Smiling to be polite, I shake my head. "Wife wouldn't approve."

"Well, aren't you a keeper?" She giggles as she rights herself and goes straight to Matthew—with the same offer, I'm sure.

But, of course, he's a lot more eager to say yes.

"Keep the seat warm for me, will ya?" His eyes dance with excitement as she drags him toward the other side of the room.

With a shake of my head, I take a swig of my beer, about to head out, when a woman happens on the dance floor, and I instantly lower the bottle, my eyes unable to stop staring.

Not because I'm attracted to her or she's suddenly my fucking soulmate. I don't believe in that bullshit.

No.

I stare because I know her.

Well, kind of.

My mouth tips up on one side. The memory of when she flipped Casius over like she wanted to cut his eyes out with her nails fills my head until I can't help but wonder everything about her.

Of course I looked her up once I noted her license plate that night.

I know her name. I know where she lives too. But I left it at that. My curiosity died there, so I stopped digging.

But now? I want to dig until my fingers bleed. Until I know everything there is to know about Kayla Jenkins.

A stripper? I didn't see that coming. Not that there's anything wrong with the profession. It pays. But she didn't seem like the type. Clearly, I was wrong.

Men whistle as they take in all of her, from the pink pasties covering her nipples to the matching G-string that barely covers her pussy.

Her light brown hair glistens as she wraps her arms around the pole and swings, like it's a friend she knows well.

Her back is concealed with a nude-colored mesh piece that connects to her panties and around her throat in a glistening choker. Her back is the only part of her she keeps hidden. And it makes me wonder why. It's possible she just prefers it that way. Likes the outfit. But something tells me there's more to this.

She doesn't see me watching her. Why would she? There are

dozens here just like me.

As she closes her eyes and flips upside down, gyrating in reverse, I can see she isn't doing this for anyone but herself.

She continues into the next song, making the men groan and say despicable things, and it fills me with disgust.

Her pasties are now gone, thrown for some poor sucker to catch, someone who'll never get a woman like that, not even in his dreams.

She is attractive. Of course she is. Any fool with eyes can see that. Beautiful by all accounts, her eyes a hazel dream, high cheekbones, and full lips. Her thighs are strong, lean muscles flexing, and I'd guess they'd have to be with the strength it takes to work the pole the way she is.

I feel as though I'm violating her by taking in her breasts, a little more than a handful, and I hate that my cock grows at the sight of her. Hasn't for the others, not unless they have their mouth wrapped around it.

My attraction to her must be based on what happened with Casius, the way she handled him. Nothing more.

She finishes her dance and gives the crowd a little smile. But as she happens to start toward the back, one of the men roughly grabs her ankle.

"Come on, baby, take off those panties. Show us that cunt," he cackles.

Two security guards immediately lunge at him. But before they drag him away, she lifts up her foot and presses her thin stiletto into his shoulder, her face set with a sneer.

I register the tightening of her fist against her hip, and that makes me grin.

Her chest pumps with the heaviness of her breaths, then she's turning toward the back of the stage while the man is heaved out of there.

While the last bit of her disappears behind the curtain, I start to wonder who this Kayla really is and why I care to begin with.

KAYLA

"You okay, honey?" Coco asks quietly backstage, not wanting the other girls to hear.

She's the one person I've grown close to, both of us with scars of our own.

I never meant for her to find mine, but the day I came to apply to work here, she walked in on me trying to cover up my scars with makeup.

My heart jumped in my throat, and I thought that was it. I'd never get the job now. She'd tell them as soon as I went into the audition. Or they'd be able to see it because how could I cover these scars all by myself? They'd see how ugly I was, and they'd tell me to leave.

But Coco didn't do that. Instead, she closed the door, went to the closet in the corner, and pulled out this mesh-looking thing, then helped me attach it to my panties. It had a hole for my neck, which she added a choker to.

"Makeup doesn't work as well. But this will, honey."

I cried. I stood there and cried as she held me and told me it was okay. Then she fixed my makeup and cheered me on as I went up on that stage and danced my heart out.

She's a good fifteen years older than me, and kind of like a big sister now.

The girls do their makeup, glancing at me, knowing how shaken up I was when that asshole grabbed me. I was visibly trembling once I was back here, the adrenaline gone and only the memories of my past remaining.

"I'm better now," I tell Coco. "Thank you."

Swiping off my ruby-red lipstick, I gape at my reflection in the mirror. I don't even recognize myself anymore.

"These men think we're whores or something," Coco says, louder now. "Like we're here to do what they want, but fuck that!" She flips her blonde hair past her square shoulders, her frame thick and muscular. "Next time, you hit him in the balls, sweetie. See how he likes it."

"She's not trying to get arrested," Cat remarks with a roll of her eyes from beside me, staring into a mirror while adding a new coat of red lipstick.

Cat's been at this club for a while. Not as long as Coco, though. I'm the newbie, only been doing this for a couple of months.

I do it because I want to. But if I'm being honest, it's because I *need* to.

One night, I passed by the club and went inside. Seeing these women bare themselves while the men watched, unable to do anything else to them, I wondered how it'd feel to have that kind of power. To show the men everything and have the upper hand. To say no, something I didn't have the luxury to do before…

So I applied. And this sense of control, that things only happen on my terms, it's freeing. It's helping.

But, of course, I can't tell anyone. If Jade or Elsie found out, forget it! They'd think I'd lost it for real. I'm sweet, innocent Kayla. Sweet, innocent girls don't go and strip. But this one does.

I tell Coco goodbye before I head out. When I step into the dark parking lot, streetlamps illuminate across several cars there.

Wearing sneakers now, my feet barely make a sound as I tread a few yards, getting closer to my sedan, when a noise carries from the end of the lot. I can't make it out at first.

But then I hear it: a muffled cry.

My hairs rise on both arms when I register a grunt—a man's grunt.

The woman, though? She continues to cry.

My stomach churns, because I know what's happening before I get the chance to see it. I've heard that exact sound from my own lips, from those of my friends as men took turns.

Removing my phone, I intend to call for help, and when I step near the tall dumpster, I see him. A man with his back to me, the streetlights providing enough illumination to find a woman I recognize by her ruby-red hair to be Ivy from the club.

"Ivy?" I call, flipping on the flashlight on my cell.

The man instantly turns, and even more disgust coils in my gut. It's *him.*

The man who grabbed my ankle.

No. Not a man. A vulture. A cancerous tumor that needs to be excised.

Anger claws through my insides, like a thorny vine wrapping itself around my limbs until I'm one with it.

Ivy turns to me, her cheek bloody and puffy, tears streaming down her face as he presses her against the dumpster.

"Get the fuck away from her!" I roar, slamming a fist into his back as he laughs.

But that only enrages me further.

"You whores should know when to speak and when to shut up," he hisses. "Now leave! So I can finish, unless you want me to finish on your face instead."

His eyes run down my body, his mouth snaking up one side.

Without thinking twice, I reach into my black tote and remove a flip knife I carry everywhere. When he takes in the blade, he cackles like a hyena, his round belly jiggling. He continues to pound into Ivy while she whimpers, sandwiched between him and the wall.

Before he can utter a sound, the knife slashes across his upper arm. He lets out a painful groan, snarling as he glances down at his bleeding arm, the crimson coating his white t-shirt.

"Run." I inch the knife toward the side of his throat. "I may enjoy this a little too much."

"You little—"

"She said *GO*." A deep, guttural voice causes me to gasp, my hairs prickling across the back of my neck.

From deep in the shadows, a man stands, watching us. A black hood covers every inch of his face, the rest of him concealed in darkness, matching the eerie, deadly aura floating around him.

My body crawls with fear.

Even the piece of filth grows scared as he pushes off Ivy and lifts his pants, fumbling with his pockets.

Something slips out of one and falls, but he's too busy running to realize he dropped his wallet. Without even thinking twice, I grab it and stuff it in my tote.

I gawk at the man in the hood. Like an angel from hell sent to carry me into the darkness with him.

"Who are you?" I call, my pulse racing both from terror and adrenaline.

But instead, he turns and stalks away, leaving me with a heavy feeling in the pit of my stomach.

One I can't seem to shake.

Not even long after he's gone.

Ivy refused to press charges. Of course she did. She was too shaken up. Too scared nothing would happen because of what she does.

Men like him always get away with it, while the real victims are cast aside. Unimportant.

After I took her back inside the club, I left with every intention of going home, but instead, I'm going somewhere else entirely.

The man? His name is Barry Mancini.

I don't even know why I'm driving to his home. But I started to wonder if he was married. If he had kids. Does his family know what a sick piece of shit they're living with? If not, I plan to tell them.

I want to ruin him. I can't stop the rage this kind of thing triggers. It feeds my darkness, feeds these thoughts I can't stop. I want to ruin them all. All the monsters. All the men who hide in plain sight, waiting to hurt us.

And that serial killer, the one the cops can't find? It could be any of them. It could be Barry or the next man who hurts a woman.

My mind starts to wonder about the man in the hood. What was he doing there? Was he at the club? Did he hear me and offer help?

Why would he want to help, anyway? Men don't help girls like me. They say we're asking for it. We don't matter. Why would I matter to him?

What if he's just like Barry, only pretending to be a good Samaritan?

Glancing at my rearview mirror, I look at the cars behind me, wondering if he's there. Doubt it though. I'm sure he left long before I got into my vehicle.

Barry only lives thirty minutes out of the city, and when I pull up to a small ranch with a wraparound fence, I find one car parked in front of it. His car. The one I saw him drive off in. The house isn't in the best condition: a broken shutter, slightly overgrown grass, a piece of the fence missing.

He clearly doesn't worry about taking care of his things. Doesn't surprise me.

Parking a couple of homes away, I slowly get out, looking all around, not seeing anyone in the vicinity.

When I start for his house, my body quivering with nerves, a light suddenly turns on through his window.

I freeze in place. Pressing my body flat against the shrub in his front yard, I see him moving sluggishly, like he's still in pain.

Which, of course, thrills me. There's something about hurting him that excites me. When he shuts the light off, I release a breath of relief and start closer toward the side door.

Not sure what the plan is. But before I know it, I'm opening the door. Of course the idiot left it unlocked. He isn't afraid of monsters. Because he is one.

I stride gradually through the dark kitchen, a counter to my right and a small foyer straight ahead. A groan comes through, and I follow the sound, tiptoeing forward.

That's when I see him lying on the sofa, his wound now wrapped, a beer resting on his belly. Another empty one on a pizza box on the floor.

The TV is on low, but I'm not paying attention to anything but him and the knife in my hand, which is somehow already clutched in my grasp.

I move slowly. Like a gazelle. But my predator doesn't see me. And if I have it my way, he won't until it's too late. I'm right behind him now. But he has no idea what's about to happen.

He shifts and it startles me, but I stay fastened in place while he begins flipping through the channels. As he does…

"What the fuck?" he snaps.

His mind can't catch up with what just happened, and neither can mine. My blade's jammed into the side of his throat, not an inch of it visible.

He jerks up his eyes to find me looming over him.

"You?" he groans, terror there as he tries to yank the knife out.

I grin and help him.

Blood shoots out of the cut.

He lets out a scream, trying to stop the bleeding, but it does him no good.

Pity.

It leaks out like a slow-moving faucet while I step back and watch. I expect to feel something—disgust at this much blood, some kind of sympathy—but I feel nothing but joy.

"You—you won't g-get away with this…" The last few words sound like a strangled whisper as he starts to collapse to the floor.

"Of course I will…"

Eyes opened, he's staring at the ceiling, crimson pooling around the pizza box, his body now on it.

I continue to look down at him until so much time passes that I don't realize I've been here for an hour. If not for a car rolling down loudly on the street, I wouldn't have glanced at my phone.

It hits me then: my fingerprints are everywhere.

Panic batters in my gut. I can't get caught. I can't go to prison.

I can't be caged again.

"Oh, God…" I rush toward the kitchen, grab one of his hand towels, and wrap the knife in it before stuffing it in my pocket.

I don't know where else I left evidence. I don't even know how to get rid of it.

But I know someone who does. The thought of calling him pains me, but I have no choice. I have to trust he'll keep this between us and not kill me for it.

My fingers shake as I find his name in my cell and call. It rings and rings, and he finally answers.

"Yeah?"

"Michael?" I sniffle. "I—I need your help. I did something… something bad, and I can't fix it alone." I pause with a soft cry. "I'm sorry."

His breathing is heavy across the line, and for one moment I'm afraid he'll tell me to fuck off.

But instead, he says, "Address. Now. And don't touch anything."

Too late.

ADRIEL

Well, well. I didn't see this coming.

Kayla is a little killer.

She already has a way of surprising me. Something no one has ever managed to do. But a stripper *and* a murderer? She only continues to intrigue me.

Have there been others, or is this her first time? Did she like how it felt? Did she feel remorse? Or was it satisfaction?

She didn't realize I followed her after I stopped that man from hurting her like he did her friend.

She didn't see my face, and that was intentional. I don't want her to see it. To know who I am. Seeing me will only make it harder for me to watch her from a distance. And that's exactly what I intend to do. Little wolf needs someone to keep an eye on her when she hunts.

And she *is* a hunter, whether she knows it yet or not. I can see it there in her eyes as she stares at the dead body with a cold glower.

What happened to her? What made her this way?

Did she grow up like me? Did she have parents who didn't give a shit? Or was she born this way? More nature than nurture?

From the window, I continue to curiously observe her, wondering, waiting to make sure she doesn't get into trouble.

She called someone, though. I heard a name. Is that who she's waiting for?

About thirty minutes later, I get my answer when a black SUV shows up, and another behind it. Two guys roll out of the first and four from the other.

I slink behind the shed, spotting them entering the house. Returning to the window, I see her throw her arms around the neck of one of the men, though from this angle I can't see him well.

Tentatively, he closes his arms around her in a brief hug before he looks at the damage she's caused.

"What did he do?" His words stomp out of him.

As he continues to speak, my pulse kicks up. Because I recognize it.

No way. It can't be.

But when he pivots toward me and I catch the thick scar on his right cheek, his eyes almost black, there's no mistaking him.

Michael Marino.

Fuck!

How the hell does this woman know my brother? Half brother,

but brother nonetheless.

Not that it matters much. He's as good as dead. They all are. And I want my mother to watch it happen.

Want to see her take her last breath, knowing it's her little darling boy who sliced her open.

She can add it to her little book of memories. The one she keeps under her mattress. Wonder if she knows I broke into her home and went through every bit of it.

But know what I didn't see? A photo of me.

"Why would you do this, Kayla?" Michael crosses his arms. "Did he try something?"

She nods.

"He…he tried to hurt my friend. I had no choice. Please believe me." She's crying pitifully now, like a damsel in distress.

"Where is she? Your friend."

"N-not here." Her voice sounds small. Scared.

I grin.

Little wolf is a good liar. I almost believe her.

"The girl ran off," she goes on. "I stayed because he made me. Please…" She grabs his forearm while the others start wrapping the dead body up in a tarp. "Please don't tell Elsie."

"I don't plan to. She doesn't need to worry about you more than she already does. This stays here. Do you understand?"

"Of course." She nods, then asks, "What are you gonna do with him?"

"That's not for you to worry about. But hear me…"

His agitation radiates out of him. I can see both Michael's and Kayla's profiles easily.

"That whole not-wanting-a-bodyguard bullshit? That ends. Today. You don't have a choice anymore. You *will* get one assigned to you tomorrow."

Fuck. That will make things complicated. How can I watch her now?

Gonna have to figure it out.

Don't worry, little wolf. I'll be there making sure he's on his best behavior.

She groans, but I can see it: she doesn't have a choice in the matter.

She clearly means something to my brother, yet she's not his wife. That's Elsie. She must be her friend. But I've never seen Kayla around when I've followed Elsie. I'll find out exactly how she knows my so-called family.

"Do we understand each other?" Michael clips out. "There's a *damn* killer on the loose. And you know someone is trafficking women for the Bianchis again. They could come after you. They may want to take you back. And now this!"

And there it is.

Her demons.

I instantly want to find the ones who took her and send them straight to hell. Is that what she wants too? Does she want to see them suffer? Is that why she took this asshole's life?

I can help her. I can bring her darkest thoughts to light. Would she let me? Or would she run?

I'm faster, little wolf. But I won't hurt you. I'll keep you safe. Even if it's from a distance.

"I won't take no for an answer anymore, Kayla." Michael continues to stare at her. "Elsie cares too much for you, and I won't watch my wife hurting anymore."

"I'm so sick of this!" she hollers, and that woman I first saw at the bar finally makes an appearance. "I don't want to live my life afraid, constantly looking over my shoulder. I want to live for once in my *fucking* life!"

He sighs and nods once, like he understands.

But he doesn't. How could he? People like him will never understand people like us.

And she and I? We're the same, in a way. I wish we weren't. No one should endure that level of pain. Especially not someone like her…

My fingertip traces the window, outlining her face.

He steps back and hands her a bag I didn't see him holding. "I need the clothes you're wearing. Put these on and put the old ones in here."

"Why?" She grabs the bag.

"Burning them. Now stop asking so many questions and hurry so we can leave before a neighbor shows up."

"Okay."

She steps backward and rushes into another room, disappearing from view. But I follow, inspecting her through another window as she strips her clothes.

As she faces my direction, her eyes appear sullen until her bottom lip trembles, and she collapses onto the floor.

Quiet sobs fall into her palms.

It's like I can feel the moisture on the pads of my fingers, outline the agony carved into her soul.

My heart drums a little faster. My fingers reach for her, wanting to…

To what? Touch her? Hold her? Make her feel better?

The thoughts ridicule me. I don't do that. I don't provide comfort. I don't even know how.

She collects herself a minute later and swipes her forearm under her eyes before she puts on the jeans and t-shirt Michael brought. Quickly, she slips the other clothes inside the bag and marches back out. Like nothing ever happened.

I follow back to the other window just as she's handing him the bag.

She peers in my direction for a brief moment, and I quickly retreat, wondering if she caught sight of me.

And this tiny flicker of hope springs to life, wishing she did. Wishing she knew I followed her. That I know what she's done. That I'm proud of her. That I will protect her.

"Make sure this never happens again," Michael's voice echoes.

Gradually, I glance through the window, seeing her attention on my brother now.

"I promise," she says, her tone sheepish.

But I know her better than my brother does.

She's gonna do this again.

And the next time, she won't need him. Because I'll be there to clean up her mess.

I'm good at that.

And soon, she'll learn all of my hidden talents.

KAYLA

I knew this would happen if I called Michael. I knew he'd get pissed and force the bodyguard on me. But what choice did I have?

It was either that or take my chances at getting rid of my DNA all by myself. And let's face it: I don't know how to do that.

But Michael does. He has resources I don't. So I had to bite the bullet and ask for help.

"You okay?" Elsie asks as we sit in her yard the following afternoon, lounging around the pool with Jade.

I can't even call this a yard. It's acres of greenery, so much land around the two-story mansion that I don't know how anyone lives in such a big home.

But Michael and his brothers are wealthy beyond measure. Private jets, homes in exotic places, they have it all. That's all nice, but I don't need that. Give me a cute cottage by a lake and I'm happy.

"Have you been seeing the therapist?" Jade squeezes my arm, her bright blue eyes kindly assessing me like a broken bird who needs mending.

"Yes, and he wants me twice a week now."

"That's a wonderful idea." She reaches for her iced tea, fixing her straw sun hat. "It helped me so much to talk to mine. As long as you're honest, you'll get a lot out of it."

"Do you both tell them everything?" I whisper, like I'm afraid of someone overhearing us.

"Yes," Elsie answers with a one-shoulder shrug. "It was hard at first, but I've gotten better."

I nod, wishing I was like them.

But I'm not. I'm Kayla. Weak. Afraid. Unable to break through the walls those bastards continue to erect around me. And every day, it feels as though they're adding more bricks, making it harder to fight through.

Elsie's cell vibrates on the table between us. She lifts it up and stares at the screen.

"Michael wants to see you for a minute." Her eyes climb to mine. "We'll come with you."

I groan because I know what it's about. "Did he say why?"

"Yep. You're meeting your bodyguard." She grins, and as though she's waiting for me to protest, she adds, "I don't want to hear it. We all need to be safe."

"I didn't say anything."

"Right…" One end of her mouth lifts. "Come on. Let's go meet him."

"He's here?" My eyes burst.

"Sure is. Michael hand-picked him, so we *know* he's good."

"Awesome…" I mumble as Jade giggles.

All three of us rise, making our way down a long path back to the home.

When we enter, the first person I see is Michael. Beside him is a tall man, maybe six-three, and he definitely enjoys the gym. Because even through his suit jacket, I can tell he's built with pure muscle. Not the kind that is overly bulky, but enough to show he cares. A lot.

His hair is dark, almost as dark as Michael's, and when he turns to me, I notice it's tapered on each side while the top is full and thick. The kind of hair a woman probably enjoys running her fingers through.

Not me, though.

I have no desire to get involved with any man. How would that even work if I can't be honest with him about who I am and what I've been through? He'd look at me differently. Treat me differently. Hell, he'd probably break things off. Too much baggage.

I am, though.

No one wants a work in progress, not someone who's as bad as me.

I don't even know if I'm capable of having sex. I'd probably cry…or stab him to death. And neither of those things would be good.

So, yeah. No, thank you.

I much prefer to be alone. It's safer that way.

The bodyguard's brows snap, as though he's somehow heard my inner thoughts. But that's obviously ridiculous. Maybe he can already tell I'm a mess.

His face is sharp and stoic as he assesses me. A deep wrinkle forms between his beautiful pale honey-colored eyes while he continues to take me in like I'm a project he's deciphering.

I instantly don't like him, and that's probably because I don't want someone watching my every move.

How in the world will I work? Because I'm not quitting. Maybe I can bribe him to be quiet.

And what do you have to offer a man like that?

My thoughts ring with the answer, though. I can offer him me. Anything to stop him from running his mouth to Michael. At least this time, I'd be using my own body for my own needs.

He continues to stare, his gaze like sand that glistens beneath the rays of the sun.

"This is Chris Embers," Michael offers. "And he will be your bodyguard for the foreseeable future."

Fucking fabulous…

"Chris, this is Kayla Jenkins. You have her schedule already, along with all the places she likes to frequent. Anything else, feel free to ask her or talk to me. Got it?"

"Yes, sir." That voice is so rugged and powerful. Like with one word, he could bring the world to its knees.

Michael's expression is tight as he regards me before his attention returns to Chris. "You start now."

I roll my eyes, and Chris's mouth twitches.

"Come on, Jade…" Elsie cracks a smirk. "Let's allow Kayla to get to know her new friend."

"Don't plan on being her friend, ma'am." Chris slips his gaze to me, intensity rivaling within it, one I match.

"Good thing because I'm not looking for any."

Jade laughs as they all stride away, Michael pulling Elsie to his side and kissing her temple.

My heart pitches at the affection, longing for that feeling of being loved and wanted and free. So free that I'd let a man touch me—crave it, even. But I don't see how I can. Even if I trusted one for long enough to tell him what happened to me, I can't be fully honest.

How do I tell a man the depraved things I desire? The things I'm afraid to tell anyone about? No man wants someone like that. A girl who's turned into *this*: a twisted-up woman.

Chris clears his throat, and I almost forgot he was here. A mere inconvenience I will have to figure out how to avoid.

"Will you be sleeping in my home?" My gaze narrows.

"No."

Thank God.

"But I'll be right outside at all times."

Oh, goody.

"When do you sleep?"

His mouth lifts into a quick grin, and it does something to me. Something I don't care to admit.

"You don't have to worry about me, Ms. Jenkins."

"You wish I was worried." I roll my eyes.

"We don't have to do much getting to know one another," he goes on. "I get paid to protect you. All I need to know is where you go, and that will be easy to figure out. Because I will be right behind you. Think of me as your shadow."

I huff. "This is insane. Completely insane. Normal people don't need bodyguards."

His gaze reduces. "But you're not normal, are you, Ms. Jenkins?"

The way he says my name, all gravelly and seductive…I'm suddenly warmer than I was a moment ago.

A tattoo peeks from beneath his deep blue dress shirt, right below his neck. If only I was able to pop a few more buttons, I'd be able to tell what it is.

Why do I care, anyway? He seems like a jerk. But the curiosity keeps gnawing.

"Something catch your eye, Ms. Jenkins?" He smirks.

The bastard caught me.

"Are you just going to keep calling me by my last name the whole time you're stalking me?"

"I am. Why? What would you like me to call you?" His deep, raspy tone only makes it harder for me to respond.

"Kayla is fine."

"Okay, *Kayla.*" His mouth tips up.

I hate him. Did I mention that?

"What kind of tattoo is that?" I go with the bold approach.

He lets out a lazy laugh. "How about we only discuss things pertaining to your wellbeing?"

"My wellbeing is just fine. Thanks for your concern, Mr. Embers."

"My…what a relief that is, curious Kayla." His eyes fill with mirth, and that tempting mouth of his gives me a teasing smile.

He's enjoying this. My torment. My dislike of the situation. Of *him.*

Well, he's going to enjoy what I have in store too.

ADRIEL

She's here with him, yet I don't want her to be. It's a foreign feeling I've never experienced and don't know what to do with.

I stare at her as she exits her car in front of the strip club, him parking right behind her.

It was one thing she refused to give up. Her right to drive her own car. Michael allowed it, especially when Elsie gave him that look which said he either agreed or faced the consequences.

And by the looks of him, he definitely didn't want to face them.

Michael has no idea I work for him. That I infiltrated his system without much effort.

It was easy enough to kill one of his men and steal his ID, then pretend to be him. No one suspected a thing. Not very smart of my brother. Maybe they should hire my company and upgrade their tech. I'd have everyone scan their retinas before they even step foot on the grounds.

They have a lot to learn.

They'll learn soon enough, though.

It's a shame I haven't seen Kayla here before. Had I, I'd have known who she was connected to before I saw her at the bar that first time.

Michael usually has me doing work outside the house. But today he needed some of the other men to travel for an overseas job, so he called on a few extras to run ops.

"What are we doing here?" Chris asks her.

She snickers, drilling him with an irritated stare. "Look, I don't need a babysitter, okay? So how about you go and get some food somewhere?"

"That's not what I heard." He crosses his arms. "I heard you very much do need a sitter."

"Wait…" Her eyes widen. "He told you?"

He nods.

Of course Michael told him she killed a man. With him protecting her, he has to know what he's getting himself into.

"Oh my God…" She squeezes her temples between two fingers and shuts her eyes for a moment. "Listen, you cannot tell anyone, okay?"

"I don't plan to. That would mean death. So, I will ask again, *what* are we doing here?"

I can see her chest puff out as she wonders what to tell him. She paces back and forth a few times before she stops in front of him.

"This may shock you, but I work here." She straightens her spine like she's ready to fight whatever judgment he's gonna dish out. "I'm a stripper, and this is something I do for *me*. So if you're uncomfortable with that, then I suggest you make an excuse and quit."

His brow lifts a fraction.

"Oh, and let's get one thing straight." She digs her index finger into his chest, staring heatedly at him. "You keep your mouth shut about it, okay? I know you work for Michael, but you cannot tell him or anyone about this. It would ruin me." Her hand returns to her side. "And the last thing I want is for my parents to find out. This would break their hearts." Her face falls as she glances down at her feet before gathering her composure once more. "They've been through enough, and so have I."

His expression grows stiff. "It's not my job to tell anyone your business. My job is to keep you safe."

"It won't bother you to see me naked?"

"Is it supposed to bother me?" His mouth hikes up, and he keeps his eyes connected with hers.

"I don't know…" she ponders, gaze wandering down his chest. "I mean, I think it'd make me uncomfortable to see *you* naked."

"Well, it's a good thing I'm not the one who's stripping, then, Ms. Jenkins."

She scoffs, and her cheeks grow pink. "Kayla."

"Right." He chuckles. "Well, Kayla, I can keep my eyes closed if it would make you feel better."

"Pretty sure you won't be able to do that."

"Why? Think you have what I want?"

"No…" Her face twists harshly and it's a bit adorable. "Because there are literally dozens of naked women at the club, and there's no way you're not going to want to look at them."

"I think it's cute how you think you know me." He chuckles.

"You think I'm cute?" She fights a bemused smile. And I very much would love to see it.

"I didn't say that." His lips turn up at each end.

She pivots on her heels and starts toward the entrance. "Sure you didn't. Now, come on. I'm running late. Stay in the back and don't kill anyone."

"I think I should be telling *you* that."

She glares at him from behind her shoulder, then proceeds inside. "It was *one* time, and he deserved it."

"He did…"

I make my way to the last row of tables and settle in, watching as she disappears into the back of the stage.

Though I don't want it to, my dick jerks at the thought of seeing her bare again.

Women come and go, dancing to a beat I don't care to hear. But as soon as I see her, my breath catches and my eyes stay glued to hers.

She doesn't know me.

It's better that way.

Nothing good ever comes from knowing a man like me.

KAYLA

His eyes are on me. Dark and brooding, jaw tensing every time he watches me round the pole while I purposely stare directly at him, enjoying his intensity.

I don't know why I'm even looking at him, but it's as though I can't help myself.

Is he my type? Do I even know what my type is?

He is attractive, though. The women here think so, at least. Coco asked me if he was my boyfriend. Wouldn't that be ridiculous? Considering he gets paid to spy on me.

The song changes, and he folds his arms over his chest, trying to keep his eyes on mine instead of my body.

I have to give him an A for effort.

But I like the attention, if I'm honest. He likes what he sees. I can easily tell he does. But knowing he can't have it? Well, that excites me.

Unlike before, in my old life, these men can't have me. They get to watch. Want. Then go home. And if they try anything, they'll die for it.

When that thought crosses my mind, I wonder if I could do it again. If I could take a life. Would it be easier this time?

But I can't do that again. I can't call Michael and have him clean up after me. He'd be furious.

Before I can think more of it, the MC introduces another girl.

I head for the back, seeing Chris rise to his feet and follow me.

When he tries to cross beyond the curtain, the security guard stops him. "Can't go past me, buddy."

While Chris shoots his attention to me, I get a thrilling idea.

He must've discovered something in my gaze, because he narrows his. "Kayla. Tell him who I am."

"Never seen him before." I wink and head to the back, hearing his thundering growl as I quickly change into my clothes.

Hoping he doesn't catch me, I grab my handbag and rush toward my car, jumping inside. Just as I roll down the street, I see his fiery gaze through my rearview.

CHRIS

This girl is trouble. She may not know it, but I do.

I watched her watching me as she danced. That sinful body swirling around the pole, her hips gyrating seductively as she flipped that luscious hair over her head, refusing to look away. She wanted me hard for her, and I was.

Fuck, I would've stroked myself if I'd been watching her in private.

It's what she wanted. To make me hungry. It's too bad nothing can happen between us. Not now. Not ever.

She's merely a job. And that's all she'll ever be. When I'm done, I'll move on to the next one, and she'll be long forgotten.

I follow her, speeding down the street as she turns right.

Once she ran off into her car, my anger boiled. But I have to catch up with her. She can't get away.

If she were in front of me, the things I'd do. My palm itches to mark her round ass and turn it red on my lap.

Would she like it? Would she want my touch between her thighs? Perfect pink pussy. I bet she tastes good.

"Fuck!" I clutch the steering wheel so tight my knuckles turn white.

Honking at the yellow cab before me, I swerve around it, almost crashing into another vehicle.

This little troublemaker likes to start fires, and I'm gonna put them out for her. Or it will cost us both everything.

KAYLA

Somehow, I ended up at a random bar. Mostly college-aged kids, it appears.

I pass a glance at the young twentysomethings laughing with their friends, drinking, having a great time.

That should've been me. I should've had a life. A future. Now, I'm a twenty-eight-year-old college student. It's laughable.

My only friend in school is Eriu Quinn, Patrick Quinn's daughter. Her father is newly married to Michael's mom, Fernanda, and her older sister is married to one of his brothers.

When I showed interest in going to college, Elsie suggested I apply to the same school Eriu goes to.

I never thought I'd get into an Ivy League school, but Michael made sure I did no matter what. So here I am, studying biology, hoping to become the oncologist I never got to be.

Those fuckers may have taken everything, but they didn't take my determination. They can pry that out of my cold, dead hands.

"Can I buy you a drink?" a guy with pale blue eyes asks, his teeth bleach white, his black hair combed back like he's from one of those Gucci ads. He's gotta be twenty-one.

"I'm okay."

"Oh, come on." He pouts. "Just one. I promise I won't bite." He leans in. "Unless you want me to."

His grin spreads, and I instantly roll my eyes internally.

Corny.

"Yeah, sure. One drink. Piña colada."

He dons a victorious grin as he settles onto a swivel chair beside me. Calling over the bartender, he orders my drink.

A minute later, I'm sipping on it while he takes a shot of his vodka.

"So, what's your name?" he calls out over the blaring rock music.

"Kayla. You?"

This is normal, right? Just talking to a guy at a bar. I can be normal. I can try at least. What if he's actually a good guy? What if he's my future husband and I'm standing in my own way?

"Prince." He laughs.

My brows squint. "For real?"

"Yes, laugh away." He shakes his head, a smile still fastened. "My parents were obsessed with him…"

I grimace. "I'm sorry."

"They're cool, so I've forgiven them."

"My name is pretty boring."

He hikes his chin a fraction. "I don't find any part of you boring, Kayla."

My cheeks grow hot. My God, I'm so easy. One compliment, and I'm blushing.

"I should go." I start to get up. "It's getting late, and I have school tomorrow."

"Where do you go?"

"York State."

His eyes widen. "No way! Me too."

I blink incredulously. "Really?"

"Yeah. Shit! Now I have more reasons to see you. What's your major? Mine is business."

"Bio."

"Smart and beautiful." He angles in close. "How about I give you my number? Maybe we can grab lunch or something."

I don't know if this is a good idea. But I'm reaching into my bag anyway and handing him my phone after I unlock it. He types into it and calls himself from it, then hands it back to me.

"Well, Kayla, I'll see you around."

He pays for our drinks, mine still full, and with one last lingering look, he walks over to his buddies. They all stare at me, then back at him, laughing and looking like he just won the lotto.

I shake my head, needing to go home. When I start for my car, the lot is empty.

As soon as my hand lands on the door handle, I register footsteps behind me.

The hairs on my arms stand up, my chest growing heavy with undulating fear.

"Hey, baby," a deep voice I don't recognize calls. "Where are you off to in such a hurry?"

The way he sounds...disgust swirls in my gut as I turn to face a man about ten years older. Maybe more.

"Going home." I start to open the door. "Have a good night."

He chuckles coldly. And as I get into my car, he rushes into the passenger side in an instant, grabbing my throat as he locks the doors.

"Drive, bitch."

My body grows icy; every memory of my time as a Bianchi whore comes smashing into the surface.

With unsteady hands, I start the car and get it on the road, wishing that Chris was here. I was an idiot for losing him.

"What do you want?" I whisper, rolling to a stop at a red light.

"You, of course. Do you live alone?"

"No."

He laughs. "Liar. Drive to your house. I wanna see where a pretty thing like you sleeps at night. Maybe fuck you on your pretty bed. Bet you haven't had anyone fuck you the way I will." His fingers squeeze my throat while he relaxes against the seat.

My heart pounds, but inside me, something grows. Something wicked and hate-filled. If he wants to see where I live, I'll let him.

Twenty minutes later, and I'm pulling up to my place. He forces me out, pushing me toward my home.

"Get the keys out."

His hand clutches my hair as I quickly do what he wants. Seconds later, and we're inside.

"Where's your bedroom?"

I point left, and he roughs me toward that direction. I wonder if he has a weapon, because I do, and when he drops his guard, I'll use it on him. Slowly, I open the flap of my handbag, fingers reaching inside, retrieving a flip knife.

When we're in my bedroom, he turns me around. As he does, I open the blade and instantly swipe it across his cheek.

"You little bitch!" he roars, rushing for me.

But I bypass him, my pulse trembling, not knowing how this will end.

Will he kill me? Or will I kill him?

There's an adrenaline rush here, fear swirling with fury as I lunge for him with a guttural scream.

As I do, he flips me and wraps his forearm around my throat and squeezes. The knife tightens in my grasp, my lungs growing hot as I gasp for breath.

My hand trembles as I raise it behind me, hoping to claw his eyes out, but he grabs my wrist and attempts to get the knife from me.

He almost does too, but as he backs up, he trips against the chair.

That's all I need to escape from him. As he stumbles onto the floor, I jump on top of him and stab him in the throat.

Roaring on a cry, I plunge the blade over and over, his blood spilling until my hands are covered in crimson, until his life has left his body.

He's dead now.

Yet I'm shaking.

Crying too. I think.

Blood. So much of it.

I don't know what I'm going to do. How I'll explain this to Michael again. He's going to kill me. There's no way I can call him. But what other choice do I have? I don't have anyone else to help me.

"Step away from the body," says someone I immediately recognize. Same deep, gravelly tone sending shudders down my spine.

With a shaky breath, I turn, facing the man in the hood standing before me.

But this time, I see his face—or should I say, the taunting mask he wears? Was he wearing it that day in the parking lot of the club when Ivy was attacked? If he was, I didn't see it.

The mask sends a curling level of fear streaming through my limbs. All white. No mouth on it, except the shape of a nose, and two black eyes where no one can see the pupils beneath. And on each one is a red bloody vertical slash, like it's been clawed right down to its cheek.

Terrifying. That's the only way to describe it.

Who is this man? What the hell is he doing here? Is he gonna turn me into the police?

Oh, God. I can't go to prison.

"Please…" I choke out. "It was self-defense. I—I didn't mean to."

But that's a lie. I wanted to as soon as he came up behind me. I wanted to kill him right there and then.

The man doesn't answer. Just stands there, barely even moving. I gulp down the fear, my arms prickling, my nipples beading.

"Are you gonna hurt me?" I ask, knowing somehow that he won't.

"My, my, little wolf, you have one insatiable appetite." He chuckles darkly, and my body grows tingly from the sound of it, from the way his tone fills with something murky and taunting.

He moves a step, and I move back, fearing him, yet draped with excitement at the thought of being caught.

"Don't call me that." The words shake out of me.

"Why? You *are* every bit the wolf, playing with danger, hunting your prey."

My body shivers.

"Do you deny it? That you wanted to kill him just like the other man whose throat you slashed?"

I gasp. "H-how did you know that?"

"I know everything, Kayla Jenkins. I know everything about you." His laugh is cold, emotionless. "But don't worry. I won't tell a soul what a *dirty* girl you are." His voice is sinful. Deadly. "I can keep your secret."

I swallow down the lump in my throat.

"Do I know you? Have we met? What do you want in exchange?" The questions rush out of me while the body bleeds across my wooden floor.

"No." He shakes his head. "You don't know me."

He moves even closer, and my breaths ring louder as he does.

"But none of us know one another, do we, now? Not at our core. We're all strangers to one another, especially those closest to us."

He takes another step toward me, and this time I wait, wanting to be near him, anticipation drowning me.

"Take you, for example," he goes on. "Do your friends know how wicked you are? How much blood is on your pretty hands?"

My chest grows tight, fear clouding my vision.

"You can't tell them. Please," I beg, my breath caught in my throat.

"I have no intentions of telling anyone. Your secret will remain between us. Because we're friends now, aren't we?"

I nod because he's a madman in a mask, holding my fate in his hands.

"I've gotta say, though..." He chuckles deep in his throat. "You need to learn how to be a little bit neater with your work." His face turns toward the man.

"Didn't exactly have that luxury with him trying to kill me and all."

His laughter is silkier this time, like being draped in a soft, pillowy blanket. I can just see his smirk too.

"Well, you sure made a huge mess the last time, and now this… There are easier ways to do it."

My stomach turns to knots. "And you know this how?"

He laughs again, but doesn't answer my question. "I'm going to clean this up for you. You're welcome."

"Wh-what? Really?" My eyes fill with disbelief.

Maybe I won't have to call Michael after all. Or maybe he's lying.

"Why would you do that? What's in it for you?"

How the hell can I trust this lunatic? What's wrong with me?

"Do you always question a gift when it's handed to you?"

"Of course." I hike up my chin.

"Good girl."

I swear, if I could see beneath his mask, I know he'd still be smirking.

"Now get me some hydrogen peroxide, lots of water, and a pair of gloves while I grab some bleach and plastic to wrap him in," he demands.

I look around, not seeing any. "Where is it?"

"Well, obviously not here." He chuckles. "Going to get it from my car while you do what I asked."

The better question would be why he has bleach and plastic in his car to begin with. Then again… He *is* in a mask and terrifying as hell.

"What will you do to him?" I peer over at the body.

"Nothing you need to worry about. Now go before your bodyguard shows up. And I don't really want to kill him. Unless you want me to."

I shake my head. "No, he's fine. He's not like them."

And he's currently pissed off at me, if the text messages burning a hole in my pocket are any indication.

"Lucky him, then."

I wish this stranger would take off that mask so I could see his face. I want to know what he looks like. Want to see his mouth move as he smiles.

I pinch my thighs together. I'm sick. The thoughts running through my head would shame the Kayla I used to be.

But I'm no longer her, am I? Not since they took me. Ruined me. Now, I'm barbaric, wanting things I can never say out loud, especially to a man.

If I'm being honest, I like his mask. Want him to throw me on the floor and wear it as he fucks me.

My God, I'm sick.

The men from my past would wear masks too…

Is that why I like his? Because I'm twisted that way?

But theirs were pretty. Deceiving. His is not. He isn't hiding. He's showing me who he is.

"What's with the stupid mask?" I blurt out, needing a distraction from my intrusive thoughts.

"You're not scared of it?" I hear the mockery, like he enjoys the fact that I'm not.

"Scared? No." I slowly shake my head. "Seen monsters scarier than that."

"So have I," he whispers, and for a moment, there's something raw in it. Something real and honest…and sad.

Though I can't see his eyes, I feel them, and my heart slams in my chest.

What were his monsters like?

What did they take from him?

Every part of me itches to ask him. To know. To feel.

But instead, I rush out of there and into my bathroom. With my back against the wall, I close my eyes and temper my breathing, needing to be okay before I head back out.

The door slams shut while I stay here wondering…

What am I even doing caring about this psychopath? I mean, he *is* a psycho. Who else wears a mask like that and isn't even fazed by a dead body?

Shit. It hits me now.

Is he stalking me? He must be. What are the chances of him just showing up here? Oh my God. I have a stalker, don't I?

This is just great! A bodyguard *and* a stalker. How did a girl get so lucky?

Not even a minute later, I hear him return.

Grabbing the things he asked for, plus some thick yellow gloves for each of us and towels from the closet, I force myself toward the exit.

I drop everything gently on the floor as soon as I'm out.

"Here." I hand him his pair of gloves, holding on to mine.

He zips his line of vision to my hands.

"What?" I snicker. "Thought I'd let you do it alone?"

He chuckles all deep, and my stomach dives, heat sprouting between my thighs once again, like a flame that won't simply put out. I hate it and love it at the same time.

"My, my, little wolf. You just keep surprising me."

"You make it sound like it's a bad thing."

"That's 'cause it is."

I stare at him, and through the mask, I just know he's staring right back.

He drops a jug of something that reads *oxygen detergent*. As he slips on his gloves, I pick it up, examining it.

"What's this?"

"Ah, I see my little murderess hasn't read the latest on forensics."

"I'm sorry we're not all career murderers like you, apparently. Promise to do better next time," I scoff.

"No, you won't," he chuckles, his leathery rasp sending an electric chill up my spine. "But that's because you don't plan it out. You just do it. That's when mistakes happen."

I hate to admit how right he is.

"So, will you enlighten me on your secret weapon, or should I guess?"

His silence greets me for a moment before he goes on. "This is a special type of bleach. Not the chlorine kind, which makes blood stains invisible, yet will still show the presence of hemoglobin. Oxygen-based bleach erases all traces of it, leaving no evidence."

"Wow…" I say almost sarcastically. "You really are a murderer."

"You sound pretty judgey for a woman who just killed a man. Two, I might add."

"Touché." My mouth quirks up, and I pause, staring quietly at him for a few moments. "Will you show me your face?"

His chest rises with growing breaths. And for a moment, I don't think he'll answer.

"Maybe. But you're not ready to know me yet."

"Have I seen you before?"

"Maybe."

"Do you always answer questions without really answering them?"

"Always."

"Are you smiling under that stupid thing?"

"Sure as hell am, Kayla Jenkins. But don't take it as a compliment. Wouldn't want it to go to your head."

"Wouldn't dream of it." I purse my lips, but my mouth burns

with how hard I'm trying not to smile.

"Fucking trouble," he mutters under his breath, like he didn't mean for me to hear it. With a heavy exhale, he says, "Let's clean up this mess before you create another one."

"For some reason, I think you're very much enjoying this."

"A little too much."

Without saying another word, he unrolls a plastic tarp across my floor, then grabs the man's body and lowers him down. Speechless, I watch him cover the dead body with the plastic until only a shadow remains.

He picks up some of that oxygen bleach and a towel and starts cleaning, while I follow everything he's doing and do the same.

Together, we make the place look as though nothing ever happened.

And the scariest part of all is that being here with him, doing what we're doing, is the most fun I've had in a while.

Seven

KAYLA

I haven't seen Chris since I ran off on him last night. Nor have I heard from Michael on how pissed he is at me, so maybe Chris didn't actually tell him.

Getting out of my car at school, I look around for the neighborhood's friendly stalker, but I don't see him, nor do I see my bodyguard anywhere.

Maybe they both decided to leave me alone.

Doubtful…

College students bustle around, talking in groups, rushing to their classes, while I grab my books and start out of the car.

As I head for the humanities building, this sudden eerie feeling washes over me. Goose bumps thread my skin. And I know instantly.

Someone's watching me.

I can't see him. But I know he's there, lurking in the shadows.

I freeze in the middle of the road, glancing around, trying to find the man in the mask. Because I know he's the one watching. Waiting.

He could be anyone. A professor. A student. The janitor I say hi to every day when I head for class.

"Hey, Kayla!"

I gasp as a woman's voice flips me in her direction.

I turn to see Eriu bouncing down the steps of the building, heading right for me. My chest still pummels heavily inside me.

I force myself to look into her emerald-green eyes and fake a cheerful appearance. "Hey. I was just…uh…heading to class. Are you done with yours?"

She nods. "Yeah, I have a little break, so I was gonna grab some coffee before the next class." Her brows stitch in concern. "You okay? You look a little nervous."

"Yeah, totally fine. Just thought I saw someone I knew."

She smiles. "No worries. I'll text you after your class. We can grab lunch."

"Sounds good." I wave goodbye before heading toward where she came from.

As I enter the building and rush toward the snack machine to get a water, someone grasps my wrist from behind.

When I pivot around…

Chris.

And his eyes are no longer soft. His jaw is clenched, his throat tight on his next swallow.

Every cell in my body pulses under that heated stare.

Well, he definitely isn't happy. Wonder why…

"Hey…it's you." I fight a nervous laugh while he grinds his jaw and pulls me in the direction of a classroom.

Before I can protest, he drags me inside, throws me up against the wall, and locks the door. I realize the classroom is empty and that he somehow knew that already.

Two palms flatten on each side of my head, the intensity in his eyes dancing with danger as they peer down into mine.

I'm cowering in fear, yet my body tingles simultaneously, like it enjoys every bit of this danger.

My lips part, my gaze zeroing in on his full mouth while my heart beats to a wild crescendo.

His eyes grow heavy-lidded, as though the way I look at him is affecting him just as much as it is affecting me.

"If you do that again…" he husks. "If you sabotage me from keeping you safe, I will handcuff you to me, Kayla."

He grabs my jaw, fingers pressing deep into my flesh. I grow aroused at the way he manhandles me. Like a thing he can play with and manipulate at his disposal.

"Do you understand me?" He drops his mouth lower until I taste the sweet mint on his breath. "You will eat, sleep, shower right beside me. Is that what you prefer?"

"No."

Yes.

Maybe.

I sound like a helpless little mouse.

His eyes remain fixed to mine, searching endlessly. His thumb reaches out to brush across my mouth.

"Don't ever scare me like that again." He blows a hard breath, and my heart beats faster and faster.

"You…you were worried about me?" My pulse speeds up.

He doesn't say anything. Instead, he threads his other hand through my hair and holds me still.

I want his hands everywhere, on every broken and bruised inch of me.

Would he hurt me like they did? Would he take care of me?

And suddenly, I'm thinking about the man in the mask. That deep ruggedness of his tone, only a little deeper than Chris's. Thoughts of all three of us together make my toes curl. My arms bound behind me while one takes me from behind and the other forces his cock down my throat.

A little moan slips from my lips, and instead of pushing off of me, the tip of his tongue rolls past his bottom lip, just enough for me to see it.

Desire unfurls through me like a hungered siren.

I realize how insane I've become, thinking of two men. Of being treated the way I want to be.

Why am I like this? What the hell is wrong with me?

Tears ache behind my eyes, and I curl my fingers against my sides.

"Get off me, asshole!" I shove him off. "Don't you ever touch me like that again!"

He immediately backs off, as though I've suddenly grown thorns.

"My apologies, ma'am." He turns rigid.

I instantly regret what I said, wanting that man again, the one who worried, who sounded like he cared.

My chin trembles, and I rush out of the room, hearing him call my name.

But I don't look back.

There's no reason to. He's not my future.

Because I don't have one.

Not anymore.

CHRIS

I slam a fist into the wall as soon as she walks out the door, tears shining in her eyes. The ones I put there.

"Fucking bastard," I scold myself.

I made her uncomfortable. I made her cry.

Kayla…

I know about her past. I know she was taken and hurt for years before she was found, and I go and trap her like that?

But I wasn't thinking. Not when I recalled how she ran off on me, leaving me worried that something could've happened to her. When I tracked her back to her place, she was there, and luckily still okay.

It's not even my job I'm worried about. I don't care if I lose it. I can't let anything happen to her, not on my watch. It's my duty to ensure her safety, and I don't fail at anything.

My pulse still races as I think about the way she looked at my mouth. Like she wanted to know how good it'd fit around hers. I bet she tastes sweet, like an innocent little flower that requires a delicate touch.

But I can't be the man to give her that. Not after what she's been through. I don't even know how to be gentle with a woman. Never was before. Never needed to be, not with the kind of women I've fucked. They all wanted it rough, and I gave them everything they craved. But I can't be that way with Kayla.

But shit, the way she made me throb. The way I wanted to find out if she was aching for me between her soft thighs. The sounds I could force out of her while my tongue's pressed over her clit…

I pinch the bridge of my nose, trying to tame my ill-fitted

thoughts so I can go and do my fucking job: watching her. I know she's in class now for the next hour, and I know where.

Taking another moment to compose myself, I head out in her direction until I reach her classroom, which is already in session. Peering through the little window in the door, I see her in the middle row, chatting with some guy her age.

My hand clenches when she smiles at him.

That's how it should be, though. Her talking to guys that aren't me. I don't belong with any woman, not with the things I've done. Least of all Kayla.

She'll remain out of reach, where she belongs.

KAYLA

When I strut into my classroom, I still have Chris on my mind. He must think I'm crazy after how I reacted.

But that's because I *am* crazy. Not like I'm in denial.

The professor strolls into the room, and I scurry to find a seat in the nearly full classroom.

"Hey," someone whispers loudly, and I startle to see where the noise is coming from.

When I find the source, there's a guy waving to me, a huge grin on his face. I immediately recognize him: Prince from the bar.

What the hell is he doing here? Were we always in the same class and I just never noticed? There are a couple of hundred kids here, so that wouldn't be so hard.

Heading in his direction, I drag a smile.

"Hey, Kayla." He removes his messenger bag from on top of the chair beside his, grinning sheepishly.

"Hey. I hope I'm not taking anyone's seat." I settle into it.

"Nah," he waves off with a smirk. "I was saving it for you."

I drop my tote onto my lap and start to remove my laptop and a textbook on European history.

"I can't believe we're in the same class."

"Wish I noticed you before." He drops his mouth close to my ear. "This class would've been a lot more fun."

"You don't like it? I find it interesting to go back in time and reexamine mistakes humans made and how they affect us today."

He shrugs. "I'm not one to focus on the past. I like to spend my energy on the present and the future. Plus, this professor is boring as hell." His voice lowers as the teacher starts to speak, fixing his red-rimmed glasses.

A door slams shut. I jerk toward it to find Chris marching inside, and every single girl in the room has her eyes set on him.

My throat instantly dries when our eyes connect.

He may be a jerk, but he's a handsome jerk.

His gaze stays glued to mine until the very last second as he makes it to the last row, taking a seat that allows him a direct view of me from behind.

I readjust in the chair, feeling hot and cold all at once.

"What the hell is an old dude doing here?" Prince laughs.

"He's like forty. That's not old." This need to defend him comes over me, and I don't know why.

But nothing about Chris is old. He's every bit man, and I want to run my hands all over his body.

Whore, the voice inside me says, and disgust grabs hold of me and refuses to let go.

I own the title, something I've been called for years. Why should now be any different?

The class passes slowly because I know he's watching my every move. I spend that time trying to pay attention in between turning around to find Chris still staring at me, an aggravated expression painted on his face.

He looks as though he's ready to punish me. Ready to grab me by my hair, force me to my knees, and pry my mouth open with his cock.

I bet it's thick and hard. I bet he fucks just as roughly.

I discreetly shift in the seat, not realizing I've been biting my lip.

"You okay?" Prince asks.

My eyes pop wildly while my entire face heats up. I wish I could hide from my mortification.

"Yep. Just anxious for it to end."

"See? Boring. I told you." He puffs out his chest and folds his arms across it like he's just proven me wrong.

But he has no idea…

Nothing about today's lecture is boring. It's just hard to pay attention with my bodyguard right behind me.

I glance back at Chris again, and this time one corner of his mouth curls, just a little. Just enough to make my heart skip a beat.

Did he notice me practically grinding all over the chair? Did he know it was because of him? Or was he smiling like that because he liked that I was looking at him?

The bell goes off, and everyone starts to bolt.

"Don't forget to read chapters ten to fifteen for next week's class! There will be a quiz!" the professor announces.

Collective groans ring through, and Prince is definitely the loudest.

I grab my things and start toward the exit with Prince next to me. But I know who's right behind us. I can feel him towering over me, the warmth of his body cascading through mine.

When I glance back, he's there, eyes on me.

He leans in, and it's like a powerful wave of electric current falling over me. "You won't be getting away from me ever again, Kayla Jenkins."

His hot breath swirls around the side of my neck.

My stomach drops, and not because I'm nervous. A thrilling feeling comes alive inside me instead.

We wrestle our way out of the building with a horde of students rushing both ways.

Once we're outside, Prince grabs my hand. "Don't tell me you're leaving me so quickly."

I nervously shiver, knowing Chris is listening and watching everything, even as he stands a few feet behind Prince nonchalantly.

But when his eyes zero in on our joined hands, his nostrils flare.

I immediately drag my hand away, afraid he'll break Prince's arm.

That relaxes him. A bit.

Clearing my throat, I say, "I'm meeting a friend at the cafeteria, actually."

My gaze darts to Chris for a second, while he's now pretending to be using his cellphone. But I know he's faking it.

My phone vibrates, and I find a text from Eriu. Just in time.

ERIU

In the cafeteria. Saved you a seat.

KAYLA

Coming.

"Uh, want to join us?" I ask Prince.

That has Chris snapping his feral eyes to mine, a hint of danger in the tendrils of his gaze. A shudder zips up my spine.

"But I'm sure you have plenty of friends," I backpedal. "And you don't actually want to."

Prince chuckles. "I do have my fair share, but none of them are you, so count me in."

He's being sweet, I know he is, but it's making me feel nothing, which wasn't the case with Chris or the masked mystery man.

That's because you don't like nice. You like crazy and rough and wildly intense.

At least my subconscious knows me well.

He strides beside me while Chris follows. But Prince doesn't even notice. A guy like that is all about himself. I know the type. Met men like that in my past life.

He's no different.

When we make it inside the cafeteria, Eriu waves us over. I rush to give her a hug and introduce her to Prince.

While we eat, she drops her face toward my ear.

"He's cute!" she whispers, while I elbow her.

"Not my type." My eyes snap to Chris's.

Apparently, my type is currently drilling holes into the back of my head.

Eight

KAYLA

When I got home from school a few hours ago, Chris followed me, his SUV sitting right outside across the street.

He didn't say a word to me after I left school, but he was one step behind at every moment. Like my personal shadow.

I wouldn't be surprised if he planted a tracker in my car, probably somewhere I'll never find it.

Pressing a few keys on my laptop, I check the latest updates on the sex registry, investigating all the new ex-cons who may have moved into the neighborhood.

Clicking a few more keys, I find one.

Fred Avon.

Five-nine. Bald. And only lives a few blocks away…

From the looks of him, he appears nice. Safe.

But he's not.

Imprisoned for thirty years.

Sexual abuse in the first degree, it says. The victim was only five years old. He was twenty-five at the time.

Nausea swims up my throat.

A quick search reveals that he also lives alone.

I flinch at the thought of how badly he traumatized that girl. What she had to go through, live with.

I have to do something. I have to make him hurt! It isn't fair that he's out. He should be rotting away in prison.

But what can I do?

I continue to stare into his eyes, now somehow appearing colder than they were a moment ago. And I know instantly. I know what I have to do.

I don't know if it'll work. Or how I'll even accomplish it with Chris watching. But I have to try. I can't let men like that get away with it.

Closing my laptop, I head for my bedroom, and as I flip the light on, I make out something on my comforter.

A single white lily and a note beside it.

But that's not all. There's a small, square brown box there too.

Fear claps around my throat and my breathing turns fast and shallow.

With unsteady footfalls, I creep closer, my fingers reaching for the box first. As I peer inside it, I let out a harsh exhale. All I find is a bunch of cleaning supplies and a pack of fifty gloves.

But it's then I realize… Those are the same exact gloves I gave to the masked stalker the night he helped me get rid of the body.

"What the…"

Quickly, I grab the note and read it.

Happy early birthday. I thought it was only fitting I leave you a little gift. I know how dirty you can be. By the way, you looked pretty in class today. I like it when you wear your hair down. Makes me want to run my fingers through it. And I hate that you make me feel those things.

See you soon, little wolf. Don't get too hungry without me.

—A

My heart hammers. He saw me in class? He likes my hair?

He knows when my birthday is?

Oh my God. He really is stalking me.

I don't like to feel those things…

Neither do I.

But I feel something for him, no matter how depraved it may be, no matter how hard it may be to describe. He brings something out in me.

My lungs grow heavy, and I keep staring at the note. I knew he was watching. Knew he was there at school the whole time. But where?

The fact that he's been inside my room thrills me.

Will he come inside my house again? While I'm asleep? Why does that excite me so much?

I start to wonder what his name is. But at least I can call him A until he trusts me with his full name.

Getting the box off my bed, I bring it into the bathroom and put the cleaning supplies away. Then I get a small plastic vase from my cabinet and fill it with water.

Bringing it to my room, I slip the lily inside and place it on the nightstand beside me. I want him to know I kept it. That I love it. That it makes me happy just to look at it.

Before I head to sleep, I peer out the window, hoping to see him, but all I find there is Chris, still in his car.

A has to be out there.

I know he's somewhere close.

I know he's always watching.

I want him to.

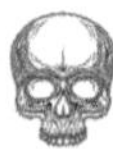

One large hand grips both of my wrists above my head, my eyes bound, the smell of his cologne invading my nostrils.

I lie there in nothing but a long t-shirt and a thong.

"Take off her panties," one man says to another.

I know that voice. I've heard it before. I know it's him. A.

I grind my hips against the soft mattress, anticipating his touch, my toes curling as hands on my panties cause my entire body to tingle.

"Mmm, look how pretty she is…" the other one groans, and it sounds like Chris.

But how can that be? Why are they together?

My heart pounds.

Someone runs the tip of their finger down my wet and warm slit.

"Come on, little wolf, spread those legs for us. Let us see how pink and pretty that pussy is. Promise we'll make it feel good."

I immediately obey, opening wide, wanting their hands, their bodies everywhere. Wanting to feel them both inside me at the same time.

Whore.

But I ignore the voice in my head, focusing on the sensations they're igniting within me.

Cold metal prickles my belly button, and I wince.

"What is that?" I whisper, and someone grabs a fistful of my hair and yanks with a growl.

"Something to tear the rest of those clothes off, baby." Chris's

deep, seductive voice makes me ache. "We want to see every stunning inch of you."

My shirt is being torn, like they're slicing it with a knife or a pair of scissors. I'm not even scared. I want more.

"Please touch me," I beg with a heady moan. "I need…"

"Need what?" A groans.

Oh my God. What is happening?

But I don't have time to think about it when one of them flicks my clit and my back bows, the sounds coming out of me loud and wanton. I don't even know which one of them just did that. I'm shrouded in utter darkness.

"Who should be the first to taste you, little wolf?"

Sensations explode through my core as a finger continues to torture my pussy.

"Should it be me?" Chris sucks my earlobe while one of them fondles me, refusing to slip his finger inside me.

Is that A? Oh, God, I want it to be him. I want him to touch me.

I'm so turned on. I know they can both see it and feel it. But I don't care. I'm too far gone to worry about that.

Fingers pinch my nipple, and I gasp and whimper, my teeth snapping around the edge of my bottom lip, the feeling so erotic it makes me twist and writhe in ecstasy. I've never once felt anything like this before.

A mouth is on my nipple now while someone else continues to touch my clit, two fingers stroking it. The sensation is so addicting, I'm ready to explode.

"Look at her. She's such a slutty thing, making a mess of the bed, wanting both of our cocks in this tight little hole."

He penetrates me just a little, and I beg and plead.

"Please, please don't stop."

One man groans around my other nipple and teases it with his teeth, biting it just enough to send a zap to my core, already on overdrive.

I'm theirs. Both of theirs. I wanted this. Fantasized about it, even. Now it's really happening.

"Does baby girl need to come?" Chris husks around my ear. "Do you want it?"

I nod. "I need it. Please. I want both of you."

"Fuck," A growls.

And the next thing I feel is the heat of his mouth around my throbbing pussy, his tongue flicking so quickly, it's like I'm being transcended to another space and time.

"Open her mouth. Put your cock inside it," A tells Chris.

The sound of a zipper resonates through the space while my eyes roll back. I crave it, feel it, want it. I want them to do whatever they want to me.

My body's flipped onto my stomach, my hands are gripped against the small of my back, and someone is tying something around them.

"Wh-what are you doing?"

"It's what you want, don't you?" A's croaky, deep voice turns me into molten lava. "You want to be tied up and used like our whore, isn't that right?"

I nod, my core aching for release that they never gave me.

"We know everything you want. We're inside your head. We know your demons, your darkest desires. And we want to give them all to you."

Before I can tell him it's what I want too, he slams inside me so hard and deep, my entire body convulses and my release washes over me. But he doesn't stop. He keeps going, grabbing a fistful of my hair.

"Open that mouth for me." Chris's cock brushes velvety soft

over my lips, and I don't hesitate to suck him right into my mouth.

"Oh, fuck," he groans, slamming down my throat with fervor while A takes me deeper, faster, until I feel it again, the sensations overtaking me.

My throat is on fire with how hard Chris's length slams into it.

"That's it, come on my cock. Look how good you take it," A praises, slapping my ass with a heavy palm.

"Take off her blindfold," he tells Chris. "Let her see us while she comes this time."

"Wanna watch us as we violate you?" With a hand, Chris forces the back of my head further down his thick erection.

I moan around it, and then I feel his fingers around my eyes as he rips off the blindfold.

"What the…?" I shoot up to a sitting position in my bed, my body heaving, my palms around my raging heart.

I stare around the room, where a shadow looms in the corner.

"A?" I gasp, blinking faster and faster…until…

Until I realize there's no one there. I'm alone. I was seeing things.

"A dream? *That* was a dream? Really?"

With a groan, I plop back against the pillows. Of course I was dreaming. Neither of them would want someone like me. I bet they can smell the damage coming a mile away.

Groaning, I turn into a fetal position, forcing myself to try to go back to sleep. But as I do, I catch sight of something new on top of the other nightstand.

A note and another white lily.

My pulse thrums, my body jerking from the shock of it.

Does this mean he was here? During my…

"Oh my God!"

How did I not hear him? Did he come through the back window

in my spare bedroom? The back door? Chris would've seen him if he came from the front.

Nervousness coats through my limbs as I pick it up and read the words he wrote.

Were you thinking about me while you slept, little wolf? Did I make you moan like that? Did you dream about me inside you? I know you did. You can't deny it. I heard you groan my name. But I heard HIS too. And I don't like it. You're mine now, and I never quite learned how to share.

—A

With lurching breaths, I jump out of bed and rush for the window, noticing that Chris is still there. But as I look to the right, opposite him, I notice a shadow lurking.

Someone all in black.

I open my window and call for him, because I know it's him.

"A! Show me your face! Stop playing games!"

I don't know what the hell I'm thinking, but I'm not. I need to know who he is! That's the only thing fueling me right now.

Hastily, I sprint out of my room and down the stairs, racing outside barefoot, where Chris is already waiting with concern on his features.

"What's wrong?" His hand is on his waistband, and I bet there's a gun there. "Did you see someone?"

I nod nervously. "There was a man in a hood. I—I think. I saw him for a second before he ran off."

"I'm gonna go check it out. Go back inside and lock the door." He drops his palm on my shoulder and gives me a forceful look. "Do not come out for any reason. Do you understand me, Kayla? This isn't a joke."

I nod. "I understand. Please…" Instinctively, I place a palm around the stubble of his cheek, and his jaw tenses. "Be careful."

A will not hesitate to kill you if he has to.

He doesn't move, doesn't speak, while my hand remains there, but I can see his throat bob before he gently removes my hand.

"Go inside. Now."

I do what he asked and lock the door behind me, while he runs off toward the wooded area.

I pray like hell that A doesn't hurt him, and that he doesn't hurt A either.

CHRIS

Rushing through the pitch-black forest, I flip on my flashlight to help illuminate the path the man ran through.

I can hear him in the distance, the quiet footfalls crackling through the branches.

Someone came for her. Someone who didn't know or care that I was watching.

How the *fuck* didn't I see him?

I failed her. He could've hurt her…or worse.

Staying in the car isn't going to work anymore. I'll have to talk to Michael about staying inside her home.

She's not going to like it. And imagining that face getting all pissy has me smiling. I like knowing I can push her buttons. I think she likes pushing mine too.

When she placed her hand on my cheek and told me to be careful, it did something to me. No one has ever worried about me. Not really. Not like her. She meant it too. I could just see it there in her eyes…

I try to keep silent as I near the assailant, his black hoodie and dark pants growing closer. Removing my nine-mil, I point it at him, aiming for his thigh, needing him alive. He will answer for this.

As soon as I fire a shot, he turns and releases one of his own, barely missing my face.

"You're gonna die, motherfucker." I chuckle, needing this, wanting a fight.

I can make out the glare in his dark eyes. Never seen him before. Don't know what faction he belongs to, if any. But I will find out.

He shoots at me again, running faster, but I'm gaining on him. And soon, he will tell me why he came for her.

I aim the barrel at his leg as I continue to chase him toward the road I now find through the clearing.

I can't let him get away.

I press the trigger, and a shot rings off right into his calf.

He instantly goes down.

I sprint toward him as he shifts his body to me, lifts up his weapon, and fires.

Crouching immediately onto the dirt, I evade the bullet, rushing for him. But just when I almost reach him, a car comes screeching down.

Two masked men fire shots at me while two others drag him away.

I shoot off a few bullets at the car, running toward it, but they press on the gas and gun out of there. No plates on the car, and nothing to go on.

"Fuck!"

Reaching into my pocket, I remove my cell, and when I do, my flashlight illuminates something on the grass.

A gold card.

A card I recognize. Michael was sure to show each man who works for him one of these so we knew how to spot it.

I instantly know what it is even before I pick it up off the ground.

Turning it over, I find a phone number there, just as expected.

Because the Bianchis, the ones who took Kayla, they operated their sex club using one of these.

The men call the number on the back, and someone in a mask picks them up, puts a bag over their face, and takes them to a secret location.

Without hesitation, I dial the number, expecting a voice, but instead, it's a recorded message, obviously disguised by a cheap device.

As I listen to it, my blood boils over, needing to spill theirs.

"Elsie, Kayla, and Jade are ours," the stranger informs. "And we will take them all back like we did the others. You can't protect them. No one can."

Yeah, we'll see about that.

Nine

KAYLA

"**W**hat do you mean, he has to stay at my house now?" I blink back at Michael with utter disbelief. "Tell me this is a joke."

Beside me, Elsie rubs my arm, but it doesn't help the situation. Not at all. How the hell am I supposed to live this way?

"It's for your safety." Michael's tone is even. Assertive.

I have no choice. That's what he's truly saying.

"After what Chris found, all of you have to lie low, and all of you are getting extra protection." He glances at Elsie.

"I'm so sick of this!" I let out a scoff. "I'm not scared. If they want me that badly, they can try to come after me too. I'm not afraid to fight back anymore."

Chris's mouth jerks at the corner.

I knew I shouldn't have come over for lunch today. I know they're trying to protect me, but I'm just… I'm just so over it all.

I'm tired.

"I understand that," Michael says, sounding wholly unconvincing. "But that doesn't erase the danger you're in. You know what those animals are capable of. Until we can extinguish them, you'll have round-the-clock eyes on you."

Wonderful.

"I know this sucks," Elsie murmurs, squeezing my hand. "I hate it too, but we have to think about ourselves. This is only temporary. Michael and his brothers will find them all and bring them to justice."

What she means by that is they're all gonna die. Which, of course, I'm fine with. The sooner, the better.

"Yeah, okay, fine."

Yet I internally protest, sending Chris an irritated glower. The bastard has the decency to shoot me a half-smirk.

"You better not snore or anything," I say to him. "Or I will throw you outside with the bats."

"Don't snore, ma'am." His eyes sparkle as that smirk only deepens. "And I like bats."

"Of course you do." I roll my eyes.

Saying my goodbyes, I spin on my heels and head for the door, needing to get to my therapy session with my doc.

Chris strides up beside me.

"Where to next, roomie?" he whispers with a hint of amusement I'd like to wipe from his smug face.

"Therapy. And no, you can't come inside."

"That's a pity. Bet you'd have a lot of good things to say about me." A knowing chuckle escapes through a breath as we make it outside.

I stop mid-stride.

"Like what?" My gaze narrows at him.

But he only laughs, almost to himself, as we step out into the driveway.

And I have a sinking suspicion I know what he meant.

He heard me dreaming. About him.

He must have my placed bugged.

Fuck me.

And I don't mean that literally.

I think…

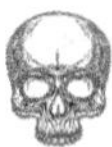

"How have the nightmares been?" Doctor Collins asks, keeping his yellow notepad on his lap, ready to jot down how messed up I still am.

"They have been the same." I shrug. "Maybe I need more meds."

I hate taking them. I just want to feel better.

But will that ever happen? Will I stop being trapped in the hell that was once my home? Will I find monsters everywhere I turn?

I just want this all to stop. I want to forget. Move on. Heal. But I can't. I fucking can't!

With a silent scream, I let the anger consume me. But the good doc can't see it. I hide it all too well.

"We can try something different since you're at the highest dose right now. Have you considered yoga or meditation?"

I bite back a laugh. *Pretty sure I'm too far gone for that.*

"I'm still boxing. I like it."

He nods through a squint. "Well, that is a good outlet too. But meditation and yoga may help center you, so you can try both if that's what you want."

"Yeah, maybe."

Not happening. I don't want to sit there doing some breathing exercises. That's not me.

"Have you considered talking in group? It may help to talk to others about what happened. Women like you who understand."

"I'm not ready to sit in front of a bunch of people and tell them how many times I was raped."

He winces. I said it so casually. But I forget most normal people aren't used to someone speaking about that kind of thing so plainly.

I should change the subject. Maybe bring up Chris again and tell him all about how much I hate having a bodyguard.

And if Chris ever finds out about the other murder, he'll tell Michael, who'll probably ship me off to some psych ward to be condemned for eternity.

Life is great!

The doctor's alarm beeps, signaling that our time is now over.

Thank God.

"If you need me before our next session…" he says. "You have my number."

"Thanks, yeah. I'll see you next week."

I scurry out of there, passing by Jade's office next door. She's really an angel on earth. She went through something even worse than we did. Having been raped by Agnelo, she got pregnant. But as soon as her son, Robby, was born, that bastard took him away. Robby was raised by Agnelo's daughter, Aida. A girl who was every bit his victim too.

Jade talks fondly of Aida, and Robby adores her. She's happy he had someone kind looking after him.

Robby is eight now and back with Jade. But before that, she'd only get to see him once a month, year after year. I don't know how she endured.

Look at her now, though. Reunited with her son, in a healthy relationship, running this place so well… It brings tears to my eyes.

She has changed so many lives already, giving these women a place to call home, a family who will protect them at all costs. Many of the girls the Bianchis kidnapped were runaways and addicts. They took the ones they thought no one would miss.

But they matter. Every single woman they ruined matters. We're all human beings. And look what they did to us.

My heart grows rigid as I continue to stare at Jade, but she doesn't see me watching her through the door, engrossed in a set of papers on her desk.

But just as I swipe under my eye and start down the corridor, she calls my name.

"Kayla? Hey!"

I pause and look over at her.

"Just the woman I needed to talk to," she adds. "Have a minute for me?"

"Sure!"

Walking into her office, I grin, trying my best to appear like I'm not always falling apart. That I'm happy. That's all everyone wants me to be.

But happiness is a weird feeling. I don't know how to be happy. I don't know if I ever will be either. So I've accepted that this is who I am now.

"So…feel free to say no…" She bites her bottom lip and gives me that look that says she really hopes I agree to whatever she's about to ask me.

I internally groan, already anticipating the worst.

"Yeah…" I pull up a chair and sit before her desk. "What are you going to make me do?"

"How do you know I'm gonna make you do anything?" Her lips pull up.

"Because. You have that look in your eyes." I squint a shrewd gaze.

"Fine." Her shoulders slump, and she leans back. "You got me! There's this girl named Cammie who's really lost right now…"

Oh, no.

"She was actually in the house with you and Elsie for a couple of years before they took her somewhere else. She could really use someone who can get through to her, someone who knows what she went through."

Please don't ask me to do this…

"I was really hoping that would be you…" She gives me that sweet, hopeful look. "She's mentioned how nice you were to her when you two were at the house… And believe me, I've tried to help her myself." She throws a hand in the air. "But I can't connect with her as well as I think you can."

"Jade…please…." I slant my head to the side. "I can barely help myself. How can I help her?"

"You're stronger than you think." She purses her lips, her compassion seeping through her angelic blue eyes. "If I didn't worry that she'd try running away again, I wouldn't ask, I swear. I know you hate talking to people about it all, but I'm desperate. I want to help her so badly, and she pushes back even harder every time. So maybe you can give it a shot and see?" She bends her face in a desperate plea.

My chest squeezes, seeing her pure goodness. Jade wants to help the world. Wants to make all the women better.

"I love you, you know that?" I say with a sting in my throat. "I wish there were more people like you in this world."

Her eyes mist, and she fans herself. "Stop it. You know very well compliments make me cry."

"Shut up," I laugh, tossing a pen at her.

She catches it. "I'm sorry I'm putting this pressure on you. I'm feeling bad about it now, so if you can't, I really understand. I just know you'd be good at it."

Releasing a dramatic sigh, I start to rise. "Can I see her now?"

Her gaze pops. "Sure can! She's in the library right now, using the computers."

"Great. Gonna go and pretend I know what I'm talking about. But highly doubt I'll be able to do much for her."

"All we have is our ability to try. So that's all I'm asking for."

"You'd make a good shrink."

"That's what Dr. Collins says." She grins. "But I'm happy to do a little bit of everything. Let me know how it goes with Cammie."

"Will do. See ya later."

She waves while I head for the elevator, entering it before it climbs up to the fourth floor. My pulse instantly throbs. I really have no idea what to tell this girl. Sure, I remember her. She was quiet. Cried a lot. Kind of like me.

Except unlike me, she didn't become a murderer, so at least she has that going for her. Silver lining and all that.

As soon as I walk in, I spot her sitting alone in front of a laptop. I remember being able to count the amount of ribs she had while they…

My gut churns.

I don't want to go back there. Not now. But I can't stop it, not when I'm in this place, seeing the woman I was once locked away with.

There were so many at the house with Elsie and me, some coming and going, others never returning again.

Because they were dead.

They'd show us photos.

Made us scared to get help.

That's what happens to little girls who don't know how to keep quiet. You're gonna keep quiet, right, Kayla?

Of course I did. I'd never risk my or Elsie's lives.

Closing my eyes for a moment, I drag in a long breath to get courage in my system before I nonchalantly take an empty seat beside her.

She glances my way and smiles shyly before she continues reading something on the screen I can't make out.

"Hey, Cammie. Nice to see you."

"Hey, Kayla." She gives me a timid glance. "You don't come here much anymore."

"Yeah." I shrug. "Usually at my place. I come here to see Dr. Collins, though. Are you seeing him too, or one of the other ones?"

"Yeah, I see him." She bites the inside of her cheek, eyeing me nervously. "He's okay, I guess."

I focus on her. She looks younger than she is. More eighteen versus the twenty-five that she is.

"He actually suggested I take on yoga and meditation. Can you imagine me doing that?" I let out a dry laugh, pretending I'm doing a meditation prayer pose and humming to myself.

Her laughter slips free. It's nice to see her laughing. I don't ever remember her doing that.

"That's crazy." She shakes her head. "No way would I even bother with that mumbo jumbo. Therapy is bullshit anyway. I don't know why those people think they can help us or something." Her features tighten, and her voice drops. "How can they help us if they have no idea about any of it?"

I nod. "You're one hundred percent right."

I struggle to say the next few words because I don't really believe them, but if I can make her believe, that's enough.

"It's why we need each other. To talk to one another. Because we understand. We know. Because we endured it together."

She drops her face and stares into her lap. Her chin trembles, and she takes a few seconds before she speaks again.

"I don't know why I'm still alive." Her tears shine in her eyes.

"You're alive because they just happened not to kill you."

Her eyes burst.

"I don't believe in God or any of that bullshit," I tell her honestly. "Nor do I believe that things are meant to happen as they should or that karma exists. Life is just filled with unfortunate events, and sometimes they happen to some and not others. But what matters is that we're still here." I take her hand in mine and squeeze. "If we're living, then we have to do whatever we can to live our life to the fullest. You know why?"

She shakes her head, staring with widened attention.

I drag my chair closer. "Because that's how we get our revenge. By living. They never wanted that for us. They wanted to use us and make us their victims, but we can't act like victims anymore."

This time, her hand squeezes mine.

"We have to fight, and every day we're living and moving on and healing, we *are* fighting. We're telling them to go to hell. And that's where they are. In hell."

She sniffles, tears winding down the slopes of her cheeks as she tucks her brown hair behind her ear.

"If you ever need me…" I say. "If you ever need a friend or someone to hear you cry, I'll be there for you. No questions asked. Because everyone needs someone."

She lets out a sob, and instantly her arms are around my neck. She cries while I hold her, crying a little too.

I gave Cammie my number, hoping she does use it. I hate to

admit it, but Jade was right. That was productive. I liked knowing I got through to her. That I maybe even helped somehow. I hope she does take me up on my offer and calls me.

After therapy, I had some classes in the evening before coming home, and of course Chris followed me in.

He appears half-dead, though, as he enters my living room, looking all over the place, examining my things, my furniture. Like he's trying to understand me as a person.

"Do you approve of my aesthetic, or do you have something to say?" I flick up a sassy brow.

"Hmm…" A wry smile twists his features. "You don't seem like the type of woman who takes critiques very well."

I scoff. "From the likes of you? Never."

He grins.

"Sit," I tell him. "I'll get you water. And maybe you should actually try sleeping tonight."

I swear he barely sleeps, and I'm sure napping in his car has been hell.

"I don't trust you enough to sleep," he teases, his hazel eyes playing.

"I wouldn't trust me either. But since you don't have a replacement, you need to get some rest. I have a spare bedroom I can set up for you."

"I'll sleep on the couch." He settles onto it and outstretches his arms across the upholstery as he leans back, his legs spread like the king of the castle.

And I swear this need to sit over his lap and feel those big, strong arms hold me completely overtakes me. A warm current coats my skin, but I shake it off, rushing into the kitchen to grab him a glass of water.

When I bring it out for him, he's standing, a picture frame of me with my parents in his hand.

Startling, he gently drops it back. "Your parents seem nice."

"They are." I hand him the cup. "They're the best." Lowering onto the loveseat across from the sofa, I wait for him to sit. "Are you close to yours?"

He finishes his water and settles back down. "I was when they were alive. But they died years ago."

"Any siblings?" I wonder.

"I've got brothers, but they're not around. Married and all that."

"No marriage proposals for you? Shocker."

"You've got jokes, huh?" His teasing, tight smirk sends white-hot shame to my cheeks.

I fold my arms over my chest. "You make it *so* easy."

He shakes his head with a grin. "Beautiful and funny."

"You think I'm beautiful?" My cheeks flush.

"You don't?"

My eyes roll. "You sound like my shrink, turning everything into self-reflection."

"He sounds like a smart man." His grin is comforting and warm, like a mug of hot cocoa on a cold day.

"He's okay." I shrug.

Thoughtfully, he stares. "Does it help? Therapy?"

He waits for an answer, curious eyes searching mine.

"I honestly don't know yet. I mean, how much could it have helped if I've turned into a murderer?"

He lets out a laugh, his entire body rocking. "Shit, you are something else, aren't you?"

"If you say so." I sound unconvinced.

His eyes darken as he drops his elbows over the top of his thighs. "You are, Kayla. Don't ever talk about yourself like that, like you're not sure of your worth. I don't ever want to hear it."

My heartbeats pound from the intense way he gazes at me, from his words filled with meaning.

"Okay…" I whisper, knowing right now I'd agree to anything he says.

"Damn, that was easier than I thought."

That tiny, crooked smirk is back, and all it does is make me feel alive, like I'm free-falling. Like maybe there'd be someone to finally catch me on the other side. What a stupid thought.

It's then that A's masked face appears, invading my thoughts, reminding me who I truly am. Corrupted and crazed for vengeance. And I don't know which Kayla I want to be, because when I'm around each one of them, I'm two different people.

Or maybe I'm not. Maybe I'm deluding myself.

Yet the way I feel around these two men…it's confusing and terrifying.

But I want them both. What has become of me? Depraved and insatiable.

At least I feel *something,* though.

At least I know I'm not dead inside.

That *they* haven't killed that part of me, no matter how much they've tried.

Ten

KAYLA

He's out cold. I poke him just to make sure. But he doesn't even move. With both hands, I lay the fleece blanket over him before I tiptoe out of there.

I feel almost guilty for what I did, but not guilty enough not to have done it.

Grabbing my duffel, I quietly slip out of the house and lock the door behind me.

Hopefully he doesn't wake up until after I leave. But those meds should give me a couple of hours, and that's all I'll need.

With a black hood over my head, my clothes the same color, I strut a few long blocks, two cars whizzing past before I stop at the house fifteen minutes later. It's dark inside, and a blue sedan is in the driveway.

My pulse pumps rapidly and my body flutters with adrenaline. With rage.

I'm doing the right thing. He doesn't deserve to be alive. But I can fix that.

Quietly, I open the latch to the back gate and slip inside. With thick black, leather gloves, I check the back door, hoping it's open. Or I'll have to resort to breaking the glass and opening it myself. But I'm prepared for that.

I took A's advice to heart. My bag is full of useful things. He'd be proud.

And I wonder if he's here. If he's watching me.

The knob turns, and a grin draws up my face.

I pull air into my lungs, and my stomach churns from fear. Anticipation. But thrill too. It's all there in this moment. Like that feeling I'd get when my favorite roller-coaster ride would slowly climb up, higher and higher, until that first big drop. Then chaos.

I live in chaos now.

I let myself in, then shut the door as quietly as possible.

Except for the small table lamp, there's only darkness here. A single staircase to my right.

It's late. Fred Avon is probably upstairs sleeping, which will make killing him a lot easier.

I want his tears. I want to watch him as he realizes this is the end.

It's as I'm about to kill this man that those faces flash before my eyes: those men, all the ones who did despicable things to us and laughed. I can hear it. Thick, cunning laughter.

I blink back the tears and welcome the fury.

That's my only friend now.

I won't be that Kayla anymore. I won't cry. I won't beg. They'll be begging *me*.

The stairs squeak as I start up.

My breaths catch in my throat as I freeze on the second step, listening for noise.

But I hear nothing except the silence of the night.

All I have to do is find his bedroom—and he only has two in this small colonial—then jam the syringe of propofol I stole from Helping Hand into his neck.

Once he's out, I'll kill him.

I'll clean the mess with the oxygen bleach A gave me and disappear.

The cops won't suspect me. Why would they? A man like this surely has many enemies. Many who hate his guts. It could be anyone in the area. Even if the cops look at my computer, so what? Looking at sex offenders in the area isn't against the law or uncommon. And I always make sure to look at those in other states too.

I'm even writing a thesis paper on sex offenders for a class. It's why I'm searching up these perverts. For school. Nothing more.

"Officer, I was merely looking at Fred Avon and the others for my school assignment. Comparing prison sentences of offenders with similar crimes. I could never hurt someone, no matter how sick and sadistic they may be. I truly hope you catch whoever did this."

When people look at me, they don't see a killer.

But A was right. It's what I am. No better than him. No worse, either.

Continuing up the stairs, I hold the strap of my bag as tightly as possible. The stairs only creak one more time, right before I reach the second level. There are three doors up here, and one is opened. Probably a bathroom. Once I pass it, I confirm that it is.

With my heart in my throat, my hand grips the handle of the first door and slowly, at a snail's pace, I begin to turn it.

I can do this. It's going to be fine.

The nerves take a front seat, but I don't let them stop me. Not when the door groans, not even when I step inside and realize this room is empty. Nothing but a desk and a chair. I release a breath of relief before I strut back out into the hallway and head for the last door on the left. It's the only room he can be in.

Knowing he's there helps me prepare. Unclipping my duffel, I remove the syringe, holding it in one hand while I use the other to open the door just as quietly.

When I pass the threshold, my body turns ice cold. But once my eyes adjust to the dark, I notice a body on the bed. I can make out a shadow of a face, like he's sleeping on his back. He lets out a moan, like he's having a bad dream.

As I creep the short distance, my arms prickle with goose bumps, hoping he doesn't wake up.

I lift the syringe, getting ready to jam it into his throat to take him out so that I can kill him in peace. As soon as it pierces his skin, I can feel it. And further, I push the meds into his system, letting the liquid enter his veins.

I'm sure the missing propofol will be reported, but I was good at covering my tracks. They're not gonna know it's me.

Just as I pull out the needle, the light switches on, the brightness momentarily blinding me.

I release an audible gasp, my mind attempting to catch up with my body. My pulse drums in my throat while my eyes adjust to my surroundings.

I blink twice, because I swear there's a large, black mass in the corner of the room.

My vision begins to clear, and I gasp at the hooded figure sitting on a single chair in the corner, a blade in his hand. His face is downcast, so I don't see if he's wearing his mask.

"A?" I shiver out, ready to hurl. "Is…is that you?"

KAYLA

He chuckles, and when he leans back into his seat and shows me that mask, my body sags in relief. For one moment, I thought it could be the Midnight Murderer, ready to take me as his newest trophy kill.

"Hey there, little wolf. Got hungry?" He extends his hand, the blade glistening as I slowly make it toward him.

"Wha-what are you doing here?" My stammering is quite pathetic, but I can't get over the fact that he's here. That he somehow found the man I was going after and…what?

I scan the body behind me and don't see any signs of death. Fred is still groaning and mumbling now, the effects of the meds taking hold.

Unless…unless A had already drugged him too.

"Did you know I'd be here? That I was after him?"

He nods once.

"How?"

"I wouldn't want to spoil the fun." He laughs. "I told you, I know everything about you, Kayla Jenkins."

"Then why didn't you kill him already? Why is he still alive?"

He tilts his head to the side and says nothing. That creepy mask is staring at me, yet it no longer terrifies me.

"I was being a gentleman, waiting for you to take care of it."

"And they say chivalry is dead." I take the knife offering, but stay rooted in place, wishing he'd take the mask off so I could see his face, know who he truly is.

"Never knew myself to be the chivalrous kind. Guess there's a first time for everything."

The handle is warm in my grip, and my eyes scan the sparkling blade. "You know what he's done? Why I chose him?"

He nods. "I do. He deserves it." Climbing to his feet, he towers over me, and tentatively, his fingers trek closer to mine, like he wants to touch me, but is afraid to. "I'd always be by your side, no matter who you chose to kill."

He would?

"Why? Why are you watching me? Covering for me?"

My pulse goes faster, my heart lurching at the thought of finally being touched by him. This man. This stranger. This killer. Someone who's like me in so many ways.

When I'm near him, all thoughts of Chris fade, because whoever this man is, no one compares.

As soon as he brushes the top of my hand with the barest touch, my whole body comes alive, this shivery feeling casting over me. My breaths still as I wait for more, needing it so damn much. But just as quickly, he rips his hand away as though I'm made of acid.

"You excite me. It's a feeling I'm not quite used to. But one I'm starting to enjoy." He grunts almost to himself. "A little too much."

My gut somersaults. "I got the lily you left. How…" I swallow down the rush of desire. "How long were you there watching me?"

His breaths are audible through the mask. Seconds pass before he speaks again.

"I just like to watch you sleep. Everything else was just a bonus."

"Why?" I whisper, my heart thudding to a beat all of its own. "Why did you want to watch me sleep?"

"Because…" His voice falls to almost a whisper. "It brings me peace."

A sudden ache hits the back of my throat. In his tone is a shred of humanity, a vulnerability I had yet to hear from him.

I want to rip the mask off and hold his face in my palms and tell him it's okay. Whatever happened to him, whatever made him this way, it's okay.

"Stop looking at me like that," he grits.

"Like what?"

"Like you feel sorry for me. Because you don't need to." He treks forward, causing my heartbeats to gallop. "The only ones who you should feel sorry for are the ones who meet me."

"I don't feel sorry for you. I just wonder what happened to you." My tenor drops.

His chest rattles up with battering breaths.

I immediately change the subject, even while wishing I didn't have to.

"How many have you killed?" I ask this time.

"Enough." His words are firm, rugged. And it turns me on even more. "Now, are you going to do this or keep stalling?"

His humor is back, and I snicker.

"I'm not stalling. I'm not afraid."

"Never said you were." Extending a hand, he follows me to

Fred, who still lies there breathing a bit shallower, moaning like he's drunk.

"Did you give him something before I came?"

"Of course. I wanted to have him ready for you. Little did I know how prepared you'd be." He gently tugs on the strap of my duffel.

"I learned from a friend." My mouth curls.

"Must be a smart friend."

"He certainly thinks so." I pop a brow. "Me? Still undecided."

He chuckles, and it sends a chill scurrying down my spine.

If I am going to do this, there's no coming back from that. This time, it's different. I chose him.

The knife burns my palm as I breathe a little faster. Lowering my duffel onto the floor, I wonder why it suddenly feels heavier now.

I swallow down the anxiety while he saunters behind me, his body too close. And when he moves into me, I can feel the thickness of his cock pushing into the small of my back.

Is this turning him on? The anticipation of seeing me kill someone?

"You're hard." My voice comes out small, sheepish, yet every inch of me feels braver now that he's right here, as though sewn into my skin, giving me the courage.

"Does that bother you? Does the fact that you make me hard scare you?" he whispers into the crook of my neck.

All the hairs on my arms rise to attention.

"No…" I shake my head lightly. "I've been to hell and back. Nothing scares me anymore. And I…"

A's hand draws out, fingers tracing up my arm, leaving my flesh wicked and wanton.

"And you what?" The timbre of his voice strokes me in places long forgotten.

My core grows tight and uncomfortable, and I hate the feeling, yet I want it too. A conundrum of sensations I don't fully comprehend. Not with this stranger, who could be anyone. Hell, he could be the Midnight Murderer himself. But I want him. More than I've wanted anyone ever.

"I like that you want me."

He growls deep in his chest. "Don't tempt the devil. He may come out to play."

"I'm every bit the devil you are."

With a groan, he takes my hands in his, the knife perched within our evil palms. "Maybe it's why I can't stop thinking about you."

The confession sends a ripple of heat down my curves. "Maybe I don't want you to."

"Fuck, you are a tempting little devil." That deep pitch has my skin prickling.

He arches into me as he lifts our hands in the air, the tip of the blade staring downward onto its victim.

"Shall we do this together?" he asks. "Shall I show you how to slice his throat?"

The man groans, but we both have long ignored him, our souls marked by the foulness of our making, the life that made us who we are.

"Yes," I breathe. "Do it."

"No, you're gonna do it. You will take the blade across the right side of his throat."

The nerves begin to dissipate, and instead I see the cunning men and their faces, so many of them. The way they grabbed me, ripped off the little amount of clothes I was allowed to wear. Watched as they took everything. Used every inch of my body like I was a toy built for their enjoyment.

I don't notice the tear fall from my eye until another comes. And behind me, he swallows a sharp pull of an inhale, his grip tightening around my hands like he saw what I didn't want him to see: the weakness there, the vulnerability when the pain comes. And it comes more often than I'd like.

My heart races with unfathomable rage. And with a roar, I jam the knife into the man's throat, over and over, until my tears mingle with my wrath, until blood pours out of him like all the years I've lost. All the agony I've endured. It's there, staining my fingers, turning my soul black.

But it's been black for a while, hasn't it? Even before I was saved from that place. I was just afraid to expose that part of myself. Because what would my friends and family think about precious little Kayla turning into this?

Oh my God. Kayla? You need help. Let us help you.

They'd stare at me with horror, the eyes of a killer. The Kayla they once knew no longer there at all.

But I don't need help. I need *this*.

I need to kill them all—the monsters who roam the streets looking for their next victim. And if I can save one of them, even one, then I have done good. My evil has served a purpose.

I stab him again and again, and I realize A is no longer holding my hands. No longer there to release the rage with me. But I'm too far gone to even care.

I plunge the knife so many times, I've made a mess I promised not to make.

I don't know how long I keep doing it, but eventually he's there, hands clasping my shoulders. I feel them—heavy, yet comforting. Lulling me with a calming voice I didn't know he was capable of.

"It's okay, little wolf. He's gone now. You can let go."

When I don't, when my hands ache with how hard I hold the

weapon, he shushes me, heaving breaths causing mine to mellow second by second.

"I won't let anyone hurt you anymore. I've got you."

I tremble, gasping with a cry.

Does he know? Does he know what they've done to me?

And with a quivering sob, I instantly push off of him, the knife still in my grasp.

"Anymore?" I ask, shaking my head, tears leaking out. "Do you…do you know what happened to me? Before?"

When he just stands there, I know instantly he does.

This feeling of being violated by this stranger surges me with so much anger, I want to use the knife on him!

With a scream, I lift it up in the air and aim it at his throat, wanting to hurt him the way I am in this very moment.

But instead, he grabs my wrist with one hand and clasps the back of my head with the other. "If you want to kill me, then do it. Whatever you need to help take away your pain. But just know killing me won't help. It won't make it hurt any less. It won't make you less angry. Less scared."

His thumb massages my nape, and I whimper, the knife jittering in my hands.

"It'll just make you regret it. But killing someone who deserves it, someone who's hurt others? Well, that? That is power. That is good, and we can be good together."

My hand continues to shake until it falls to my side, the knife plundering to my feet. And instead of running this time, I hold on and I don't want to let go.

And his arms? They tentatively drape around me too, just a little, just enough to make me feel it—the fact that behind that mask, there's a man who cares.

I cry into his chest while his strong arms hold me like he doesn't know how to do this, but wants to anyway.

I grab a fistful of his hoodie, and I let it all out, a cleansing of my deepest pain, the kind of release that you know will make you feel better when you've reached the precipice. But I'm not there yet. There's so much to let go of. The ruins so ingrained in my scars that I don't know if I can ever get rid of them.

But I try anyway, knowing that they will never have me again. I don't care who is out there, trying to take women in the name of the Bianchis, but it won't be me. And if I can help it, it won't be anyone ever again. But I don't know who these people are and how to help the women they've taken so far.

Too much evil runs these streets, and I'm not enough to save them. But maybe he is. Maybe we can do this together.

"Do you know who the killer is?" I perch back and stare at an invisible man.

"Why? Do you think us murderers have each other on speed dial?"

"Shut up." I swipe under my eye and find dark liquid on the finger of my glove. Blood clearly.

Fabulous.

"Let me clean you up." Without waiting for a reply, he reaches into his pocket and removes a small packet of wet wipes.

With one, he gently rubs away the evidence of my treachery, and the heat skating down the length of me warms me to my deepest core.

"You shouldn't have," I tease, trying to ease the heaviness.

"You're right, but with you, I can't seem to help myself."

"Still hard?" My brow rises.

I swear I've never ever dreamed of talking like this with a man, not after everything, but somehow with him, I feel safe enough to do it.

"Why? Wanna feel it, baby bird?"

"How many pet names are you gonna give me?" I tip up my chin, staring into the mask I've come to hate and like equally.

"As many as I want to." His fingers reach toward my face, tucking a strand of hair behind my ear.

"I like them. I've never had that." My heart tightens in my raw and aching chest.

"Never had what?" His fist clamps against his side, then opens, like he wants to touch me again, but is fighting it, while the skin across my nape tingles from where his hands have been.

"Never had a man care enough to give me an endearing nickname…" The words cause my own heart to break.

"That's alright, 'cause I'm here now." The warm, dark sluice of his voice sends my stomach soaring with butterflies. "You will never need anyone else."

The air thickens and my pulse scurries out of my throat.

I bet behind that mask, his eyes are dilated, his breaths warmer.

"And why's that?" I ask, wanting him to say that he wants me. What would that feel like?

He cups my jaw, his face nearing mine. "Because you're mine, little wolf. I thought we established that."

"Yours?" I scoff. "And how will that work exactly? We kill together, you wear your mask, and then what? You won't take it off. You won't let me know you. And I want to know you, whatever your name is. Because for the first time since I was rescued, I'm able to be myself with someone. Do you even know what that means to me?"

His breaths grow heavier, and he lays his forehead against mine.

"Yeah," he husks. "I do. Because for the first time in my life, I'm able to be myself too."

My heartbeats quicken, and my hand snaps to his mask, wanting to rip it off, wanting to kiss him. My God, the need surges so powerfully, I don't know how to stop it.

But in a flash, he grunts and clutches my wrist in his beastly grasp. "No."

One word. One rough word ends it.

Defeated, I lower my arm to my side and huff. "You say I'm yours, but it doesn't feel that way, now, does it?"

"I—" he attempts, but the ringing of my phone in my duffel stops him.

I let it ring, not caring who it is, wanting to toss it into the nearest toilet just to hear what he was gonna say.

"Gonna get that?" he muses.

"Probably not."

He removes his rubber gloves and stuffs them into a black garbage bag beside us. Before I realize what's happening, he's unzipping my duffel and taking out my phone.

"What are you doing?" My eyes pop and grow even wider when he answers.

"Hi there," he says like he's the sweetest man on the planet. "Yes, Kayla is here. She's just getting something to eat."

"I'm gonna kill you," I whisper.

"I'm a friend from school, ma'am." He pauses again. "Yes, she's a great friend. Always has my back, and I have hers." He nods. "I don't want you to worry, Mrs. Jenkins. She has me now. No one will hurt her. You have my word." He pauses. "There she is. Let me give her the phone."

With a heated stare, I glare at him.

He chuckles lowly and places the phone to my ear while his mouth drops to my other. "She sounds nice. Maybe I can meet her soon."

"Yeah, good luck with that," I breathe.

He chuckles, all low and gravelly, shooting a tingling sensation between my thighs.

"Honey, you there?" my mother's worried tone comes through. "Who was that man? Is he really a friend? Why haven't you told me about him?"

I'm visibly annoyed as I whisper, "Thanks for that!"

His shoulders rock.

He finds this funny, huh?

"He's a friend. Nothing really to tell. We were just studying at the coffee shop. Why aren't you sleeping?"

She sighs. "I couldn't sleep. I had a feeling you would be up too." A few seconds of silence pass. "Are you okay? Do you need anything?"

"Mom, I'm fine. I'm getting by. I'm doing the work. Going to therapy. You know I love you, but you don't have to ask how I'm doing every time, okay? It's gonna take me some time, but I *will* get through it."

Yet the bloody knife stares at me from the floor, as though daring the truth from my lips.

She sniffles. God, I hate knowing I'm making her cry.

"You wanna come over for dinner tomorrow night?" she asks. "I'll make whatever you want. Just name it."

I know what will happen when I go there. My parents will fawn over me, treating me like a little kid who needs extra attention. They mean well, but I hate it. But I also can't say no.

"Sure, Mom. Maybe some roasted potatoes and pizza burgers. I love those."

"Of course! Your dad will fire up the grill. You can even bring that nice friend of yours. We would love to meet him."

I snicker to myself. "He's got something to do."

"No, I don't."

I swear he's having fun with this.

"What did he say?" Mom retorts.

"Nothing. He just said he's *very* sad to miss it."

"Aww. Next time, then. How's six?"

"That works. Well, okay, Mom. I've gotta go now. Have to finish studying and get home."

That's when I remember Chris.

Shit. What if he is awake now and tracking me here?

My body goes all pins and needles.

"Okay. Good night, honey. Happy I got to hear your voice. I'll go back to bed now. I love you." She waits for me to say it back.

"Love you too, Mom. Night."

He hangs up for me and removes the cell from my ear, stuffing it back into my bag. I turn and snap my glare at him, removing my own gloves. He takes them from me and throws them where he tossed his.

"Are you insane, talking to my mother? What if she tells people and then they ask questions?"

"About someone you go to college with?" A small chuckle rolls out from his lips. "And how will that lead anyone to me? Are you worried for my safety?"

I want to rip off that smile I know he's wearing under that godawful mask.

My hand instantly snaps to it like before, but he pushes my hand off.

"Don't you ever touch my mask!" he roars. "I won't tell you again. Do you understand me?"

For the first time in a long time, I grow fearful of this man. The heavy breaths falling from his lungs, the way he sounded: like he'd tear me to shreds for what I wanted to do.

Would he really hurt me? Would I be his next victim?

"I should go," I quickly say.

"Like that?" He laughs coldly. "How do you expect to go back home all bloodied up?"

"I—I have a change of clothes…"

That I completely forgot about because you were ready to lose it on me.

"Let me clean you up, then you can get changed. Leave your clothes. I'll get rid of it all."

I jerk back. "Why the hell should I trust you? How do I know you won't use this evidence against me?"

But I know I sound ridiculous. He's already done this before, and I haven't been arrested yet.

"Fine." He pops a shoulder. "Take it with you. Do whatever you want. But don't come crying to me when you get caught."

"What do you do with the body? Can you tell me that?"

He steps up until his chest meets mine. A finger hooks under my chin and he lifts it up, staring down at me.

"I send them back to hell, Kayla. Where they belong."

Twelve

KAYLA

I send them back to hell.

My heart skitters at his taunting voice. And before I can ask more, he turns toward his bag and kneels, removing a bottle of water and a large towel. He pours some onto the cotton and approaches me, gently wiping my hands, my face, until I'm clean.

"Now be a good girl and take off your clothes. We need to get out of here."

Heat sprouts through me at the way he said that. I know it was dirtier in my head than he meant to make it sound. Or maybe he meant it exactly how I took it.

His thumb reaches for my lips, and he brushes them with the softest touch not meant for a man like this.

"You have a pretty mouth, Kayla Jenkins," he whispers gruffly. "I hope you think better of it before you kiss him."

"Wh-what?" My breath hitches. "Ki-kiss who?"

"That *fucking* bodyguard who wants inside you." He grunts like the idea pains him. "But you wouldn't let him do that, would you?" He groans, popping my mouth open with his thumb, his breathing storming out of him. "You wouldn't let him have what I want. What belongs to me."

"You want me?" I ask softly, still so unused to hearing something like that from a man, it's as though I need the constant reassurance.

He chuckles, and if it had a color, it'd be black. "Your flesh, your insatiable appetite, your deepest, darkest desires… I want it all, baby bird."

"Believe me," I mutter. "If you knew me, knew the things I think about, you'd never say that."

"That's where you're wrong. I want to know everything about you. Everything you think about. And you *will* tell me. Because you and I, we're the same. I can feel the rage inside you, and I want to consume it. I want to make you scream until there's nothing left but your beating heart and the naked truths seeping through your soul. Do you want that, Kayla? Do you want to scream with me?"

My chest rises and falls with chaotic breaths, tears weighing heavy within my eyes.

"Yes." I nod with a tremble. "I've never wanted something more."

He inhales and holds it in his chest before he sets it free. "Good." He traces my lips once more. "Go on now. Change. We need to go, even though I don't want to."

I realize Chris is probably going to be following me to my parents' tomorrow, and A won't be happy.

"Don't do anything stupid tomorrow." I quirk a brow.

"Like what?"

He cups my cheek, and every single inch of me grows languid. I fall into his touch like he's the apple to my Eve.

My eyes fall to a close, and I'm consumed in this tranquil feeling, never wanting it to end. "He's gonna go to my parents' tomorrow, and I'm afraid you're gonna lose your shit."

He chuckles. "How do you already know me so well?"

"Intuition." A slow-growing smile falls to my lips as I look back at him.

"So he gets to meet your parents and I don't?"

"Well, it'll be a little hard for me to introduce you. You know, with that mask and all. Mommy would definitely not approve."

He growls in frustration. "I don't like him, Kayla. And do you know what I do with people I don't like?"

I scoff. "Let me guess? You kill them."

He chuckles. "Right again, my little wolf." He runs the back of his hand down my face. "I've always considered myself an ethical kind of murderer. Now? Imagining him doing the things I know he wants to do to you? Knowing there's some part of you that wants him too? Not so much."

"What would you do if he kissed me?" I play with danger, wanting it. "If he touched me…"

"Touched you where? Here?" He brushes a finger between my thighs, and I let out a moan, wanting him to reach inside and touch my throbbing clit.

"Yes…" I gasp as he pushes a finger into me.

"I'd rip out his heart and make him watch as I burned it, right before he got a taste of the flames too."

My eyes widen.

His laughter reverberates in every part of my being. "Does that scare you? Do you see me now? The real me?"

I shake my head. "You don't scare me. You make me feel a little bit safer, knowing you're there lurking in the shadows, watching me. Wanting me…"

He hisses, grabbing a fistful of my hair. "What did I tell you about tempting the devil? Do you like to play with fire? Do you like the burn? Do you crave it?"

I nod, shame filling my cheeks.

"I do too," he confesses. "One day you'll tell me everything you want. Everything you *need*. And I'll be the one to give it to you, even when that's all I'll ever have to offer someone like you."

"Like me?"

He nods once. "We may be the same, but we're more different than you'd imagine. You have a heart, and mine? Well, let's just say I never truly had one to begin with."

I place my palm against the center of his chest, feeling the weight of his pummeling heartbeats. "I don't believe that. Maybe you do. Maybe that's all you see, but I see more. There's more inside you. Maybe you're the one afraid of it, but I'm not."

"If only my mother saw it too," he whispers.

The back of my throat stings. "Your mother? Did she hurt you?"

I ache for him then, hearing that pain in his voice, letting a fragment of his true self slip away.

"Never mind her. She's not worthy enough to be spoken about between us. Now, please change before I do something we both regret."

"Maybe you'd regret it, but not me."

My gut recoils as I imagine how disgusted he'd be if he saw my body. Saw the cuts that no longer bleed, the scars that no longer throb.

"I'd never regret you." He says that as though it's as true as the sky is blue.

But that's not the truth, now, is it? He can't know that, not until he sees it for himself.

I move back, my body trembling inwardly as I clutch the hem

of my hoodie and start to take it off, pushing it over my head.

My entire body fills with nerves I can't shake, my hands quivering.

"What are you doing?" he barks, anger radiating in his tone.

But I continue, hands on my sweats now, rolling them down slowly until I'm able to step out of them. Even as the anxiety settles inside me, I maintain eye contact, knowing he's looking right back.

"Kayla," he warns. "Don't."

My cotton panties come next, and this part is not even the hardest. I've done this before. Taken off my clothes in front of strangers.

The cotton drops to my ankles until it's forgotten. His fists clamp tight, knuckles white.

"You can't be doing this." He forces himself to turn.

"No!" I stamp out. "Look at me, God damn it!"

"Kayla…" The word strangles in his throat.

"Please, I need you to see me. All of me. I need you to know everything."

It's as though I'm begging for acceptance. Begging for someone to finally see every inch of me and tell me it's okay.

It's then he slowly returns his attention back to me.

I start to remove my tank top, my breasts popping free. And once I let my shirt fall and I turn around, that's when he grows completely silent.

He growls, more animal than man.

"Who—" He pants. "Who did that to you?"

There's pain and rage in his words as I let him see me. Marred and cast aside.

"Savages," I tell him without looking his way. "The ones who took me and my friends, the ones who tried to make me turn on

Elsie when she escaped. But I wouldn't give her up. No matter what they did to me." An ache catches in my throat. "They thought I was weak. They thought they could break me." I grin even through the tears. "But they never realized I was already broken."

"Tell me their names, and they will never know another sunrise." He sounds so brutal, like he'd burn the world for me.

Tears bathe my eyes just as he marches forward until he's there behind me. His body heat radiates in waves.

Before I can wonder what he'll do next, I gasp as his fingers gently trace one scar, then another, and another. I heave a gasping cry, standing there until he's outlined every single one.

"This is just skin, Kayla. Beautiful skin. It doesn't matter to me what it looks like."

Silently, I cry, not knowing if I even believe him.

Strong hands turn me until I'm tucked against his chest, his arms just a little surer as they safeguard me against my heartbreak.

Pulling back, he cups my face in his palm. "Don't cry, little wolf. We don't let them win. We destroy them."

"Most of them are dead or in prison," I explain. "But this? This is what I am now."

"No." He cinches his grasp. "This is just flesh. Who you are is Kayla, and Kayla is *beautiful*."

I fight back the endless river of tears as they storm out until they cloud my vision, over and over, blinding me.

I'm naked before a man I've never known, and he's made me feel like I'm floating.

We stand like that together for long moments in unbending time, as though it's frozen for us while my heart weeps to see his face. To touch it. To kiss every inch. To feel his mouth on mine until my soul aches. But that's not our reality. He's a secret keeper, and I'm afraid he'll never let me know his.

"What now?" I ask, not wanting him to go. Wishing he'd come home with me and hold me until I fall asleep.

But we can't do that either. Not with Chris around.

"I don't know." His arms tighten around me just a little more. "Am I doing it right?" he whispers hoarsely.

"What?" I'm completely unsure of what he's asking.

"Hugging you. Am I doing it right?"

His voice…it's so vulnerable, so real and raw.

And achingly beautiful…

I blink faster through the blanket of tears. Has he never been hugged? Never hugged someone in return?

I clasp my arms as tightly as I can around him, wanting him to feel it.

"Never been held better in my life," I practically sigh.

"You liar."

I grin and burrow into him some more. "Stop ruining the moment, stalker."

"What the hell have you done to me, Kayla Jenkins?" he breathes.

I'm not sure. But I think it's the same thing you've done to me.

Thirteen

ADRIEL

Her eyes are soft, endearingly gazing at me as she watches me finish cleaning.

And me? I don't know what's happening. I don't know what these feelings are or how to process them.

What is it about Kayla Jenkins that makes me want to keep her safe? I've never worried about anyone before. Not once. But with her, it's somehow different.

There's something stirring within me, something that's tethered to her, and the more I'm around her, the stronger that feeling gets. And the harder it'll be to let go of.

I can't make sense of it. I don't know if it's sympathy for her plight or this notion of protecting her, but something is hidden beneath the rubble, and it's aiming for her.

This obsession is more than just physical, it's spiritual. I can feel it deep enough where I know it's there, waiting for something

I can't yet name.

I've tried to fight it. I've tried to keep my distance, but every time I did, I found myself watching her all over again.

I can't seem to stop.

And I've never been the kind of man who couldn't control his urges.

But after what she showed me, that back covered with scars… fuck…the need for vengeance, to scorch the earth with the ashes of her enemies grabbed hold. Desire to find every last one of her transgressors took root until it grew into something stronger. Palpable. And it spreads with every second I look into her eyes.

My heart…it beats a little faster, my anger raging out of me at the thought of someone hurting something so beautiful.

They will pay. I will find every last one of them. I will steal their breaths until they're burning with their demons.

The things she's endured…

Those scars were all over her back. Like someone had fun carving her up.

My nostrils widen. Prison won't stop me from killing every single one who hurt her. And I will give her that. I will give her their hearts, and she will know I did it all for her.

While I start to roll the dead man into the tarp on the floor, she plays with the hem of her shirt.

Why do I feel this way? Why do I want to be the one to wash away the blood from her broken body, to erase the evidence of our sin, to clean her and dry her and dress her? I want to do all those things.

But I can't. I can't let her see my face. Know me. It's never been part of the plan. I must resist the temptation.

The nuns would approve.

I force myself to focus on the body before me.

The furnace waits for this child molester, one of many that have known the flames. Casius comes to mind. The way he screamed. The way he begged. It's too bad I had to drug this one, or he'd have begged too.

There's something fascinating about hearing them scream like that, knowing you're doing it to them. There's power. Power stripped away, power given. A mutual exchange.

The news of Casius's disappearance has begun to spread, but the police haven't found a body, nor will they.

And no body means no crime. It's beautiful how the system works.

His friends have told the authorities that Casius had begun gambling again, that he may have owed the Albanian Mob a lot of money. And those guys don't like it when you don't pay them back. They take more than just a finger. They take your life, and it seems like Casius was next on their list.

What a shame. He had his whole life ahead of him.

If only he hadn't been such a piece of shit.

I finish with the body and start on the few rug stains she left behind when she kept stabbing him, probably seeing the faces of the men who hurt her instead.

I get it more than she realizes. Sometimes, as I'd kill, I'd envision the nuns who beat me, the families who took me in for short periods of time, swearing to take care of me before they turned to monsters too.

My scars may be different, but they're just as deep.

She clears her throat, her arms around herself, her silky hair draped over her shoulder. I long to feel it. Want to get lost inside her. To own every inch of her. To know that there's a way to feel more…more of the feelings she brings out and less of the rage I've been born into.

"Are you sure you don't want my help?" Her mouth flutters.

"No." I shake my head. "Don't want your DNA anywhere."

Nodding, she says, "Thank you for helping me with this."

Her eyes are doleful and down right sweet. She's tempting me even as she does nothing but stand there.

I grow hard again at the sight of her, my cock throbbing and heavy, wanting to feel her pretty cunt clasp around it. But I can't fuck a woman who's gone through what she has. I can't be the man to give her that. I can't give her anything. Nothing but my undying promise to always stay one step behind in case she needs me.

But then I realize she's going to have a future. She may not know it yet. But she will one day, and I'll still be there, watching.

But as long as she's not wanting to fuck that bodyguard, I'll be okay.

"Fucking liar."

"What?" she asks, a puzzled look on her face.

Jesus, I'm talking to myself now.

"Nothing," I mutter. "You should go home. He's gonna be looking for you. I'm sure those pills you gave him won't keep him down too long."

Her body tugs back and she straightens her spine. "How did you know I gave him pills?"

When I don't answer, she blows an exacerbated breath.

"You could make a woman crazy with your silence."

"I've got news for you, babe. You're already crazy."

She scoffs, and for a moment, I think I've hurt her feelings, but then she bursts out laughing.

And I would die a thousand times over just to hear her laughter all over again.

KAYLA

He called me *babe*. My stalker called me *babe*.

Most girls would run, but me? I want to go back inside instead and ask him to call me that just one more time. I stayed as long as I could. Until he was practically done. Nothing left but getting the body into his car.

With a sigh, I walk faster. I'm almost back to my place, hoping Chris is still there sleeping, or I'll have a lot of explaining to do.

Reaching my door, I find it quiet as I step inside. Nothing out of the ordinary. Relief washes over me. He would ruin everything. He'd tell Michael, and Michael would eventually tell Elsie that I'm up to something, and then my parents would find out. That would be the end of it all.

But I can't quit this. I need it.

Reaching the bathroom in the hallway, I quietly flip the light on and shut the door. Staring at myself in the mirror, I barely recognize the woman staring back at me. How did she become this?

I've killed. And yet I want to do it again.

They may not be my enemies, but they're someone's. They've left behind victims just like me. Just like all the other women and children who were held like I was. Like Elsie and Jade were.

I do this for all of us—getting rid of those who should never have been born. All they've done is ruin the lives of those who did nothing to them, and now I take their lives away. And I'm not sorry about it.

Needing to force myself to get some sleep so I can actually wake up for classes tomorrow, I head toward where Chris is sleeping before I head upstairs to my bedroom.

But as I pass the sofa, my heartbeats explode.

Shit.

My eyes drown over the empty spot, the blanket lying haphazardly on the edge. He's not here. But his car was. What the hell?

"Chris?" I call, my voice simmering with fear.

Nothing. I have no idea where he could be.

Quietly, I start to climb the stairs, the old wood groaning beneath my feet as I listen for any hints as to his whereabouts.

Wouldn't he have called me? Tracked me? But there's not a word from him.

Reaching into my duffel, I grab my phone and press a button to ring his number.

It goes off immediately.

From upstairs.

My body breaks in a shiver. The place is dark except for a small sliver of light coming from the outside window.

Once I make it up, I head for my bedroom, hoping that maybe he's in there, but when I peer inside, I find it empty.

A series of small noises I can't pinpoint comes from the bathroom, causing every hair on my body to rise. I turn toward it.

"Chris?"

Nothing.

Oh my God. What if A did something to him?

But how? He wouldn't have had time to hurt him this quickly.

But we're talking about A here. He is capable of anything.

I grab the door handle. But as I try, it flies open and Chris is there, hair damp, a towel wrapped around his hips, a simple white t-shirt over his chest. But even through it, I catch the way his abs contract.

A slow-growing smirk makes it to his lips, and when I look

back at his eyes, the way I should've been, his smirk deepens.

"Hey there, Kayla. Where have you been?"

My stomach somersaults.

Think!

"I, uh…"

That's not helping!

"Um, I went for a…walk. Needed to clear my head, and you were sleeping so soundly, I didn't want to bother you."

The words tumble out quickly, and I force a trembling smile, even though from the look of him, I don't think he's buying any of it.

"Mm-hmm…" He chuckles.

He doesn't believe me.

Of course he doesn't, 'cause he's not an idiot!

"I woke up a bit ago and found you gone," he explains with amusement flanking his features. "I did track your phone and you were close enough for me to come and get you if I needed to, so I let you be for a little bit. But next time, wake me. Okay? If something happens to you and I'm not there…"

He grabs my jaw, eyes boring into mine so intensely, all I want to do is look away. But I'm lost within them, not knowing why.

His jaw tenses, and he exhales deep from his nostrils. "Go to bed." He straightens. "I'll be on the sofa, and I'll be up all night. So don't try anything again."

"Like what?"

"Kayla…" His tongue slips out and strikes across his bottom lip. "Do you think I don't know when I've been drugged?"

Shit.

My pulse kicks up. "What? I—I didn't—"

"Stop." His tone is unforgiving, and I think his cock jerks beneath the towel, but I'm too fearful of his harsh expression to really notice. "I know you did it, and I'm not mad. Not really. I expected it."

"You look kinda mad." I grimace.

His laughter is like nails carving me on the inside. "Trust. Me." He punctures those words. "This is me not mad. But I swear, you pull that again, and I'll tell Michael to assign a second guard to your detail, then you'll have more than one of us to deal with."

That's the last thing I need.

"Fine. I'm sorry, okay?" I throw a hand in the air. "I needed some time on my own. I hate being suffocated by people. Like I'm caged again. But I know what I did to you wasn't right, and I am sorry."

He nods, sighing deeply. "I get it. But don't ever fuck with me like that again. If you want to be left alone, just tell me."

"And you'd just be a good sport about it. Right…" I arch a brow.

"I'd take it under consideration, depending on where you're going and if I'm able to track you, because that is my job."

"Track me. Yes, of course. I always forget that I'm a child who needs tracking."

"Kayla…"

I throw a palm up to stop him. "Don't say anything else. It's fine. I'm tired. Going to bed. Sorry for drugging you. Hope you slept well, at least."

"Slept like a fucking baby." He grins.

I turn on my heels and head for my bedroom. "You're welcome."

He laughs as I shut the door, pressing my back against the wall and calming my racing heartbeats.

I got away with it. He's not mad, and he doesn't know where I was and what I was doing.

Maybe I can do this. Maybe no one will know.

Or maybe I'm only fooling myself.

I guess we'll find out.

ADRIEL

The next day, my mind is still racing with all things Kayla. Watching her take the knife to that man's body, feeling her in my arms, feeling her blood racing through her veins, knowing her heart was beating faster the more I held her…it did things to me. Things I never even knew could exist for someone like me.

But her pain, I understand it. I feel it like it's my own. The things that were done to her are unforgiveable. And if there was a way to bring them all back from the dead, I would. Just so I could make them a sacrifice. For her. I'd set her on top of her throne while they bled before her feet. It's what she deserves. But not all of them are alive for me to do that.

As for the ones who are? Well, they're going to wish they weren't.

Right now, one of my clients who has a brother in prison is passing him the names of four men who were part of the ones arrested for trafficking women. Two of them are the same ones who took Kayla and her friends off the road. The other two are businessmen who were caught using the club for their sick pleasures.

See, the thing with having the kind of business I do is I know a lot of people. And not all are clean. In fact, most are dirty. It's why they want my products. To use them on their enemies. But having some of my most loyal clients in prison…well, it comes in handy.

Like now.

My cell rings. Just in time.

"Yeah?" I greet. "Is it done?"

"It is. Four days. He will deliver."

I grin. "Good. Thank you."

"No. *Thank you.* The added investment into the charity was a welcome surprise."

"I do whatever I can."

"That you do." He laughs before ending the call.

I dial my friend Abel at the morgue next.

"Hey. Is it set?" he asks.

"It is. Expect it in four days."

"I will see you then."

He doesn't question me before he hangs up. He knows what I do. He used to do the same. It's how we met, aiming for the same target. But he gave it up a few years ago when he started working at the morgue. I think he still dabbles from time to time, just doesn't tell me.

My mind focuses on why I'm doing this.

For her.

The play's in motion. Now I sit and wait.

Fourteen

KAYLA

"**H**i, sweetheart!" Mom flings her arms around me in a tight hug, refusing to let go, while my father smiles softly beside her.

His hair was once a vibrant brown, but is now all gray. Yet that sparkle in his eye that I recall so vividly as a child is still there, and that brings me comfort.

Mom finally backs off and gives Chris a glance, his tailor-made suit making him look like…well, a bodyguard. How the hell am I supposed to pass him off as a college kid?

"And who might this be?" Mom perches back and gives me a curious stare. "Is this the young man from—"

"From college?" My heart races.

She was about to blow my cover and tell him who I was with last night.

"Yeah, he's a friend from school."

I nervously fumble backward and give him a *you better follow my lead or die* look.

His mouth twists, and he advances toward Mom, extending his hand in greeting. "I'm Chris, and yes, we go to school together."

"Oh, I'm glad you were able to come after all."

His brows gather, and his attention bounces between Mom and me.

"So!" I quickly say, needing to end this dreadful conversation. "What are you making, Dad?"

"Well, I'm grilling up those pizza burgers you like and some roasted vegetables, plus some chicken wings because I remember how much you loved those."

My chest tightens. He'd barbecue all the time. We'd sit around every weekend in the summer while Dad made us a meal. He loved to feed us.

"I still do, Daddy." I throw my arms around him.

His hugs are home and warmth. Tears burn my eyes, but I force them away. They have no place here.

"Come on, let's eat." He pats my back and kisses my forehead. "I missed this."

Me too.

It's my fault, really. I didn't want to do anything after I was rescued, drowning in my own despair. And my parents didn't push it. But maybe these barbecues are just what I need to remind me of who I once was.

You'll never be her again. When will you accept that?

I will my mind to stop, straightening my back as we settle around the yard, laughing and eating and smiling until our faces hurt. Even Chris is smiling, telling them about his brothers when they were younger.

His eyes jump to mine in the midst of all of this, and his smile swells. I give him one in return, but as I do, something in my gut lurches because this is wrong. I shouldn't be smiling at him this way, feeling happy.

Because he isn't A and he'll never be. Mask or not, A's the only one who truly knows me. Truly accepts me. He doesn't judge or scold. He'd hand me the knife and ask who's next. If Chris knew who I really was, he'd never look at me the same way again. He'd think I'm sick. Depraved. A broken little girl who needs mending.

But not A. To him, I'm perfect. He doesn't even have to say those words out loud for me to have felt them. Who else would tell a woman with as many scars as I have that she's beautiful? That her scars are nothing but skin? Who else would watch her kill a man and hold her as she cried?

No, Chris can never be anything. No one can. No one but A. If he even wants me.

None of this is real. I'm just pretending, even with my own family. Smiling for the crowd.

I know he's here. Know he's watching. Seeing me with my family, smiling with another man. Is he jealous?

And why do I want him to be?

I wish he were here instead. I wish I could introduce him to my family. Will I ever be able to?

But until he tells me who he is, this is all we have. Strangers by day, friends by night. If that's even what we are. Nothing with him makes any sense.

I stare out past the bright green lawn and through the shrubs, wondering if he's there, watching our every move.

"You okay, honey?" Mom asks.

I quickly jerk my head toward her, light brown eyes shining brightly.

"Just fine. Never been better." I take a sip of my beer.

"We should do this more often, don't you think?" she goes on.

"We should. I think it's good for me."

Her emotions shine in her gaze. "I'm so happy to hear you say that."

"Me too, kid." Dad nods. "We've missed you."

I take a deep breath and throw on a grin. "I missed me too. But I'm back. I promise."

Just not the version you remember.

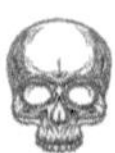

ADRIEL

I hated knowing she was with him yesterday. Him meeting her parents like he's her fucking boyfriend.

"Fuuuck!" I shout, wanting to be the one with her.

But at the same time, I don't even know how to be that man. To give her what she needs. How the hell do I become someone I've never wanted to become? Be someone who could love her?

Love…

Yeah. The concept is laughable. I don't even know what love looks like. Feels like. I've been empty. Love never existed in my life.

And it's all thanks to one woman: my mother.

Staring at the woman who gave me life while she shops at the supermarket, I pretend to be examining peaches while she looks at plums like they're a fucking science project. Just pick a few and go. How hard is it?

Kayla's parents looked like they actually gave a shit about her. I'm glad I don't have to kill them.

Maybe they're available for lessons. Mom could use some of that.

My rage pierces through my calm demeanor. She'd never suspect what I'm going through being this close to her. The way my knife burns in my pocket, aching to make her throat its home. But every artist needs to be patient. And so will I. She will meet the end, and it will be by my hand.

"I can never tell with these things." She laughs, looking at me.

My heart barely even budges. You'd think your mother talking to you after knowing she gave you up like trash would spark something emotional. But not for me. All I want is to see her dead.

Well, I guess that's an emotion too.

Inwardly, I smirk.

"You just squeeze." I strut over, my arm almost touching her shoulder.

I pick up a plum and demonstrate, imagining it's her throat instead. I grip it so hard it bursts.

Oops.

She inhales and clears her throat. "Well, that is one way to tell for sure."

I bite into it and grin. "Sweet."

She laughs nervously and throws some into a clear plastic bag. "Thanks for your help, young man."

"No worries. My mother always taught me to be helpful in every way that I can."

She pinches her mouth and throws her fruit into her shopping cart. "I've always taught my boys the same. All three of them are men I can be proud of. I'm sure your mother is too."

"Wouldn't know." I shrug, eyeing her intensely. "She's been dead for a while."

"Oh." Her face crumples. "I'm sorry to hear that." Her compassion shines through as she places her hand on top of mine, and it burns. "As a mother myself, I know that your mom is very proud of you."

"Wouldn't count on it. I was never perfect. And she never let me forget it."

Her chest rises with a ragged breath. "Well, I'm sure she tried her best."

"Yeah. Unfortunately, sometimes our best is simply not good enough."

She sighs. "You're right. It's not. Anyway, thanks again for your help."

"You bet, ma'am. See ya around."

And I mean that literally.

I'll be coming for her.

Real soon.

I follow her to the park where she meets with Sophia and Mabel, Sophia's babysitter. She doesn't stay long, though, kissing Sophia goodbye ten minutes later and leaving the little girl alone with Mabel.

Instead of following Mother, I stay back and watch Sophia. I can't explain why.

How would my mother feel if she were to disappear? If her precious granddaughter was taken? I bet it'd hurt. Would she cry for her the way she never did for me?

A pang hits the center of my chest, but I push it away.

It doesn't matter, though. I'd never take the girl. I don't hurt children. No matter who their parents are.

The little girl laughs as she runs with her friend, chasing a soccer ball. I stare at her for long seconds, envying that. I've never laughed like that before.

My world was a stark contrast to hers. All black and colorless.

All I ever knew was pain. But this child? She's happy. I wonder who I'd be if I were once happy too.

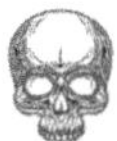

"Get up!" Sister Mary whips my bare back as I weep on the floor, unable to stand.

The burns on my feet hurt so much.

She told me she was teaching me a lesson for not wanting to study the word of the Lord. Because I was a sinner. And sinners get punished.

All the time.

"Get up, I said!" She slashes my back again, and I know she's making me bleed.

How do I make her stop? I can't even catch my breath.

"You're seven, and this is how you behave? Like a whiny, willful child? Do you realize how lucky you are to still be here?"

Another whip, harder this time.

"That we allowed you to stay after every family who has tried to help you sent you right back?"

Another slash.

"Aren't you embarrassed at how unwanted you are?"

And another.

"I've tried so hard to make someone love you, want you, but it's been for nothing! Because you'll never learn!"

She hurts me over and over while I cover my face with my hands, sobbing for someone to help me. To save me. But no one ever comes.

"Even your own mother didn't want you." She laughs. "Handed you to me while you were straight out of her womb."

Her laughter is mean, but it doesn't hurt like it hurts knowing my mommy hates me.

"She must've known what a waste of a breath you'd turn into, so she left you here. But even I couldn't help you."

She hits my arm with the whip, and my skin rips, blood dripping down my fingers. My stomach hurts, and I vomit on the ground.

"Pathetic! You can't even take a whipping like a man!"

My weeps only grow, and right here and now, I wish to die.

"Get up!"

She doesn't stop hurting me. I lose count of how many times she does.

I try to rise, but as I do, as the soles of my feet throb, she forces the whip across my chest, and I fall right back down to my knees.

Will she kill me? I want to die.

"Wh-what's my—my mother's name?" I stammer, needing to know.

If I survive, I want to find her. I want to ask why she left me here. What did I do that she didn't love me? I knew I was given up. Mary told me all the time how my mom abandoned me when I was just born. That I was a burden, and I was not God's child.

But there's no God here. This is the house of the devil. And even he'd be kinder than this.

They hate kids here. They hurt us, and no one does a thing. Because nuns are supposed to be nice. They don't hurt kids. They help them.

What a lie.

When I get older, I'll make the world see what this place is really like. I'll burn it to the ground.

"Your mother didn't want you to know her name." She sneers. "She didn't want to be associated with a weak, ugly thing like you."

I cry again. Everything hurts.

"No!" I shout even as the tears leak from my eyes. "She—she'd

l-love me if she met me."

She chuckles so hard she almost drops to the floor. "Oh, that is hilarious. She doesn't want you, Adriel. She left you here for a reason. She never once asked about you. Never called. Never even wrote a letter to ask how you were."

She kneels and grabs my chin, tilting up my eyes to her demonic ones.

"You meant nothing to her or your father. I bet she would've gotten rid of you while you were still in her belly, but her mother was religious, and she'd never have allowed that. Or your mother would end up in hell like you."

"This—this is hell." My chin trembles.

Her face grows with unrestrained rage and her eyes, almost black, grow closer until her nose is touching mine.

"You don't know hell." Her fingers bite into my skin. "This place is a gift for wicked little boys like you. You should thank us instead of being so ungrateful."

She stares at me in disgust and hits me again, the whip right across my back.

"Sister Mary!" Sister Agnes calls. "That's enough for today."

She's older. Her superior. But she's no better.

"Go on, Adriel. Go to Sister Laura," Agnes says. "She will clean you up."

I grab my clothes and run out of there, hiding behind my whimpers as my feet throb and ache with the burns she put there. But I ignore it, needing to escape as far away from her as possible.

Entering my room, I put my underwear back on, dropping to the floor as I sob.

"Why?!" I ask as though my mother can hear me. "Why did you leave me here all alone?"

But no answer comes. She never cared about me then, and she doesn't care about me now.

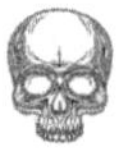

My hand clamps against my thigh as I concentrate on Sophia, needing to forget Sister Mary and all the others who ruined me.

It wasn't the first time she did that, beat me until I wanted to die. Through the years, it was all she did, reminding me she was in charge.

But she's dead now, along with all of them. Their sins exposed. It's what I did before I burned that place down. I collected the evidence, the photos they took, the videotapes, showing all the ugly things they'd done. It was like they wanted to keep them as keepsakes of their depravity.

But as they sat there tied up in a circle, screaming through the gags, I told them what I planned to do. Reveal all of their sins, make the world know who they all were. Then I swore they'd burn. And I kept every single word. I'm anything but dishonest.

I grin, enjoying this memory now. Sister Mary's screams are a comfort, like I'm still that boy who needed saving. And these memories? They give him that.

Give *me* that.

Watching Sophia, who was about my age when I was hurt that way, I can't imagine it happening to her. I'd never let it.

Sitting on the bench, out on a rocky path leading up to a walkthrough, I see her well, but she doesn't see me. This is the only bench here, so I can watch her from a distance, a small shrub covering me from view.

I don't even know why I'm still here.

I haven't had many reasons to follow the girl. She's not involved in any of this. And sure, maybe I don't have to kill her father, but if it hurts my mother, then even her pain is worth it.

Sophia kicks the ball hard, and it heads in my direction, rolling closer and closer. Until it hits my foot.

She bounces after it, telling her friend she'll be a second.

I pick it up, waiting for her to run over to me. When she does, I hold it out for her.

"Here you go." I get to my feet, reaching out my hand to hers.

"I hope I didn't hit you, sir." She grins, toothy and adorable.

Sir. That makes me laugh internally.

"That's okay."

Her brows squint. "You look a little familiar. Do I know you?"

"I don't think so." I settle back down.

She taps her temple with her forefinger. And then her eyes pop. "Oh! From Grandpa and Grandma's wedding! You told me you weren't Daddy's friend."

Shit. How the hell does this tiny human have such a good memory?

"Hmm. Don't recall. Who is your daddy?"

"Michael Marino."

"Ah, yes." I nod thoughtfully. "I do know of him."

Definitely can't lie to little Satan. She'd know.

"And yes, I did attend your grandmother's wedding. She looked happy."

"She is! Grandpa Patrick is the best. He's so funny! Did you talk to him at the wedding?"

"Haven't had the pleasure."

She sits right beside me. "He makes the best food. Do you know how to cook? Because Daddy says everyone should know how to cook."

But she doesn't let me get a word in, continuing in her bubbly kind of way.

"He taught me how to make tomato sauce from scratch! I also

know how to make bread and calzones!"

"Well, you're definitely better than me. I'm not much of a cook."

Of course, I lie. I cook quite well. Had to learn, living on my own.

"Oh, then you really should meet my grandpa. Because he can teach you."

Pretty sure he doesn't care enough about me to teach me anything.

"He once made pizza from scratch, and it tasted better than the best pizzeria in the city! Can you believe that?" Her eyes sparkle, and I can't help but smile.

"What else does he make?"

"He makes seafood broth, which all the grownups like, but…" She makes a gag face. "I don't like that stuff. Too fishy." She giggles.

"I don't like fish either." The confession comes easily.

"Really?" Her face lights up, eyes wide-eyed. "What do you like to eat?"

"I like pizza, steak, or burgers."

"Oh! Maybe you can come over sometime and have some with us! My dad loves to barbecue, and my mommy, Elsie, makes the best macaroni and cheese."

"I appreciate the offer, but I don't think your parents would want me there. They don't really know me."

She waves off the comment. "Everyone is a stranger to each other at first until they become friends."

Where did this kid come from?

"That's pretty insightful for…uh…how old are you?"

Of course, I already know her age.

"Six. What does insightful mean?" Her brows furrow in an

endearing kind of way.

"Means you're smart."

"Oh, duh!" She rolls her eyes. "I knew that already."

I let out a laugh.

"My daddy says I'm super smart all the time."

I nod. "Everyone has to be right about something at least once…" I whisper that last bit.

"Do you know he saved me when I was a baby?"

My curiosity is piqued. "Did he? How?"

"My birth parents died in a fire, and he rushed in and saved me. He's a hero!"

"Mm-hmm…"

I didn't know that.

She tilts her head and examines me like a tiny spy, trying to get inside my head. "Do you not like my daddy?"

No.

"I mean, he's okay…"

She giggles. "You're funny."

"Sophia!" Mabel calls. "Where are you?"

"Uh-oh." She grimaces and jumps to her feet. "I gotta go before I get in trouble. Thanks for the ball." She gathers it in both hands. "Maybe I'll see you next time, sir."

"Maybe." I give her a half-smile as she turns to rush off. "But, Sophia?"

She stops and glances back over her shoulder. "Yeah?"

"Be careful, okay? There are a lot of bad people in this world. Don't make it a habit to talk to strangers."

"But you're not a stranger. You were at Grandma's wedding, silly, so it means we're friends now." She grins.

"Friends, huh?"

"That's right! What's your name, by the way?"

Don't tell her.

"Andy."

"Nice to officially meet you, Andy."

"Nice to meet you too, Sophia."

"Bye!" She waves and rushes away.

I watch her go, getting up to make sure she gets to Mabel before I start back to my car. And I know right here and now, I'd do anything for this little girl.

Anything at all.

No matter whose name she carries.

Fifteen

KAYLA

I've been a good girl the past three days. I haven't killed a soul. And A has been awfully quiet too. Haven't even gotten a note from him.

I quite miss them. Miss *him*.

I hate admitting that. But I can't deny it's true.

I want to see him again. Talk to him. Feel those sensations he brings out in me.

Why hasn't he reached out?

Did he get sick of me? Did he move on to some other damaged girl who's less broken? Maybe he's better off…

I've done all I can to get my mind off him. Had a session with Dr. Collins. Went to work at the club. Studied. Went out to eat with Elsie and Jade. Sat in the park and watched the sun rise.

I even read a book. I hadn't read one since before I was taken. It felt nice. Too nice. And I knew sooner or later it would all come crashing down.

And today, it did just that.

My heart races at the headline on the television screen.

MIDNIGHT MURDERER STRUCK AGAIN.

This time she was an eighteen-year-old redhead with a beautiful smile, attending an Ivy League university to study biology. Her mother sobbed on the television screen, telling the world what was robbed from her.

Like me, this young woman wanted to become an oncologist. Her mother was a cancer survivor, and Bella wanted to help those battling the horrible disease, like the doctors who helped her mom did. And this animal, he took that from her, from the world. All the good she could've done. He wiped away her dreams and stole her future. For his own selfish, sickening pleasure.

If I could, I'd kill every single one of them. Every depraved soul that walks these streets. They're all like the ones who took me and my friends. They don't see us as people. We're just toys for their pleasure.

But how do I find this killer? He doesn't even have a type. I can't make myself prey.

I would if I could. I'd lure him in, and then I'd be the one to kill him.

Or at least I'd die trying.

My phone goes off suddenly, yet I still stare at the TV screen as I pick it up, glancing to see who it is, thinking it's my mom again.

But it's a text from a number I don't recognize.

That gets my attention.

ANONYMOUS

Hey.

My body grows ice cold. Is it him?

I swallow past the thick anxiety crawling up my throat. I make it to the window and glance outside, but see no one except Chris, who's in his car giving me space.

KAYLA

Who the hell is this?

ANONYMOUS

Did you already forget about me, little wolf?

KAYLA

A? Jesus, could you maybe let a girl know you have her number?

I want to ask him where he's been. Why all of a sudden he's reaching out. But that'd be pathetic. It's only been a few days. He's not my boyfriend. He's just a man I kill with. Nothing more. Two crazy people doing crazy things. That's all we are. That's all we can be. Maybe that's why he kept his distance. So that I don't get any wrong ideas.

A

Did I scare you?

KAYLA

No. I was just watching the news. He killed another girl.

A

I know.

He won't touch you, I promise. No one will.

KAYLA

I'm not afraid of that. I want him to come after me. I want to be the one to kill him. Please tell me if you have some idea how to find him.

If he did, I wouldn't hesitate.

A

If I did, I'd have killed him by now. But, Kayla? I'd never allow you to make yourself the target.

KAYLA

I don't remember asking for your permission.

Silence. He doesn't respond for minutes, and I wonder if he ever will. My cell rings, and it's his number.

My heart speeds up, and as I answer, I clear my throat.

"Yes? How may I help you?" I tease.

"Kayla, I don't know what the fuck is going through your head. But when I tell you I will never allow it, I mean that!" His howling breaths register through the line.

A shiver coasts up my body.

His voice… He sounds worried. And I very much like the sound of that.

"He isn't like the other men you've been playing with," he goes on. "He's different. He will kill you, and I will never let that happen."

"But you'll be there, won't you? You're always there. So if he tries, you can stop him. We can work together to put an end to him. He must be stopped before he kills more innocent women."

My pulse throbs in my ears.

He must die.

My breathing grows faster. My lungs tighten.

Their faces… Those men.

My hand balls tightly as I try to concentrate on A's voice.

"Absolutely never gonna happen. Do you hear me?! I'll be the one taking all the risk, not you!" The words leave him in a gritting tone while I try to calm the panic, unable to withstand the weight of the world crashing around me.

My chest is heavy; I'm drowning in it until I'm clawing at it, the phone almost slipping.

"You're not to look for him or do anything stupid," he continues, oblivious to my turmoil. "You can play with the other men. And I'll watch. I like to watch you. But not him. Do I make myself clear?"

My exhales grow shallower.

"Kayla? Are you there?"

"Mm-hmm." I try to act like I'm fine, but fail.

"You don't sound okay. Do you need me?"

Yes. Tears prickle my eyes. *I need you to hold me.*

"No." I clear my throat and swipe harshly under my eyes. "I'm fine. I can handle myself, okay?"

"This is nonnegotiable, Kayla. I'm not above sending Chris a note about your extracurricular activities. And if he tells Michael, you're done. You realize that, right?"

Anger radiates through me, my limbs tingling in its wake. "Why the hell do you care what happens to me? You haven't called in days! So stop pretending like you give a shit, whoever the fuck you are. I endured hell for nine years. I can endure anything after that!"

Thick silence greets me. Until I glance down at the phone to make sure he's still there.

"I know you have. But I—"

"What, huh?! You care about me now? Can't live without me because I mean so much to you?" I let out a sardonic laugh. "We don't even know each other! We're both just messed up. That's all we have in common."

Another laugh bubbles out of me, yet my heart? It breaks, because every word I said was a lie.

I'm just letting my anger win. The rational side of me knows that, but this other side, this girl trapped inside me, she wants to push him away. She wants to be alone. To hurt. To suffer. To bleed in silence.

"You know more about me than anyone in my life ever has, Kayla Jenkins," he whispers. "And I think I know you pretty well too. Does that scare you?"

He pauses, making my pulse quiver.

"Because it scares the fuck out of me."

All the air's trapped in my lungs. I want to say so much, yet nothing comes out. Something in me feels like I know him, or maybe it's because I want to desperately. Want to see his face.

"You will *not* go after him." His voice grows lower, huskier. "You will obey me. Because you don't want to know what happens when you don't."

I scoff. "Is that a threat? You gonna hurt me?"

"I'd never hurt you, baby bird. I want you safe. That's what this is about."

My throat aches from the sincerity in his words. He somehow does care, even if he won't actually say it out loud.

Before I can utter another word, I register a beep on the other end of the call, and when I look at the screen, I see Cammie's name.

"I have to go. Someone's calling."

"Alright. I'll see you soon. Be a good girl for me and don't cause trouble."

Then he's gone, like a phantom.

With a heavy exhale, I answer Cammie's call.

"Hey, Cammie!"

She sniffles, and I register her quiet sobs.

My heart instantly races.

"Cammie? What's wrong?" I jump to my feet, rushing for my keys.

"I—I did something," she sobs, barely able to catch her breath. "Can you...can you please come?"

"I'm on my way." I jump out the door and charge into my car, keeping her on the line as I drive off, Chris immediately in my rearview. "Talk to me." I put her on speaker. "Tell me what happened."

"I—I called my mom," she cries. "I thought that this time... may-maybe she'd wanna talk to me, you know. But—but she said she never wants to see me or hear from me. That I shamed her and got myself raped and am playing the victim."

She snivels so hard, my heart rips into two. How could her mom say that? It wasn't her fault she was taken. She was an escort at the time and came from a religious family. They had no idea what she was doing on the side, and when she was taken, the police told them the truth.

When they got her back, they shunned her. Her father and brother called her a whore. Told her she brought shame upon their congregation. She thought her mother, someone she was once close to, would eventually forgive her and take her back, but she didn't. And all that girl ever wanted was for her family to love her again. But they never truly did. Because loving someone in the shadow of who you thought they were isn't love. True love is unconditional.

But I wonder… Would my own family and friends love me if they found out what I've done? Or would they treat me like Cammie's family has?

I think the answer scares me.

"Oh, Cammie, I'm so sorry! I know how much you wanted their acceptance. But sometimes we never get that. Sometimes the truth is hard because it hurts so much. And nothing I say will make it hurt less. But I'm here for you, okay? I'll be there to listen, to let you cry as much as you want. We can even go to one of those ax-throwing places and imagine it's your mom's face."

When she stops crying and silence erupts, I wonder if I overdid it a bit. Then again, her mother deserves it.

Her laughter bursts out, and I breathe a sigh of relief.

"Glad I didn't lose you with that one."

"No." She chokes on a laugh. "I actually would like that."

"It's a date! I'll be there in about fifteen. Just stay with me, okay?"

"I'm here," she whispers. "In my room."

"Good. You don't ever have to feel alone. We're your family now. It may not be the same, but we're here for you, and we'll never turn you away, no matter what."

"You were…" She starts crying again, attempting to catch her breath. "You were always so nice."

Yeah, nice. That's always been me. Can't say I'm that nice anymore…

We continue to chat about inconsequential things until I get to Helping Hand and get out of my vehicle.

Chris leans against his SUV and nods. "If you need me, just call."

"Thanks."

I rush inside the building and scan my card. Passing by a security booth, I enter the elevator, heading for the dorms on the second floor.

As soon as I exit the elevator, another security guard greets me, and I rush for Cammie's room. Once I'm at her door, I knock once, and she opens.

When I see her, mascara running down her cheeks and her eyes streaked red, my own tears throb behind my eyes. But as I glance down at her arm, I notice she's holding a towel around her wrist.

Oh, no…

My stomach churns.

She didn't. Please tell me she didn't.

I gradually step in, and she backs off, peering down at the floor.

"Cammie… What happened to your arm?"

"Please don't tell anyone. I—I…I won't do it again."

Shit.

My heart lurches.

"Cammie, I can't keep this to myself."

How can I not tell her therapist? Jade? Someone?

Because the next time could be worse, and it'd be my fault. I have to convince her to tell someone. To get help.

"Please!" she begs, fat tears running down her cheeks.

"Can we sit somewhere?"

She nods and leads me to the sofa. She settles first, and I sit beside her.

"Are you still bleeding?"

She moves the towel off her arm and looks at her gash. "It's better now." Her body sags. "It was so stupid. I've never done this before, but…" She bows her head with a tremble in her lower lip. "But when she said those things, I was so angry. I just took a knife, and…and I cut myself."

She sobs, and I instantly hold her to me. Because I know exactly what this feels like. That pain you can't get rid of, needing an outlet for it, something to mask it.

"You just needed to control the pain inside you. I get it."

She perches back and her brows furrow. "Have you ever?"

I nod. I can't believe I'm admitting this, but if it helps her, then I'm happy to tell her.

"When I first got out, I would burn the insides of my thighs with a lighter. It felt good to have some kind of way to release all the things I was feeling. I didn't understand why I did what I did, but I knew it felt good, even while it hurt like hell."

"Do you still…"

"No. My wounds were superficial, and they're healed now. Then, once I started therapy and told Doctor Collins about it, he helped me manage it."

"How?"

"He gave me a diary and told me to write what I feel as soon as those thoughts came, no matter how bad they were. At first, I didn't think it would work, but over time, I did it less and less. Until I stopped altogether."

She shakes her head. "I'm not a good writer."

I shrug both shoulders. "You don't need to be. This is just for you. No one will read it."

"Maybe I can try it."

"How about I get you a journal and you can see how it feels?"

She nods. "Yeah. Okay."

"Let's go take care of your wound so it doesn't get infected."

Every room here has an emergency kit in the bathroom, and together, we go inside and grab it. As I start to help her clean and dress her wound, I notice the marks on her skin, evidence that this isn't the first time she's done this. And if this isn't the first time…I know she won't stop. Not until someone intervenes or she's dead. I have to do something. I have to help somehow.

"Wanna watch a movie with me?" she asks once her arm is wrapped and we're headed to the living room.

"Of course." My heart tightens with empathy as I glance at her. She's hurting. I know what that feels like.

She settles on the sofa, and as she scrolls through the cable channels, she passes the news, and I see her again. The latest girl who died.

"She's so pretty," Cammie whispers. "I can't imagine being that pretty."

"You *are* that pretty." I drop a hand on her shoulder.

"Do you think they'll ever catch this guy?" A little furrow forms between her eyes. "He seems so much smarter than the cops."

"Every killer eventually gets caught."

And I realize that means me too.

CHRIS

I'm at Michael's the following day for a briefing on the situation with the traffickers. All the Cavaleris are here too, the brothers who took out the Bianchis.

They all know what it means for this city and the world if the trafficking is allowed to continue. Destroying anyone who associates with the Bianchis means a lot to these guys.

"They are running their trafficking rings all over the country now and are sending girls overseas," Michael tells the group.

There are about thirty present for this meeting. All hands on deck. Everyone needs to be prepared for what may be coming.

"How the hell do you know that?" Dom Cavaleri narrows a

glare at Michael.

It doesn't take much to see he doesn't like the Marinos at all. Dom's the oldest Cavaleri and the leader of their gang of killers.

"Because…" Michael glares. "Two days ago, we found a guy who was kidnapping girls for them. He didn't know who was in charge, but he knew that his assignment came from someone low on the food chain, someone who is taking orders from another. But he said that whoever is leading it is keeping his identity completely hidden. He communicates only by notes given to him by one of his trusted guys and uses a burner we can't track."

"And he just told you all this?" Dom snickers.

"No." Gio grins and hands Dom a phone, pressing play as a man screams. "We gave him some incentives."

"Is that his hand you're holding?" Dom fights a laugh.

"Yeah, the right one." Gio grins. "He was really attached to it."

Enzo Cavaleri chuckles and high-fives Gio.

"So, anyway…" Michael goes on. "We don't know shit yet. Just that they had a cellar in the city that they were operating from. But now they've moved their headquarters to Boston, the asshole told us."

"Did he know why they moved it to Boston?" Dom asks.

Michael nods. "Yeah, they dismantled their operation in New York after Gio's friend Bryce was killed and had connections here."

Gio's face tenses. Bryce was his good friend. And to save himself from a gambling debt, he began working with these pricks to traffic women until he was murdered by someone who didn't go down without a fight.

"The Quinns are looking in Boston," Gio adds. "They have every one of their people on it. But whoever is doing this knows how to hide."

"Are you saying we won't be able to find him?" Dom glares. "Because we will. Even if my brothers and I have to burn this goddamn country to the ground to do it. Everyone associated with the Palermos will die."

Gio lifts both hands in the air. "Listen, man, you won't get any arguments from me. But take it easy a bit. You look like you're gonna pop a vein in that large forehead of yours."

"Shut up, Gio." Raph shakes his head. "Excuse my brother. We know how much this means to your family."

"I'm just fucking with you." Gio grows serious. "They'll get what's coming. We'll all work together. They won't be able to hide from us."

"You don't know these people." Dom drops back in the chair, his eyes cast into the distance like he's remembering the past.

From what I heard, the Bianchis killed a member of his family and did a lot of messed-up shit to them.

"I've gotta get back to Chiara." Dom peers down at the cell in his grasp. "She's not happy I'm here without her as it is."

"She could've come," Michael offers. "Faro Bianchi was her father. She could have info."

"Believe me, I know everything she does. I don't want her here reliving all the shit she's been through."

"I understand." Michael gives him a long, faraway look. "Elsie is scared. She's having nightmares again…" His voice drops before he catches himself and his face hardens. "I will not rest until she feels safe. So whatever resources you need, we're at your full disposal."

Dom nods. "Same goes for you."

"Aww, we're one happy, fucked-up family, aren't we?" Gio grins.

"Yeah, don't push it." Dom and his brothers start for the door.

"I'll be in touch." He eyes Michael before he heads out.

"I swear he's grumpier than your ass," Gio tells Michael.

"I heard that!" Dom's voice rings over from the foyer before the door bangs shut.

As the men all start out of the room, Michael calls me over.

"How's everything with Kayla? Is she being a handful?"

"No, sir." I grin internally. "I've got her under control."

"You report directly to me if she does anything again."

"Of course."

He dismisses me with a curt nod.

As I head out, I look at my phone, seeing that Kayla is behaving for once and is actually at school.

Sixteen

KAYLA

I woke up with a damn migraine this morning. Reliving what Cammie did to herself had me up most of the night.

She told me she's gonna talk to Doctor Collins about cutting herself, though I don't know how true that is. Not like I can verify it. I didn't want to mention the other marks I saw. I didn't want her to feel cornered. That never helps anyone. But I told myself I couldn't just do nothing either.

So I do something I really don't want to do. But in the end, if I don't and something happens to her, I'll never be able to live with myself.

Knocking on Jade's door, I strut inside when she invites me in.

"Kayla! Hey!" She pushes away the stack of papers she was looking at. "I'm so happy you stopped by. I was just thinking of you."

Please don't ask me to talk to any more girls...

"Oh, yeah?"

"Wondered if you were free for lunch later."

Relief washes over me. "Of course."

"So, what made you stop by this morning. Everything okay?"

My stomach turns to knots; I'm unsure how to start this conversation.

"Whatever it is, you can always tell me." Her voice is a calming sea of tranquility, and I'm ready to confess my own deepest, darkest secrets.

"It's about Cammie."

"What about her?"

I blow out a breath and say the words before I change my mind. "She's cutting herself, Jade."

She inhales sharply. "Oh, no. Did you see it?"

I tell her what transpired yesterday.

"Okay, I'll deal with it without giving your name away. I promise."

"Thanks. I really think she trusts me, and I don't want to do anything to jeopardize that," I say.

Her smile grows. "You've always been someone people can count on. I'm proud of you."

A lump lodges in my throat, even as I fight to make it go away. Because she wouldn't be proud if she knew what I've become. She'd be terrified.

"Look who's talking," I quickly change the subject. "What you've accomplished here is amazing. You're doing so much good."

Her mouth thins. "It's what they deserve. To have a place to sleep, to eat. A place that offers them all the resources they can't get out there."

"I'm glad you found what makes you happy. It's important to

do things that make us sleep better at night."

"And what helps you sleep better at night?" Her eyes narrow, as though she's attempting to dig up everything I so desperately try to hide.

"Oh, you know…" *Murder.* "A good show, a long drive to clear my head."

She grins right before her office phone rings.

Quickly, I rise, grateful for the momentary break. "Go get that. I'm gonna go help the girls in the rec room, and then we can get lunch."

"Perfect. Thank you." She slants her hand with a smile, waving goodbye while I rush out of there, hoping I'm done being interrogated for today.

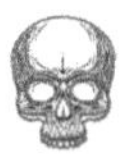

After lunch with Jade, I went to class before coming home. Eriu texted a bit ago asking me to go to a bar with her to celebrate my birthday, which isn't for a couple of days.

I figured, why not? What else would I do on a weekday? Best not to sit around and think about things I shouldn't. Like what the Midnight Murderer is doing right now. Whether he's scouting for his newest victim. Maybe he'll be at the same bar as us.

That puts a grin on my face as I get ready, slipping into a black strappy dress that hits above my knees and matching heels. Shooting off a quick text to Chris, I let him know I'm heading out.

He's stayed away from me these last few days, barely saying a word, which is fine by me. The less he's in my business, the better. And the quicker the murderer is found and the traffickers are killed, the faster I can get Chris out of my home. Permanently. This whole sleeping-with-your-bodyguard thing sounds a lot better in books than real life.

Not that we're sleeping together…

Grabbing my keys, I hop into my car and take it on the road, driving through traffic to get to the city.

This was a terrible idea. No one enjoys driving in the city. But I hate taking the train, being crammed in a small car with people I don't know. This is safer. I have control when I drive.

Finally getting there and parking almost two hours later, I make the short distance to the rooftop bar where Eriu waits for me, waving her arms while a man with chin-length dark hair and cutting blue eyes looks at her, not threateningly, but longingly. Like he wishes he could touch her.

I don't recognize him at all, and if he knew any better, he'd stay away from someone like Eriu. She's the daughter of the Mob. Not to mention Iseult Marino's little sister. Iseult happens to be Gio's wife and an assassin for the Irish Mob. That bit of information probably wouldn't be so shocking to anyone who has the misfortunate to get on her bad side. So I pity any idiot who tries to hurt Eriu. They'd find themselves in a load of shit. Between her sister and three older brothers, that girl has an army behind her.

"You came!" she screams over the music, shaking her hips as she grabs my hands and forces me to dance to some annoyingly obscene pop song.

I drop my mouth close to her ear. "Did you drink without me?"

"Maybe!"

I laugh. "Who is that man staring at you?"

I pass my attention to him, and he narrows a glare.

"Oh, that's Devlin." With that, her face falls and her shoulders drop. "He used to be my bodyguard. That is, until he went to prison. And now he's my bodyguard again. Yay…"

"What?" I blink.

"Don't ask. Long story." She sighs. "He came out of prison a few months ago, and when I came to New York, he followed me. Follows me everywhere, actually."

Her eyes go to his, and he holds her stare. She closes her eyes for a moment before she looks back at me.

"I know he's here because of my father. Definitely not because he wants to be around me. That would be a miracle." She scoffs. "Probably told my father he'd be a good little soldier and watch out for his pride and joy." Her gaze turns to slits. "I hate this. I hate wanting him the way I do! God! I wish he'd just leave. I've wanted him for so long, but all he does is turn me down."

She grinds her jaw and shakes her head.

"Wait." I jerk back. "He's your bodyguard and you *like* him, like him?"

"Just look at him. How could I not?" Her brows gather, and she stares yearningly at him while he pins her with his own gaze.

Except his is dark and brooding, like he's fighting not to pin her up against the nearest wall.

"How about we start at the beginning?" I suggest.

Her chest rises and falls with a quick sigh. "He works for my dad. And at one point, he was my bodyguard. But I've always had a major crush on him. One day, I drugged him and—"

"You did what?!"

"Don't look at me like that! I was so sheltered, I wanted to let loose, so I went to a club with a friend."

My brows curve. "Not judging. Just surprised." I grin.

"I surprise a lot of people, it seems." She snickers. "Anyway, while I was at the club, I did something bad, and Devlin took the fall. Ended up serving time for me."

"Wow, this just gets better." I can't help but laugh.

She narrows a glare as she goes on. "I wrote him letters while he was in prison, visited him there. I wanted him to know how sorry I was. That I was willing to take the fall, but he wouldn't allow it." She flicks her gaze upward and sighs. "Once he got out, I thought maybe we could be together, but he told me it would never happen." Tears shimmer in her eyes, caught between her lashes. "He's never going to want me. I have to come to terms with that. So now, this is all we have. Him following me around and stalking me." She huffs a breath.

Well, looks like I'm not the only one with a bodyguard and stalker. She's got the two-for-one special, though.

"Maybe he just thinks because you're younger and your dad's his boss, it won't work."

"Well, I can't wait around for him to change his mind, now, can I? He's the only man I've ever wanted, and he's just going to stand there and watch me instead of being with me? I know my father will eventually arrange a marriage for me, and Devlin will do nothing about it."

I know that arranged marriages are still a thing in her circle, and I feel sorry for her. She should marry someone she falls in love with. It's the natural thing.

"Maybe you should give him something to motivate him a little…"

"Like what?" Her tone catches with curiosity.

"Ladies!" Prince happens to walk right past us with a friend I don't recognize, maybe another guy from college.

A leery grin happens on my face. Sometimes all a man needs to inspire him is a little healthy competition.

"Prince! Hey! What are you doing here?"

"We just happened to end up here after hopping at a couple of nearby bars!" he hollers. "Glad we ran into you ladies."

He winks at Eriu before giving me a showstopping smile.

"You know…" I say, giving Eriu a knowing look. "Eriu was

just telling me how she wishes she had someone to dance with."

"Ugh, I did?"

"Yeah, don't you remember?" I pop my eyes and bounce a quick glance at Devlin, hoping she understands where I'm going with this.

"Oh! Yeah. Must be the margarita I had earlier, already going to my head." She laughs. "I'd love to dance with you."

Prince holds out his hand, and she places hers in his.

And that's when I see it: Devlin's fist curling at his side until it trembles. But the man doesn't move an inch, carefully watching her as she heads for the dance floor, leaving me with what's-his-face.

"I'm Tim," the stranger announces, nervously peering around the room. "Wanna dance maybe?"

"N—"

But then I think about how I can make my own stalker a little jealous. He could surely use a little motivation. Maybe then he'd actually rip off his mask and kiss me so no one else can. Not that I'd let anyone kiss me. No one but him…

But he doesn't need to know that.

I wander my attention around the bar, knowing he's here somewhere. Knowing he'll see me dancing with a man that isn't him. Knowing it'll make him crazy.

At least I hope it will.

My smile stretches before I say, "Okay, Tim. Let's go."

Seventeen

KAYLA

Islide up beside Eriu, Tim coming up behind me, hands on my hips as I let the music consume me. My eyes closed, I drown in the beat while a man I don't know dances behind me, real close.

Too close.

I don't know how long we dance, but one song slips into another, and when I look around, I don't find A anywhere. Then again, he wouldn't wear a mask here, would he? He'd wanna blend into the crowd.

Chris is watching from some obscure corner while Devlin is still glaring at Eriu, probably thinking of ways to kill Prince.

When the current song ends, I excuse myself and head for the restroom. This has been kinda fun so far.

I hate celebrating my birthday. Being the center of attention isn't something I ever looked forward to, and I know my parents will want to make a big deal about it, and so will my friends. But today is nice. Just being out with Eriu, dancing, having a drink, is enough. So I want to enjoy it for what it is before reality sets in.

"Excuse me," I say to someone just as I round the corner toward the narrow pathway leading to the restrooms.

It's kinda sketchy here, even with the few drunk women laughing as they strut past me.

Before I can enter, I feel someone behind me. Breathing heavy, warmth of a body practically touching mine. An uneasy feeling washes over me, scurrying up my arms like a deadly threat.

When I try to look behind me, a hand snaps to the back of my neck. "Look straight ahead and make a left past the bathrooms."

That voice…

"A? Is that you?"

"Keep walking, little wolf, and don't turn around."

His tone sets me ablaze. Feels good to hear the command in it. His other hand grips my hip, pushing his torso into me to propel my body forward. All I can do is want more of whatever this is.

"Are you angry?" I ask.

He pushes me further with a quiet chuckle.

"You were dancing with someone, his cock practically grinding on this perfect ass, and you're asking me if I'm fucking angry?" he seethes under his breath. "Yeah, Kayla, I'm furious. I'm even angrier knowing you were purposely trying to get to me, and I let you. You knew what that'd do to me. Knew the way I'd want to rip his lungs from his throat for touching you. So yeah, I'm angry. You win. And now you get to see what happens when you do."

A shiver glides up my arms, and I grin.

I won and he lost. It's exactly what I wanted. Well, not quite. I did want to see his face, and I still haven't.

He shoves me down the corridor until we're beside a door.

"Open it," he demands.

And I do, while my body practically jolts with tingles he put there. He thrusts me inside, and when the door shuts, all I know is darkness.

I can't see him, yet I feel him. My hands reach out for him, anything I can grab on to. At first, I feel nothing but air, hear his audible breaths rushing out of him.

"Is this what you wanted?" he asks, all silky soft, yet rough around the edges. "Did you want to make me jealous?"

"Yes," I whisper, fisting his shirt when I find it and pulling him to me, and he lets me. "Did it work?"

"Does it look like it didn't?" he groans, and his mouth drops to my ear, his body pinning mine against a hard surface behind me. "You know it did. You know what you do to me."

His lips run down the space behind my ear, the tip of his tongue circling seductively. My head snaps back as I let out a moan, realizing that if I can feel his mouth on me, it means…

"You're not wearing your mask…" I breathe.

His cock is jutting through his pants. I can feel how hard and heavy it is against my belly.

I need to see him. Need to see the face of the man who makes me feel this way. After all this time, after everything that's been done to me, I can feel something.

"Don't need it here. You can't see me." There's amusement in his tone.

"Please," I beg. "Please…"

Show me your face. Touch me. Make it feel good like it never has before.

"What are you begging me for, baby bird? Tell me what you want."

"I—"

His hand curls around my throat and squeezes. His warm breaths skate across my lips, making me whimper and sound like I never have before. Except in my dreams when he was there too, taking things I never gave a soul.

These things I'm feeling, they make no sense. It's as though I'm dreaming. Like this is someone else.

But I am someone else now, aren't I?

"Oh, God," I groan with a heavy throbbing between my thighs.

"Is this what you're asking for?" He squeezes my throat a little more. "Is this what you need?"

"Yes, I—I…I want you to be rough with me."

"How rough?" His other hand runs up my bare thigh, slowly lifting up my dress, fingering the strap of my cotton thong.

"Rough enough to hurt." The words fall without shame, because I know he'd never make me feel that way.

"Fuck," he hisses, fingertips running up and down my slit.

My toes curl, my hand snapping to the back of his head. His hair is soft as I fist it, forcing his mouth into my throat.

He kisses and nips, his palm pushing into my pussy while I grind on it, my body trembling with desire the more he touches me, the more he sounds like he's losing control.

"Tell me your name," I beg him for crumbs I know he won't give.

Instead of answering, he flips me around, one hand around my throat, the other roughly lifting up my dress until my bare ass is exposed. But he can't see it, and that just makes it all the more erotic.

"Hands flat against the wall and bend that beautiful ass over."

My palms meet the wall, while my body curves willingly for him.

"This is all you'll get from me," he breathes with a harsh

baritone. "This is all we'll have. Blood and bodies stroking in the dark. Can you live with that, Kayla?"

With a finger around the strap of my panties, he slides them down to my upper thighs.

"Yes," I cry out, never having felt this level of need before.

Never knew I was capable of it, yet somehow he brought it out in me.

But this isn't enough. I want so much more. I want him to tie me up and fuck me on the ground until tears drip down my face, not from pain but from overstimulation.

He suddenly moves back, and for a second, I think he's leaving.

"Where are you going? Please don't go!" I sound pathetic, but right now, I'm too far gone to care.

But he doesn't answer. Instead, he grips my wrist, then the other, and binds them behind my back with something tight.

"Wha-what are you doing?"

I should be afraid. It's what the men did. But I'm not. Because deep down, I know he won't hurt me. He's proven that already. This is exactly what I wanted.

"It's what you want, isn't it?" He repeats the words spinning in my mind. "You want me to fuck you like my personal whore. Tied and gagged, crawling to me." He runs his palm against my core, and my body jitters as I whimper. "Want me to use this body. Want to be my cum slut, isn't that right, babe?"

Babe.

That word again.

Pain lodges in the back of my throat.

"Y-yes," I stammer, overwrought with emotion.

"Are you crying?" Concern lines every word, and suddenly his hand stops moving.

"I'm fine. Don't stop. Please. I want this."

He grunts. "Hate that I want this too."

His palm connects with my behind, and the sound echoes in the room. He spanks me again, harder, faster. My skin aches, wanting every bit of the burn.

Every inch of my body throbs, needing this man to take me however he wants.

"You have no idea how badly I want inside you." His frame falls over mine, hard body forming against my soft one.

"Then fuck me," I say. "I want that with you. Please, A, please…"

"Shit…" His fingers trace my pussy, one sliding in to roll around my pulsing clit. "I can't, but I will give you this."

He pinches me there, and I cry out with a shudder.

"Every time you're alone in the dark, you'll think of me and the things I'm about to do to you."

Then, without warning, he thrusts his fingers so deep inside me, my body vibrates from the sensation. His palm presses into my throat, fingers cinching tighter the harder he fucks me, groaning every single time I moan with undulated pleasure.

His thumb circles around my clit while he keeps up the rhythm, making me tremble and cry out for more.

"You feel too good, baby bird. Like a needy, filthy thing made just for my depravity."

"Oh, God!" I flinch, my hands coming to form fists against the small of my back.

The need to touch him, to feel his body against mine, overwhelms me. Stars break before my eyes the more he hits that spot inside me, the release ebbing until it's ready to reach the cusp.

"I want you to come for me…" His teeth rake my throat, and the more those heady sounds come from deep in his chest, the harder and faster I need that release. "I want you drenched and flushed and begging to be mine. Because that's what you are. *Mine*."

With another flick of his finger against my center, I scream out, "Yesyesyes!"

And he's there, palm around my mouth as I free-fall into the most amazing feeling of my life.

It doesn't end. The more he rams into me, the harder I come. He doesn't stop, not even as my body's overwrought with sensitivity.

"I—I can't—fuck!" I gasp on a whimper.

"One more. I want to feel you do that around my fingers one more time."

As though by his command, I feel myself rising again, my core spasming.

"I've—I've never done that before," I pant, the truth falling from me easily.

He growls against my ear, rubbing his palm between my thighs, my eyes rolling back again.

"I've never wanted this before," he says. "Never wanted to make a woman feel good the way I wanna make you feel good. You don't know how badly…"

"How badly what?" I breathe.

Instead of finishing the sentence, he thrusts his fingers inside me again, as though wanting me to forget what he just said. But I can't.

"Tell me what you—you were gonna say," I groan.

"Never mind that. Now quiet while I make this pussy drip down my hand, because it's what you did, Kayla. It's what I make you do."

Before I know what's happening, he pushes off my body, and the next thing I know is his mouth sucking on me there, the tip of his tongue snaking around my sensitive flesh.

I feel for his head, grabbing on to his hair while he eats me to my core, his growling vibrating through my veins like crack. I need more of this. More of him.

"Yes, yes, yes, don't stop!" My cry morphs into a series of gasps, needing the wave of release so badly, I'd die just to feel it.

His fingers ram back inside me while his tongue does sinful things to my core.

This is better than oxygen. I'm addicted—to him, to what he does. I can't give this up, and he hasn't even been inside me. Hasn't even looked into my eyes as he entered me.

Would I like it? Would I be scared?

I don't know, but I want to find out.

But this? This right here is the best I've ever felt, so anything after that will be even better.

He flattens his tongue and moves it in circular motions. My hands are shaking, my knees buckling.

"I'm gonna…" The words die in my throat as the most powerful release I have ever felt pummels through me. "Yes! Oh God, A!"

His growling sensations only push me further over the edge while his teeth graze me there as I spill on his tongue. He sucks me into his mouth, and when he's done, he kisses the insides of both of my thighs, then up my stomach, until he's on his feet again. He flips me around until I face him, and he reaches behind me, undoing my hands and setting them free.

His body is back against mine, and his breaths are heavy while mine burn through my lungs.

"Beautiful and sweet," he says. "Just like I knew you'd be."

"A…" I cry, my hand reaching out, palm cupping his cheek.

When I feel his skin beneath my fingertips, an ache lodges in my throat. I run my fingers across his full, soft lips, tracing them. Down I go, drawing around his stubbled jaw and to his other cheek. My God, I want to see him. But this, right now, is enough.

I place his cheek within my palm once more and pant from the weight of my emotions.

Instead of running, he delves his face into my touch, like it's the most powerful thing in the world. Together, we stay this way for seconds or minutes, but neither of us is counting. And all I wish is for us to stay this way forever.

"Kayla…" My name is a throaty rasp.

"Yes?"

"I've never let anyone touch me this way before."

Tears burn within my eyes because I feel his pain. Feel it etched into every word, into his every molecule. The love he's lacked, the affection that has never been shown to him, it burns in him. He needs it so badly. He doesn't have to say it. I can sense it as though the pain is my own.

"Do you like it?" I run the back of my hand across his mouth. "Do you like my hands on you?"

Instead of answering, he grabs my jaw, not hard enough to hurt, yet strong enough to feel it burning through my skin.

With his other hand, he catches my wrists and pins my arms to the wall above my head, and slowly, he moves his body closer until it's trapping mine.

His lips… I can feel them hovering there against my mouth, like they're fighting for a taste.

I'm afraid to say a word, afraid he won't kiss me. A moan slips out from my lips when he brushes his with mine.

I bury my fingers in his hair, careful not to push him into me, wanting him to want it himself.

"My baby bird… You're my curse and my sanctuary."

Before I can question the meaning of those words, he slams his lips to mine and ends this grueling torture.

I groan with everything in me, my hands gripping his head, hair, anything I can grasp. His fingers are everywhere too—running up my thighs, my arms, tangled into my hair as his sensual growls beat with utter abandon.

His heavy cock rocks between us, and I want to get on my knees and taste him, make him mine in every way possible. There's no shame. No mistaking my need for him even while it may not make sense.

But I don't fight it. I don't want to. Those monsters from my past don't get to ruin a single thing about this moment. They don't deserve that. They never will. Every day, I'll fight. I'll fight their hold on me until I'm the one who wields the power.

I lower one hand and grip his length in my palm. He nips my lower lip, grunting as I stroke him.

I want this. I need this.

He sucks my tongue into his mouth, matching my movements, dropping his hand to my center.

Without warning, he thrusts multiple fingers inside my soaked pussy and curls them, driving into me so roughly, stars erupt behind my eyes.

"Mmm," I whimper around his mouth, fisting the crown of his cock in my palm, so hard he grunts.

With a quick jerk, he yanks my head back by my hair. "You need to stop touching me like that. You're gonna make me come, and I'm not coming in my pants."

"Yes!" I gasp when he flicks my clit. "I—I want you…in my mouth. Inside me. Everywhere. Please. Give me that. Force it… Oh, God… Force it into my mouth."

Maybe I'm sick for wanting things this way, but it's what I want, and I'm tired of feeling shame for it.

"God damn you, Kayla! You make me want to shackle you to my bed and never let you go."

My hands move to find the button of his pants while his fingers wrap around my throat like a collar I'd willingly wear.

He squeezes, making me dizzy with desire while I unzip him, needing to feel his silky, hard flesh in my hand.

When I do, when I reach inside and feel him…

"Shit," he groans, fingertips pushing into my throat.

He wants this badly.

"You sure about this?" he husks out by my ear.

"Yes."

One word… That's all it takes for the switch to flip, and the monster I've been waiting for comes out to play.

Eighteen

ADRIEL

This woman is slowly killing me. With her smiles and those eyes and the way she wants things the way I want them.

Part of me wants to give it all to her, yet another part wonders whether she really needs it this way. What if she needs someone to hold her instead?

I'm not that man. And she knows that by now. But this? This I can do.

I roll her long, luscious hair around my wrist and force my mouth on hers, kissing her with every breath in my lungs, consuming her rage, her pain, her suffering. I'd take every single scar she's been made to wear, add them to my collection, just to know she never endured any of it.

Her tongue dances with mine, and those sounds she makes only make me want inside her. To feel her clench around me, to know I did that to her, made her feel this way, the way I feel.

She moans around my mouth, and I swallow her lower lip, wanting to kiss every inch of her.

I'm gradually losing it. Losing everything to her. But I can't resist it.

I wrench back and wish that I could see her face, her eyes, the lust within them. "Once I feel your mouth wrapped around my cock, I don't think I'll be able to survive it."

"You'll manage." She laughs with a groan as I rub her wet clit between two fingers.

Her hand curls inside my pants, rubbing my hard-on.

"Fuck!" I growl. "You're my little sinner, taking me to hell with you."

"We've already been to hell. Maybe this is our reward."

She strokes me faster, making my teeth snap. Maybe she's right. Maybe she's my reward. Or maybe the devil's tricking me, tempting me with something I can't have.

But the thought of thrusting into her throat…I'll take that trick.

With a hand to the top of her head, I force her down hard. "On your knees, little wolf."

I feel her lower, both hands grabbing my belt.

"Take it out and fill your mouth with it."

Her breaths rise, mingled with the darkness surrounding us.

She drags my pants down, my heavy length in the softness of her hand, and the next thing I know is her heavenly tongue rolling around the crown of my cock.

"Jesus Christ…" My head falls behind me, one hand in her hair, fingers spreading, gently holding her still, until I lose all self-control.

I grab a fistful of her luscious waves and jerk her head back.

"I want you gagging on it. Want you full of me until you can barely breathe. Want my cum running down your chin, even though I can't see it." I let out a low growl. "I want to own you, Kayla. I want to ingrain myself in your DNA until you can't fucking live without me."

Jesus, I sound insane. But I don't give a shit right now. I want this woman on a level I can't even comprehend. My mind is unable to catch up with my mouth.

"Want that too…" she says.

My God, what the hell is wrong with her, wanting someone like me?

My chest squeezes, and I brush the back of my hand down her face. "My baby bird. Made perfectly for me. Yet I don't deserve you. Never deserved anything."

I grab my dick with one hand and keep the back of her head steady with the other. Roughly, I push her down, so hard she gags just the way I want it.

"That's it. That's my good girl. Take every inch of me down your tight little throat. Gonna think about your pussy while you fuck my cock with that mouth."

Her little whimpers pulse through me as she sucks with fervor, making me gasp for fucking air because this woman's robbing me of it.

I ram her head down deeper, harder, over and over until I hit the back of her throat, my thick cock stretching her in the way I wish it could stretch her pretty pink pussy.

She moans around me, squeezing my balls as I bury myself as far as I can go, thrusting until I lose every hint of reservation, giving it to her as rough as she wanted it.

She's *mine*. This thing between us, it's mine. It's ours. No one will have her after this. No one but *me*.

With a roar, I release myself into her, warm liquid dripping down her throat, and I swear I've never come this hard before. Never felt an ounce of what she makes me feel.

What the fuck is happening, and how do I make it stop?

The span of my palm grips her nape, not letting her move as I give her every single drop of me until she's consumed it all. Taken my essence into her very soul. Until all she knows is me.

When I'm through, I slowly let her go and slip out of her mouth.

She stays that way, on her knees, heavy exhales rushing out. The back of my hand runs up and down her cheek.

"Did I hurt you, little wolf?"

Because I don't want to do that.

She grabs my hand and kisses my knuckles again and again, then fastens my palm around her face.

"No," she whispers, twining her fingers through mine. "I needed that."

Needed that too.

With a sigh, she rises to her feet, and her arms? They fasten around me and hold on for long seconds, or minutes, or maybe hours. I don't know, and I don't care. Because with her, time seems to stand still, and I want to stand still with her.

My arms come around her too, getting used to the feeling of holding someone for the first time in my life. It's strange, this feeling. Part of me wants to push her away, and the other part wants to hold her tighter.

But she's here. She's in my arms, and somehow, I'm in hers. She knows the things I do, the lives I've taken, and yet she's still here. She still wants me in some twisted way. Maybe it's because she's messed up. Maybe one day she'll wake up and realize that someone like me will never be good enough for someone like her.

And maybe then I'll lose her. Lose this.

But right now, I just wanna hang on. Because it's all I have.

I've never had anything close to this before. Never felt whatever is happening between us.

And I want it. Even when it doesn't make sense to want things that were never meant to be mine.

I lower my mouth against her temple and kiss her, breathing her in like she's the only thing keeping my blood pumping.

"I have a present for you," I whisper against the shell of her ear, having completely forgotten the gifts that await her back in my home.

Goose bumps rise on the back of her neck.

Did I do that?

"But it's not my birthday yet." She exhales and buries her arms deeper into my muscles.

"To me, every day is your birthday."

"Oh, A," she gushes playfully. "And you say you have no heart."

I smirk. "Just wait until you see the kind of gift I got you before you claim I have something I don't."

She rests her forearms on my shoulders, and I can just see her mouth form a smile. "And how do I get this present?"

"I'll take you there." I move back a step, lowering my hands to slip her panties back around her before stuffing myself inside my pants and zipping them up.

"When?" she asks.

"Now."

"What? How?" I can sense the excitement in her voice.

"I'll leave here first while you give me a few minutes before you come out. Then you're gonna tell Eriu you have to go home. Better yet, tell her to go home too. She shouldn't be out here alone."

"Wait. How do you even know her name?" She pauses. "You know what? Never mind that. Where are we going?"

I take a few seconds before I answer, unsure if I should even be doing this. But that's the only place it can happen.

"My home."

She gasps. "Really?"

"My black SUV will be waiting for you in the front, and yes, my mask will be on this time."

She releases a frustrated exhale, but doesn't say anything else.

"Now turn around and face the wall, and don't look behind you." I drop my lips against her throat, her hammering pulse quickening beneath my lips. "I'll know if you did. Don't disappoint me."

When she refuses to move, I chuckle.

"Stubborn girl." I lower my mouth to hers and kiss her slowly, feeling that poison fill the marrow of my bones.

She groans, and her fingers snap to my scalp, holding on so tight, like she doesn't want to let go.

I don't want to either. I want to escape with her. Be the kind of man who can hold her and love her and do all the things someone normal would be able to do.

But I'm not normal. I'm this. And he doesn't know what the hell love even means.

With my heart heavy, I hook my arms under her thighs and lift her up in the air, kissing her wildly while her legs wind around my hips.

This is what I can do. All I'm capable of.

I slam her up against the wall, dropping her a fraction lower while I rock against her, unable to stop this maddening need to own every inch of her. To shackle her, brand her as mine. Like a hostage. Because I'm hers.

"Fuck…" I press her forehead to mine. "We need to go before it gets too late."

"I'm not the one who kissed you like that." Her warm breath

bathes my lips, heat spreading through me.

I laugh, and damn, does it feel good.

Settling my lips to the corner of her mouth, I say, "Stop tasting so damn sweet, then."

"Can't help myself." She slants her mouth against me and hungrily kisses me again until, in a flash, she rolls back. "Shit, Chris is still here. He's probably looking for me."

"Don't worry about him. I took care of that."

"What? Please don't tell me you killed him."

"No. Not exactly…but he won't be an issue anymore."

"What the hell does that even mean?"

Is she worried about him?

I grab her throat and grit my teeth.

"It means he's not going to be around anymore, distracting you with things I can't gi—" I stop myself before I finish that.

"You what?" Her voice drops.

"I didn't like how close to you he was getting. I saw the way you were looking at him at your parents'. You want him, don't you?"

"So you were there…"

"Of course I was. I'm always there." I nip her lower lip. "It's why you dreamed about him. Isn't that right? You're attracted to him. You can see yourself with him."

The way you can't with me.

Of course she can't. I have nothing to offer except this need to possess every inch of her.

"Well, I'd be attracted to *you* if you actually showed me your damn face!" she fires out.

I can't help but grin even as the envy within me grows, because I don't want anyone else on her mind but me. My body spirals with my rage, dueling between wanting to tell her everything about me and wanting to get away from her as fast as I can. But when I think about never seeing her again, never feeling her arms around me, something within me snaps.

"This is just fun and games to you anyway," she goes on, her tone growing irate.

The fact that she even thinks that makes me angrier.

"You don't even want me like that! Which is fine." She scoffs." I don't care."

But she does care. I can hear it in her voice. I wish she didn't. She shouldn't want me. But the idea of her not caring hurts like hell.

Palming my chest, she attempts to push me off unsuccessfully. "I should go. Thanks for the orgasm."

My pulse beats in my neck, and all I do is hold her throat a little tighter.

"Does it look like I'm having fun right now?" I snap, my heart racing. "To not be able to stop fucking thinking about you every goddamn second of my life? To think about what you're doing. If you ate. If you're having a nightmare again when I'm not there. Fuck, Kayla. This isn't fun!" I brush my lips with hers, gritting my teeth. "This is *torture*."

"You…you think about me?" she whispers, her mouth whisking over mine.

"Let. Me. Finish." I wrench back an inch, needing to get it out before I kiss her again, and then we'll never get out of here. "I've never felt whatever the hell you're doing to me. Never asked for it. Never wanted it. Never even knew that it existed. Until you, Kayla fucking Jenkins. So don't you dare tell me what I want. Because you have *no* idea what you're talking about."

Silence.

Complete and utter silence.

My heavy breaths take hold until they echo through the room.

Is she gonna say something? Or is she gonna stand there and make me feel like a jackass?

"Wow."

Finally. She speaks.

"Okay." She laughs nervously. "That was…uh…very insightful."

"Insightful, huh?" I exhale so loudly, it sounds demonic. "That's all you're gonna say?"

"I mean, what do you want me to say? You're clearly obsessed with me."

Ahh, there's that sarcasm.

"It's kinda unhealthy. Have you talked to a shrink?" She laughs.

This goddamn woman. With a growl, I grab her jaw and kiss her one last time, not knowing when I'll get to do it again. Because here, in the dark, I can be me. No barriers. Just us. And it scares me how badly I want that.

She sucks my tongue into her mouth, and before this goes any further, I yank her head back by her hair.

"Turn around. Face the damn wall. And come outside in five minutes. You got it?"

"Fine. I'll do as you wish. But know this. One day soon, I'll rip that mask off and you'll let me kiss you when I can see your face."

If only…

Then I rush out of there before I make that fantasy of hers come true.

Nineteen

KAYLA

"What do you mean, you're leaving?" Eriu pouts, still dancing, while a grumpy Devlin shoots daggers at another guy she's now dancing with.

"Yeah, I have a headache. Went outside for a bit to get some air, but it's not going away."

"Oh, no!" she yells over the still blaring music. "Okay, I get it. I'll probably go in a bit too."

"Get home safe." I give her a quick hug, and from behind me, I watch Devlin approach us.

He gives me a curt nod as I separate from Eriu.

"We're leaving, Eriu." His Irish brogue is hard to miss.

"I'm not done yet." She pops a brow, grabbing the guy's hand and starting to dance.

Devlin's jaw clenches, his blue eyes simmering with danger.

Clearly Devlin has a lot more self-control than I realized. But he looks ready to lose it, and fast. I'd be kinda worried right now if I was Eriu.

"Like hell, you're not." Before my eyes can comprehend what's happening, he flips the guy's hand back until he mutters a curse and runs away like he's on fire.

Her eyes burst wide. "What are you doing?"

But she doesn't get an answer. Instead, he lifts her in the air by her hips and throws her over his shoulder, carrying her out of there.

"At least he's touching you!" I giggle as her horrified expression locks with mine until she disappears from view.

Deciding that five minutes are up, I head for the exit, pushing through hordes of sweaty bodies, trying to get out of this hellhole.

Cool air hits my face as soon as I rush out of the doors. Scanning for a black SUV, I don't see one until it catches my eye from the left, a few cars away.

Quickly, I rush over, crossing the street carefully until I'm pulling open his door. And this time he's wearing that damn mask like he said he would, with that hood on. I can't even see his hair, except for a bit in the front, the dark strands teasing me.

He looks my way for a few seconds before he puts the car in drive and gets us the hell out of there.

We ride in silence for a few minutes before I ask, "How long until we get there?"

"About forty-five."

That has me wondering where he lives. That's around the distance to my home.

"How far away do we live from each other?"

"Give or take?" he muses playfully. "Ten to fifteen."

My eyes widen.

"Does it bother you to know I'm always near?"

He wants me to be bothered. I can tell from his voice.

"No. I just… I didn't realize you lived by me."

But I like knowing he's close. That he's watching me. It's comforting.

He doesn't say anything after that, driving in silence while I stare out the window, watching the streetlights flicker until my eyelids grow heavy.

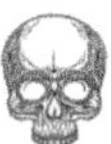

The next thing I know, we're pulling up to a two-story brick colonial with dark shutters and a wraparound white fence. I rub at my eyes and look back at him.

"Morning, princess." He chuckles all leathery soft, yet set with a darkened edge. But everything about him is dark and eerie.

"I didn't realize I fell asleep." I yawn into my opened palm, staring out the window. "Nice house."

The home is large, yet not overly so. Somehow fitting for him.

"Glad you approve. Now let's go inside."

"Oh my God. My car. I completely forgot about it."

"Don't worry. I'll bring it back to your place tomorrow before you wake up." His palm lands on my upper thigh and squeezes.

Images of him throwing me up against the wall, touching me, tasting me, come roaring back. I can make them out in my head as though I can see them. Recreating them from the feeling of him on my skin.

"You have my car key?"

"Of course." His bemused tone has me angrier by the second. "I made myself a copy."

"Are you serious?! Let me guess, you also have a key to my place?"

He doesn't say anything.

"Oh. My. God. You *are* insane!"

"You're finally catching on." He chuckles, looking my way, chest rising and falling steadily, making my pulse rise. "It's for your protection, Kayla." He grows serious. "I want to be able to get to you, no matter what. I want to keep you safe."

A lump lodges in my throat, but I fight it. These stupid emotions, this sinking feeling that I could possibly mean something to him. But nothing can happen between us, not when he's still hiding.

"Right. For my protection," I scoff. "You're no better than everyone else, trying to cage me and treat me like a child."

Grabbing the door handle, I push it open and march toward his place.

His heavy footfalls sound behind me, but instead of appearing by my side, he yanks my wrist hard and pulls my body up against his. His arm loops around the small of my back.

"Don't do that." His harsh, yet vulnerable tone makes me yearn for everything he has to say. "Don't be mad at me. I don't think about you that way at all, babe."

His hand brushes down the side of my face, and my heart… It leaps, throbbing with pummeling beats. I place my palm over his hand, and my skin heats up instantly like he's the warmth keeping the fire lit in my heart.

"The thought of something happening to you, and me being unable to get to you…" His words drown out in the pain I register in every word. "It's why I did it. But if you want them back, I'll give you the keys."

He wanted to protect me. In his own messed-up way, he cares.

"No." I shake my head. "Keep them." I throw my arms around him and sigh. "You were gonna keep them anyway, weren't you?"

He chuckles, curling his arm around me just a little tighter. "Of course I was."

I snicker, slapping him playfully on the chest before I pry myself out of his grasp and start toward his door. He sidles up beside me and grabs my small hand in his enormous one, like it's the easiest thing in the world. But the weight of it, the enormity of its meaning, is beyond measure.

He freezes, both of us breathing heavy, both of us facing forward as though realizing at the same time that we both somehow mean something to one another.

Tingles rush up my arm as his thumb slowly rubs my skin, and my gaze widens, tears stinging my eyes. Because he doesn't get it. He doesn't comprehend what this small gesture just did to my soul. My chin trembles, and tears start to fall, dripping from my lashes. I try not to cry. I swear I try to fight it, but it's too much. A small whimper escapes.

"Kayla…" He sighs, and it only makes me cry even more, trying my best to keep it silent, to keep him from seeing the weakest parts of me.

I can't say anything back, all words lost to the breaking of my heart. Because I can't fall for this stranger, this man who keeps more secrets than even I do. Yet somehow, I think I am. I think I have. I think I like my stalker. A little too much. And I think he likes me too.

Clearing my throat, I pull on his hand.

"Come on." I throw on a lighthearted tone. "I want to see my gift already."

But I fail to sound like I didn't just cry.

He stays still, unmoving, holding my palm even tighter.

"You make it so easy to wanna kiss you." He exhales roughly, causing my breath to still in my lungs.

"We're not in a closet anymore," I whisper.

"We can change that." He yanks me to him again, like I've always belonged here.

"I think what would be better is for you to show me who you are and kiss me in the light."

"You *are* the light, Kayla Jenkins. All I see is darkness without you."

My heart unfurls with so many emotions. It's moments such as these when I so badly wish to see him.

He clasps his hand over my cheek, the span of it holding the entire side of my face. We stay this way for a few moments before he pulls me forward, like it's too much to be this way with me.

With my heavy sigh, we make it past the door he opens and into his home.

"This way," he instructs, leading me past a side table with a small vase and fresh lilies.

The house is dark, except for a few flickers of light coming from the two lamps he left on.

"We're going into the basement."

"You do realize that this is how many scary movies start, right?" I've been catching up on all of them since I've been out.

"Promise I'm not here to kill you," he laughs.

"That's probably what every murderer wants you to think."

"I guess we'll find out." He inclines his head as he leads me toward the staircase. "You first." His arm outstretches toward it.

I'm not even nervous as I head down the brightly lit space. Whatever he has to show me is bound to be good. I just know it.

He follows closely, footsteps thundering behind me.

"Why is the gift down here?" I ask, glancing behind me for a moment.

"They were too big to carry."

My brows furrow as I make it past the final step. But as soon as my eyes take in the four bodies lying over a plastic tarp, my pulse increases.

The realization finally sinks in.

"Two of the men are the ones who took you that day." His face drops to my ear. "And now they're yours to do with whatever you see fit."

He throws an arm over my shoulders and tugs me to him.

"Think of them as a blank canvas, and you're the painter, the sculptor, their *fucking* god," he snaps through gritted teeth. I can practically hear them rattling.

I spin around and clasp the side of his throat; my emotions bubbling out of me. Tears fill my eyes, my heart beating so quickly I'm afraid I'll grow dizzy.

"You did all of this? For me?"

He nods. "They hurt you. That was enough."

I throw my arms around his large body, fisting his shirt, my cheek lying against his chest while I cry.

I feel him as he holds me in his embrace, so gently it doesn't quite fit, except it also does. Because this is him too: this man who hunts with me, yet holds me when I cry.

"How did you do it?" I wonder.

He'd have had to break them out of prison. That's not an easy thing to do.

He clasps my nape in his powerful grasp. "Someone owed me. His brother is in prison, same one they're in, and he's in good with the guards. He slipped them each a drug, a paralytic that stopped their hearts for a brief time. It makes a person appear dead." He snickers. "That's all I needed for them to be sent to the morgue. They may look dead, but they're conscious. They know what's happening to them, yet they can't scream or move or do anything."

I stare, bewildered.

"My friend at the morgue kept them for me until I was able to pick them up and bring them here earlier today."

"That's a lot of effort," I whisper. "I can't believe…" The words choke up in my throat. "I can't believe you did all of this for me."

"I'd kill them all for you if I could, baby bird. But you should be the one to do it. So I'm giving you the chance you never had. Their lives are in your hands. Take them."

My heart hammers, adrenaline coursing as I face the bodies while we drift toward them hand in hand. All kinds of weapons lie across the plastic.

"Pick your poison. Anything your heart desires."

I let him go and kneel, running my fingers across the knives of all different sizes, brass knuckles, a bat, large-looking scissors, and a homemade garrote constructed from wire and tied between two pieces of wood.

I've never killed this way before. Never had someone catch them for me. Can I do it when they don't fight back? Will it be easier?

I stare down at the first man. I remember when he pretended to help me and my friends before grabbing us off the road, shooting us, hurting us. My veins fill with contempt.

I pick up a knife with a long, thin blade. I want to kill them. I want to rip them open and make them hurt. Make them bleed. Make them beg.

Just knowing that they will feel what I do to them is enough. It's actually more satisfying. They don't have the power anymore. It's been taken, the same way they took it from all of us.

I see them, the things they did. The way they'd laugh as they hurt us. It doesn't matter what their faces look like. Because they're all the same. Every single man who hurt the women and children, they're all the devil's hand. And I will return them back to him.

Back to hell, where they will burn for eternity.

My lips twist as I lower the knife to his face, and I etch a line down his cheek, being careful to dig it deeper the more I go. When I'm through, his face is bloody, and my smile swells. I start on his other cheek, then his forehead, his jaw, lower until I carve his throat, his arms. I slice him until blood pools, until there's too much.

But I want more. I want every drop. Until he's empty.

"I remember you." I stare into his open eyes. "I remember what you did to us. The way you laughed. The way you smelled. I even remember that stupid brown t-shirt you wore with a red stain on the collar. Like you dropped some ketchup on it. Or maybe it was blood. Maybe you hurt someone else before you hurt us."

My heart races, my stomach dipping with every ounce of resentment.

"I hate you." I lift the knife in the air, holding it in both hands. "I hate that you're still alive. That you get to walk this earth. But that ends today." I jam the knife into his stomach and grab another. "Does it hurt?" I grin. "Does it make you want to die? Because I won't let you. Not yet. Not until I've had enough, and I haven't come close."

With a roar, I unleash, everything spilling out of me. All the hurt left inside me suffocates me until I'm lost to it, lost to the agony I've lived in all these years. I sink the knife into his thighs, his cheek, his stomach. I stab his body until there's no more space. Until blood covers my hands, my clothes. Until the last strike, until the weapon sinks into his throat. Until he's gone.

Hands hold me as I rise, breathing heavy. "Are you alright, baby bird? Do you need me to finish it?"

I turn to him and shake my head, both corners of my mouth curving. "No. I want to be the one."

He nods once, brushing his knuckles down my face. "Then go and make them hurt, and don't stop until they do. Let your rage rain."

I grab the bat this time, wander toward the second man who took me, and swing the wood in the air, grinning down at him. "I know you couldn't see what I did to your friend, but I promise it was quite the show."

I smash the bat into his nose, cracking until blood explodes from his face. My pulse pummels as I come at him, blow after blow, shattering his kneecaps, his fingers, his tibia. Every bone I can smash splinters in his body. The fury overtakes me until I'm lost to its power, made one with it, like we're connected. Unbreakable.

Screams echo. My screams. My battle cry. I've won. I made it out of there while they're here, dying.

Maybe I've become like them. An animal. Someone society would never accept. But I'm okay with that. I got something so many people like me never get. I got to torture them. I made them hurt. *Me*. Weak little Kayla.

They had no idea how strong I truly was. No one did. Not even my friends.

But here, with A, I get to prove my strength. My perseverance. He's the only one who sees the true me, the one I fight so hard to hide. But with him, I never have to do that. He's like me. He understands.

With the final blow, I smash his skull until his face collapses into itself, until there's nothing but brain and blood. It makes me want to vomit, but I hold it in, dropping the bat and collecting myself.

"Are you okay?" A asks, clasping my face in his now-bloody hands. "Let me hurt the other two for you. Please," he whispers. "It would be my honor."

I nod, knowing I can't handle four bodies on my own. Those two were enough. They were my victory.

A makes it to one of the men, picking up a pair of brass knuckles. "You will all die here." He stares at them. "You will all burn, your ashes never to be found. This is your last day in this world, and I promise it will feel like an eternity."

Then he's smashing the man's face with the knuckles until he's no longer recognizable.

He collects a knife next and slices his throat open until it bleeds like a slow-moving puddle. When he rises and gets to the other man, we're both covered in crimson, and something about it is beautiful. He's killing for me. Hurting for me. It's a bond beyond anything I've ever known.

He does the same thing to the last man, unleashing himself the way I did, his wrath spilling through every blow he enacts until he's through. Until they're all dead.

If only I'd known him when I was stuck in there. Maybe he could've saved me before I turned into this.

But it's too late now. This is Kayla, and I have to accept her. I have to become her instead of wishing I could be someone else. Someone who didn't have the life I had.

I once felt alone. That there was no one like me.

I don't feel that way anymore.

Not with A.

He drops the knuckles with a clanking and grabs my hands, our fingers twining as one.

Blood to blood.

Sin to sin.

A connection forged through anguish. Through pain.

That's us.

And we're all kinds of beautiful.

ADRIEL

She stares at me with this longing in her eyes, and I don't know what I'm supposed to do with it.

I don't know how long I can go on this way, unable to control my emotions around her. I don't even know what to call it except this need to make her smile. To let her eyes shine as brightly as they did when she killed those men. And fuck, did she make me proud.

She let them see what they did to her. She made them feel it. It's exactly what I envisioned when I planned this.

"How are you feeling?" I ask her, my hands still clasped with hers.

And I don't want to let them go. Not now. Not ever.

"Free." She smiles tightly. "I never thought I'd get this chance. To hurt one of them. But two?" She shakes her head in disbelief. "You're something else, stalker."

I chuckle. "You've got a way with words."

"But seriously, thank you." Her mouth forms a tight line. "Words don't feel like enough. I don't know how to thank you."

"Seeing you smile is the only thank-you I need."

Her eyes grow wet with unshed tears. "What now? What will you do with the bodies?"

"Ah, you haven't yet seen the special place these assholes all go into. Let me demonstrate."

I lead her to the far wall, pressing the button to reveal the furnace. When I open the door to it, her eyes snap wildly between me and the contraption.

Within my mask, my grin grows. "It's a furnace."

I flip it on, and the flames erupt like a sleeping beast.

"This is amazing," she whispers. "I couldn't even tell that was there."

"That's the look I was going for." With my laughter, I savor her adorably bewildered expression.

I start for one of the bodies, slipping my hand under his armpits and dragging him across the floor. Hoisting him up by his waist, I push his head into the opening before lifting the rest of him. And when he's all the way in, I shut the door.

"Wow. That's all it takes, huh?"

"That's it."

She swipes a drop of blood dripping from her cheek.

"How about you get cleaned up? Then I'll worry about the other bodies."

"I don't know how I'm going to go home with these clothes." She grimaces, glancing down at herself. "Chris is gonna know what I was up to and immediately tell Michael."

"Don't worry about either of them."

She furrows a brow. "What have you done?"

"Nothing for you to be concerned about. Now, how about this? I wash your clothes and you take a bath in the meantime."

"And what do I wear after I'm done?"

"One of my shirts."

The thought of that bare body in something I own, it smelling like her long after she's gone… Fuck.

"Uh…" She swallows nervously. "If you're sure that's okay."

"I'm pretty sure I can handle the thought of your beautiful body beneath my clothes." My cock throbs.

"You should probably stop giving me so many compliments. It's bad for your rep."

I let out a laugh. This woman and her sense of humor.

"And what rep is that?"

"The scary, murderous kind."

"I'm only scary for those I don't like."

Her lips perk up and her eyes enlarge.

My pulse only beats faster at the sight of her shocked expression. The thought of liking her shocks me too.

"Now, come on. I'll run you a bath while I wash your clothes and get rid of the bodies."

I head for the stairs.

"Run me a bath?"

I glance behind my shoulder as she gasps, popping her mouth wide in mock horror.

"You're really not helping your persona right now."

She's covered in blood, but all I'm picturing is ripping off her clothes and thrusting inside her up against the wall, my fingers tracing crimson around her pink nipples. My heart batters in my rib cage as I stare at her. Those eyes gleaming. And before I can change my mind, I'm on her, hand wrapped around her throat, body backing hers up against the wall.

I lean in real close to her mouth and squeeze her soft, delicate neck. "How's my persona now, baby bird?"

"A much-needed improvement." She groans.

My dick grows hard at the sound, at the way she looks, all heavy-lidded, cheeks growing rosy.

She's dangerous.

One wrong move, and I'll step onto a grenade and she'll blow me to bits. I'd probably like it too, which makes this even worse. This addiction. This woman. This light so bright, I can't see beyond it.

Beneath my thumb, her pulse pummels.

"You're making me think things I have no business doing to you, Kayla, yet I want to. You make me want to." I drop my face closer, picturing the sounds she'd make if I fucked her. "Why are you doing this to me?"

"Sometimes you should give in to those urges. Might make you feel better." She bites the edge of her bottom lip.

And the thought of removing my mask, letting her see me, becomes too strong. It would make things easier. She would know who I am, and we could…

We could what? What the hell am I even thinking?

As I start to back away and tell myself how ridiculous it was to even consider being with her, my car alarm goes off outside.

My body instantly goes rigid.

Someone is here.

That was a calling card.

"Stay here," I snap. "Do you understand? Don't go upstairs."

"What? Why?" Her face upturns with confusion. "Is something wrong? Alarms go off all the time. It was probably a bird or something."

She has no idea the kinds of people I've encountered. That was not a bird. Or an accident. I intend to check my computers later to confirm that, but for now, I intend to stop that annoying alarm.

Luckily, I don't live near others, so this won't draw any unnecessary attention. The only nearby home is about a mile away.

"I don't know what it is," I tell her. "So, until then, you'll stay here."

I don't wait for her to fight me on it like I know she wants to. I rush up the stairs and out of the house, reaching into my pocket to grab my keys to finally shut off that godawful sound.

But just as I start to turn toward the house, I notice something on the windshield. A small piece of paper.

I fucking knew it.

Quickly snatching it, I unfold it, reading the words over and over, my anger rising each time I do.

I hear you've been looking for me. But I've always been right here. Right under your nose. We're not that different, you and me. But you seem to think so.

I've met your pet. I don't know what you see in her. I was thinking of introducing myself properly. Getting to know her more. Becoming good friends. You know you can't keep an eye on her 24/7. You're bound to slip, and I'll be there, taking her away from you.

-MM

While I've been watching her, he's been watching me. I've been careless.

With a roar, I crumple the paper in my fist and stare out onto the open road, knowing the Midnight Murderer has found me.

Found my weakness.

And now he's coming for her.

KAYLA

As soon as he walks back in, I know something's wrong. His body is rigid and tense, his shoulders shuddering with hurried breaths. I stride up to him and place a hand on top of his shoulder, but he only turns around, clutching something in his fist.

I stare at his hand, an uneasy feeling in the pit of my stomach. "Tell me what's wrong."

"Nothing," he snaps, and the tone of his voice sends a shudder through me.

As though sensing the effect it had on me, he pivots and cups my cheek. "Let me get you a towel so you can take that bath. Take off your clothes in the bathroom and hand them to me."

I nod, knowing whatever he's holding has him really upset.

But I don't pry. He isn't the kind of man to open up that easy. But I will find out what he's keeping from me.

One way or another.

ADRIEL

She's in the bath I made her, rose petals and some jasmine thrown in the water. I picked all that up last week, just in case there was a reason for her to use it.

And here she is, in my home, naked in my bathroom. And all I want is to be with her.

But I'm not. I'm here, looking through the surveillance cams, rewinding all the ones around the vicinity of my home. Someone in a dark hoodie left that note. Average height. Average build. Literally nothing to fucking go on! I slam a fist on the top of my desk and grind my molars until my jaw aches.

How the hell did he find me? How long has he been watching me? Watching *her*?

Fuck! He could take her at any moment. How the hell do I keep her safe?

I press another key on the laptop and watch the video over and over until I memorize his movements. Everything he does.

He didn't come with a car. I tracked him for miles until I lost him. Smart not to have used one. Makes it harder to locate him. If I wasn't enraged, I'd be impressed.

The rushing of water from the bathroom informs me Kayla's done. She's going to ask me questions, and I'll need to keep avoiding them. Because I can't tell her. She'll get scared. And I don't want her to be. I want her to feel safe, especially knowing I'm always watching.

Reaching inside a drawer on my desk, I retrieve a small square box. I intended to give her this sometime in the future. As a token of…I don't fucking know. But I had it made for her, and I need her to have it.

Quickly, I turn off all the computer screens and lock the door with a key. Wouldn't want her wandering in here, seeing the videos I have of her. She doesn't need to know I planted cameras in her trees, her home. That I'm always watching. Night and day. I know everything she does. Every moan she makes. When I'm not watching her sleep, sitting in her room, her quiet breaths lulling me into a calming state, I watch her from my phone.

Heading up a flight of stairs, I meet her in the den as soon as she comes out of the bathroom. My shirt is draping her body, the hem flirting with her upper thighs. Smiling softly, she holds a hairbrush in her hand, and I have the urge to run it through her hair, to have her in my lap as I brush it.

"Feel better?" I ask, grinning behind my mask too. She does that to me.

But that's the fucking problem, isn't it? She weakens me. Makes me careless. It's the reason he found me. Found *her*.

"I do. Are you done with the bodies?"

"Not yet. Come sit with me." Lowering onto the sofa, I pat the space beside me, leaving the box behind my back.

She stares curiously, but doesn't hesitate, coming to settle so close her knee touches mine. And I feel it: this current of immense power she wields through me. Like she holds the weight of my world in the palm of her hand and there's nothing I can do to change it.

"Turn around." I take the brush from her hand just as she pivots, giving me her back.

Dropping my face to the crook of her neck, I can smell the scent of jasmine on her skin. She awakens me just from being this close. She makes me want things that I can't even put into words. Makes me feel things I can never feel with another. With her, I want to discover parts of myself I never realized existed. Is that even possible?

Gently I brush her hair, taking my time, savoring her long, shallow breaths as though she's savoring this moment too.

I want to take care of her, in all ways. I just don't know how to do it.

She reaches behind her, a hair tie in her grasp.

"Can you braid it?" Her voice is a soft cadence, stilling my heart until it beats to a song only she awakens.

"I don't know how," I whisper.

"I can teach you."

"Okay." I nod, the back of my hand brushing down her cheek from behind, causing the hairs on her arms to stand at attention.

To know I did that is a gift.

I know she feels this too. This unexplainable connection. This palpable magnetism between us.

She takes me through how to properly braid, laughing as I get it wrong the first few times.

"It's perfect," she breathes, running her fingertips over her hair, now settled over her shoulder.

"It's not anywhere close to perfect."

"It is." She faces me, tucking my large hand in her small one. "You're too hard on yourself."

I just want to be perfect for you.

Extending my hand behind me, I retrieve the box there, and she catches sight of it. "This is for you."

Her eyes dance between the box and me. "What is it?"

"Open it."

My heart beats so loudly, it'll rip right out of my chest. What if she hates it? What if she doesn't wear it?

Her eyes light up as she takes it in her palm, gently popping the top of the black box. Her gaze widens as she registers what's inside: a silver chain with a pendant of a wolf's head attached to it.

"This is…" She chokes up. "It's beautiful." Her eyes swim with tears.

"Let me put it on you." My chest warms, seeing her this happy from something so small. Something *I* gave her.

I slip it around her neck, witnessing the vein there jerk when my fingertips brush against her skin. Gently, I clasp the back of the chain, and when she turns to me and I see it on her, I grin like a motherfucker. Because it looks perfect. As though made just for her.

Her fingers trace the wolf with its one red sparkling eye.

"Happy birthday," I say.

If only I could kiss her. Feel her arms around me as I do. This woman. This poison she's soaked me in… I can't fight it much longer.

"Never gonna take it off." She presses it to her chest.

"I'm glad you like it. How about I take you to the bedroom now so you can rest while I clean up? Then I'll take you home."

"Sure, sounds good." She yawns with a grin. "You're such a considerate killer."

And her smile? It breaks me, because a huge part of me feels undeserving of something *so* unexplainably beautiful.

I stare at her, unable to peel my gaze away. This unfathomable sensation pours into my veins until I'm lost to it, as though waiting to be found. I've been waiting for so long, not realizing it. Yet I know she can't be the one. No one is. A man like me isn't meant for anyone.

An unfamiliar twinge builds in the center of my chest, and I fight it. Fight it like I fight what she does to me.

"Come on, let me take you to bed." I gesture toward the stairs, climbing up behind her, trying hard not to stare at her ass as I do.

Of course, I fail. It's a beautiful ass. Don't need to see it to know that. I felt it in my hands, the soft skin there aching against my palm. She'd look good over my knee with that shirt over her back as I do that again, making her pretty skin red, make her groan and throb for me.

My hand reaches out and wraps around her hip just as she makes it to the top. Out of nowhere, her body jolts as though my touch scared her. Her mouth twitches into a barely there smile as she swings around.

"S-sorry. I—" She swallows harshly.

"Don't need to explain. I understand. I'm sorry."

"No. Don't. It's me." Her long lashes flutter like there's something wrong with her. "It's just I didn't expect it, and it was behind me. It…uh…it took me back there for a split second."

Shit. I feel like an asshole for not realizing that.

"You don't need to explain. I'm not angry. I won't touch you like that again."

She nods, her lips curling on one side, forcing herself to appear okay. "But you're still gonna touch me, right?"

"Just try to stop me."

She releases a weighty sigh as I march up beside her, pointing toward the room.

"This way." I pop open the door and let her in first. "You can relax here as long as you want to. I won't be too long, though."

"Okay, thanks." She plays with her fingers, biting the corner of her bottom lip, making me want to be the one to suck it into my mouth.

When have I ever felt such strong sensations for a woman?

Never. It has never happened. And I'm not sure why it's happening now. With her.

"If you need anything to eat or drink…" I tell her. "The fridge is downstairs, right past the den."

I start to go.

"Wait…"

Instantly, I freeze, as though she's got the key to my body, to everything I am.

"Yes?" I look over at her from behind my shoulder.

Her fingers reach for me, and I badly want to touch them, but I don't. Not with the blood soaking through my clothes.

"Thank you." It appears as though she wants to say more, but changes her mind at the last moment.

"No need. I'll be back."

I have to get away for a bit before I do something I have no business doing to her.

She nods, pulling the comforter back and sitting on the edge. And the way my mind is picturing me lying behind her, that body curled around me, it's downright wrong. I have nothing to give her. Nothing but blood and sin. Nothing but the broken child trapped inside me.

Heading back into the basement, I throw her clothes in the wash while I finish with the bodies and burn my own clothes. I plan on burning hers too. After she goes home, I'll get them and get rid of them. Any evidence is evidence, washed clothes or not.

Once I'm done, the entire basement is clean and I've got new clothing on.

I make it back to my bedroom, peeking inside to find her eyes closed, her curves curled in a fetal position.

"Kayla?" I whisper.

No response. Her slow breaths make her body sway up and down, and that calming effect she has on me returns.

I remove my mask, getting some much-needed air as I sidle closer, my knuckles reaching for her beautiful face, needing to touch her skin. To be one with it. With her.

Featherlike, I glide my knuckles down her cheek, because this is the only way I can touch her. "I'm gonna take care of you, baby bird. I'm gonna take care of you like no one ever took care of me."

The moment those words leave me, I know they're true. I'll do anything for her. Before I convince myself not to, I slip in beside her from the other side and throw my arm gently around her.

Something catches in my throat, and instead of fighting

it, I embrace it. Embrace all these intense sensations burying themselves inside me like they're burying their roots into my soul.

Kayla.

It's as though my heart calls for her.

The beauty to my beast. The rose to my thorn.

An angel to my devil.

Because no matter what she thinks of herself, she's not like me. Not really. She's good. There's never been anything good about me. My mother made sure I knew that.

Kayla makes an adorable little whimper and turns to me, burying her face in my chest like I somehow make her feel more at ease.

How's that even possible?

I pray like hell she doesn't wake up and see me. But part of me wants her to. I want her to see who I am. To want me as I am. To need me.

I want to own this woman, body and soul. I want her surrender. Her obedience. The marrow from her bones. I want everything she is.

I kiss the top of her head, inhaling that scent of jasmine in her hair. When she starts to move, I place the mask back on, knowing now isn't the right time for this. Not when he's after her. I can't have distractions.

Once she knows who I am, everything is going to change, including whatever is happening between us.

And I'm not ready for that. Not yet.

Maybe not ever.

Twenty-One

KAYLA

Light drips through the slits of my eyes, my arms stretching above my head. And for a moment, I'm not sure where I am and why it's so bright in here. As I open my lids and blink around the room, I realize I'm not home.

It's then I remember I'm in A's home. In his bed.

I shoot up to a seated position, realizing he isn't here, but my clothes are lying neatly on the foot of the bed.

I fell asleep here! Shit. How did I manage to do that? One second, I was lying in bed; the next, I'm waking up in the morning. The clock on the wall reads eight.

Chris must be going insane, searching for me. Probably called Michael and they have a search party looking for me.

But then the very thought infuriates me. I'm a grown adult. I can sleep over at anyone's house. I don't need to sneak around. I'm not a teenager.

With a harsh exhale, I flip my legs out of the bed and find my cell on the nightstand, waiting there with a bottle of water and a note.

I pick it up, and warmth instantly fills my limbs.

I like knowing you think about me even as you sleep. You said my name so many times. I just lay awake beside you, listening to you. You entice, babe, even when you're unconscious.

Come downstairs. I made you breakfast. Your favorite.

—A

Babe.

That word…it does so many things to me.

A smile pulls at my mouth, but then the sudden realization hits.

Wait a minute. My eyes pop wide.

He slept next to me? I said his name in my sleep? And…he knows my favorite breakfast? How…

He's been watching you. That's how, you idiot. What part of stalker is hard for you to comprehend?

I get to my feet, quickly slipping out of his shirt before putting on my clothes, then head down the stairs. The aroma of freshly brewed coffee hits my nostrils. And suddenly, I'm a little less peeved with my stalker. I mean, he made coffee. And breakfast. After breaking out those assholes from prison and letting me kill them. I say he gets a major pass.

His back is to me as soon as I step into the kitchen, his muscles rippling and flexing beneath his black hoodie as he stands in front of the stove, flipping something on it.

Hope springs to life that maybe he forgot his mask and I'll finally learn who he is. But as soon as he turns around, holding a plate with a burrito on it…

Fuck me. That thing isn't even scary anymore. It's funny now. The entire fact of this masked man making me breakfast would make the outside world think I've gone mad.

But, I mean, let's be real. I kinda have.

I give the plate a glance. He does know my favorite breakfast, doesn't he? I don't even need to bite into it to know he made me an egg-and-cheese burrito with avocado. It's what I eat every single day.

Pulling a stool before the counter, I settle onto it and place my cell down.

"Morning, baby bird. Slept well?"

The seductive twinge in his tone does something to me, heat coiling between my thighs as I fight the urge to curl my arms around his biceps and pull him in for a kiss.

The fact that I want to—that I desire something normal after everything I was put through—is tremendously scary, yet beautiful. He's made me want things I once never dreamed of wanting. Now I'm here, in his home, in his arms at night and being fed by him in the morning. There's something warm and safe about him. You know, when you're not thinking about the secrets and the mask… oh, and the fact that he's a killer. We're a match made in hell.

"As per your note…" I say back. "I slept quite well. If I'd known you were asleep next to me, I'd have awakened to pull that mask off your face and kiss you."

His burly, defined chest jolts.

"Then what?" he asks, practically groaning.

"Then I'd go back to bed." I grin, yanking the corner of my bottom lip.

He inhales a sharp breath, his feet slowly advancing toward me like a predator about to make me his willing meal. Placing the steaming plate beside me, he flips my stool around to face him.

With a towering frame, he pushes himself between my thighs, opening me up, bare and pantiless.

He cups my jaw in his palm, thumb stroking across my lips, hips jutting out into my core, eliciting a wanton sound from my lips.

I swallow down the ball of nerves, anticipating his next move. He drops closer, leaning his torso into mine. His fist snaps around my hair, yanking my head back, his chest pressing into mine.

"The fact that you think we'd stop at kissing is the cutest thing I've ever heard."

I gasp a quiet breath, mouth parted slightly, just enough for him to push his thumb inside, pressing it down onto my tongue.

"Fucking beautiful," he rasps, and my body peaks with awareness, with harrowing need.

I wonder what he'll do next. Say next.

I jump back as my cell rings, over and over. He doesn't move, except his free hand as he picks it up and examines who the caller is.

"It's Michael," he announces before he decides to answer for me, placing him on speaker.

"Kayla."

"What the hell?" I whisper to A, my expression horrified.

I had no intentions of answering this call.

"Hey, Michael. What's up?"

"I wanted you to know that you have a new bodyguard assigned. His name is—"

"I'm sorry, what? Where's Chris?" My eyes widen at A.

He did something to him. He had to have. It's why he said not to worry about him.

Oh my God. Did he burn him in the furnace?

"Chris had a family emergency. He had to go out of the country to take care of his mom, who's dying."

"Oh, no. That's so sa—"

A cold, icy chill drowns out the rest of my words.

Because Chris doesn't have a mom. I remember exactly what he said. His parents died years ago.

Did he lie to me? Or did he lie to Michael?

"What is it, Kayla?" Michael's concern is evidence. "What do you know?"

"Are you sure he said his mom was ill?"

"Yeah, why?"

I can hear his beastly breaths across the speaker.

"Because…"

Beside me, A squeezes the phone so tight, his knuckles turn white.

"Because he told me his parents are dead."

The phone goes silent. Seconds trickle by.

"Michael?"

"Are you sure that's what he said? You have to be sure, Kayla."

"I—I'm sure."

"Okay. Look, if he contacts you or anything, call me." I hear him shuffling around like he's in a hurry.

"Michael, you're scaring me."

"You don't have to worry. Terrence is at your house already. If you look out the window, you'll see his black SUV."

Chris didn't even tell him that I didn't come home. I can't shake this eerie feeling.

"I have to go," he says. "If anything comes up, call me."

"Sure, yeah."

Click. A hangs up too and places the phone down.

"Did you kill him?" I ask him point-blank. "I need you to be honest with me."

"No." He shakes his head. "But he's as good as dead. Now eat your food so I can take you home, and I swear to God, if you let the new one anywhere near you, I will most definitely rip out his heart and make you watch as I burn it. Do we understand each other?"

He roughly grabs my jaw and grunts when I squeeze my legs around his outer thighs.

"Yes," I whisper. "I understand."

"That's my good girl."

"I'm not your girl." The need to fight him, to let me hear him say I am, overwhelms me.

He chuckles all slow and seductive. "That's what I keep telling myself. But unfortunately for you, you are. And there's nothing either of us can do about it." He places his palm on the center of my chest. "Feel that? Feel the way your heart races at the mere feeling of me?"

Yes. This is exactly what I wanted. To hear him say how wrong I am.

"I own you, Kayla. You're mine. Your heart. Your mind. Your fucking *soul*. I own it. And soon…" He slips a hand between us and circles his thumb around my achy clit. "I'm gonna own this pussy too."

"Oh, God," I hiss.

"Make you beg and cry and scream my name. My real name," he promises. "And that's the moment…"

He pushes a finger inside me, and I whimper with a gasp.

"That's the moment you're gonna own *me*."

Then he's off, returning to the stove, leaving me there breathless and gasping for air.

Because he owns that too.

He owns everything, and I can't even deny it.

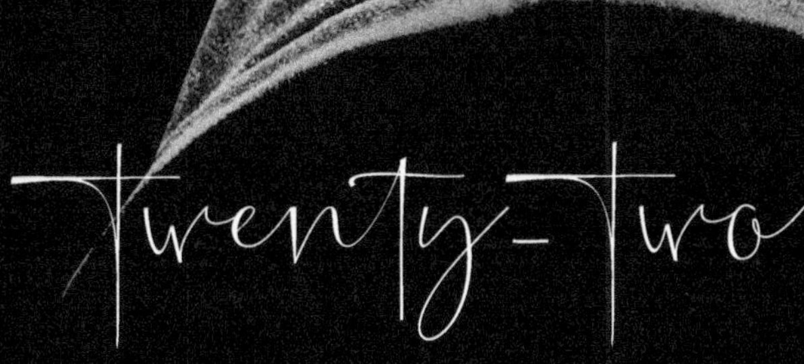

Twenty-Two

ADRIEL

I drop her off back at her house, careful to avoid the unassuming Toyota parked across the street. I already got the license plate and a picture of her new bodyguard. I'll be doing a little digging later today. Want to know who he is. Can't be too careful when she's involved.

"You can leave me at the back," she says. "I can go around the yard."

I hate that she has to sneak around with me, but I can't exactly expose myself either.

"I'll be around. Call me if you need anything. My number is in your cell."

She grins. "I know."

Winking back, she hops out and gives me one final look before she disappears into the house.

Rolling back onto the road, I start back toward my home, but at the last second, I change my mind. I didn't intend to do this now, not when there's a killer and damn traffickers after her. Too many fucking variables I can't control.

But I can control this. I can take what I've been wanting to for so long, since the first time I found out she didn't love me.

That I was dispensable.

Now, it's her chance to repent and beg for my forgiveness. And when I'm through with her, I'll deliver her body to her sons in pieces. The only sons she ever gave a fuck about.

Keys jingle in the door, footsteps slowly creeping closer while I wait in her kitchen. My mother has no idea what I look like. She never even realized I was hers when I talked to her in the supermarket. I was just a random guy. If I had a heart, it'd break.

But I don't have one. She made sure of that.

She hums a tune, switching on the light and illuminating the space already bathed by the rays of the sun.

I keep myself well-hidden behind a partial wall while still being able to see her.

Her cell rings, and she instantly answers.

Fuck. I need her off it.

"Hey, Raph. How are you, sweetheart? How's Nicolette?"

There's a few seconds of quiet, my pulse ripping through my throat at the sound of my twin's name.

I hate him with equal fervor. Hate them all with a passion so deep, I ache to spill their blood. But she's the one I want. The one whose death I've been imagining my entire life.

As I got older, I'd lie there and close my eyes as the nuns whipped me, and I'd see her throat ripped open as though I had done it with my own teeth. An animal of their creation. A beast who haunted their dreams, turning them into nightmares.

And I'm her grim reaper. Wicked as they come.

"Of course I'd love to come to the party," she gushes, and my teeth snap. "Tomorrow night is great. If the girls need help, I'd be happy to."

My hands ball. *A party tomorrow? Too bad she won't be making it.*

"Sure, honey. You go. I'll see you all tomorrow. I love you, son."

I love you, son.

I wonder for a moment how it'd feel to have her say that to me.

Pinching my eyes shut, I take in deep breaths, steadying the ravaging of my exhales. She will get what's coming soon enough, and she will see my face as I rob every quaking breath from her lungs.

She drops her keys and cell on the counter, not seeing me as she opens the fridge. Not knowing there's a monster lurking behind her, quietly prodding closer until my arm curls tightly around her throat.

"Hello, Mother," I chuckle humorlessly. "You look so happy. I can't wait to take it all away from you."

She gasps, her body jolting, trying to turn to look at me. "Oh my God!"

My laughter echoes.

"Please, please, don't hurt me! Just talk to me!" she pants.

My forearm snaps tighter, suffocating her, enjoying the way she claws at my bicep. She knows exactly what my name is. She named me.

I drag her backward toward a chair around her table and shove her into it. She notices the mask, the knife in my hand, the blade sharpened to perfection. I didn't intend to use this one on her. I had a special one custom made just for her throat. But here we are. Improvisation has always been a strength of mine.

Her eyes fill with terror, and her hands shake.

Good. She deserves this. Deserves worse.

Reaching inside my pants pocket with my other hand, I remove a pair of zip ties, twirling them around my finger.

Her tears come heavy now, her eyes rimmed with regret, with pain I can't seem to care much about. She didn't care about me. Why should I extend this woman, this stranger, that courtesy?

"You won't need those." She inclines her chin toward the ties. "I won't be going anywhere."

My lips wind up, and I stuff the ties back inside. "You're right, Mother. You won't be."

I take a single step toward her, tipping up her face with the edge of the blade, nicking the underside of her jaw. Drops of blood pool around the metal, and her eyes? They hold mine, brows furrowed as her chin quivers.

"I'm sorry," she cries, sniffling back. "I—"

"Shut up!" I roar. "I don't want to hear your bullshit fucking apologies! That isn't what this is about. What's done is done. And today, you will finally pay for what you did to me."

She sobs, shutting her eyes, trembling from how hard she cries.

"Open your eyes!" I holler. "Open them or you die right here, right now!"

She slowly reverts her attention back to me and blinks through the moisture building.

"Did you even care?" I wrench back. "Did you even wonder about me?"

She nods. "All…all the time. I—oh, God, I'm sorry. I'm so, *so* sorry." Her words strangle out of her. "I hoped and prayed you had a good life, but I—I was wrong, w-wasn't I?"

She shakes her head, wails like this is somehow all about her.

"You were." I smirk wickedly. "Guess I wasn't important enough for you to check on me."

"I'm so sorry!" she continues to repeat that same shit over and over, and it only enrages me.

"You keep saying that! But sorry isn't going to change anything! You abandoned me, left me at the hands of those monsters, where I spent years wishing that my mother would come and save me. But you know what happened?" A stoic laugh emanates from my lungs. "She never did."

"A…" Fat tears roll down her face.

"I want you to know! To see what they did to me! Those nuns. Those vultures." I line the knife against her throat. "You're no better, even when you pretend to be."

She snivels, unable to catch her breath, while I flip the knife to a close and stuff it back in my pocket. With both hands, I remove my mask, not afraid of her knowing who I am. Let her see me. She won't be coming out of this house alive.

When she sees my face, her vision grows.

"Oh my God…" she gasps. "The store! I—I remember you."

I grin, relishing the shock on her features.

"I knew something about you felt familiar," she coughs out with a whisper. "But I…I just thought it was because of your eyes. You still have those big, green eyes."

Her bottom lip quivers as her sadness reeks like her death will.

"My father's, you mean." I grin. "I know about Patrick. Know about your sons. Your granddaughter. You have quite a beautiful family. You must be proud."

"Please, don't hurt her! I beg you. Do whatever you want to me. But not Sophia. She's innocent!"

Her hands tremor on her lap, fear for the one she loves

encroached around her like a vise.

I grab the hem of my shirt and lift it off my body. "I was innocent too."

Turning, I give her the brutality that was carved onto my skin, my flesh reborn into something even a mother wouldn't love.

Her breaths come in jerky, panicked gasps. "Oh—oh my God. Wh-what have I done? My-my baby."

Those treacherous sobs of hers return, making me want to choke them out of her. I've waited for this moment all my life, needing her pain, wanting to own it, to make her feel it as she takes her final breath.

"Don't pretend you had no idea where I was, or that you couldn't find out! You didn't fucking care! You left me crying for you, needing you. Wanting you! And now? Look at me!"

She shakes her head and shuts her eyes, endless tears stamping through her vision.

"No! You fucking look at me, *Mother*!" I grab her throat, and she instantly returns her attention to me. "This is what you did to me!"

But she continues to sob, and I want to put a knife through her fucking throat so she stops.

"They used to tell me stories about how you didn't care," I tell her. "How you left me when I was a newborn. They'd whip me, tell me what a sinner I was. How no one would ever love me when my own mother didn't."

"That's—that's not true," she weeps. "I loved you. I still do!"

Tears fall endlessly down her face. But I don't for a second buy into her bullshit. She'd say anything to get out of here alive, to save Sophia, who she has no idea I'd never harm.

"You never loved me." I squeeze her neck even tighter. "You never will. Your actions have proven that time and time again. You had so many fucking opportunities to get me out of that place, to tell me you were sorry for the mistake you'd made. But that never happened. So stop lying!"

All she does is cry, sniveling through her breaths like a dying animal.

"I've waited so long for this moment. To make you pay for everything."

"I deserve it, son." She blinks back her tears and nods.

"Don't you dare call me that!"

"I don't deserve to. You're right. Do whatever you need to do to make this better for you. I will forgive you."

"Who the hell says I need your forgiveness?! I need nothing from you. Not anymore!"

"Regardless, you have it." Her voice cracks.

"Did he know?" I grind my molars. "Did Patrick know you gave me up?"

"No." She shakes her head. "He—he only found out after you left that note at Gio's wedding," she pants.

I knew it…

"Before you kill me…" She sniffles. "Can I please just know your name? Please. I never knew it."

I cough up a laugh. "What do you mean, you never knew it? You named me, didn't you? The nuns told me you did…"

She shakes her head. "They lied."

My pulse throbs in my ear, swallowing away the silence.

Fuck. What else did they lie about?

Doesn't matter. She's gonna be dead soon enough. She's just like them.

"Adriel," I tell her.

"Adriel… Thank you." Her chin shakes, and she forces a smile, tight with melancholy.

Her eyes fall to a close, and she takes a long, deep breath, like she's preparing for her final moment.

I slide the knife out of my pocket and flip the blade open. Lining it against her throat, I watch her swallow harshly, her body shaking as she silently cries.

"I never wanted this for you," she swears. "If I could go back and do things differently, I would. I would've given up my life for yours. But I failed you, Adriel, and I see that now." She sniffles. "For that, I deserve to die."

She shoves her throat toward the blade.

"So do it," she whimpers. "Kill me. I'll still love you in the end. I need you to know I never stopped, no matter what you think."

All I want to do is slice her throat right now. How fucking dare she say that to me?

"Please, just go into my bag and get my wallet. I beg you!"

My heartbeats echo in my rib cage, the sound drowning out the plan I've always had for her.

Her eyes seek for refuge, for forgiveness. Tears continue to leak down her cheeks, but she doesn't cower. She stares right into me as the knife edges deeper against her throat.

She's gonna die.

I have to kill her.

I have to get my revenge.

It's what I've been waiting for.

The one kill I've desired above all others. And right here, right now, it can be mine.

"Please, Adriel, just look in my wallet."

With a growl, I remove the knife from her throat, grab her bag off the counter, and retrieve the wallet she's dying for me to see.

"Open and unzip that small left side."

I do it quickly, reaching inside and finding a small colored photo.

My gut tightens with knots. In it is her, but younger, a baby in her hands.

"That was you." She sobs. "That was you and me, Adriel. My boy."

"Liar!"

"A nurse, she took a photo of you and me." She can barely speak now, consumed by pain I can't seem to understand.

She left me. She abandoned me. Why is she crying like it suddenly matters now?

With a roar, I lift the knife up in the air, clasping the photo with my fingers.

"I'm sorry," she weeps just as I slam the knife down.

"Fuck!"

She sobs heavier now, the blade carved into the wood of the chair, right beside her thigh.

I can't fucking do it. After all this time, wishing for this very moment, I can't do it. I can't kill my mother.

I stare at her, unable to understand.

She means nothing to me, and yet…

"Fuck!" I pull the knife out and return it back to my pocket, turning around and rushing out of here.

She's bound to tell Michael who I am. They'll come for me.

Let them. I'll give them a war like they haven't seen before.

I'll kill her sons. Leave her with nothing.

"Adriel! Please wait!" she screams for me. "Please talk to me. Don't go!"

But I'm already slipping out the door, where I'm safe from her lies.

I couldn't kill her this time. But I was close. I'll get another chance, and next time, I won't fail.

Because I can't.
She must die.
And I must be the one to do it.

Twenty-Three

KAYLA

"Surprise!" The room erupts as I step into it. People, so many I don't even know, all smiling at me.

"Happy birthday," Elsie whispers from beside me, squeezing my forearm with a huge grin.

I force one too, not having the heart to tell her how much I didn't want this. I told them so many times, but my friends always have the best intentions. Unfortunately, they make a habit of not really hearing me.

"I know you said you didn't want a party," she goes on. "But your mom really wanted you to have one, and Jade and I figured a surprise would be fun!"

I laugh dryly. "Yeah, uh, this is great. Ish."

She throws an arm around me, walking forward and dragging me with her through her den that is now fully decorated for a party.

Tables, a DJ booth at the end. Food, more than anyone needs in a lifetime, set at different stations. This is definitely more than I ever needed. I would've been fine with a quiet dinner with my friends and parents.

Jade rushes up to me, her son, Robby, running off with Sophia, who's only a few years younger.

"I'm sorry if we went a bit overboard." She grimaces. "But we figured after everything we've been through, we deserve to all celebrate something as important as your birthday." She rounds her arms around me and gives me a little squeeze.

"Yeah, we do deserve it," I echo her words, almost to myself.

"I heard about Chris." Elsie changes the subject. "Kinda weird how he called Michael in the middle of the night and told him he had to leave ASAP. I mean, of course things happen, but I don't know…it gave me a weird vibe."

Me too.

"What did Michael say?"

I wonder if he told her what I told him about why Chris left.

"Not much." She shrugs a single shoulder. "Only that he had a family emergency."

I wonder if I should tell her more, but I don't think that's a good idea. Better not to involve them with anything that could be dangerous.

"Do you like the new guy?" Jade asks, sipping on a class of champagne.

"Not sure. I haven't really talked to him. He kind of lurks around." I laugh.

"There's my girl!" Enzo swings his arm around Jade and kisses her temple, giving her a lustful gaze. "Come dance with me, baby."

His arm curls around the small of her back and he kisses her—and not a quick peck, either. One of those open-mouthed, passionate kind that sears into your soul. And it instantly has me missing A. Wanting his mouth on me once more. Like in the closet. Where I can feel him everywhere.

"Okay, you two, get a damn room," Elsie teases while grinning, clearly happy for Jade.

She deserves to be happy. And Enzo, he makes her feel that every day.

"Excuse me," I say, clearing my throat, needing some air.

Because inside, I'm envious. Tears prickle my eyes as I head for the outdoors, running past Fernanda, who fixes the fancy red scarf around her throat. Not sure why someone needs a scarf, but she makes it work.

From the corner of my eye, I see my parents heading toward me. I give them a little wave as they approach.

"What a party!" Dad says. "Your friends sure know how to throw one."

"Yeah, it's nice." I force a smile.

I force a lot of them these days. But with him—with A—that's when every single one of them is real. I wish he were here, holding my hand, dancing with me. Like we're a real couple.

Mom's eyes water over, moisture building within them. "I'm so happy you and your friends are together." Her chin trembles, but she saves herself from falling apart.

"Me too." My heart lurches as I glance at both Elsie and Jade.

We escaped. We got the chance that so many girls never did. For that, I'll always be grateful. No matter what we went through, we're still breathing.

"Could you guys excuse me for a sec?" I say. "Wanna get some air."

"Oh, sure, honey," Mom waves off. "You go. Your dad and I are gonna get something to eat."

"Oh yeah, we will." Dad pats his rounded belly. "I hear there is lobster tail," he whispers, making me laugh.

"Don't forget the crab legs." I grin.

"Alright, I'm gonna go stuff myself before someone else eats it all." He chuckles.

Mom shakes her head, watching him go. She turns to me then, her expression growing serious. "Are you okay, sweetheart?"

Pretend.

My lips spread into the biggest smile I can muster. "Absolutely. Having everyone here is the best gift I could ask for."

She nods and swipes a finger under her lower lashes. "It sure is a gift." She clears her throat. "Anyway, you go and do whatever it is you need to do. Dad and I will be around. I love you, babe." She squeezes my hand before she turns to join my father.

I look at them—together, happy, still so much in love. And I wonder if that will ever be me.

Before an ache builds behind my throat, I force myself in the opposite direction, hoping to actually make it outside this time.

"Hi!" Sophia bounces over to me.

Her light pink, puffy tulle dress and ballerina bun make her look like a little dancer. Her cheeks are stained with a hint of rosy blush.

"Happy birthday, Kayla." She grins, her gaze shining brightly up at me. "You look really pretty!" She notes my black knee-length dress and the pair of nude sandals with a bit of heel.

"Not as pretty as you, though!"

She fans her lashes and purses her lips. "Thank you! Mommy did my makeup."

"She's very good!"

She nods, brows knitting. "She is. Not as good as me, though. Want me to do yours?"

"Oh, you leave her alone, princess." Michael struts over, pushing off some hair off his forehead.

"She's fine." I give Sophia a little wink.

"I'm gonna go see if Uncle Gio will let me do his!" She practically bounces with excitement. "Uncle Gio!"

She runs over to him, and he grabs her in his arms, spinning her in the air.

"How are you doing?" he asks me, and suddenly I'm nervous.

Does he know what I've done? The others I've killed?

"I'm fine. I…uh, actually just wanted some air. Excuse me."

"Has he called you?"

I stop and look back over my shoulder. "Chris?"

He nods stoically, his jaw clenching.

"No. I'm sure I misheard about his parents."

"Maybe. But he did text me back and sent a photo of him with some old lady in a hospital. Could be his mom. Could be he's lying. But we're verifying."

My spine tingles with a chill. Why would he go through so much trouble? Something gnaws in the pit of my stomach.

"Well, if he calls, I'll let you know."

"Watch your back, Kayla. There are snakes everywhere."

His eyes are haunting as they stare at me for a second before he's heading toward Elsie, grabbing her face, and kissing her like his life depends on it.

Could Chris somehow be involved in something bad?

No, I refuse to believe it. He may not have been A, but I don't think he'd do anything to harm me. Or maybe I'm wrong. Maybe I just don't know how to read people.

With a deep sigh, I rush out into the yard and breathe in the fresh air.

Finally alone. Only a few people mulling around, not close

enough to bother me.

I stare out into the expansive yard, acres upon acres of land. All the Messinas own mansions. I don't know why someone needs to have a home this big. I'd feel lost inside these walls. I prefer something cozy.

I drag my phone out of my small handbag and check to see if there are any texts from A. But I find none. My heartbeats rap across my ribs, aching to hear his voice. To feel him. To know him. I don't know anything about him. Not really. Not in the ways it matters. But I know he cares about me. I can feel the way he does. And I want that all the time without hiding my feelings for him.

"Hey, Kayla."

I gasp, turning to the sound of Cammie's voice, her eyes downcast, her arms covered in the long, see-through sleeves of her dress.

"Hey, Cammie! I'm so happy you're here."

She shakes her head and looks as though she's about to burst into tears.

"What's wrong?" I place a hand on her shoulder, concern weaving through me.

"You told her." She sniffles. "You told Jade about my cutting."

"What?"

My pulse quivers in my throat. Jade would never break my confidence that way.

"Don't deny it. It had to be you. Dr. Collins brought up self-harm rather discreetly, and coincidently after Jade mentioned to me how she noticed my arms and wanted to talk to me to help me. How could you?" Her tone rises, tears bathing her eyes. "I trusted you!"

My heart breaks watching hers do the same. I don't want to lie to her. It wouldn't be right. But I hate to think she'll be even more upset with me. I take both her hands in mine and stare into her eyes.

"I'm sorry." I'm crying now too. "I'm sorry you're upset, but I'm not sorry I did it. Because you matter to me, Cammie, and if I could prevent something bad happening to you, then it was worth it. So you can be mad at me, but maybe, just maybe, I did the right thing. Maybe I saved your life. Because I want you to be here."

"Why?" she snivels, shaking her head, wanting to rip her hands out of my grasp.

But I don't let her run. I want her to hear me. To see herself the way I do.

"Why do you care what happens to me? I'm not Elsie or Jade. I'm not your friend. I'm a nobody! No one gives a fuck about me. Not even my own family!" She sobs heavily, and I take her in my arms and hold her against me.

"I give a fuck, Cammie. Jade gives a fuck. You're loved. You matter. Your life matters. And your family? Well, they can go fuck themselves if they don't see how special you are. We will get you help. We will do whatever we have to for you. And years from now, you'll look back and realize maybe I did the right thing and maybe you'll hate me a little less."

Her laughter is a blubbering mess. "I don't hate you."

"That's a relief." I pitch back, clasping both of her shoulders. "Jade told me she's helping you find a job. How about tomorrow we go and find you some interview clothes?"

"Really?" Her eyes widen. "I was just gonna get some donation clothes from Helping Hand."

"I think you deserve something that is just yours."

My heart warms at her bright smile.

She blinks back through her tears before throwing her arms around me. "Thank you."

"Of course. You never have to thank me. It'll be fun."

"Yeah." She huffs out a breath. "I should go get some rest back at the dorms. I'm exhausted."

"Yeah, go. Thanks for being here."

"Always. Thanks again." She gives me one final look before she heads out.

I don't like the idea of her driving by herself in the dark while upset. I intend to text her in an hour to make sure she's back.

As I turn back around to head inside, Dr. Collins is behind me, his expression grim for a moment.

A sudden cold shudder rushes up my back.

But quickly, he recovers and his mouth twitches. His fingers perch his glasses up on his trim nose. "I didn't mean to eavesdrop. I hope you know I didn't mean to cause you any issues with Cammie."

I smile faintly, unsure why he's even here to begin with. Did someone invite him? Did he just show up? That's kind of odd. We aren't friends that way.

"It's okay," I say. "She's just upset. I'm glad she has your help and Jade's help."

"She's a very troubled young woman." He tsks with the shake of his head. "I do worry for her wellbeing. What she could do to herself… But I will do everything I can to help her."

He takes a step toward me and grabs my forearm, looking intently at me.

My stomach churns.

"You have my word, Kayla."

"Uh…" I laugh uncomfortably. "I believe you."

Why is he being so odd?

"Well, I hope you have a great time at the party. I'm gonna go and talk to Jade for a moment."

"Sure, I'll just go and see myself to all that food." He grins and appears more himself now. Yet I can't shake this weird feeling.

I give him a smile before rushing off, slipping between people to find Jade and Elsie dancing together.

"Hey, there she is!" Elsie grabs my hands and forces me to dance with her.

For a second, I resist, but then I do. I slide my hips, throw my arms in the air, and let go, throwing my head back to the upbeat song. Being here, living another year, being with my friends and family, I'm so lucky.

My eyes scan the glass doors I came back into the house from, and as I stare through it, I find a large black mass peering at me through the distance.

The hair of my arms rise, prickling against my flesh.

"A?" I whisper, my heart beating. "Is that you?"

My body stills, staring at the hooded figure, unable to see him. Is he wearing a mask? Is he hiding out there without one?

"Excuse me," I tell my friends, my voice lost, barely audible.

But they're too busy having fun, Enzo now joining them, dancing between them with a beer in hand.

I slowly head back outside, needing to know if it's him. If he's here, watching me. My fingers reach for the necklace he gave me, and I have yet to take it off. It's with me always, like he is. This man who has somehow pierced himself into my very soul until all I know is him.

Rushing out the doors, I don't see him anywhere. I dash in every direction, my head turning this way and that. Waiting. Hoping. Needing to see him.

Disappointment echoes in the chambers of my heart, tears prickling behind my eyes as I sprint further down the estate, running toward the fountains.

Almost breathless, I stop in the middle of the empty place, knowing I imagined it. Knowing he isn't here after all.

Sadness unfurls within me as I shake my head, starting back toward the party.

A crack of something catches my attention. Like a twig breaking in the distance.

Fear creeps into my veins, and I start a mad dash toward the house until a strong arm grabs me from behind.

A scream rips from my lungs, but a hand cups my mouth.

"Shh, it's just me, baby bird. You can relax now."

My heartbeats pound in my throat as he loosens the palm around me, allowing me to turn toward him as I try to calm the ravaging of my breaths.

"I'm sorry I had to do that. I couldn't risk anyone seeing me." He remains standing within the bushes he came out from, that mask covering his face.

"My God, you scared the living shit out of me," I whisper. "Next time, warn a girl before you jump out and grab her, will ya?"

He chuckles. "I promise. Now, how about we leave this place? I have a little birthday surprise for you."

My eyes narrow. "Haven't you given me enough gifts?"

"No. Not even close. If I could rip the moon from the sky and give it to you, I would."

My chin trembles even as I fight the onslaught of my emotions. Why does he have to say things like that? Why do I want him to?

"Will you come with me?" he asks, extending his hand for mine. "Will you let me give you this one last gift?"

Without hesitation, I take it, and he pulls me to him, chest to chest, and if he didn't have that thing on his face, our lips would be close enough to touch.

He cups one side of my face, his thumb brushing softly over

the corner of my mouth. "I love the way you trust even when you shouldn't."

"I do. You're one of the few I do trust."

He inhales harshly like there's more he wants to say.

"Don't," he whispers, his voice raw with something unspoken, and I'm afraid to ask why.

Because I'm afraid that all of this, whatever it is that we have, will be ripped from right under me until I lose him. Until I lose the one man in this world who became something I don't yet understand. But I know no matter what happens, I will never forget him and the way he's made me feel: like I'm not alone anymore.

"Come on, we have to head this way to my car. It's parked a couple of blocks away."

"Are you gonna tell me where we're going?"

"It's a surprise. But I promise you're gonna like it."

And from his wicked tone, I have a feeling I will.

Twenty-Four

ADRIEL

She sits beside me, her knee bouncing up and down as she stares out the window of my car while I steal glances at her. This beautiful creature I can't seem to stop thinking about.

I couldn't help myself. Needing to see her. Needing to break into the party and watch her. I knew she couldn't see me. Until I wanted her to.

Until I couldn't stand another moment not being with her.

The last thing I wanted to do was see my mother or the rest of her family. But none of that mattered. Not when Kayla is all I want.

My pulse picks up when I picture her seeing what I have in store for us. She will love it. She will savor it the way I do. Together, we'll raise hell on those who deserve it. The way I promised her we would. One unified force; that's what I want for us.

I drop my palm across her leg, right above her knee, and squeeze. And that single touch alone makes my heart beat faster, like it awakens for her alone.

Her chest expands with a shallow breath and she looks at me, those eyes like soft glistening stars across the sky. I'd give her the moon. I'd give her anything she wanted just to stay with me. To kill with me. To hold me the way she does.

I'd like to say I'd be a bigger man and let her go if she wanted to leave me, but I can't. I won't be able to. Will stop at nothing to keep her until my dying day.

"Don't be nervous," I say, rubbing my fingertips up and down her thigh, smirking under this mask when her cheeks flush.

"I'm not." She tugs on her bottom lip, making me want to be the one to do it.

We pull up to a residential block on the outskirts of New York City. Nothing but darkness and silence.

"Where are we?" she asks, getting out of the car while I do the same, coming to stand beside her.

Her hand reaches for mine, and she holds it tightly, twining our fingers. My chest cinches, and I can't even explain what it feels like to have her take my hand this time, to hold it like I'm hers and she is mine.

Is this what normal relationships are like?

But as I say that to myself, a laugh cuts through. Because I'm pretty sure normal couples don't go killing together.

"What's so funny?" she asks.

"Nothing. Come on, let's go inside."

I pull her with me, and she matches my steps as we enter the back gate, nearing the door.

"Whose house is this?" she whispers, clasping my hand tighter.

"A man who does awful things." I stop and clasp her face with both palms. "I told you we'd hunt together. We'd kill together. Do you still want that?"

Her eyes expand. "Yes. More than anything."

"Then let's go hunting, little wolf."

The door is open, and I let her in first before following her. The man inside is already tied to a chair, gagged so no one hears his screams.

When she finds him there, her eyes jump between us. "What has he done?"

"Well, Ivan here has been a very bad man. Haven't you, Ivan?" I kneel to pick up a stake, like the kind you use to stab a piece of meat.

I trace it across his bare, hairy chest, chuckling when he jumps in his seat as I roll it down to his balls.

"He's been hurting children. Little girls and boys. He got out on a technicality. His lawyer has been paid top dollar to see him out of prison. Most kids don't want to testify. Too scared. But there was one. She was nine, and she spoke against him, told the court how he hurt her. But the judge's hands were tied. His lawyer claimed there was something wrong with the chain of custody for a crucial piece of evidence, then told the court the child was lying because Ivan used to date her mom before the accusation and the girl wanted to get rid of him. But see, I know she wasn't lying. Was she, Ivan?"

He screams through the gag as Kayla reaches down for a torch gun, flipping it on and creeping it closer to his eye.

"You vile piece of shit!" she hollers, her body vibrating with rage.

It's like she's back with her kidnappers, back in the hell she's endured. Seeing her this angry, it should bring me some level of happiness to know we are the same. But it doesn't. I hate that she knows what it's like to live with a past that won't ever escape you. I want more for her.

Yet this is all we have.

She lines the flames against his eye, and his wrenching screams rain through the night. It's beautiful to see her work, and I can't help the smile it brings out in me. Her gaze, it's beastly as she watches him, her body trembling with chaos born from her scars.

The torch goes dead as my hand glides up her spine, fingers raking through her hair.

"You're beautiful, Kayla. He's yours. You get to play with him however you want. Do your worst."

I hand her the stake in my grasp and settle on the chair across from him, allowing me the perfect view to watch.

She gives me a long look, her face upturning with fury before she's on him, the stake penetrating him through the side of his stomach, the torch now at his feet. She lets herself go, roaring with her rage while she mutilates him, piece by piece.

The blood drips to the floor, creating a pattern like artwork. Her art.

Somehow, the bastard still breathes, and if I cared, I'd feel bad for him. But I'm glad he is, glad he gets to suffer like he made those children suffer.

She picks up the torch again, and his body quivers, tears rolling down his cheeks as he watches her turn it back on.

His sobbing wracks through him, and once the flames eat through his shriveled-up dick, his screams are like nothing I've heard before.

She selects a knife next and edges it across his throat.

"Go fuck yourself," she whispers as she cuts across his flesh, crimson staining her hands with the color of retribution.

When he's finally dead, she stands tall, staring at what she's done, and for a moment, I think she'll regret it.

Instead, she turns to me and smiles.

"So…" She swipes the back of her hand against her bloody cheek. "When can we do that again?"

KAYLA

I can't believe I enjoyed that. The blood. The gore. But the more I do it, the easier it becomes. When I kill them, I'm able to focus on their actions rather than the fact that I'm a murderer.

Maybe it sounds like an excuse, but it's valid to me. They're animals, and some animals need to be put down.

I've been scouring the newspapers and the television for any reports of the murders I've committed, but so far there has been only one about Fred Avon. An online newspaper mentioned him going missing. *Convicted and registered sex offender gone missing*, it said. But A has assured me we're clean. That no trace of any of the bodies can lead back to either one of us.

Sitting beside him in his car, I pass glances at his large hand currently occupying my thigh, his fingers thick and masculine as they grip me like they own me.

A woman like me should loathe the idea of being owned by anyone, but with him, it doesn't feel like a bad thing. It feels as though he's rescued me, made me accept who I am now more and more every day.

After he cleaned the blood in the house, he took me back to his place so I could wash away the evidence while he got rid of the body.

When he took a shower, I had every intention of sneaking into the bathroom and seeing him. What the hell would he do to me?

He'd never hurt me. I know that like I know the sky is blue. But when I tried to open the door, it was locked. Of course it was.

We drive silently back to my place, and as we reach my driveway, he stops the car and turns to me.

"You still have the necklace I gave you?" he asks, whisking me from my thoughts.

I grin. Fingering the pendant from beneath my t-shirt—well, his t-shirt since I needed to borrow one of his to wear back home—I tug the necklace up, showing him that I in fact kept my promise.

"It's always with me. Never gonna take it off, remember?"

He nods. "Good girl."

The pads of his fingers massage my inner thighs, and I squirm from the way my core heats from a single touch.

He groans as he registers my discomfort. "Go, before I do things I'll regret."

"I doubt either of us will regret a thing."

"Kayla, after everything you've been through… Are you sure?"

Is he considering it?

But I won't sleep with him with a mask on. I want to see him. Touch his face. Feel his mouth on mine.

"I know what I want and how I want it. And I want it all with you. But first…" I lower my hand on top of his. "I need you to trust me and show me your face."

"Fuck," he mutters, clasping the top of his head, the black hoodie he always wears around it. "You need to get out of here, baby bird." His tone grows huskier. "I'm this close to saying fuck it all and burying myself inside your pretty pussy right here. And that's the last thing I wanna do because the first time I'll have you is when I can spread you open and see every breathtaking inch of you."

My body grows ragged, a warm shudder of desire rolling hot

through the apex of my thighs, needing him there.

"Go, Kayla. Now." There's demand in his voice, and everything in me wants to disobey.

"Fine," I say. "I'll go this time. But you'll give in soon enough."

"Fucking Christ," he mutters.

Laughing, I open the door and smirk over my shoulder as I head toward my home. He stays there until I lock up, and then I hear his car go.

I look out the window and don't see my new bodyguard anywhere. Last I checked, he was still at the party. So easy to sneak away from these guys. I was able to lose him in the crowd, and he definitely didn't see me with A when I left. If he did, he'd have shown up at the house we were in.

I lock both of the bolts on my door and make sure to secure the back one too. I can't be too careful, not with everything going on.

Heading for the shower, I turn on the water, the spray pounding against the tiles like heavy raindrops. I strip away my clothes, feeling as though I need to wash it all away, even though I did that already at A's.

Maybe it's all the blood. Maybe it affects me more than I want to admit.

As I enter, something catches my attention, a distant sound like someone dropped something on the floor.

My heart races and my chest grows rigid as I grab a robe from the hook and slip into it. Taking a pair of scissors from the medicine cabinet, I open the door, listening for sounds. Maybe it's Terrence coming in to check on me. Or maybe it's just old wood or something outside. I can't live in constant fear.

Once I'm in the living room, I scan the entire perimeter, not seeing a thing out of place.

"I'm being ridiculous." I laugh to myself and head back into the bathroom, keeping my cell close just in case.

I shut the door and lock it for good measure before I take a shower. Of course there's no one in the house. My fingers massage the shampoo into my scalp. It's normal to be scared. Anyone would be.

After I wash away the suds, I rinse off and dry myself quickly, needing to get to bed. Yawning, I drape the robe back on and head toward the staircase leading up to my bedroom.

The stairs creak in an ominous tone and fear prickles up my arms like a premonition or a warning. But I know I'm only scaring myself for no reason. A is close. He wouldn't let anything happen to me.

I quickly get dressed and return a few texts from my friends to apologize for leaving the party early and thank them for such an amazing day. I make sure to let Elsie know I'll pick up my car tomorrow, that I didn't want to drive when I had something to drink.

Dropping the cell on my nightstand, I flip my comforter and slip under the cool cotton. It feels good to be here, but it would be better if A was beside me, keeping me warm.

My eyelids are heavy as sleep comes quick before it consumes me, and I let the darkness win.

KAYLA

Quiet, muffled voices wake me, growing steadily. It's as though I'm dreaming. Floating. My body is languid and tingly.

"Make it quick," one says to another in a whisper. "He's gonna be looking for her."

Make what quick?

Where am I?

Groaning groggily, I try to pry my eyes open, but I can't seem to. Darkness entraps me, like something is shrouding my eyes.

Panic suddenly hits and I start to scream, and it's then I realize my wrists are tied and I'm blindfolded. The pull on my wrists as I shout and jerk my body around causes my skin to burn.

"Shh. Don't fight."

I can't make out the voice too well. It's like I'm slipping in and out of consciousness even as my adrenaline fights to keep me awake.

"We need to hurry. Someone is going to come."

Who's saying that?! Where am I? Am I still home?

Sudden cool air hits around my breasts.

I'm naked? Oh, God….

My chaotic heartbeats echo in my ears as I continue to fight, even though I know it's pointless. But I won't give up. I won't let them have me without giving them hell. Though I continue to scream, no real sound comes out.

My limbs jolt in a tremor. It's happening again. They took me. They're bringing me back.

"No!" I holler, but all that comes out is an unintelligible sound.

"Shut the fuck up," a man fires, and I try to concentrate on the voice, try to make it out.

But it's to no avail. My mind is too clouded, but I know deep in my heart that I have heard that voice before.

"Hurry up!" he repeats. "Do it now!"

And that's when I feel it.

I let out a bloodcurdling wail as I register the sharp, agonizing throbbing in my stomach, like someone is slicing me open.

I wail, unable to move. Something tight is binding my ankles. I'm completely helpless as I shriek, tears leaking out of the edges of my eyes as a monster cuts me.

"A, where are you? Please! I need you. I need you," I weep and beg and plead for him to hear me.

But he can't. He doesn't know what's being done to me. Who is doing it.

Could be anyone. Could be the Midnight Murderer…

My pulse kicks up. It's him, isn't it? He came for me. He's branding me like the others. Oh, God!

But there are two people here. Who is he working with?

I shriek as another agonizing slice pierces through the cloudy fog in my head. It's like I've been drugged.

"Shh. Don't worry, this will be over quickly."

Am I going to die? Will it end this way? The way it began? Taken. Trapped. Unable to fight. Is this my destiny? Was I fooling myself into believing I could take him on? This killer. This monster.

A's words ring in my head.

He's not like the others.

He told me to be careful. But the killer found me anyway.

"The drugs are gonna wear off. Hurry up."

Oh, fuck. They drugged me! That explains why I feel like I'm underwater, as though I drank too much.

The pain, it's unbearable. Screaming against the gag does nothing but let the monsters win. So I stop, biting down instead, my hands fisting as my heartbeats quicken and my chin trembles. But they won't have my screams, not anymore.

The brutality lasts for minutes, hours, I don't know. I've lost all sense of time as they carve me up for their pleasure.

"He'll find you soon enough."

Does he mean A? Was this about him?

Oh, God, it hurts. It fucking hurts!

But I lie here, screaming inside my head, wanting their blood on my fingertips, wanting their deaths.

The sound of a window opening terrifies me even more. I hope they're leaving and not taking me with them.

Time passes on a loop until I realize they're actually gone. That I'm naked and alone, unable to get up or do anything.

Tears continue to fall as I cry, unable to stop now. Not sure what I can do but lie here, hoping A finds me. Because no one else will.

Emotions battle inside me, and I go there, to the one place I swore I wouldn't. To the day I became someone I never imagined

I would be. I bottled it so deep after it happened that I didn't think it'd ever come out to haunt me. But here, with my own tears, I remember hers.

Because I killed her.

I played their wicked game and I lost.

It's what they wanted. To break us. To chip away every human thing about us.

Her face is clear in my mind, as though she's standing right in front of me.

"Why did you do it?" she asks, a bullet in her throat, blood rushing out of the wound like an endless river.

"I'm…I'm so sorry," I cry, my body trembling as I reach my fingers for hers.

But she's out of reach.

With her other hand, she removes a gun from her pocket and aims it at my chest.

She laughs at my horrified expression. "Say goodbye, Kayla."

While I do nothing else but cry.

She pulls the trigger.

And I return to darkness, yet I still see her face.

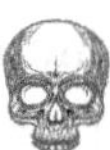

Our bodies are bare, six of us standing in front of Chad, one of the cleaners who works for the Palermo crime family. And by cleaners, I mean the ones who disposes of us when we're no longer needed.

Each of us knows that someone is gonna die today. Who? We don't know. How many? No one knows that either.

"So, ladies…" He grins. "We have a little problem at the club today. Someone poisoned one of our customers. And do you know what happened to him? Hmm?"

He shoves the gun under my jaw, and I shiver, breathing faster, afraid that the bullet will enter me at any moment.

"Do you know what happened?" he asks me, his eyes darkening.

"N-n-no." I shake my head in a hurry, one arm covering whatever I can of my body.

But it's no use. They've seen it all. Touched and invaded every inch of me. Hiding is useless. They'll always find me.

He slams the butt of the weapon into my jaw. Pain erupts, and I fall to the ground, large tears welling behind my eyes.

"On your feet, whore!" he bellows so loud, the other girls whimper.

Cammie reaches down for my hand and helps me to my feet. He lets her.

"How about you?" he asks Talon, another girl here with us.

"Is…is he d-dead?" she asks.

"Now, how would you know that?" Chad pops a brow.

"I didn't, I promise! I j-just assumed since you're mad."

He cups her face and strokes it with his knuckles. "Now, aren't you just smart?"

He mocks her, but her eyes seek for shelter, for warmth. For love. But there's none of that here. All of it was depleted from our souls so long ago, we don't know when it's real and when it isn't.

"Be my good girl and tell me who did it."

She sobs, shaking as she looks at Cammie.

No. No, she couldn't have.

"Her?" he asks.

"I—I'm sorry!" Talon cries. "I'm sorry."

Cammie's eyes pop. "No! It was her! She did it! I swear! I'm not stupid!"

He huffs, all dramatic. "Well, we have ourselves a situation, girls, don't we?"

The whole room explodes in snivels, and I know this is the end. He's either gonna kill them both or kill one of them, but someone is definitely not coming out alive.

"What do you suggest I do here, girls?" He points the gun at Cammie, and his finger moves over the trigger until she trembles and huddles against me.

My hand curls around the back of her head.

"Shhh," is all I manage, not knowing what else I can say.

Everything will be okay *seems useless, because nothing is okay.*

Chad stares at me, his eyes cunning, a wry laugh escaping his ugly mouth. He's a vile piece of filth, and not much older than me, around twenty-five. Brutal as ever. He doesn't care who he has to kill. I don't think he sees us as human beings, or he wouldn't be doing what he does.

Does he have a mother? A sister? What would he do if this happened to them?

Is Chad even his real name? I think it is. These men are arrogant. They don't think giving us their actual names will do anything.

"Stand straight!" He wrenches her away from me.

And when he glares at me this time, something devious brews in the sliver of his gaze.

He watches me swallow, and a slow-growing sneer fastens to his mouth. "I have an idea. I'm gonna let one of you decide who killed him. It'll be fun!"

He walks around the room, chuckling like a sadistic madman, pointing the gun at each of us. This isn't the first game he's played. They all play these games to mess with us. Agnelo made Elsie kill a girl when she did something wrong. It was her punishment. So whatever Chad has in store will be just as bad.

"Let's see, which one of you should have the honor?" He points

the gun toward each girl until it lands on me. "You."

No. Please. No. Not me. I don't want to do it. I don't want to kill anyone.

I know that's what he'll make me do.

"Who do you think did it?" he asks me, his eyes glistening like this is exciting to him.

"I—I don't know." My bottom lip juts out and fat tears roll down my cheeks. "Please…"

"What are you begging me for? You have no idea what I'm even asking for except your opinion."

Nausea swirls in my gut as he takes a few steps closer until the mint on his breath suffocates my nostrils.

He grips my jaw and pushes the barrel of the weapon into my gut. "Pick one. You get to decide their fate. One of them did it, and it's either all three of you die or one of them does. And you are the lucky girl who gets to pick the winner."

"No!" I sob. "I—I c-can't. I won't do it. I won't take a life."

His fingers deepen into my jaw, and through gritted teeth, he says, "Did I tell you that you had a choice? Because you don't!"

He wrenches back and grabs Cammie by the hair until she screams.

"Her?" He throws her on the ground, flat on her stomach as she cries, over and over until her voice seeps into the marrow of my bones. "Was she the one?"

"No! No, please! I can't! I can't do it."

"That's a shame." He grabs Talon and throws her right beside Cammie's naked body. "I guess it will be the both of them, then."

My body wracks with my heavy sobs. "I can't."

I shake my head. How can I kill either of them? But how can I let them both die?

"You have 'til the count of three to decide. Or I will decide for *you. One.”*

“Please, just don’t do this! They didn’t mean it!”

“Two.”

“I’m—I’m s-sorry!” I stare down at both of the girls, their bodies shaking in fear, unending pain seeping out of them.

“Three.”

“T-T-Talon,” I sob. “Talon. Oh, God!”

“No! No!” Talon screams, turning to me, her eyes round with shock. “Please don’t kill me! Pleasepleaseplease! I don’t wanna die.”

“Seems like she’s decided.” Chad pats me on the shoulder. “Now, here.” He shoves the weapon toward me. “You get to do the honor.”

“W-what? N-nooo,” I cry, words trembling.

“You heard me, bitch. Take the fucking gun before I blow all of your brains out.”

He shoves it into my hand and wraps the weapon around my shaky fingers. Quaking as I stand there, my emotions wrench out of me. I can’t kill anyone. I’m not a killer. I’m not like them.

“Tick-tock!” He grabs a fistful of my hair and pulls so hard my scalp throbs. “You have three seconds!”

I lift the gun in the air.

“One.” He shoves me closer to Talon, who’s sobbing as she holds Cammie’s hand.

“Don’t hurt me! Please!” Talon’s glassy blue eyes connect with mine, begging me not to pull that trigger.

“Two.”

“Please, just kill me instead. I—I can’t do it!”

“If I say three, the whole room dies! What will it be?”

Panting, trembling, my chest heavy, I aim the gun at Talon. Instead of turning to face the floor, she looks at me, her eyes immortalized in my soul, like a statue of her doom. Something I know I'll never escape.

"Three!"

Pop.

The bullet hits the back of her neck, blood pooling around her.

I drop to the floor, rushing for her, covering the wound, my fingers soaking with crimson.

She doesn't die right away. She suffers, her eyes still holding mine until her life slips away, second by second.

Then she's gone.

Yet I will live with this forever.

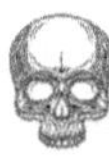

It plays in my head over and over, like I'm watching it on a TV screen, while I lie here dying, or wishing I was.

ADRIEL

After dropping Kayla off, I drove back to the party. Been watching my brothers, my mother with that fucking scarf on her neck, covering what I did to her. She didn't tell them. If she had, they'd come after me. But things have been quiet except for them putting all their resources into finding the trafficking ring.

I hate seeing my mother's face, that photo of me as a baby still burning a hole in my pocket. I don't know why I still carry it. I don't know why she did either. Her lies were exactly that. Maybe she feels some form of guilt for what she did, but it doesn't excuse her not looking for me. She had her chance, and now it's mine.

People have begun to leave, and I spot my twin, Raph, with his wife, Nicolette, his arms wrapped around her. He's happy. It's too bad I'm gonna take it all away.

Suddenly, Sophia jumps into his arms, her smile bright, making my lips twitch. From where I am, I can't hear her, but she clearly loves her uncle. And I wonder what that feels like, to have a niece, to know her love.

She would never love me like that. I'm nothing like him. I don't nurture. I don't love. I'm this. A monster of my mother's making.

Michael strides up beside them with Elsie, and Gio soon joins with a tall redhead, who I know as his wife, Iseult—my half sister.

If I wasn't banking on the Marinos trying to kill me, I bet she would love to. But I have nothing against her. I don't exactly have anything against my brothers, either. Not really. It's always been about my mother and how I can hurt her. I know the way to do that is through her sons. Taking one of them from her would kill her.

Raph sets to go, while Nicolette pats him on the shoulder. She struts off with Elsie while he nods at his brothers and kisses his mother on the cheek before heading out. I follow him, watching as he gets into the car, and I get into mine.

He drives some distance while I stay far back, making sure he doesn't get suspicious. I don't know where the hell he's going. I thought he'd be returning to his home. But it's not his usual direction.

I slow down, the road empty. Dark. The remote in my hand is steady as I ready to press a button. In another life, maybe I would've actually liked him. He seems decent enough. But in this life, Raph dies, and I'll be the one to do it.

As he turns right, I don't wait another moment. Pressing the button, I anticipate the bomb in his car going off.

"Three. Two."

The car swerves and stops.

"One."

Boom.

It explodes like fucking fireworks, the vehicle lit up with a blaze so wide, I stare in awe at the vivid orange and yellow inferno, knowing he's burning inside it. Knowing this will break my mother's heart. I grin.

Needing to see him, I slip my mask back on and grab the fire extinguisher as I head out the door. The car burns, so close to exploding. As I reach it, I extinguish the fire inside the driver's side, unable to stand my excitement at the thought of his charred body.

Except when I look inside…

"What the…"

He's not here. There's no one here.

I growl, staring out onto the open road.

How the hell did he escape?

The car swerved. Did he get out? Did he know? Did he hear something?

Fuck! My tech is undetectable. What did he use to find the fucking bomb?

Rushing for my car, I gun out of there, needing to figure out what went wrong.

But as I do, a notification pops on my phone. The cameras in Kayla's home register extra bodies. I immediately turn on the app, and my heart completely stops beating.

She's on the bed, tied up as two people with ski masks are on top of her, stripping her, blindfolding her as she barely fights back.

"FUCK!" I scream, slamming my forehead with a fist, going 130 miles per hour to get back to her while still watching her on my phone.

The muscles and veins strain against my skin, filling with rage. Too much of it, I can't contain the quaking of my body.

And when she screams, when they take a small carving to her stomach, I know instantly. The Midnight Murderer has Kayla. Two of them as a team. Now it makes sense how they've managed to get away with it for so long.

They have her. They will kill her.

I should've been there instead of avenging a past I should've let die a long time ago. Because of my carelessness, they came for her. Now I'm gonna lose the only person I have left in this world.

If I'm too late…if they kill her…my life is over too.

"I'm sorry, baby bird!" My voice bleeds with an indescribable level of agony. "It's all my fault. Fuuuck!"

My chest rattles, and something registers in my eye. I fling at it so I can still watch Kayla. As I do, I glance down at the back of my finger, seeing something I haven't seen since I was a child.

My own tears.

It hurts. It fucking hurts so goddamn bad to see her cry, to watch them do this to her.

"I'm coming! I swear I'm gonna kill them for this!"

But I fucking hope like hell I can make it back in time to do just that.

Twenty-Six

KAYLA

"**S**hh. I've got you, baby bird," A's soothing voice lulls me, yet I'm still unsure where I am or who I'm with.

It sounds like him. My A. But I don't know what is real and what isn't.

I can barely move my body, darkness still creeping in until hands against my face pull down whatever's been covering my eyes.

"A?" I blink back, still hazy, hoping this isn't some dream.

Did he really come for me? I try to pry my eyelids ajar, but they feel as heavy as lead. A whimper escapes me, and it's like I hear myself, yet it sounds like someone else. Someone distant.

"It's me… Fuck," he groans with anguish bleeding through. "I'm so sorry. I'm sorry I failed you."

It feels like I'm being lifted, carried, or held. I can't be sure.

I sag against him, feeling somehow lighter now that I know he's come.

"I'm gonna take care of you. I won't leave your side."

I whimper, hands tingling as I grab on to something. Maybe his shirt or his hair. His arms tighten around me, like a heavy blanket keeping me warm.

"You can sleep now," he says softly.

With a sigh, I melt further into him. Pressing my face into this man I barely know, I fall back into darkness, knowing he'll find me and bring me back to the light.

Twenty-Seven

KAYLA

Light filters through the narrowing of my eyes, and I stretch my limbs, my body achy and sore for some reason I can't quite recall.

My breathing intensifies as I glance around the room, and panic grips its ugly hand around my throat. Where the hell am I?

It appears to be a simple bedroom. A bed and a loveseat in one corner, plus a cherrywood dresser and nightstand.

I've never been here before. What am I doing here?

I try to sit up, but throbbing in my stomach makes me fall back down. As soon as I do, I remember.

Being home. The attack. My stomach…

Oh, no…

I'm afraid to look at what they did to me.

I remember A rescuing me. It wasn't a dream? Is this his place?

I'm in my own clothing, but different than what I had on when

I went to bed. I think. Someone dressed me.

"A?" I call for him.

Where is he?

My pulse thrashes at the thought that maybe I imagined the entire thing. Not the attack, but my rescue. Maybe someone else has me.

"Hello?" My words are croaky, weak. "A? Are you here?"

Keys chime at the door before it opens, and there he is, mask and hoodie on, and somehow that brings me comfort.

"Hey, babe. How are you feeling? I made you some tomato soup for when you feel like eating."

I fight to sit up, groaning from pain. And he's instantly there at lightning speed, helping me up to a seated position.

"I have a headache." My fingers massage my temple.

He takes the bottle of meds and the water, the ones I hadn't noticed on the nightstand, and gives me two pills. I take it, returning the water bottle back to him.

"What happened to me? How long have I been here?"

His chest rises and falls in quick succession. "Two days."

"What?!"

How's that possible?

"Kayla, I'm sorry."

"Tell me what happened, please."

I know I won't like it, but I have to know. I have to know what he knows.

He wrestles with what to say, clenching and unclenching his hand.

"Two people came for you. It was him. The killer." He chokes up with rage in his tone. "He…"

It's then my fingers reach for my stomach, feeling the cotton there.

Panic sets in. Adrenaline kicking through my bloodstream. Suddenly, I'm on my feet, breathing heavy. Dizzy.

Oh, God. What did they do to me?!

"Show me!" I yank up my shirt and try to pry the gauze off. "What is it?" I tremble, angry tears filling my eyes. "Show me, God damn it!"

His hands clasp mine and his thumb brushes my skin there. "It's okay. You're safe here. Just relax and sit down. I'll show you whatever you want."

My body goes rigid, and I nod as he settles me back on the edge of the bed.

"Is it bad?" I wonder.

He doesn't answer, lifting up my shirt, which I hold up while he slowly removes the tape around the gauze before it's off completely.

When my eyes dart down, I gasp with quick, jerky breaths.

"No…" I shake my head with a cry. "Wh-what is it?" I pant, staring at the star carved onto my stomach.

"That's his brand," A clarifies. "He knew I've been looking for him. He left you alive for me to find. He wanted me to know he can get to you whenever he wants." He growls. "I'm sorry I brought him to you. I'm so fucking sorry."

My heart races and I jump to my feet. "I need to get out of here!"

Winded inhales assail me as I rush for the door, attempting to pry it open. But when I turn the knob, I realize it's locked.

I spin around to him. "Let me out!"

"Kayla, you need to lie back down. You're gonna make yourself bleed."

My mind returns there, playing it over and over. "Let me out!"

I suddenly feel claustrophobic, my knees bucking, my head

spinning.

When he stays rooted in place, I march toward him, hating that this happened to me. That I was a victim again.

Weak, pathetic Kayla. I'm over being weak.

"Just wait a minute, okay?" he pleads. "You need to rest. Please. I want to take care of you. That's all."

Pain swirls in the back of my throat as he goes on.

"I got your car, and it's in my garage. I also made sure to text your friends telling them you went on a little getaway by yourself, a lake house upstate. They were understanding. So were your parents, though your mom was worried, but I calmed her down." He takes a step forward. "Sent her lots of texts and photos of a beautiful cabin by a lake so she doesn't think you're off doing something crazy."

My mouth widens as I cut the rest of the distance between us. "You have this all figured out, huh?"

"I was just trying to help. This is my fault."

I ignore the pain in his voice. "Let me out of this fucking place!"

"I hate seeing you this way." He cups my cheeks, and I succumb to his magical touch, my heartbeats slowing a little, like he's the antidote to my heartache. "I just need you to get a little better before I let you out."

"Excuse me?" I shrug off his touch. "Who the hell are you to decide that for me? I will never be imprisoned again. Do you hear me?!"

"I'm not keeping you prisoner. For fuck's sake, Kayla! Do you know what it did to me to see someone hurting you and be too far to stop it?"

He saw it? Oh, God.

"Do you understand that the mere thought of losing you made me wanna fucking *die*? You don't, do you?" He chuckles coldly.

"Because you've always had people you cared about. Me? I never have." He snaps his hand around my jaw and pulls his face near. "Not until you." His thumb strokes my lips. "I can't take it, feeling the things you do to me, the things you make me wanna do and say. So yeah, I'm keeping you here until you get better, and then you're free to go."

A lump lodges in my throat until fresh tears skim down my cheeks. His admission was huge for him. I know it was, and I don't take that for granted.

"I'm not mad at you." I sniffle, taking his hand in mine and kissing his knuckles.

Our fingers twine together and stay that way, forging a connection much deeper than most have in a lifetime.

"I don't know what's happening to me, Kayla." His raw truth pierces through once again.

"I don't know what's happening to me either." I wrap my arms around his middle and cry against his chest.

He holds me tightly across my back, tighter than he's ever held me before, like he doesn't ever want to imagine his life without me.

"You're gonna be okay," he assures me. "We'll get them. There'll be a reckoning, I swear it."

"How did you find me?" I perch back, wanting so badly to see him, to look into his eyes. To know this man who's come to mean something to me.

"I—"

"The truth, A." I know there's more.

I didn't miss the fact that he said he watched me get hurt. How could he have seen it? Did they send footage to his phone?

He releases a long huff. "I have cameras installed in your home."

A flush creeps up my cheeks. "I'm sorry, *what*?"

"It's for your protection, Kayla."

"How dare you?!" I push him off with two palms across his chest. "How could you violate me that way after what I've been through?"

My head, it hurts. I hate this. I don't want to exist like this. Being watched, preyed on. I can't trust anyone anymore.

"I needed to make sure the killer wasn't after you, that the traffickers didn't return for you. But I fucking failed. I know that!"

"Get out!" I snatch a fistful of his shirt. "Get the hell out!"

He grabs my wrist and brings my body flush against his, and before he knows what's happening, I grab his mask and yank it off his face.

But once I see who's behind it, I stumble backward, a cold rush creeping up my spine.

"No!" I trip, trying to get away, my pulse pounding in my ear. "It c-can't be you." I tremble out the words, unable to process the face I'm looking at.

How could I not know? How could I have been deceived this way?

"Please, Kayla. Let me explain."

"No, g-get away from me!" My voice comes as a whispered shout, tears leaking out of the edges of my eyes.

"Please don't run from me, baby bird. I can't stand the thought of losing you." His throat bobs as he draws closer while I back into the door, slamming right into it.

Two palms cage me as his lips, those lips I've dreamed about kissing when I could finally see his face, hover above mine.

"I won't stay here another moment! Not after this!" My heart aches, the betrayal soaking in so deep I don't know how I can ever forget it.

His lips curl on one side and his gaze grows sad.

He reaches for my face, knuckles feathering down slowly as those eyes, those bright green eyes, pin mine. "I'm sorry, Kayla. But I can't let you leave."

KAYLA

I don't want to leave either. All I want is to make him put that mask back on and pretend. I want to return to a time when I didn't know who he was. Didn't know that he spent all this time lying to me.

"Get away from me, *Chris*." My teeth rattle from how hard I bite down.

It can't be him. All this time? How? How did I not even suspect it? Am I that stupid?

But he didn't sound like A. Didn't have those green eyes he has now. He made a fool out of me!

"You need to open this fucking door!"

He sighs, clutching my face with both palms, ignoring my pleas, forcing me to look at him and him alone. Those full lips drop closer, brushing against mine.

"That's not my name. Never was."

He kisses me. Just once. Just a touch of our mouths, and my soul weeps. It cries out for him, needing him, this man who's made me feel as though things I once dreamed of are actually possible.

But now? All we have are lies. He isn't A. Not my A. Yet he is. And reconciling these two things is getting harder by the second.

My head spins, trying to put all the pieces of the puzzle back together. How can he be Chris? I don't understand.

"You can't be A. How is this even possible?" My vision clouds, moisture building within my gaze.

"Just let me tell you everything before you leave, alright? Just give me a chance to make things right. Please, Kayla."

His eyes search mine, helplessly begging for something I don't know if I'm capable of giving. But he's A. He's been my A this whole time. How can I not hear him out?

"Fine." I nod. "Tell me everything. But this doesn't mean I forgive you."

"I deserve that." His eyes go downcast, and he exhales. "I need to start at the beginning."

He takes my hand in his, and those tingles I've come to love whenever he touches me grow even stronger. Instinctively, my hand tightens around his.

"Kayla…" he whispers, my name a plea for mercy. "You've been a gift in my life, and I've never gotten one of those before."

I suck in a breath, crying softly, caring so much for this man, hating that he's never even had the things every person should. I ache to hold him and tell him that he's the gift. That knowing him has made me a better person.

But I can't say any of those things because he's been playing me this whole time, pretending to be two people. He had so many chances to tell me, but he didn't. I want to forgive. But how the hell do I trust him again?

"A, I don't know how to do this." My brows furrow, not wanting to lose him.

Yet I can't forgive him. Not now. Not yet. Maybe not ever.

"I don't know how to do this either, but you and I, whatever this is, it's real." His gaze bores into mine. "And I need to know that for once in my life there's a person worth fighting for. Worth finding out whether I'm capable of things I never thought I was. And you, little wolf, you gave me all that. You changed something inside me. I can't deny it. Even while I can't put a name to it."

"Why couldn't you just tell me?" I cry, shaking my head.

"I couldn't. Not at the time."

"What's your name?" I ask. It's as though I've been waiting for this moment all my life.

His lips start to move, and I wait there, needing it like oxygen.

"My name is Adriel. And my mother is Fernanda... Fernanda Marino."

"W-w-what?" My heart climbs into my throat. "I—I don't understand."

He pulls me toward the bed, and when I try to sit down beside him, he gently curls his arms around my hips and carefully settles me on his lap.

I try to get off, but he hardens his grasp on me.

"Don't. Just stay. Let me be honest with you. Let me give you parts of myself I've never given anyone before."

My heart's heavy, seeing and hearing his anguish. And before I can stop myself, I lower my mouth to the corner of his and kiss him.

He breathes in sharply and snaps his palm to the back of my head. Keeping me there. Silently, our hearts beat as one. I'm afraid to move or breathe because in this moment, I forget he's Chris. I forget that he's lied. He's my A, and he always will be.

"When I was a newborn…" he starts. "My mother gave me up. I'm Raph's twin, and she didn't want me. So, as soon as I was born, she gave me to some nuns, where I spent sixteen horrible years."

I blink back tears, knowing this story is not going to end well. Not with everything I know about him so far.

"You once showed me your scars, but what I didn't tell you is that I have mine."

He lifts me a little and places me on the bed while he rises from it, dragging up his shirt and showing everything.

I throw a hand over my mouth, anguished at what he endured.

"I'm so sorry," I pant, knowing the agony all too well. Seeing his scars, it makes me feel even closer to him. "Who did that to you?"

He returns to me, placing me back on his lap, an arm swooping around me. "Those fucking nuns." He scoffs. "All because of my mother. I vowed to kill her for leaving me at the hands of women who should've cared. Who should've shown me what it meant to love and be human. Yet all I found there was the cruel reality of human nature."

He forces his head back and sears his gaze to mine, and I feel it everywhere. This man, he makes me want to hold him in my arms, like a broken little boy who just needs someone to love him.

"I'm so sorry, A." My throat closes up.

"Don't be. I met you." His smile is wrapped with melancholy. "I'd take another sixteen years of that torture just to meet you again."

"You stupid man," I cry, wrapping my arms around him and holding on. "Why didn't you just tell me? I wouldn't have told anyone. I'd have kept your secret."

He chuckles gravelly, staring back at me. "My beautiful Kayla.

Had I known you'd be the kind of woman I'd want to lay down my life for, I would've. But we don't get second chances."

Don't I know it…

"How did you come to work for your brother?"

He snickers. "Well, he doesn't know who I am. No one does. Except my mother now."

"What do you mean? How does she know?"

"I tried to kill her the other day."

"Okay. Wow. Do go on."

"I didn't end up doing it. Nicked her throat a little."

"Oh, crap. Is that why she had a scarf on at my birthday party?"

"Yep." He shakes his head with resentment ripping through his features. "I waited years for that day. Years to find her and kill her, and I couldn't fucking do it. All because of that damn picture!"

"What picture?"

He reaches into his pocket and retrieves it, handing it to me.

"Oh my goodness. Is that you?" My gaze jumps between him and the photo of a baby and a woman who looks like a younger Fernanda.

He nods. "Apparently. She had it in her wallet, said she never forgot me. That she loves me. Can you believe that?"

I slant my head to the side and feel for him. "Maybe she does. Maybe she had her reasons. Have you asked her for an explanation?"

"Whose side are you on?" His voice trips with irritation.

"Yours, of course. But I don't want you to carry this anger that she's the root of if there is maybe a good reason for what she did."

"No. There's no good reason. She left me and never even looked for me. Not once."

I nod. "You're right. I'm sorry." I lay my palm against the stubble on his cheek. "Tell me more."

"I infiltrated my brother's army, wanting to be close to them. To know their whereabouts so that I could make my move when I needed to."

"Did you pick me? Or did Michael assign you?"

He laughs. "I wanted him to choose me. From the moment I saw you with that man from the alley—the one you killed, then called Michael to clean up your mess—I knew I needed to know you. Needed to have you."

"W-wait." I shake my head, drawing back further. "You saw me kill that guy?"

He nods. "I followed you after you saved that girl he was hurting. And once I heard he was assigning you a bodyguard, I was the first to volunteer. It was my way of making sure you didn't get yourself into trouble."

"So why did you stop? Why did you lie to Michael about your mother being sick?"

"Because...I hated the thought of you growing closer to someone else, someone who was me, yet wasn't. I hated that you could fall for him, kiss him, and fuck him. Instead of me. I was jealous." He scoffs. "I can't believe I just admitted that."

"You were jealous of your own self. You sound insane. You know that, right?" I tease, unable to stop smiling.

"I *am* insane, Kayla. Been for a long time. But with you, I've never seen the world clearer."

"And your voice, your eyes... They're different. How? I mean, I know contacts are a thing, but your voice is different than Chris's."

"I know." He smirks. "I run a high-level tech company where I create lots of things like voice changers. I created a tiny black circle that sticks to the roof of your mouth and can change the pitch and sound of your voice to whatever level you desire."

"What the..." My eyes grow. "Are you some kind of genius?"

"Some say that." He grins.

"But wait a minute. The night I killed Fred, you were there. But…but I drugged you."

"So you thought." He grabs my jaw and growls. "You make me crazy, you know that? I've never been so out of control, so lost to my emotions, until you."

"Stop distracting me. Tell me how you managed to un-drug yourself."

He chuckles. "I never drank it. I knew you'd try something."

My mouth pops wide. "But you were at the house taking a shower."

"I drove back with my other car. Not the one I use as Chris."

"I can't even process this right now."

"I know. It's a lot, and I'm sorry."

It's beyond too much. It's like I've been thrown into a loop and I can't stop spinning.

My eyes go to the tattoo on his chest, the one I once wanted to see. A gravestone peeks proudly in between what looks like two dark-hooded figures, like monsters, the moon high above. A black crow sits obediently at the center of the stone. And on it are the letters RIP with the letter A right below.

"What does it mean?" I ask, tracing the letter.

"It means I'm dead. But with you, I'm reborn. And I wanna stay that way."

I place my cheek against his beating heart until something hits me.

"Shit… Michael." I sit up straighter, slapping a hand around my mouth. "The thing I told him about your parents. Oh my God… He's gonna come for you! He's gonna kill you, A. What have I done?"

His smirk grows. "You're worried about me?"

I roll my eyes. "Of course I'm worried about you. I may want to stab you right now, but I don't want anyone else to."

He laughs, and his entire face brightens before it turns dark and brooding. He searches every inch of my face, his eyes cast with a tender ache.

"I don't deserve you."

"Of course you do." I pick up his massive hand and place it against the center of my chest. "We're both so used to feeling unwanted, unloved. It's easy to get used to that. But you deserve someone's tenderness and affection. I want to give you that."

His eyes fall to a close for only a moment.

"I never knew, Kayla. I never knew how it felt to have it." His eyes glaze over. "Not until you."

His fingers slice into my hair, and gradually, he brings my lips to his, a breath between them.

"What now?" he asks, like he's afraid I won't forgive him.

But, see? I have already, because how could I not?

"Now we just focus on finding them. Until then…I wanna do this."

With a palm to the back of his neck, I pull him in, and I kiss him slowly, tenderly, just like he deserves.

With a growl, he fists my hair and takes the air from my lungs as he kisses me back with everything he has and more.

Twenty-Nine

ADRIEL

One day bleeds into the next, and she's sleeping in my arms, her head resting on my bicep as I stare down at her with my elbow propped.

When I let her rip off my mask, I was afraid it was over, whatever the hell we have torn to shreds. But I wanted her to know. I was sick of her not being able to look into my eyes, to see me, to know what she has come to mean to me. It was the only way I could show her. I don't have the words to give her.

It was close. She was gonna walk away, but somehow, I managed to save it. I don't know what I would've done if I couldn't. Because I need her. She will never truly understand the degree to which I crave her, the connection between us seared to last eternity, even after we're gone.

She starts to wake, groaning as she stretches her arms up. A smile twines over her mouth, and I can't help returning it. I hated pretending when I was Chris. I wanted her to know me as Adriel, not some persona I had created to serve a purpose.

I never intended to meet her. But once I did, it was too late. I couldn't risk her telling Elsie or any of her friends who I was. I didn't know what her reaction would ultimately be. So I pretended. I was two people, and I despised every moment she spent with him. Because he wasn't me, not in the ways that mattered.

But now I have her. I can be me. I can be the one she leans on. I no longer have to hide behind a mask.

Her fingers reach toward the stubble of my jaw, her half-lidded gaze assessing me deeply, making me want to get lost inside this woman. It's a feeling most akin to being drunk, a loss of control. My heart beats faster when she looks at me, my gut tightening for reasons a man like me will never understand.

"What?" she asks, her sleepy tone not helping my desire for her.

Instinctively, I clasp a hand over her cheek. "Nothing. Just staring at you." I smirk. "You make it difficult not to."

"I like being able to look back at you." Her hazel eyes glisten.

"Is it weird?" I whisper. "Without the mask?"

"No. Just weird that you're Chris. I still can't believe you're him and he's you. I—" She sighs. "I don't even know anymore. I just know that I have to forgive you because I don't really know how not to." She clutches my wrist. "For the first time since I've been rescued, someone sees me. I'm not afraid of being judged. I'm not seen as broken. Not with you."

"Broken? Nothing about you is broken. You're safe with me. I'm your home now, little wolf, and you're mine."

She grins, and the way my heart beats, it's unexplainable.

"How are you feeling? Need more pain meds?"

She shakes her head. "I'm better. Just a little throbbing. Nothing

I can't handle."

I release a harsh exhale. "I don't want you to hurt at all. So if you need something, I can give it to you."

She throws an arm around my shoulder. "You've already given me so much."

"I want to give you more. Because you deserve it."

As a crease forms between her brows, my body falls over hers, keeping myself up on my elbows so I don't hurt her.

Staring into her eyes, my chest tightens, and something passes between us, something heavy and bleeding life into the both of us. My finger softly runs down her cheek and her lips tremble. And in this moment, all I want is to kiss her. So I do.

I smash my mouth to hers, grunting as her fingers twine into my hair, her tongue meeting mine, the passion dripping between us.

My palm clasps around her throat, a thumb pushing up the underside of her jaw as I deepen our kiss, needing more of her.

"Mm," she moans, wrapping her legs around my hips, pushing herself further into my hard-on.

She needs this as much as I do.

"Are you sure?" My lips fall to her neck, kissing her. Nipping her. Groaning as my tongue tastes her there.

"Yes…" She clutches my hair and forces me back, kissing me roughly, biting my bottom lip so hard it has me growling.

"Fuck," I grit, my hand wrapping around her delicate throat as I look down at her, seeing the desire pooling in her eyes. "You're gonna ruin me."

"I thought I already had."

Then she kisses me again, reaching a hand between our bodies, her fingers curling around my stiffness. She strokes me to the rhythm of our mouths moving, making me sound depraved, a monster of her making.

Catching her wrist, I throw it above her, pinning both with a single palm. Using my other, I reach inside her leggings and feel her bare and wet, circling her clit as she cries out. Mouth parting, she locks her gaze with mine.

"You're so fucking beautiful." Gently, I slip a finger inside her, curling it as she bucks, her walls clenching around me.

I want to rip off her clothes and take her like an animal, but I'm trying to be different. I want this to be special for her, however she needs it.

"Harder," she begs. "Please…"

"I was trying to be good," I hiss, adding another finger. "I wanted to go slow for your sake." My digits ram all the way inside until she screams. "But if this is what you want, then I'll give it to you."

Adding another finger, I thrust hard and fast, and her eyes close, the sounds she makes sending me straight to hell.

I yank a fistful of her hair. "I want you to look at me while I finger-fuck this perfect pussy. Don't you dare look away. Understand?"

She nods.

"That's it. Good girl… Give me those pretty eyes."

I roll my thumb over her clit, and her lashes flutter, but they don't shut. She stares at me as though she can see inside my soul, and this feeling between us, this undeniable connection… I feel it everywhere at once.

I give it to her rougher while her body jolts and quakes beneath me. I know she's close, fighting the temptation to close her eyes.

Feeling her, seeing her in the throes of passion, I don't think there's anything quite like it.

"A…" she rasps. "D-don't stop, I'm gonna come!"

A groan escapes between my teeth, wanting to feel those

ripples. It's different this time, not like the closet where I couldn't see how breathtaking she is submitting to me this way, giving me her body, trusting me with it. I'd never do anything to betray that.

"Come for me, baby bird. Now." I pinch her clit before thrusting back inside her.

And she does, screaming my name.

"Yes, A! Don't stop!"

"Don't know how to." I take every drop she has to give, needing more of it, more of this.

Before she has a chance to recover, I flip her around on all fours and yank her leggings down, shoving her thighs apart with my knee.

The material gathers around her ankles as I thrust my fingers back inside her, tugging her head back by her hair as she screams my name. "Tell me what you want, baby bird. Tell me how you want it."

She's slick and wet, and I add a third finger, spreading her wider. She writhes and moans, looking so damn good, I want to taste every inch of her body.

"I want you to tie my hands behind my back."

"Then what?"

Her voice goes all hoarse the more I slip in and out of her. "I want you to force me. Force yourself inside me even when I tell you to stop."

Her eyes slam to mine from over her shoulder, and there's no shame in them. I like that. I like that she can be herself, give me her darkest fantasies, so I can be the one to make them all come true.

My dick's rock hard, wanting to take her with the same level of depravity she craves. With my foot, I yank her leggings off the rest of the way, and I slide out of her. She pops her ass in the air, and I slap it hard, leaving a nice handprint.

"Stay still. You're making it difficult for me to concentrate."

She bites into her bottom lip, her gaze molten, needing to come so badly I can taste it. I push her face down on the mattress, her ass in the air as I grab both of her arms and bring them behind her back. Using her own leggings, I tie her wrists together. The double knot ensures she can't escape.

"You look so damn good," I groan as she locks her knees tight. "I can't wait to use every inch of your body until I've been everywhere, tasted and fucked every hole."

"Oh, God. Please…" She cries out, and I don't even know if I've ever been this hungry.

"What does my little slut want?" I fit my palm between her thighs and rub against her warm cunt.

"Yesss," she whimpers as she attempts to stay propped on her knees, her arms straining against the small of her back.

"I need you to fuck me and force me to come. Please, A." She swallows harshly. "Don't stop no matter what I say or do."

With a grunt, I roll her hair around my wrist and yank her head back. "Do you know what it's doing to me to hear you beg for my cock?"

"Show me…" Her eyes narrow. "And don't wear a condom. I'm on the pill."

"Shit!" I grasp a fistful of her ass and give it another slap. "I need that shirt off of you."

As I quickly get off the bed, she watches me while I reach into the top drawer of the dresser and remove a flip knife. The blade glistens as I walk back to her, running the tip down her spine, beneath her bound wrists.

She flinches, but her cheeks flush and her toes curl. The knife rolls down to her ass, gently sliding over her pussy. Before she has a chance to say no, I cut the shirt off of her body, the fabric slicing in two down her spine.

The material falls beneath her, those round tits waiting for me to suck them into my mouth. But that can wait. My hand returns to her hair, snapping her head back before I push her down on the mattress, leaving the knife on the nightstand.

"I've wanted to fuck you since the moment you killed the first man."

My fingers trace her scars, beauty and strength in each one. She doesn't even recoil. She trusts me with them. Knows that there's nothing about her I wouldn't find beautiful.

"Something in me saw you…" I go on. "And I wanted to know more."

I rise on my knees as she stares at me over her shoulder, while I work my pants down, my thick and heavy cock springing free.

"But that wasn't the first time I saw you." I chuckle, remembering the night with Casius. "I was out at a bar, and you were there flipping the guy over for touching you."

"You saw that?" She can barely get the words out, straining as her whimpers increase.

I nod once. "He was a client. A real piece of shit."

I start to work her clit against my palm while she tries to close her thighs around my hand. I don't let her, forcing my knee there, keeping her open for me.

"He was hurting women, and I knew you were gonna be next. I killed him that night. I had planned it before I saw you, but I would've done it for you no matter what. I know that now."

"Adriel!" she cries as I fondle her clit between my fingers.

It's the first time she's called me by that name, and hearing it… My heartbeats still.

"I wanna ruin you," I vow. "I wanna make it so you never

forget me. Not in this world, not even when we're both rotting in the ground." I slam two fingers inside her. "Do you want that? Do you crave this as much as I do?"

"Yes!" she pants, gasping for air.

My hand curls around my cock, and I rub the crown against her wetness. "I'm gonna treat you like my filthy whore." My free hand fists her hair in a tight grip. "'Cause you're my whore, aren't you?"

I hate using those words with her, knowing she was called worse when she was with those animals, but I know it's what she wants. What she needs. She wants to own her power, and I will be right here to give that to her.

"No, please," she whimpers, being my good actress.

If she wants me to force my cock deep inside her, then I will do exactly that, and I will enjoy every *fucking* moment.

"I don't need your permission to fill you up." I press my body over hers, my front to her back, my teeth nipping her lobe. "I get to play with this little cunt anytime I want. Any way I want. I get to taste it, suck it, and fuck it."

Without warning I enter her, hard and fast with one quick motion.

"I own it now," I growl. "It's mine. Just like you."

"Oh, God!" she cries. "Please…no!"

But her perfect behind meets every one of my strokes.

I reach under her and play with her clit, my lips on her neck as I kiss there, teeth sinking into her sweet flesh. "Look how wet you are. So easy for my fat cock to stretch you."

My groans grow deeper just as I slide out and ram all the way back in until her head meets the headboard.

"N-no. Stop, please," she chokes even as her groans get closer together.

Because she doesn't want me to. She wants me to go faster. So

I do, pounding so deep, I become one with her.

"Shit, oh God," she chokes out. "Don't do this. I'll be good. I—I promise." Her voice goes breathless, head bending sideways, eyes meeting mine.

"Mm, you *are* being good. Look how good you take every inch of me. Stretched around it to perfection."

My hand edges up and fastens around her neck, the span of my palm covering her throat. Her pulse raps violently, those eyes boring into mine with lustful need.

Her chest pressed to the mattress and her ass high, she lets me hit deeper, the sound of flesh meeting flesh sending me even further over the edge.

"Oh, God. I'm gonna come. Please don't make me..." Her fingers curl against her back, tightening into fists.

"You keep saying that and I'll make you come all night until you can't talk anymore. Better yet, maybe I should gag you." I slip four fingers into her mouth, and she bites, whimpering around them.

"Fucking hell!" I deepen my strokes, unable to stop the maddening way I want her. "Come for me. Let me feel you drench my cock."

She groans around my fingers, biting down hard, but I only welcome the pain.

"Shit, look at you..."

Her pussy gushes all over the bed, and it's a beautiful thing to know I made her do that.

"Look at you squirting around my dick." I thrust faster as she continues to come, like she can't stop herself.

I increase my pace when I feel she isn't done. She's gonna have another. Jesus Christ. She chokes on her own moan when another orgasm hits her only minutes later. This time, I let her scream, using the fingers that were in her mouth to flick her clit.

"Yesyesyes! F-f-fuck!" She can barely catch her breath, gasping with her cries of pleasure.

I could die right now and feel as though I've served a purpose on this earth: to make this woman come the way she is right now.

I tangle her hair around my wrist and pull my mouth to the shell of her ear. "I'm gonna come inside you, baby bird. Make you take every drop, because everything I am is yours."

"Please." Her eyes beg me for it.

She pushes her ass into me, and my release hits me almost instantly, rushing out with a vengeance. The hardest I've ever come.

"Kayla…" I hiss as I spill into her warmth, never wanting to come down from this high, my balls squeezing until they ache. I give her every drop I own.

My pulse thumps almost out of my throat while I slow my movements until I'm done. Yet slipping out of her is the last thing I want.

So I don't.

Instead, I untie her wrists and curl one arm around her front. Pulling her up against me, my front to her back, I remain buried inside her.

"What are you doing?" she asks breathlessly.

"Making myself at home." I kiss her shoulder. "Now close your eyes and go to sleep. You need to rest."

She yawns and nods. "After what you just did, I think I do."

There's a smile in her voice, and knowing I put it there makes me smile too.

This would be the perfect way to go. Die right here in her arms, 'cause I know death is coming for me soon enough anyway.

I bring the blanket over us and watch her fall asleep, hating that in a short while I'll have to leave her.

But there's something important I need to take care of. Someone else I have to keep safe. And knowing what the Midnight Murderer is capable of, I know he has no lines he wouldn't cross.

Thirty

ADRIEL

"**H**ey! It's you again." Sophia bounces over with her soccer ball, me on the same bench I was on when we saw each other last.

"Hey, kid. You love that ball, don't you?"

"Yeah." She shrugs her shoulder, popping a sassy brow. "What can I say? I'm good at it."

A half-smile falls to my mouth. "How have you been?"

Now that I'm not Chris, I don't know what's going on. Don't know the intel about the traffickers or anything else I was able to get from my so-called brothers.

"Not much! I started a new dance school, and that's a lot of fun. Grandma was supposed to come to my first class when I went with Daddy, but she was very sad and stayed home." She pouts as she settles beside me. "She's been sad a lot lately. Even Grandpa can't cheer her up."

"Why? What happened?"

"I don't know." She flips her hand in the air, twisting her mouth in an adorable way. "She doesn't talk about it, not even to me. Which is weird because she always talks to me. I'm her favorite." She grins.

I chuckle. "Sometimes grownups don't want to make the kids sad, so they keep things to themselves."

"That's stupid. Because I'm already sad since she's sad. Maybe if she told me what's wrong, I could help her."

Such innocence. Such hope in her eyes. That's what childhood should look like. Not the way I had it.

"And Daddy is being ultra-grumpy lately, telling me I can't go out with Mabel a lot, and he won't tell me why either. I know there are bad people in the world. I'm not stupid."

She rolls her eyes, and I laugh to myself. She's something else. A force to be reckoned with.

"He's just trying to keep you safe." I can't believe I'm defending that idiot.

"Yeah, well, that stinks, 'cause I was supposed to go to Jackie's party yesterday and Dad said no. He didn't even tell me why!"

"Well, you're out in the park now with your friends, so that's good."

"Mm-hmm." She narrows her eyes and purses her lips. "Whose side are you on, anyway?"

My laughter falls freely. "On yours. Of course. I'm just helping you see both sides of this situation."

"I don't like both sides. I just like mine." She crosses her arms over her chest. "I should go." She sighs. "Before Mabel catches me and tells Daddy, then I'll be locked away in my room like Rapunzel."

"Before you go, I have something for you."

Her eyes grow with excitement as I reach inside my pocket and retrieve a black jewelry box.

"A present? For me?" Her lashes bat.

"Well, you did say we're friends. So I figured I'd get you something." I open the box, and a small pink heart-shaped ring grabs her attention.

Her gaze is radiant, her mouth widening. "It's so sparkly! Can I put it on?"

"Sure." I remove it and slip it on her middle finger. "It looked like something you'd like."

She stares at it with awe. "This is my favorite present. Thank you, Andy."

"You remembered my name."

"Of course I did, silly. I remember all my friends' names." She starts away from me, but as she goes, she glances back. "My birthday party is coming up soon. Maybe you can come?"

Doubt that's ever gonna happen, but I don't want to ruin the kid's day.

"Maybe. Thanks for the invite."

"You're welcome. I'll see you. Bye!" She gives me a big wave before she skips down the hill and back to her friends, who were too busy running around to notice she was gone for a few minutes.

I watch her for a few more minutes before I head back out, needing to return to Kayla. Her wound is getting better, but the fact that she has it? Fuck, the rage in me can't be stilled.

My desire for vengeance knows no bounds, not when it comes to her.

And when I find the people responsible, they will not be spared. They will know what true evil looks like, and it'll be my face they see last.

KAYLA
FIVE DAYS LATER

Adriel makes us dinner in his kitchen, his bare back the only view I care about. His muscles, tanned and ripped, have me shifting uncomfortably in my seat. It's still a strange feeling to want him as I do after everything I've been through. But I can't deny that what I want and need is him.

A has been nothing but kind and warm and sweet to me in these last few days. With each passing day, we've grown closer while I've been healing, mentally and physically. I didn't realize how much what happened really affected me, not until he made me talk about it. Late nights were spent in each other's arms while he listened and let me cry and held me as I did.

He did let me out of the basement the day after he brought me there. He knew I wasn't running. I no longer wanted to. Being with Adriel is the safest I've ever felt. With him, I know that I have someone who's always watching my back. That the killer won't get me here.

I wish I could stay with him forever, but I know I can't.

With my new bodyguard on my tail, staying here long term is impossible. If Michael finds out he's Chris, he'll kill him. I'd never let that happen.

But I can't go back home either. It's been tainted, the rotting smell of what was done polluting the space.

I don't know where I'll go. Maybe I can spring some of my cash from work for a hotel room on a more long-term basis. Nothing fancy. Something cheap and livable. Then I can look for a place to rent. I can't have Michael or anyone getting me another home. That wouldn't be right.

"You okay, babe?" he asks, that word always bringing a blanket of warmth over my body.

He carries two plates filled with seared tuna on a bed of saffron rice and places one before me. My God, it smells so good.

"I was just thinking about where I'm gonna live," I confess. "Can't go back to my own place for obvious reasons."

Slowly, he lowers into his seat, dark brows drawn down tight. "I thought you'd stay here."

He appears offended. And seeing this big, tough man sulking is so incredibly sexy.

"A…" I rise and head for him, settling on his lap as my arms fall across his shoulders. "You know that is impossible. I have the bodyguard, and after I come back from my amazing vacation…" I grin. "He'll know who you are and will report you to Michael."

The vein in his neck throbs, and those eyes, they seem to burn into mine. "I can handle Michael." He runs the top of his hand across the underside of my jaw. "You'll stay here. With me."

He says it like it's been made into a decree, but I won't risk his life.

"I'm sure you can handle anyone, but I don't want either one of you getting hurt. So please, promise me not to do anything stupid. If I could stay here, you know I would."

His chest puffs out. "I like having you here, and I refuse to let anyone from my family stop me from having what I want." His voice grows low and husky, his knuckles crawling softly down my cheek.

My skin instantly tingles, his touch alone making me want him.

After that night when we had sex, he hasn't attempted it, and neither have I. Though I've wanted to, I've liked getting to know him more than anything. Part of the reason I think I wanted to sleep with him was to see how broken I truly was. Considering I didn't cry or attempt to murder him, I'd say it was a success. And the way he gave it to me was perfect. I owe him so much for that.

Leaning in, I kiss his mouth, and an approving growl rumbles against my lips. Fingers slicing into my hair, he pushes me in deeper, tongue snaking out for mine, sucking it into his heady mouth.

Breathlessly, he fists my hair back, eyes smoldering. "Don't kiss me like that. I have very little self-control thanks to you, and I'm one move away from fucking you again."

"Why haven't you?" My rapid heartbeats beat to a chaotic rhythm.

"Because…" His thumb brushes against my lips, causing my arms to prickle. "I can sense it's not what you really need. So I'm trying, Kayla." His eyes grow glassy. "I'm trying to be the kind of man that you need. I don't do hearts and flowers, but I can do this. I can listen. I can hold you, even when I don't do it quite right. I can braid your hair. Make you dinner and turn you into my dessert. It's what I am, baby bird." He shrugs like any woman in her right mind would ever turn any of it down. "I don't want to just be the man who fucks you, though I did enjoy that, quite a bit."

His one-sided smirk causes flutters to erupt simultaneously with my own tears.

"Hearts are overrated and flowers die. But *you* are priceless." I grab both sides of his face. "Do you even know how amazing you are? Aside from your murderous ways, you literally are the perfect man."

"Say what now?" A disbelieving chuckle rises out of him.

"Come here." I open my arms and hold him to me, pressing my cheek to his shoulder. Staring up at him, I smile. "You have beautiful eyes."

"Nowhere as beautiful as yours." He drops his lips to mine, and now he's the one kissing me, clutching my jaw as he deepens our connection.

And I swear, I could get lost in this feeling. We're both so torn apart, and maybe that's why we found one another. To give each other something to hold on to.

"Are you sure you can't stay here?" he asks, practically pouting, and a bubble of laughter escapes me.

"Are you sulking?" I ask, a teasing tone greeting him. "Because I think you're sulking."

"I don't sulk." He raises his chin, a hint of that smirk returning. "But I—" His throat vibrates as he swallows, something heavy crossing his eyes.

"You what, Adriel?" I love saying his name. It's so beautiful.

"I'm gonna miss having you here." He clenches his jaw. "I've never…I've never missed anyone before."

Oh, my heart. My chest gets all tight with my unruly emotions. How is he this amazing person, and he doesn't even know it?

"I'm gonna miss being here with you every day too." I clasp him to me, my eyes closed as he sighs. "But you're still going to be stalking my every move, I'm sure, so it'll be like I never actually left."

"Uh-huh. You're hilarious." He narrows a playful gaze, huffing out an exhale as he reaches into his pocket, getting his cell out.

"What are you doing?" I question, sitting straighter as he continues to press on his screen multiple times, concentrating as he does.

"Booking you a hotel for a week not far from here. After that, we'll figure it out."

"You're still banking on me moving in with you, aren't you?" I giggle, placing my head back against his shoulder.

"I'm not the kind of man who gives up that easily. You should know that by now."

"Your tenacity is one of the things I love about you."

His body grows instantly rigid, and he stares at me. Like he's about to bolt.

Crap.

Why did I say that? He'll think I meant *love*, love.

The man didn't even know what missing someone felt like, and you're using the L word? Are you insane?

By the time I'm through yelling at myself, my pulse is so loud I feel nauseous.

"I…uh…" I try to explain. "I didn't mean love as in…in *love*. I meant, you know, the other way, like I like that about you." I laugh nervously. "Not that I couldn't love you, because I could, but we barely know each other, and you know…" I think I finally take a breath.

My face heats up while he just stares at me. Seconds pass, and he hasn't said a word.

Okay, this is bad.

"You should see your face right now." He bursts into a fit of laughter, and I almost collapse from relief. "I knew what you meant, Kayla. I'm not an idiot. I know you're not in love with me." Some emotion briefly flickers past his gaze.

Why did he just sound so sad when he said those last few words?

But I don't question it. Instead, I play it off.

"Geez! Maybe don't get all serious when I throw that word around." My heart races so quickly, I try hard to mellow it. "I swear I thought you were gonna race out of here and never see me again."

A crease forms between his brows. He cups my face in both hands and gazes deep into my eyes.

"Is that what you think of me? That I'd just leave you? I'd never do that Kayla. Never." He pins his forehead to mine. "You don't understand what you mean to me. You can't," he whispers. "And that's okay. Because I'm glad you don't. But you? You're my whole world now. If you're gone, so am I." He kisses my temple before he steals my heart away with another searing look. "I don't know what happens between us tomorrow or a year from now, but I'd never willingly leave you. I'm gonna be in your life until my last breath. Whether you want me there or not."

Affection swells in my chest. "That's so romantic."

"Also, I should probably tell you I got us a penthouse suite."

"Us?"

"That's right." He winks. "I'll be staying with you. No way in hell would I let you stay in a hotel all by yourself."

The back of my nose stings. Because I never truly knew what happiness felt like until this very moment.

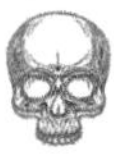

The following day, I'm with Elsie and Jade out to grab lunch. They have been worried about me since I left on my very peaceful lakeside trip. I've managed to calm them. I know they worry I could spiral, especially since I've missed the last few appointments with Doctor Collins. But after that incident at my party, then the attack, I haven't felt comfortable enough to return. I will have to face him later today and tell him I decided to switch to a new therapist.

I was going to tell Jade my concerns, but what do I have to go on? My gut feeling? What do I even say? *"He was being kinda weird, and I don't know, something felt off."* Wouldn't be right to get him fired over something that is probably nothing. Jade did say she invited him to my party, so it's not like he was there at random.

I will have to figure out what to tell them once I move to the hotel, though. They're gonna find out from Terrence. I'll need a reason why I'm moving. Maybe I can say someone broke in? But what if Terrence gets fired because of that? Michael will blame him for not doing his job. I have to think of something believable.

"You haven't touched your burger." Elsie looks at me, picking up hers, and takes a bite. "It's so damn good. The bacon is cooked perfectly on mine."

Jade picks at her salad, stuffing a piece of grilled chicken into her mouth. "Tell us more about that lake house. How was it? It was so out of the blue."

"It was relaxing." My mouth thins. "I needed that."

"Well, we're happy that you took time for yourself," Jade says.

I nod, forcing myself to eat. I haven't had much of an appetite since I left Adriel's. Everywhere I turn, I wonder if the killer is there in the shadows, watching me. Wonder if they'll find me and end what they started. Adriel wasn't able to get to me then. What if he'll be too late again?

"There's something I wanted to tell you guys." I take the glass of water to my mouth and pull a few sips.

"What is it?" Jade places a palm to the top of my hand.

"I'm gonna be staying at a hotel for a bit. I—"

"What?" Elsie straightens her spine. "Did something happen?"

"I don't know. With everything going on, I don't feel safe at my place. I'm alone there. I think it would be better to be with a lot of people around."

"So why don't you stay with us?" Elsie's brows furrow with concern. "Why would you go somewhere else? We have plenty of space."

"That's sweet of you guys, truly," I tell her. "But you have done enough for me. I need to do this on my own. I can't depend on everyone else. I have to learn how to handle things on my own."

Elsie twists her mouth in disapproval, but doesn't say anything.

Jade squeezes my fingers before she returns her hand to the table. "I think she's right, Elsie. This is good for her. She knows what she needs."

"Fine. But I'm not happy about it." She pouts before she grins at me. "It would've been fun to have you around again."

"I can always come over for a slumber party."

I was only half-joking, but Elsie's face lights up.

"Like the kind we used to have in high school? My God, those were fun, weren't they?" Her eyes build with moisture.

"Yeah…" Jade's gaze turns distant. "We had the best times together."

"Things are so different now," I say. "So much has changed."

"Maybe some things shouldn't." Elsie's attention bounces between the two of us, grabbing both our hands from across the table. "Some things are worth holding on to."

"We're lucky, you know." Jade glances at Elsie, then at me. "For all the things they broke, they never broke this." She lifts our hands off the table a fraction. "This will never change."

But it could.

If they find out what I've become, they may never want me in their lives again.

And that will only kill me.

Thirty-One

KAYLA

Nerves skitter in my gut as I clutch the door handle of Dr. Collins's office. We have to break up today, and it makes me sad because I did like him. But after that night at my birthday party, I can't shake off the unease.

Hopefully, he'll understand. Blowing a quick breath, I open the door before I change my mind.

"Hello there." He looks up from his yellow pad, his glasses perched low on his nose.

Suddenly, the nerves return, and I bite my upper lip as a smile trembles out of me.

"Please have a seat, Ms. Jenkins." He straightens his spine as he takes me in. "I was beginning to worry. You have cancelled our last few sessions."

"Yeah, uh…" I lower onto the brown leather. "I had tests and stuff. Had no time."

He nods. "I understand the pressures of school, but you must put your mental health first or else you will fall back to your old habits."

My heart beats faster. "Right, yes."

"How are you doing otherwise? Have the nightmares been recurring? This madman is still on the loose. I can't believe they're not able to catch him yet."

"The nightmares have been better."

I ignore the part about the killer. It's the last thing I want to think about, not after everything…

"Well, that is great. The medication is working, then."

"Yes."

Or maybe the murders are. It's been cathartic. Killing those men. Sometimes I forget they're not the men from before, from my past. To me, though, they're all the same. Same soul, different face. And in the end, your soul is all that matters.

"There is something I wanted to talk about," I tell him.

And there goes my pulse, ricocheting in my throat.

"Of course." Concern fits his thick gray brows. "What is it?"

"This is a bit uncomfortable for me, but I was thinking…"

"Yes?"

"I was thinking of switching therapists."

"Oh?" He narrows a gaze. "Any particular reason?"

"I think you may have been right. It's difficult for me to talk about what I went through with a man. It'd be easier with a woman, you know?" I play with the hem of my t-shirt, hoping he buys it.

His mouth thins. "Of course. I understand. I can recommend someone within the center, unless you're looking to go outside of it."

"No, I'm going to stay in the center, and I already do have someone in mind."

Complete bullshit, because I have no clue. There are numerous therapists here, and they're all free.

"That's wonderful." He grins. "The most important thing is for you to get the help that you need. I'm glad you felt comfortable enough to talk to me about it. I do wish you all the luck in the world, Kayla. You have come so far. You're doing great."

I nod with a tight smile. It almost makes me feel guilty for leaving because right now he seems just like the man he always was.

"We can cut this session short if you'd like."

"Yes. That would be great. I have to study before my classes later."

"Well, it was nice knowing you, Ms. Jenkins. I hope you have a wonderful rest of your day." He nods as I get to my feet and head for the door.

ADRIEL

While Kayla is meeting with her therapist, I scan the police files online in my basement. Hoping to find some new piece of evidence on the Midnight Murderer, I look through everything the cops have.

I never expected there to be two killers. One was taller. That's all I was able to get from the recording the night they hurt Kayla. Their faces were shrouded in ghost face masks. Nothing to go on at all.

I need to find them before they come for her again.

My phone vibrates on my desk, and when I stare down at it, I see Michael's name.

Shit. I've been avoiding him. He's gonna have questions,

especially about the whole my-parents-being-dead thing. But when I was Chris and told Kayla my parents were dead, I wasn't thinking it would come back to bite me.

My parents *are* dead. Both of them. They may as well be. But now, this could fuck me. I have to figure out what the hell to say to him.

Slipping the voice changer into my mouth, I answer the call. "Hello?"

"I've been calling for days. Why haven't you answered?" The tight flare of his quiet rage fills my ears.

"My mother's hospital has poor reception. I apologize. I've been here night and day."

"Your mother not doing well?"

"She's not. She's on her last breath. Any day now."

"I'm sorry." He doesn't sound like he gives a shit. "But we need you back. Things with the traffickers have taken a turn. Dom Cavaleri and his brothers have captured a few who have given up some of the smaller rings around the country, and it's all hands on deck. I need you here. You're one of the best I have."

Fuck!

I thought I had more time. But I can't lose this fucking job. I need to stay on top of this family.

"I get it. Let me see if one of my brothers can stay with her. Can I let you know tonight?"

"Sure. I'll be waiting. Take care." He hangs up, while I try to figure out what the hell to do.

Returning to the computer screen before me, I hit a few buttons, seeing that Kayla is back at the hotel. I have to get out of here. The less she's alone, the better.

"What the hell do you mean, you're going to be Chris again?!" She gawks. "You can't do that! Michael is gonna kill you!"

"No, he won't." I grab her hips and fit her on top of my lap where she belongs.

Her eyes are two pillars of rage.

My smirk widens, deepening with her concern. "You worried about me, baby bird?"

"Yes, you idiot! I am! I can't lose you, do you understand that?" Her brows weave tight. "If you go back, he'll kill you. Michael is dangerous."

"Babe, so am I. And did I mention how sexy it is when you worry about me?"

"You know what's not sexy?" She narrows her gaze. "Your death."

"Kayla." I palm her cheek and stroke my thumb over the corner of her mouth. "You think I'd go unprepared? I'm always ready for war."

"Not much of an army when you're alone."

"I don't need one when I have the kinds of weapons I do."

She shakes her head. "Why are you so infuriating?"

"I don't have a choice. I have to go. If he was telling the truth about the traffickers, I want to do everything to help. It's one thing I agree with the bastard on. But if it's a trap and they're trying to get me, then I'll be ready."

I grab the back of her head and lower my forehead to hers.

"I have something to live for now," I whisper. "I have you. And nothing and no one will take me away from you. I swear it."

"You don't know that," she breathes, her lips softly kissing mine. "You're not invincible."

"Sometimes with you, it feels like I am."

"Adriel…" She sighs and smashes her lips to mine, kissing me deeper.

And with a growl, I lift her off the chair and throw her onto the bed. "I need you."

With her eyes boring into mine, she says, "Then need me."

And I get lost inside her for hours, wishing we could stay this way forever.

thirty-two

KAYLA

I can't believe he wants to come back as Chris. It's the worst idea known to man, but he's stubborn as hell and changing his mind was impossible. He's gonna do whatever he wants, and I'll be there paying for the consequences.

My gut churns at the thought of Michael killing him. He won't care that they're brothers. Adriel will be considered the enemy. His deceit alone will make him a target, but when Michael finds out what he did to Fernanda and the bomb he set to Raph's car, he'll annihilate him.

It doesn't matter how many weapons A brings. He'll be all alone with no one fighting beside him. If I could, I would. Maybe that makes me a horrible friend to Elsie, but he means everything to me. I can't allow him to die.

Maybe I can talk to Elsie. If she knew everything, she wouldn't want this either. She wouldn't want Michael hurt.

Shaking my head in frustration, I enter the lecture hall, finding my seat beside Prince. He grins, inclining his head in greeting.

"Hey. Just the girl I wanted to see."

"Oh, yeah?" I reach inside my backpack and retrieve my laptop. "Why's that?"

"Well, me and my friend Tim, the one you met that night, we're hitting up a bar tonight. A local rock band is playing, and we wanted to invite you girls."

"You mean you want Eriu there." I snicker.

"That obvious?"

I laugh. "Yeah. You might as well be blushing."

"Well, she's cute. Put in a good word for me, will you?"

"I'll see what I can do. But just so you know, she has a crazy older sister, so if you hurt her, she will kill you."

He chuckles.

I give him a deadpan stare. "I'm not kidding."

His face tightens. "Noted. But still…" He's back to grinning. "I want a shot. She may be worth dying for."

I shake my head just as the professor walks in.

"Alright, class," he calls for attention while I start my laptop.

Prince has no idea who he's interested in. Dating the youngest daughter of the Mob is definitely not something to be taken lightly. Not that I can warn him. But Iseult would have his balls. I'd be more afraid of her than Eriu's three older brothers.

Once the lesson begins, I focus on it, trying to put everything else out of mind. Acing all my classes is a priority to me. I want to make the honor roll this semester like the last one, and I know I can. My grades have been exceptional so far, and I won't allow anything to get in the way of that.

As I type more of what the professor is saying, my cell vibrates in my pocket. I ignore it. Whoever it is can wait. But it goes on again and again, even as I shut it off with the press of a button.

Frustrated, I remove it when the phone vibrates for the fourth time, and once I see Cammie's name, my body grows ice cold. Four missed calls. All from her. Something is wrong. She hurt herself. She must've.

Gathering my belongings, I start to get up.

"What happened?" Prince asks.

"An emergency. I've gotta go. Please take good notes."

"Yeah, sure. Let me know if you're okay." His expression grows with concern as I nod and hurry off.

Once I'm out the door, I call her back. "Cammie?"

Silence.

Except the heavy breathing. A man's breathing.

And I know exactly who it is.

Chills quake across my skin, and panic tightens my throat. "Hello? Who's there?"

The man's cold laughter pummels through my bones.

"Don't you fucking touch her!" I rush for my car. "Tell me where you are! Tell me what you want."

It's then I hear her crying.

Oh, God! What is he doing to her?

I start the engine, not sure where to go.

Fuck!

"Just tell me where you are! You can have me instead! Just let her go!"

When she sobs, pain lodges in my throat. He's gonna kill her. No...

"You'll get a text," he says. "Come alone."

The phone goes dead.

My hands tremble, and the cell slips from my fingers, landing right against my feet just as a beep informs me of an unread message.

Panting, I grab it and read the text.

CAMMIE

Parking lot. Your strip club.

Dropping the phone in the cup holder, I rush down the street, hoping I can get to her in time. Hoping I'm not too late.

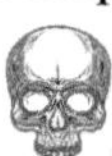

When I arrive at the club, there are only a couple of cars there. No one but management is here during daylight hours, and I doubt they were checking the lot for suspicious activity. They're usually in the basement of the club, going through finances or whatever else they have to do.

As I get out of my car, I don't see anyone. My whole body shivers.

I already texted A, telling him what's going on. He told me to wait for him, but I couldn't risk something happening to her while I did.

My legs are weak, my footfalls drudging across the concrete as I glance all around me, wondering where the killer is. Where Cammie is. Whoever hurt her could be hiding. Unless he took her already.

No. I can't be too late.

I keep walking toward the large dumpster where Ivy was once attacked. And at first, I don't see Cammie. But once I round the corner, my shaky hand cups my mouth. Cammie lies facedown, ankles and wrists tied with zip ties, her mouth gagged.

"Oh, God!" I drop to my knees and lift her off the ground while simultaneously slipping off my jacket to put around her back.

Her chin tremors, and she starts to weep as I pull down the

black material he tied her mouth with. I don't know how to get these damn ties off of her!

"Who did this to you? Did you see him? Is he hiding?" My heart races, needing answers.

"P-p-please," she chokes out. "Please, don't make me. Please!"

She buries her face in my shoulder, cotton soaking up the tears.

"It's okay." I release a shallow sigh, stroking her back, and as I do, I feel something wet on my stomach.

What the hell? I push her back a little, catching the blood seeping into my shirt from her stomach, her pink t-shirt setting with a dark red stain.

"You're bleeding!" I gasp for air, starting to remove my shirt so I can use it to put pressure on the wound. "He cut you?"

"It's a star," A's voice rings behind me, and as our eyes connect, we both know who did it.

He removes his own shirt and hands it to me.

"I f-f-fought him off." Tears leak down Cammie's cheeks. "Then he ran when he heard a car. I—I think?" Her voice trembles, and I fight like hell not to cry.

"You did good." A nods, removing a pocketknife as he kneels and cuts the zip ties off. "We have to get her to a doctor."

Her eyes widen. "No! Please. I—I can't go. I don't want to. I don't like hospitals."

"Can you do something about the wound?" I ask him, pressing his shirt into her wound.

I don't want to put more stress on her. It doesn't appear she has injuries anywhere else. We can take care of this.

"Okay. We'll take her to the hotel."

He brings his attention to Cammie. "Can you walk?"

She nods, and we help her to her feet while I continue to press the t-shirt around her midsection.

"I'll take her to the penthouse," he tells me. "And you drive your car. We stay together, okay? I will follow you."

"Okay, let's go. But I think you're gonna need another shirt," I tell him with a faint smile.

"Got a few in the car."

He safely places Cammie in the front and secures the seat belt around her while I rush toward my vehicle.

Together, we head back to our temporary home, hoping Cammie has a lead for us to go on.

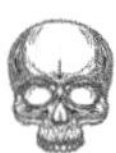

Once we're in the hotel and Cammie has been bandaged and given pain meds, we wait for her to finish the tea I made her.

I don't want to push her to talk, but we have to know if she saw anything. It could mean life or death. He's gonna be hungry for another kill. I can't let that happen.

"Cammie?"

She looks up, her eyes streaked with red.

"Please, you have to tell us."

Fear clings to her pupils as her gaze jumps to A.

"He's safe," I tell her, knowing exactly what she's thinking. "He's a friend. He helped me when…"

I have to tell her. She has to know that I too was attacked by the killer. It'll make her feel like she can open up to us.

"You what?" She places her cup down.

"It's better if I show you."

A places his hand on top of mine and gives it a reassuring squeeze. As I look back at him, my heart warms. Those green eyes feel like safety and home for once since my world was stolen.

Getting up slowly, I lift my shirt and show her the star on my abdomen, no longer needing to be bandaged, but raw and angry.

"Wh-what? I—I don't understand. Why do you have that? Who did that to us?"

Tightening my mouth, I sit back down and take her hand in mine. "There's something you need to know. The murderer from the news, the one killing all those women, he brands them with a star on their stomach."

Her eyes pop. "Oh my God…"

I nod. "When I was attacked recently, there were two of them. They drugged me and did that. Andy found me."

I give her the name A uses for the ones he doesn't trust, though she could very well identify him as Chris. But we can cross that bridge when we get there.

"So…so the person who came after me was the killer? Oh my God. I'm gonna be sick." She clutches her stomach. "Ow, shit."

I grimace. "You okay?"

"It hurts like hell."

"I'm sorry." My face falls.

"Was there only one person you saw?" A asks her.

"Yeah, I didn't see two people."

"I wonder if they both do it and take turns," he muses.

That does sound plausible. It'd make so much sense.

Cammie grabs my hand, hers trembling as she leans into my ear.

"Are you sure we can trust him?" she whispers.

"Yes, I swear," I breathe.

She perches back, and fresh tears pool in her eyes. "I…" Her attention jumps between us. "I saw him. Just as I kicked him, I… I hit his mask and I s-saw him. I know who it was."

This is it.

My adrenaline kicks in. This is how we get him.

"Who was it, Cammie?" A's tone grows with urgency. "Who's the killer?"

Thirty-Three

KAYLA

"I—I don't know if I can tell you," Cammie whimpers, clutching my hand so tight, it feels like my bones are going to shatter. "What if he—"

"We promise to protect you," I attempt to convince her. "Anything you say will be kept between us."

"You don't understand," she cries. "If I tell you, he'll know it was me, and he'll come after me!"

"No, he won't." A stares down at her. "We can keep you safe. Believe me."

"Come on, Cammie. You can do this." I peer at her as tears swim in her eyes.

I can just imagine how afraid she is. Giving up the one who hurt you, someone dangerous, someone still out there, is terrifying. But she has to do this. We have to know who it was so we can torture him. Then we can find out who his accomplice is and destroy them both.

"I couldn't believe it." She drags in a heaving breath, unable to stop her hands from shaking. "He was so nice to me. He was helping me. How? How could he?"

"Tell me." I search her gaze, fearing her next few words even when I ache to hear them. "Who was it?"

"It's…it's… It's Doctor Collins."

An icy shiver races through my entire body.

No. It can't be.

My chest rises and falls with pummeling exhales. "Are…are you sure?"

How can he be the one doing all of this? How? It makes no sense! Or maybe it does, and I don't want to see it.

"It was him, and he knows I saw him, Kayla. He knows!" She wraps her arms around herself.

A is already on his phone. "I'm going to his place. You two stay here."

"Wait! What if he knows you're coming?" Concern tramples through me. "He knows you're looking for him."

"I'll be fine." He nods sternly. "Call Jade. Find out his work schedule. Then let me know. I want to see what I can find at his place. And if he's there, I'll end him." He grabs the back of my neck. "I'll be back, I promise."

"You better," I whisper. "Don't you dare die."

"Never, babe." He drops his lips to my forehead before he heads out the door, and I can't help but worry about him even as my own rage finally registers.

The man who's been pretending to help me all this time has been the one who hurt me, hurt so many. But he won't do it anymore. Now that we know, his time will come.

I retrieve my phone and quickly call Jade. She answers

immediately.

"Kayla, hey!"

"Jade, listen, can you check if Dr. Collins is at the office?"

"Why? What happened?"

"Just please check now. It's important."

"He actually left early. Said he had an emergency. Should be back tomorrow. What happened? Talk to me."

"I can't say anything right now, but I promise I will. If you see him, don't let him leave. Make security keep him in the office."

"Kayla, you're really scaring me."

"I wish I could tell you, but I can't right now."

Then I hang up and tend to Cammie, who's even more shaken up than she already was.

ADRIEL

As soon as I arrive at the good doctor's place, I know instantly he isn't here. But the evidence is. He didn't do much to hide it; his basement was covered with it. Newspaper clippings of the dead girls, every instance the killer was mentioned he attached to the wall, like a shrine to himself.

But the most damning evidence was the photos. All the girls who have been killed were in a photo album he kept in his desk. A snapshot of his brutality. And on the last page was Kayla, Cammie's photo not yet entered into his memory book.

My muscles and veins strain against my skin as I clutch her photo in my fist while I take snapshots of the wall, the album already in my trunk.

Now all I have to do is find him. Tracking his phone should be easy enough. Once I get to my house, I will do just that.

Kayla texted me, letting me know she spoke to Jade, but didn't tell her anything. She didn't want Jade telling Elsie or anyone else. That would mean my brothers would be here with an army of people, discovering that Chris is in fact not with his dying mother after all.

But tomorrow, I'll have to face them. No choice in the matter. Maybe I'll plant some evidence about the doctor so they can look for him too. The more eyes, the better. I can't do it alone. He needs to be stopped before he comes after Kayla again to finish what he started.

But I'll never let that happen. I failed her once. I won't do it again.

Thirty-Four

ADRIEL

I head to meet Michael at Gio's house the following day. Checking on Kayla's location, I'm assured she's in class with that bodyguard on her tail. Hopefully she's safe there until I'm done with this bullshit with my brothers.

I've yet to speak to my mother, not knowing if she opened her mouth to them about our little reunion. But I don't think she's told them yet. Maybe she never will. If it's because her guilt's eating at her, then I'm glad. I hope it always does. I hope she suffers every day knowing her sins grew a monster. And that monster is me.

Arriving at a gated community, I park in the three-car driveway before I'm greeted by two men I recognize.

"They're inside." One tilts his head toward the door.

I nod before I open it, finding a few others on Michael's payroll. As soon as they see me, they greet me.

"How you doin', Chris?" He gives me a sharp look. "How's

the mother?"

"Not well."

"Shit, man." He frowns. "Sorry. Lost mine last year. I get it."

"Thanks. Where's Michael?"

"They're in the den." He points in that direction.

"Why aren't you guys there?"

"We're not on the intel for this assignment." He shrugs. "Not high enough on the food chain."

I snicker as I walk past, anticipation buzzing through my marrow. If my brothers are here to kill me, there are enough men here to ensure I don't escape alive.

Rounding the corner, I head for the wide foyer, a few other men greeting me before I continue further past the large dining area, hushed voices coming through.

"We will get it done," Gio says, then everyone goes quiet.

"Chris, that you?" Michael asks, and my hand immediately goes to the nine in my waistband.

"Yeah. Sorry if I'm late," I say as soon as I enter, seeing my three brothers there plus a few others I recognize.

"Sit," Michael instructs.

"I prefer to stand." I grip the back of the chair with on hand, keeping the other close to my waist.

This is a fucking ambush. I can feel it.

"So…" Michael starts. "A few of the Cavaleris have taken hold of a couple of men. They're being interrogated. We've also located more trafficking rings overseas connecting to whoever is running the show in Boston. We'll be setting up teams to head to those locations. I'm putting you three in charge of those teams."

He looks to the two other men, then to me, his eyes cast tightly.

"What do you think about that?" His question is directed at me.

"Whatever you need."

"What I need is…" He paces closer. "Men I can trust." His eyes are expressionless. "Think I can trust you?"

"Of course you can." My tone is steady. My pulse too. Not a shred of evidence that I'm anything but a loyal little puppet in his army.

He drags in a long, deep inhale. "Where were you, Chris? Were you really with your mother?"

"I told you I was." I stay rooted. "You saw photos. What is this about?"

He clenches his hand, and Raph clasps Michael on the shoulder as he passes by. Now Raph's the one slowly marching up toward me. His eyes search mine, like he's trying to find something that isn't there.

"Who are you?" he asks.

And I know for certain.

They know who I am.

While he's distracted with me, I reach a hand inside my pants pocket, quietly finding the keychain inside.

My forefinger on the button, I wait for the right moment. The instant they know that this will either end in their deaths or mine.

"I'm Chris." I chuckle dryly. "I don't know what the fuck is going on here, but if you no longer want me here, just say the word."

"Who are you?" Gio asks this time, his teeth clenching as he gets to his feet, the other two men slipping out the door.

Instead of denying it, a slow-growing grin curls up the ends of my mouth. "Why don't you ask me the real question? You know you want to."

Michael's gaze narrows; Raph's eyes grow a fraction.

"Are you…" Raph's mouth starts to move, but no sound comes out. There's a tightness in his features that wasn't there before.

Michael carves away the distance, staring me down with an icy gleam once he nears. A flush creeps up his neck as the tension grows thick between us.

"Are you A?" Glaring anger pours from his eyes. "Are you our brother?"

An infinitesimal twitch of my lips has his upper lip curling.

"Fuck yeah, I am," I laugh just as my finger presses a button and everything goes BOOM.

Smoke and chaos surround us as I rush out of the room, removing both of my weapons, the one in my waistband and the other in my ankle. I have another two strapped to me and more bombs around their property.

This one took out one side of Gio's house. Oops. It was a nice house.

"You're fucking dead!" Michael roars. "I never liked killing a brother. But you? I'll gladly take out, especially after the bomb you put in Raph's car. We know it was you."

"Sure fucking was."

My gloating chuckling has him roaring in rage.

"Never had a brother!" I shout over from behind the bar. "Not a mother either. She tell you what I did to her?"

Raph growls this time. "You fucking hurt our mother?"

Guess Mommy really did keep her mouth shut.

Pop. Pop.

Two bullets whiz past my right.

"I would've killed her! She's lucky all she got was the little scratch my knife left on her throat."

"You're fucking dead!" Michael snaps. "When I'm through with you, there'll be nothing left to recognize."

"You keep saying that, but I'm here alone and managed to blow half of Gio's house away. So let's see you try, *brother.*"

"Don't you call me that!" He shoots at me through the bar while I slide my hand out straight ahead and fire back at him. I can tell where he is from the direction of his voice.

"You try anything else…" I warn. "And I blow your house too."

"You son of a bitch! My fucking daughter lives in that house."

"Yes, my lovely niece." My laughter echoes. "Sweet little girl. What a great soccer player too. Definitely didn't get it from you."

"You ever come near her, and I'll take everything from you!" His beastly sound reverberates through the space, and he bellows as he rushes toward me.

I'm ready for him. Ready to take him on. Because I won't die today.

Never had anything worth losing.

Except now. Except her.

My baby bird.

I hurry to my feet and open my arms with a cold, calculating grin. "Let's see what you've got."

He guns for me, rushing forward while I do the same.

I've been waiting for this. If I can kill one of her sons, one of the ones that actually matter, maybe that'll hurt. Maybe for once, she'll know what true agony feels like.

Michael swings a hit into my jaw, and that's all it takes for the demons to come out. I kick him in the gut while the other two brothers point their weapons at me, waiting, hoping. But at the same time, they want to give him this chance to hurt me or kill me.

Don't they realize? I'm already dead.

This is child's play.

Laughter spits from my lungs while I lick the blood from my own mouth, unsure if it's his or mine. Either way, it's victory. I got to him. I got to all of them.

They must know what a fool I've made of them.

"Do you know how fun it's been to pretend to tolerate you while I hate you?"

He kicks me hard in the thigh.

"Knowing that you had no idea who I really was." A blow hits him right in his scar. "Your enemy right under your nose."

He groans and tries to flip me over, using his foot against my ankle, but he's unsuccessful.

"Let's just kill him already!" Gio adds.

"Of course you'd want it the easy way." I laugh, catching his tight, enraged glare.

"Fuck off, you piece of shit!" he thunders. "You've hated us for nothing! We've done nothing."

I strike my foot into Michael's ribs, and when he goes down, I force myself on top of him, smashing the butt of the nine into his nose. Blood gushes out while I use my fist next.

When Raph tries to get to Michael, I point the gun at him. "No, don't you dare. You come closer, and I blow him away. Can you live with that?"

He flays me with a thunderous look. "You're angry." His tone is even as he raises his hands in the air. "How about we all just talk? Maybe we can figure this out."

"Fuck you all! I'll nev—"

A bullet rings out, and we all turn to face a mob of angry fucking women. Iseult's with her own gun pointing at the ceiling, her bright red hair like flames across her shoulders.

"Are you *fucking* kidding me?!" she snaps. "A bunch of grown-ass men behaving like children! What the hell are you doing?" Her body visibly shakes with rage. "Other than destroying my goddamn house!"

Shit, even I'm a little afraid of her.

It's then I see Kayla move from behind her, tears in her eyes.

Baby bird. I'm sorry.

Elsie's holding her around her shoulders, while Nicolette is staring at Raph, crying against my mother. That woman, though… She stares at me. And there's no anger there, just sadness.

Iseult bravely walks up to Raph and Gio. There's a tightness to her face, her eyes flashing.

"Give me your weapons!" She holds out her palm. "Now!"

Gio exhales a quick breath, giving her a hard stare.

"Did I stutter, husband? Now! You too, Raph!"

"Yes, ma'am," Raph mutters as they both hand her the weapons.

She struts off to Michael and me. He's still beneath me, both of us covered in blood. It's all over my hands. His face. Our clothes.

"You too!" Her cold tone matches the icicles that now adorn her eyes.

I swear if I look hard enough, they're about to shoot out of those green eyes and kill us both. My half sister is fucking insane. I have something in common with one of them, it seems.

I grin.

"What's so goddamn funny?" Her stormy gaze hits me without blinking.

"Nothing," I chuckle.

"Just do what she says, man," Gio grumbles. "Better not to fight it."

I tip up my chin and hand her the weapon. She snatches it, then takes the one from Michael.

"Great!" Her lips thin. "Now, you're gonna talk it out. And I swear if I hear anyone killing each other, I'm gonna kill you all. 'Kay? Bye." She waves her fingers in a feigned goodbye and gives us her back. "Come on, ladies. Let the children learn how to use their words."

"I have nothing to say to this asshole," Michael throws out.

"Well, sweetheart…" Elsie eyes him with disappointment. "You're just gonna have to figure it out while us girls are gonna be right outside this room."

She comes to stand before us, and I finally get off him.

"Because this whole putting-yourself-at-risk-and-being-reckless thing is not gonna work for me." She chokes up. "Or Sophia."

"You have no idea what he's done." Michael jumps to his feet and takes her hand, but she shakes it off.

His nostrils flare.

"I'm aware of everything. We all are." She peers behind her at the women. "Your mother told us. None of us are happy about any of it. But trying to kill each other is not gonna help anyone. So talk! Understand each other! Because this is the breaking point. You either make up…" She looks up at me before staring back at him. "Or you all stay the hell away from each other."

"Gladly," I tell her. "I have nothing to say to anyone here."

I head for Kayla. The only person I need. I take her hand in mine and kiss the top of it.

Giving my mother a lethal look, I say, "I'm done with you. You can all rot in hell! I have no family. I never did!"

"Good," Michael snickers. "We didn't want you anyway."

Something in my chest tightens, but I brush it off.

"Michael!" Mother Dearest reprimands. "Don't say that!"

"Come on, babe, let's go." I drag Kayla out of there while she gazes back at Elsie.

"I'll call you," Elsie tells her.

"I love you," she says to her friend as we exit the room.

Need to get the fuck out of here.

Just because Kayla is friends with Elsie doesn't mean I need to be around my brothers. I'll skip all the family events. My lips curl.

Wouldn't wanna get trigger-happy.
    Time for me to move on.
    I feel better anyway.
    Even if my mother still breathes.
    I have Kayla.
    That's all I'll ever need from now on.

KAYLA
THREE DAYS LATER

The last few days have been quiet. As quiet as a life like ours can be. I've been in his arms while he's been in mine. We've left the hotel, and I've been staying in his house. Not officially moved in, but kinda getting there.

He wants me to live with him, but I don't know if I'm ready to let go of my own place. Baby steps is where we are, and he's okay with that.

Though he may not say it, I know he needs me after what transpired with his brothers.

It was exactly what I was afraid of. Them finding out and trying to kill him. So when he went to them, I called Elsie and told her everything. It was one way I could ensure that he'd be safe.

Elsie was with Fernanda at the time, who told her everything, and together, they called Iseult. Of course, once Nicolette found out Raph was in the middle, she came too.

We figured if we all showed up, they wouldn't want to put us in harm's way. The only thing we worried about was whether we were too late. But luckily, we weren't. Other than superficial wounds, they were all alive. With Iseult there, we knew she'd make them stop. She has that effect on people.

"Does your nose still hurt?" I ask, cupping his face while I lie on his chest, his fingers stroking up my bare spine.

"You need to stop worrying about me so much, little wolf. I've never been better." His eyes glaze over as he raises his head and kisses the top of mine.

"You should talk about what happened. You need to talk to someone."

"I'm fine." His fingers continue to brush sensually.

"It helps to get it all out. To say how you feel without guilt."

"Pretty sure if I told a shrink what I'm thinking, they'd have me arrested."

I let out an exacerbated sigh. Propping myself on one elbow, I turn to him, chin on his chest. "You have to heal from this. You never got to talk to your brothers or your parents about what happened to you. Really talk. It will eat at you. Please, A. Do it for me. Talk to them."

He shakes his head and stares at the ceiling. "Nothing good will come of it. It's over now. I just have to forget them."

My lips meet his ribs. "I'm afraid you'll never get over it."

He doesn't say anything, just continues to stare at the ceiling while my heart simply breaks. He deserves to heal. To tell his side.

He's been hurt so badly. His scars are deep. None of them truly understand it. Maybe they never will, but he has to try.

"Do you have work tonight?"

He clearly wants to change the subject, so I let him. Pushing will do nothing but make him close down. He needs to feel like he's in charge of this.

"Yeah." I drop my cheek against his chest. "But I have to quit tonight." My gaze wanders off, hating that I have to. "I can't possibly work there with this scar on my stomach. It's enough that I covered the ones on my back with the mesh. I can't do that with my abdomen."

He sits up, curling his arm around me as he pulls me close. "I'm sorry, babe."

I shrug. "I don't even know if it's the right thing anymore." A rush of a breath leaves me. "I used to like it because it allowed me to have this sense of control, you know?" I smile stiffly. "But now, with you, I have that. I'm finally in control."

He picks up my hand and kisses my knuckles. "I'll always give you what you need. Anytime you need it."

"Well, don't sound too disappointed about me not stripping anymore."

He chuckles, then hisses. "Ow, fuck me."

His hand curves around his nose. He can't laugh without feeling pain these days.

"That's what you get." I pop a brow.

The back of his hand caresses down my cheek, and he gives me a long look. "You know I'd never tell you what to do. It's your body. But I'd be lying if I didn't say that I'm happy you won't be stripping anymore."

"Oh, yeah?" I grin. "Why's that?" My finger runs down his abs, lower, stroking his Adonis belt, causing him to growl low in his chest.

"'Cause now that you're mine…" He grabs my jaw and steals a sordid gaze. "I don't want anyone else to see what belongs to me."

A moan escapes me as he flips me beneath him and those lips

meet mine in a passionate exchange.

Breathlessly, he captures my eyes with his as he lifts one leg and throws it over his shoulder, the other wrapped around his hip, my foot resting on his back.

"I need to fuck you slow." He slips the crown of his cock inside me while my fingernails dig into his bicep. "I need to savor you until you're all I know."

And with one thrust, he enters me.

"Oh, God," I cry as he plunders in and out, lips nipping my neck, the fingers of his other hand lightly pinching my nipple.

"Adriel…" I whisper and groan as he continues to unwrap every piece of my soul.

The more his eyes bore into mine, the stronger the connection between us. I crave it, feel it raid my heart and fill my veins. He's my whole universe.

Lifting my other leg, he throws it over his other shoulder and rises on his knees. Eyes heavy-lidded, he increases his pace, staring down at where we meet.

At the sight of him looking there, the veins of his arms rippling, my eyes roll back.

"I'm gonna come…" I touch myself there, fingers circling my clit as he watches me.

"Fuck, you're so beautiful. I need a taste of you."

Before I can catch hold of my release, his mouth is on me as he sucks and licks and flicks until I'm lost to oblivion. Lost to him and us and the things we create together.

There's no reason to hide anymore. We're free. We can be together. No one will stop us.

"A!" I scream out as an orgasm springs to life, his tongue inside me now, feeling me ripple and tighten.

"Mm…" He engulfs my clit in his warm, seductive mouth until

I slowly climb down.

Those lips trail kisses on the insides of both my thighs before they climb up my body until he smashes his mouth to mine. His fingers curl around my throat as he rams his thick cock back inside, my body jolting, craving every inch.

The power of his large frame over mine, the way he gives me just enough air to breathe while our eyes are locked… I never imagined it could ever be this way—pain and pleasure creating something beautiful.

When I come this time, he joins me, his warmth shooting through my limbs.

Owning me.

And I've never liked being owned so much in my life.

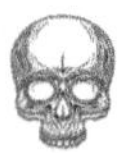

Arriving at the club, I slowly get out, my nerves getting to me. I can't believe I'll never work here again.

I like the women. The friends I've made. But sometimes growing as a person means letting things go, and I'm ready to let this part of myself go.

I haven't even been here long, but I grew attached to the people, to the feeling it gave me when I took off my clothes and not a damn soul could do anything to me, not like before.

I'm also not the same woman I was when I first started. So much has changed in my life. I wonder what's next.

But no matter where my life takes me, I know for certain that A will support me, even when he thinks he's terrible at all things relationships. Yet he somehow still says all the right things, does all the right things. Together, we'll be unstoppable. No matter what, I'll always have his back.

A security guard greets me as I enter the club, the loud music beating through the speakers. I head toward the back, another man opening the curtain to allow me access.

As soon as the girls see me, they all greet me. I missed a few nights after I was attacked. Told the owner I was sick. He's good about that. Doesn't give us a hard time.

"How are you feeling, sweetheart?" Coco asks, running a long red fingernail through the front of my hair. "I tried callin'. You never called back. Had me worried." Her thin brows curve with concern. "What did you have? The flu?"

I hate lying to her. I'm so sick of lies.

"Can we talk in private?"

"Sure, yeah. I've got a few minutes before I'm up. But you'd better get dressed soon. You're up after me."

My eyes go downcast. "That's what I want to talk to you about."

Her gaze widens.

"Girls," she calls to the three others. "I'll be right back. Tell Yonie I'll go after Cat."

She gives Cat a look that says she'd better not give her lip.

"Fine!" Cat throws her hands in the air. "I'll go. Geez."

Coco scoffs as she pulls me into one of the private rooms and shuts the door. "Tell me what's wrong."

With shaky hands, I lift up my shirt.

"Oh, Jesus Lord," she gasps. "Who did that to you, honey?" She clasps my hands. "You poor thing."

"It doesn't matter." I try not to cry, but fail, tears slipping with my sad smile.

"You're leaving, aren't you?" She sighs.

"I have to." I shrug a shoulder. "I can't work like this. It's time."

"If you wanna stay, I'll talk to Yonie. I'll make him understand." Her eyes plead for me to stay.

I widen a tight-lipped smile, my vision blurring. "No." My head shakes. "He won't want me here looking like this, and I don't want to face his rejection. I came here to say goodbye, Coco." An ache weaves its way through my chest. "Thank you for everything."

Her arms close around me and hold me tight, rubbing my back. "You stop that, okay?" She clears her throat, but her emotions seep through. "You have nothing to thank me for. I'll always be here for you. Just one phone call away."

Both of her palms fall to my upper arms as she stares at me with kindness.

"You're a good soul, honey. Not many like that left out here in this cruel world. You come to me if you ever need anything, okay?"

I nod. "You too. I love you, Coco."

"Oh, hell. I love you too." She holds me once again, and together we cry, holding on to one another.

Somehow stronger for it too.

Thirty-Six

ADRIEL
TWO WEEKS LATER

I hate being useless. Hate being unable to find Dr. Collins or whoever his accomplice is. It's killing me. But the murders have stopped. So far, at least.

Maybe he left. Maybe he took his brutality somewhere else.

But what good is that? He's just going to hurt others. I need to find him.

I've looked everywhere. Every traffic light in the state. Every fucking airport. He hasn't been there. If he has, he's heavily disguised. His car is still at the house, his phone undetectable. Probably tossed it somewhere. It's what I'd do.

He may never be found, and I can't live with that. He has to die. Until he does, she will always wonder if he'll come after her. If his accomplice will. I won't let that happen.

I've been keeping tabs on my brothers through the bugs I have planted at their places, and at Mother's too. They keep killing low-level scum traffickers, but they haven't been able to locate the ringleader. One of the men they killed said the boss keeps himself hidden. Only a few know who he really is. They don't have a name or description. They report to someone higher than them, but not the actual top dog. It's a pyramid. And killing the leader is how we topple it.

Looking at my cell, I find Kayla out shopping with Elsie and Jade. I let her be. As long as I know she's safe, I let her live her life. Elsie has two bodyguards on her, so I know they've got eyes there too. Michael would never let anything happen to his wife.

When Kayla gets home, I'll have a surprise for her. I've had a feeling she was itching for it, though she hasn't said anything, probably thinking I've wanted to stop. But my needs are still there, only now I have someone to share them with.

KAYLA

"We really need to figure out how to help them." Elsie sighs as we sit around a smoothie place after a day of bonding and shopping. "I hate that Michael and the guys are still upset about the whole thing with A." She looks at me with melancholy. "I'm sorry he's been through all that. I feel so bad. Thanks for trusting us with that. I'm gonna talk to Michael. Make him understand."

I nod. "He's been hurting for so long." Tears lodge in my eyes, but I blink them back. "He's been alone. Never had anyone love him or care or anything." I swallow past the lump in my throat. "The first time he hugged me, he didn't even know if he was doing it right."

Jade's face falls, a hand against the center of her chest. "That's heartbreaking."

Elsie shakes her head. "I'll make Michael see that this family needs healing, not war or hate. My God, there's already too much hate out there. We don't need any more."

I puff out an exhale. "He's done so much. I don't know if they'll ever forgive him."

"They're gonna have to." Elsie picks up her berry smoothie and sips. "Adriel is still their brother, and they have no idea what they would've done had they gone through what he has."

"Thanks for saying that." I squeeze her other hand.

"Of course." She stares up at the ceiling for a moment, lowering her cup. "They have to do this for Sophia's sake. She keeps asking questions."

"Like what?" I stare curiously.

"She likes to eavesdrop." Elsie laughs. "I think she heard some stuff Fernanda said when she was over at the house after it happened. Because Sophia asked if A was her uncle."

"What did you say?"

"I told her the truth." She shrugs. "I wasn't gonna lie to her. Michael was pissed when he found out, but I told him he can't deny who his family is. That it was time he accepted it, regardless of whether he'll welcome Adriel into the family or not."

"Did he say anything?" I ask.

"Nope." She rolls her eyes. "I swear they're so damn stubborn. I wish we could force them into an intervention or something."

Jade laughs. "That would be something."

"If only there was a reason for them to see eye to eye. Make them realize how much they actually have in common."

"Wishful thinking." Elsie drags in a long inhale. "But we won't let this break us." She gives me a hard stare. "Right?"

"Of course not." I slant my head and smile. "Their problems

are their own. We'll never let them tear us apart."

I hope...

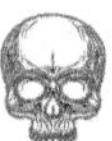

After I got home, A made me dinner and had me for dessert, and now he apparently has a surprise for me.

"What is it?" I wonder as he leads me blindfolded.

"Okay. You can stop." His hands languidly undo the blindfold.

Blinking back, I adjust to the light. When my vision focuses, I find us in the basement.

Two bodies are there.

Both are sitting on chairs, heads lolled forward like they're dead. Gagged and hands tied behind them, they groan when he walks over and kicks them in the shins.

"Rise and shine," he mocks.

"Who are they?" My heart races, the thrill of what this means feeding me in a way the club never did.

"Meet Gustavo and Hermit."

They both groan in unison.

"Nice names." I grin. "What did they do?"

His smirk sets me ablaze. "Very bad things. Right, boys?"

"I can't believe you did this." I eat away at the little distance between us and grab his hand, kissing the center of his palm.

"I didn't know if you still wanted to." He cups my face and brings his lips to mine.

"Of course I did," I whisper, my mouth stroking his.

I was afraid he wouldn't want this anymore, but part of me still needs this. Needs to end those who hurt others.

"I have another surprise for you."

"Show me." My eyes fill with delight.

He reaches inside a duffel by their feet and removes an intricate black and gold wolf mask.

"I thought we could each wear one." He grabs his own from within the bag and slips it on. His is black and silver, made of the same hard material as mine.

My teeth trap my lower lip as my smile widens before I put mine on too.

"You ready?" he asks.

"Yes, just tell me what they did."

He reaches back into the bag, retrieving a knife with a long, thin blade, handing it to me. "Child molesters. Both of them. Kids were all under ten."

That's what I need to hear before the knife enters Gustavo's balls.

And when he screams and his eyes fill with terror, all I do is laugh, twisting the blade deeper and deeper until he passes out.

But I wake him up and start the nightmare all over again.

Thirty-Seven

ADRIEL

My bloody little princess holds the knife as she stares at her kill. She's glorious, her eyes shining, her grin deepening. I gave her that.

My queen.

My world.

I am but her servant. I'd do anything to make her look this happy.

She turns to me, and something in her eyes calls to my depravity. I start to slip off my mask, intending to drop it beside hers on the floor, but she shakes her head.

"Keep it on." Her chest rises as she struts closer while my cock grows hard at the sensuality flitting through her features.

I crook a finger, beckoning her to me. "Strip."

I lower myself onto the black leather sofa, waiting for her to start.

She doesn't hesitate. Dropping the knife, she tugs up on the hem of her t-shirt, exposing her perfect tits before she throws the blood-soaked cotton on the floor. She continues to remove her pants and then her panties until she's bare and bloody, her crimson fingers drawing up her abdomen.

She kneels and gathers the knife back in her palm before she starts for me. But when I shake a finger, she pauses, her mouth curling, bottom lip tucked behind her teeth.

"Crawl to me and keep the knife."

Her brow arches, right before she falls to her knees, crawling slowly, her eyes trapped with mine.

My cock grows harder the closer she gets. I grab a fistful, stroking myself through my sweats, hissing when she stares up at me from between my thighs.

"Now what?" She's all doe-eyed, innocence and danger tucked within her gaze.

"Take it out…" I lift my shirt off and toss it.

She stares at my chest, a tattoo of a crow sitting on top of a headstone with the letters RIP on it. A grave to myself. Because I've always been dead inside, and I wanted to honor that. But now, with her, I'm not so sure.

Her soft fingertips skate across my abdomen as she slowly brings my sweats down and reveals my cock.

With her hunger smoldering, she closes her palm around my length, her fingers barely able to connect, and she moves it up and down.

"Fuuuuck," I grit, my hand sinking into the back of her head, wrapping all that silky hair around my knuckles. I yank her head back. "I can't stand the thought of you not in my life, Kayla."

"I'm right here…" She pushes her mouth toward the head of my dick, her tongue swirling around it until I mutter a curse and jerk my hips.

"This feels too fucking good," I groan.

"I think this will feel a lot better…" Then her mouth is sucking me hard.

I push her deeper until she gags, until she takes every painstaking inch of me.

She works me like a pro, and I hate that it's because she's done this unwillingly. Been hurt and used. The fucking thought puts me into a homicidal state.

But I refuse to ruin this. She doesn't deserve for them to destroy what we share.

With me, with us, it'll always be different. Because I'd never hurt her, and I'll kill anyone who tries.

She continues to suck me whole, moaning around me as her head bobs, and that heated tingle in my spine comes roaring.

I can't come like this. I need inside her. I need to fuck her until we're both bloody and spent, our hearts beating as one.

With a quick snap of my hand, I tug her head back. "On your feet, little wolf. Come sit on my lap. I need to feel my cock slowly sink inside you before I fuck you like the animal I've always been."

Her eyes narrow. "Promise to make it hurt?"

I grab her hips and settle her on top of me, staring into her eyes while my knuckles draw down her cheek. "Promise to give you what you need."

The crown of my hard-on gradually enters her as our gazes stay locked, our souls twined into something unexplainable. Inch by inch, I sink inside her, never letting go of those eyes.

Her mouth parts, that knife in her grasp, her wrist on my shoulder, while she swallows me all the way into her warm and pretty cunt.

"Fuck me," she whimpers while I slowly circle my hips.

"You're on top, babe." I smirk. "I want *you* to fuck *me*."

"I—I never…"

She has never been in control. I get it now.

"You can with me. See if you like it. If not, I'll take over."

She nods, swallowing harshly before she starts to move. And the faster she moves, the more my chest burns with the passion I feel for her.

Her palms press into my chest as she moans, those sounds of hers sending me over the edge. Her free hand fastens around my throat and squeezes.

"That's it, baby bird. Squeeze harder."

She does, crying out as I fuck her deeper, giving her what she gives me. The blade knicks my shoulder, and I groan in pleasure, the pain only fueling my desire.

An audible breath escapes her as she sees the blood pool.

With gritted teeth, I raise her wrist and place the knife against my throat. "Cut me. I want your blade on my skin. I want your fury. Want to devour it. I want to *feel* it."

When she doesn't do it, I take her hand and use the blade to pierce the skin on my chest.

Her eyes go there even as her hips move faster, making us both groan in unison.

"Cut me." I draw her head back with a fistful of her hair. "Hurt me. Give me what I know you wanna give me."

When her nostrils flare and the edge of her mouth curls, she unleashes her fury and lets the blade sink into my chest. Deeper and deeper until she's drawn a K beside the gravestone of my tattoo.

I chuckle as I flip her beneath me and take over. Her back on the sofa, I grab both of her ankles and throw them on my chest, raising her hips until I'm back inside.

The knife slips onto the floor as I increase my pace, unable to stop myself from giving her all of me. She cries out and begs for more, her body shaking, eyelids fastening.

"Eyes on me. I wanna watch as you come. As my blood drips onto those perfect nipples."

"Yes! Don't stop," she gasps.

"Fuuuuck!" I moan, unable to stop myself. "You're gonna come on my cock when I let you, and then you'll come on my tongue before I fuck you again."

"Oh my God, yes, that's it!" Her nails dig into the leather as she maintains our eye contact, obeying me.

I've never looked into a woman's eyes as I fucked her. But with her, everything is heightened. Everything is raw. This connection between us has sunk so deep into me, I feel it embedded in my marrow. I'm one with her. And no one will dare take her from me.

"Adriel!" My name is nothing but a choking scream, her release bursting out, her body writhing, while I stare at her incredulously.

"How can someone this perfect want to be mine?" I whisper, sure she hasn't heard me.

Throwing my mask to the floor, I fall to my knees, spread her thighs open with my palms, and feast on my queen before I take her again.

With every passing day, I grow more attached, afraid that it'll all vanish. Because someone like me will never truly have someone like her.

KAYLA

"What are you surprising me with now?" I ask A as he slips on a Rolex while I try hard not to stare at his ass in those black dress pants.

The dove-gray button-down he has on leaves nothing to the imagination. Every sinew, every muscle traceable, lickable.

My mind instantly goes to yesterday when he took me the way he did, when he let me do what I did. I was nervous. At first. But then something in me liked it. To draw his blood, to know I did that. The power. I think I'm hungry for it. My therapist would say I'm overcompensating. But if I can have it, why wouldn't I take it?

He strides over to me and places his palms on my shoulders from behind, watching me through the full-length mirror. His languid gaze strokes down my body, taking in my black pencil dress, hitting right above my knees.

His jaw flexes. "I wanted us to go out. Like a…you know…" He grimaces.

"A couple?" I giggle. "You're so adorable."

He snaps his teeth, yanking my head back by my hair. "Don't call me adorable."

He fights a smirk, but it only causes me to laugh even more.

"But you are, especially when you get all uncomfortable with everything relationshipy."

He snickers. "I'm not uncomfortable. And that's not even a real word."

I continue to laugh, and he grabs a handful of my ass. With a growl, his mouth falls to my neck as he kisses me, his eyes on mine through the mirror.

"You look beautiful." His heated words leave a trail of waking desire across my flesh.

"Are you trying to distract me from teasing you some more?" I groan, fighting a grin when his fingers stroke between my thighs, yanking my panties to the side.

"Is it working?"

"Quite effectively."

He pinches my clit, and my eyes roll back.

"Fucking hell, babe. You're so gorgeous. But if we don't go now, we may never leave this house." He removes his hand and straightens my dress. "You ready?"

"Yep. Let's go."

As soon as we're out the door, he grabs my wrist and yanks my body to his. His palm snaps to my nape, and his gaze darkens. With his frame, he throws me up against the door and cages me between his palms.

His chest sways to the beat of his rapid exhales, his eyes lingering on my eyes, my lips, before they drag down my body as though unwrapping the dress from my limbs.

"It does make me uncomfortable. To talk about relationships and everything they entail. I'm not..." His voice trails, and he slants his forehead to mine. "I'm not made to care about another person, yet somehow I've come to care deeply about you. So much it hurts, Kayla."

I clutch the back of his head, my heart aching so much for him. "I wish I could go back in time and give you all that you deserve."

"No." He perches to stare back at me. "I wouldn't trade a moment of my life for what I have with you. I don't know if we'd be who we are if we hadn't gone through what we did." He holds my face in both hands. "For once in my life, I believe in something. I believe in us." His eyes grow beautifully sad. "I will never give you up."

My hand wraps around his wrist. "I'll never let you."

But a part of me fears that maybe people like us don't get the kind of life we finally have. Maybe this is merely an illusion, and soon we'll wake up.

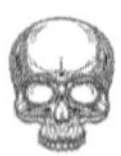

We arrive at a fancy steakhouse, the lights dimmed, people dressed up and occupying every table while a server leads us to ours.

"A waiter will return to take your drink orders." She nods politely, giving A a sheepish glance before she scurries away.

"I think she liked you," I say as he pulls out a chair for me and allows me to sit.

His face is stoic as he takes his own seat across from me, grabbing my hand and holding it in his large one. "I don't care who likes me, because I only like you."

His smirk appears as he winks, just as our waitress arrives. She eyes him too, her cheeks flushing. Great, another one who has obvious eyes for my…

The rest of the words are trapped in my head. Because I don't know what he is. We never even talked about titles. Is he my boyfriend? What else would he be?

She takes our orders before she goes, and my mind is still on what to call him. I can't decide whether I should ask him. I don't want him to think I'm childish. But at the same time, I've never had a boyfriend. I kinda want one.

"What is it?" Concern fits his features.

"It's nothing." I force a tight smile and try to pry my hand away from his, but he holds it tighter.

"Kayla." His brow bends.

With a roll of my eyes, I huff out, "You're gonna think it's stupid."

"Try me."

"Can you maybe not look at me as I say it?"

"Absolutely not." A half-grin dons his face.

"You're an ass." I shake my head with a laugh. "Fine. I was just wondering what we were exactly. Are you my boyfriend? Am I your girlfriend? I don't know, I—"

"Kayla." His face hardens.

"See, told you it was stupid."

He gets to his feet, towering closer as he drags my chair right beside him before he settles down again.

"I'll be whatever you want me to be." He tucks my chin into his palm. "But just know there is not a word in the dictionary that is adequate to describe what you are to me, Kayla Jenkins. So if you prefer it, you can be my girlfriend. Hell, you can be my wife. An extension of my fucking heart. Use any words you deem necessary. I want to make you happy."

My heartbeats quake in my chest, emotions warring within me.

"I clearly can't be your wife," I scoff. "Uh, girlfriend is fine."

Wife.

That one word made my gut sink with something foreign and exciting. Would he want to marry me? Or is that him just telling me I mean a lot to him?

The answer may scare me. Because as soon as that word left his mouth, I knew I wanted that. I want to be his wife, and I want this man to be my husband.

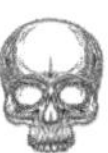

Once we return home, my mind is still on his words and the earth-shattering way he confessed his feelings to me. I know how much that meant to him. For someone who has never had this, saying all of that took a lot of courage.

I wonder where we will be years from now. Will we have the kind of life we both deserve? Will I be an oncologist? Will we be married? Kids?

No… I don't want them.

"Can I ask you something?" I raise my head and look over at him, while his fingers lazily trace up and down my back.

"Anything." His eyes fill with warmth, and I burrow closer, seeking more of it.

"Do you want kids?"

His eyes widen. "Wow, we're going there, aren't we?"

"Sorry." I grimace. "I figured we should discuss this stuff. It's what normal couples do, I read."

He chuckles. "We're not normal, babe."

"I know." My heart tightens in my ribs. "It's why I wanted to see if we were on the same page."

"Do you want them?"

"I don't think so? I can't see myself as a mother. I don't want to bring a child into this world."

"Neither do I." He sighs. "I don't know what a parent should be like. I'd never subject a child to the likes of me."

"Don't say that." I place a hand over the stubble of his jaw. "You're an amazing person. Just look how you are with me."

"It's different with you."

"No, it isn't. You have never been with anyone and look how well you treat me."

"Are you trying to convince me to have kids, or…"

"I'm just saying that isn't a reason for you not to. Even if one day you're with someone—"

"Don't you fucking finish that sentence." He lifts his head and kisses me. "There's no one else for me in this universe. No one but you. No one will be enough. No one will matter the way you do."

"I just worry that this will come to an end." My heart shatters at the thought.

"Not if I can help it."

"I hope you're right…"

With a groan, he flips himself on top of me, and his emerald gaze sinks into mine. "How about I give you a little something to hold on to?"

Then he's inside me, kissing me raw, reminding me why we have to live in the present even when the future may be a scary place.

Thirty-Eight

KAYLA
ONE MONTH LATER

Our life falls into place with each passing day. We fall deeper. Closer. More than I've ever imagined.

But here we are, cementing ourselves in the present, hoping for a future neither of us ever thought was even possible.

But things aren't perfect.

The killer has yet to be found. No trace of Doctor Collins or his accomplice. The only good thing is there have not been any new murders.

Though I do watch my back, and so does A, I don't let fear control me. I go to school. I see my friends. A and I still kill together, the bodies burning away in his furnace.

Maybe one day when the reaper comes for us, we'll burn too, but for now, we live and we breathe, and we destroy those who don't deserve to walk this earth.

Sitting in a café with Elsie and Jade, I stare at my two best friends. They're so normal. So well-adjusted. While I'm me. I don't think I'm ever going to change. Nor will I ever tell them what I do. What A does.

No one will understand us.

We don't need them to. My friends know the important things about me, and that's what matters in the end. I wish A had his family. It would help him. But they're still at odds.

Elsie has yet to convince Michael to speak to A, and I've been unable to fix the situation either. Adriel still hates his family, and I don't think that's ever going to change.

Picking up my iced coffee, I close my eyes and savor the hazelnut. Everything I eat or drink or see is special. I don't take a single thing for granted anymore.

"I really don't wanna go back to work." Elsie groans, and Jade joins her.

They're both heading to work at Helping Hand, while I have to reluctantly get to class.

"I so don't wanna sit through another chem lesson." I twist my face in displeasure. "But I really have to go too."

"This was nice." Jade smiles. "Maybe we can grab lunch again tomorrow."

I start to rise, grabbing my schoolbag. "Sounds good. See you guys."

"Talk soon!" They both wave as they head in the opposite direction from me, their car on the other side of the lot.

As soon as I slip into my vehicle, my phone rings in my bag. Reaching inside, I look down on the screen and find Cammie's name. I don't get nervous when she calls anymore. She's been doing so well with her new therapist and adjusting to what happened to her. I'm proud of her progress.

"Hey, Cammie."

Breathing. Heavy breathing.

"Cammie?"

"He…he's coming," she whispers.

And my heart instantly trips over the fear in her voice.

I start the car, my body shivering, unsure of what's happening, but knowing it isn't good.

"Who?" I make a sharp right, not even sure where I'm going. "Cammie?"

"Doctor C-Collins. He's at my parents'."

I can hear someone there, someone calling for her, but I can't make out the voice.

"Oh, God. I'm coming. Tell me the address."

I don't ask why she's at her parents'. I don't care right now.

I've been by her family's home, but don't recall the address. She once made me drive by, just wanting to see her family. Then when her mother came out and greeted her father, she made me leave. It breaks my heart for her to not have a family who loves her no matter what. Maybe she went there because they wanted to reconcile.

"554 Main Street. You remember the town?"

"Yes. I'm fifteen minutes away. Maybe I should call the cops."

"No! Please," she whispers. "You know they're connected to the Bianchis. We can't trust anyone."

She's right. The thought was stupid. But I have to call someone. I quickly shoot A a text with the address, saying Cammie is in trouble and I'm heading there to stop the killer. He will get angry, but I can't just sit here and do nothing.

Adriel's out at a meeting with a new client. Someone wealthy who owns a robotics company overseas. But I know he'll drop everything to come and help.

I could call Michael. I should. He can help too.

"Cammie? Are you there?"

She snivels quietly. "Y-yes. He's looking for me."

"Okay. Just keep hiding. Please just don't talk. I promise I'm on the way."

"I'm scared." She softly cries. "I don't wanna die."

My heart shreds into pieces. After everything we've been through, we don't deserve this. We deserve to live, something we never got to do. But now this bastard is after her. After me. And he needs to be stopped.

He probably has no idea she called me. Maybe I can surprise him. I reach into my pocket, feeling for the flip knife A gave me. I also have a gun in my handbag. He was going to give me a small blowtorch too, but I convinced him that a blowtorch would be harder to hide. Now I kinda wish I had it.

"He's coming!" Cammie whisper-shouts. "Oh my God!"

Her inhales and exhales pick up speed while I drive even faster, not worrying about the cops.

"No!" she shouts. "Get away from me! Help! Kayla!"

"Cammie?" My body spreads with a desperate panic, icy fear clawing through me. "Cammie!"

"No!" she continues to scream, her voice growing dimmer by the second.

Until it's gone for good.

ADRIEL

This meeting is taking way too long. When I agreed to it, I hadn't expected this woman to have as many questions as she did.

Not that I mind them. I get it. They're giving me a lot of their money. But what I do mind is being underground with no cell reception. Apparently, she's the owner of the company for which she's looking to purchase some of my products. She personally came down to meet me. And she owns this club too, the one she insisted we meet in. Glancing around the darkened, empty space, I have a feeling they sell a lot more than wine and scotch here.

She crosses her legs beneath a short black skirt, a hint of flirtation in her eyes. Which, of course, does nothing for me. All I'm thinking about is when this will be over so I can get back to the one woman who matters.

"So, Mr. Smith." Her blood-red lips curl. "I did love everything I heard. It's why I would like to contract you to work for my company. Permanently. But unfortunately, that would require you to stop your own…personal endeavors, shall we say?"

I release a chuckle, uncuffing the sleeves of my dress shirt and dropping my elbows across the tops of my knees. "If you came down here to proposition me into quitting my own company, I'm afraid your trip was quite useless, Mrs. Tretoria."

She smiles tightly. "You do realize I can pay you more than you have ever made doing this. It is your wish to make as much money as possible, yes?"

"No, it isn't." I climb to my feet.

This meeting is over. Her men quickly stand. I give them each a seething glare.

"I will not work for you. So next time you have any inclination to call me, don't. I'll be seeing myself out. You have a safe flight home."

"You're making a mistake," she calls out coolly.

"Yeah, well, I'm kinda used to that." I scramble up the stairs, grabbing my cell to check for any missed calls or messages from Kayla.

But as soon as I exit, my cell rings.

I freeze.

Because I know the number instantly. I don't know why she's calling, and I don't even want to answer. But something in me tells me to. Like a ghost whispering in my ear to pick up the phone.

"Hello?"

"Oh, thank God." My mother's words swim with anguish.

I shouldn't care. I shouldn't talk to her, yet I find myself unable to stop my pulse from rising.

"What's wrong?"

"Please, you have to help her! He…he didn't wanna call you," she sobs.

In a flash, I'm running for my car. "Who?"

But she ignores me, crying and continuing. "Your brothers are stubborn, you know, but I knew I had to call you. I knew you'd wanna help."

"Who needs help?" I ask again, rage and dread shooting into my veins.

"Sophia," she wails. "Someone took Sophia."

A cold dread washes over me. "How long ago? Any witnesses?"

"An hour ago. I think. I…uh… I heard Michael tell Raph that she was at the park and was playing soccer, then her friends saw someone hooded with a mask. It was a scary mask, they said. It had no mouth and had a slash in each eye."

Fuck! He came for her. He knew I was watching her. He knew what I wore. He knew more about me than I did about him. I'm ashamed of it. Ashamed that I was careless. Stupid. It's my fault that little girl was taken. Probably killed by now.

Unless he wants me there.

My fingers curl viciously around my phone as I browse through it for the app I need.

"Please say you're gonna help her. Please!" She shatters right there across the line. "I know you hate me and this family, but please, please don't hate her. She's—"

"Ma. I don't hate her."

She gasps.

That word. I shouldn't have.

"I'm gonna find her. You can tell them. I don't care. Right now, my priority is saving her. So you tell them I will find her, dead or alive."

"Dead? No…" She weeps. "Please don't say that."

"It's a possibility." Though it's the last thing I want to think about. "I've gotta go now. I'll let you know when I find her."

"I—I'm sorry," she cries.

"This isn't the time."

I quickly drop the call and look through the app that connects to the ring I gave Sophia.

"Please, kid, tell me you still have it."

It instantaneously pings a location, twenty minutes from here, a house on Main Street. Relief washes over me. There is hope she is there unharmed.

Before I start the car, I find a text from Kayla and immediately open it.

And my heart… It's never known pain quite like this before.

KAYLA

> Hey, babe. Cammie called. Says the killer is at her parents' at 554 Main Street in Lake Anges. Please hurry. I'm heading there now.

Main Street? No…

ADRIEL

> Kayla! What are you doing? Do NOT go there alone. Tell me you're not there yet. Please!

Silence. Minutes trickle with not a word from her, and my heart only sinks further into absolute, mind-bending fear. Something I've never known or felt or experienced. How the fuck do people deal with this shit? To care about another person the way I care about her…

No…

If something happens to her…

"Fuck!"

I pound a fist across the wheel, over and over, speeding down the highway, hating myself for not being there for her. Hating that I was in some meeting for my company that means nothing in comparison to what she means to me.

"Fuuuck!"

I can't lose her!

Pressing a button on my cell, I track Kayla's location using the GPS installed in the eye of her wolf necklace. It reveals what I already knew. She's with Sophia.

The killer has them both.

I know for certain someone is gonna die today, and I pray it's me.

Thirty-Nine

KAYLA

My heartbeats skip to a fast crescendo as I park my car across the street from Cammie's parents' home. My knees jerk and the pulse in my throat beats faster, but I get to my feet anyway.

I can't let the fear of what's inside that house stop me. She needs me. I can't let her die after everything she survived.

But life isn't fair sometimes. It takes and takes until you have nothing left to give but the bones in your body. But even that isn't enough.

For all the people who have endured what we have, I wish life offered us more. Yet it doesn't. It never has.

The home stares back at me. Calling to me. Two stories. Plain white with navy shutters. Simple. No other homes in the near vicinity. Nothing but acres of fresh, green grass. No one to hear the horrors transpiring inside those walls.

With my knife clutched in my palm, I give my cell a final glance, but don't yet see a message from Adriel. I know he's probably not checking his phone while at his meeting, and right now I wish he was. I need him. There aren't many people I trust in this world, and he has quickly become number one on that list. Maybe that's foolish after he lied to me about his identity, but in the end, does it even matter? He did it because he had to, and he spent his days making sure I was safe. Who has ever looked out for me that way except my friends and my parents? No one.

Coming here alone may cost me everything, though. Him. A future we could have. But I refuse to be the girl I once was. Scared of my own shadow. The life I had while being the Bianchi whore has changed me.

If I'm honest, I changed the moment Elsie ran off into Michael's car. When they beat me and raped me to make me talk, when they held me in a cage for days without any food and only just enough water to survive. But I didn't talk. I think that's when something truly shifted inside me and I became part of the woman I am today. I'd do anything for the people I care about, and that includes Cammie now.

On the way here, I sent Michael a message about where I was going. I wasn't going to, but in the end, I thought the more people who knew where I was, the better. I'm not an idiot. I know I can only do so much by myself.

Unfortunately, though, he never responded. Which is unlike him…

I thought maybe I should text Elsie too, but thought better of it. She'd worry and stress. I don't want that. She's done enough worrying about me.

I can do this. I have a plan. Maybe a stupid plan, but a plan nonetheless.

I figure if I can offer the killer something he may want more in exchange for Cammie, then I can buy us some time until someone shows up to help. Maybe the killer will even let Cammie go.

I guess we'll find out.

With a heaviness in my throat, I cross the street and slowly reach the door. The pressure in my chest increases, my pulse skipping and unsteady.

Before I even turn the knob, I know it's already open. It creaks as I push it further, reeling as the sweet, metallic odor hits my nostrils almost immediately. My eyes widen and fear grips my throat.

I know that smell well.

Blood.

And a lot of it.

Terror powers through my veins, and my pulse pumps furiously. Every inch of me trembles as I cross the threshold, unsure if she's already dead. If it's her blood I'm smelling. I want to call out for her, yet I don't know if that would alert Dr. Collins.

As soon as I step further inside, I see someone's bare foot on the ground. A woman's foot.

"Cammie!" I call out, rushing for her, unable to stop myself from caring if he's about to jump out and kill me. "Nonono!"

My knees hit the ground as soon as I'm near her, and when I look at that blank expression staring back at me, her back covered in blood, I realize it's not Cammie at all. She's older. Her mother? Oh, God!

"Cammie, where are you?" I whisper-shout, not hearing anything.

Not footsteps. Nor anyone's cry.

Dread that she's gone, that I'm too late, fills me with urgent despair.

She can't be dead! He must pay for what he's done!

I scramble on my shaky feet and plod down the foyer, and when I enter the living room…

"Cammie!" I shout, rushing for her, closing the knife and stuffing it back in my pocket.

She's lying in the corner, blood pooled around her, two more bodies not too far from where she is.

That must be her little brother and father. A fucking massacre. He killed them all and left!

"Oh God, Cammie. No!" I sob, sinking to the ground and lifting her body into my lap.

Rocking her, I cry, the blood from her shirt penetrating mine.

"I—I was too late," I bawl. "I'm so sorry I failed you."

Fingers reaching for her neck, I pray that there's a chance that she's still in there somewhere.

"Please! You have to be okay!" Tears slip down my cheeks just as two fingers press into the side of her throat.

I gasp, a cold shudder of relief flailing over me when I feel the pulse there.

"Thank God!" I hold her and sob. "You'll be okay." My breaths come in whimpering pants. "I'm gonna call an ambulance."

Reaching into my pocket, I grab my phone, and when I start to dial, her hand whips out, fingers wrapping around my wrist.

Her eyes pop open.

With a stunned gaze, my mouth starts to move, but no sound comes out.

It takes a moment for my mind and my body to catch up.

"C-C-Cammie!" I breathe out. "You're…you're okay."

"Yes. Yes, I am." She grins, her grin cold as she flips me down onto the floor, settling on top of me. "But unfortunately for you, you're not."

Then, she's pointing a gun at my throat.
And shoots.

Forty

KAYLA

I groan, whimpering, unsure of where I am. My arms ache as I try to move them. Voices… They seem distant, but I hear a woman, and that's when it all comes crashing down. The moment she pointed the gun at me, the altercation, when I pushed her off and the bullet flew right past me.

That fear—the icy, blood-chilling fear that I was gonna die—is something I can't even explain.

We fought. I remember that. She pushed me off, and…and I hit my head. I recall the throbbing pain. Remember when she hit me again, and that's when I stop remembering.

Yet I'm still alive. She hasn't killed me.

I…I don't even understand any of this. Why would she hurt me? I came to help her. Why is she doing this? Where's Dr. Collins?

"Mm," I grunt, my eyesight blurry as figures dance before me.

Or maybe it's just her and I'm seeing double.

Someone cries. Very close by. I don't understand if it's me or someone else. But who could it be? No one else was here, and her family was dead. Did she kill them? Did she want to hurt them for not accepting her? Did I become the next target? But why? What do I have to do with her family?

Then something else settles in my mind, something darker and far scarier. But I can't yet wrap my head around that possibility. The one that includes Cammie as *the* killer. The Midnight Murderer herself.

That makes no sense though. Yet…there were two the night I was taken. Two people were hurting me. What if Dr. Collins has been her accomplice? That would make more sense.

Too many questions swim, and I need answers. I won't rest until I get them. Grumbling, I force myself to open my eyes a fraction, and as I try to sit up, a soft touch lands on my arm.

"I want her gone," Cammie says, voice muffled, but still clear enough for me to hear everything.

I can see her growing less dim as she paces several feet away from me.

"I want her far away where he won't find her," she says to someone. "That would be so much worse than killing her."

She laughs with a darkness so eerie, the backs of my eyes sting. Who has she become? Where is she sending me, and who is she talking to?

A man chuckles, just as depraved, but I don't recognize the sound.

"Wake up, Kayla. Please," a child cries, her hand squeezing me. "Wake up."

It's then I turn my head slowly and blink several times, as though my eyes are playing tricks. They have to be. She can't possibly be sitting right next to me. Must've really hit my head hard.

"Kayla...I'm scared. She's crazy."

"Sophia?" I choke.

"Yes, it's me." She nods.

"Oh, God!"

No, no this can't be happening! Why would she take Sophia?! Elsie and Michael, do they know yet?

Then it hits me: that's why Michael never replied to my text. He's looking for his daughter. Oh, no! They can't hurt her. I won't let them!

"Aww, look, the princess is awake." Cammie grins, and when she kneels, I clearly make out her face. She snatches my hair in her tight grasp. "Open your eyes and look at me!"

She slaps me hard against my cheek, and that has me instantly waking up. My body quivers and I register my hands tied in front of me, Sophia's tear-stricken gaze and trembling bottom lip jutting out at me.

"You'll be okay," I lie to her. "I'm right here, sweetheart."

"Stop talking to her!" Cammie fists my hair tighter. "She's not going to be okay, and neither are you!"

Sophia wails, and Cammie grunts.

"Shut up! I've heard enough from you!" She points her gun at the poor, innocent child.

"Don't you point that at her! She's a baby! If you want her not to cry, put it away!"

She snarls and grinds her teeth, but lowers it. Her chest swells, her face bright red, the blood on her shirt still present, but clearly not hers.

This was a setup, wasn't it?

"Why, Cammie?" I whisper, my heart rapping so fast I fear I'll pass out again. "Why are you doing this? Why have you killed all those girls?"

I don't even let her deny it. I know it's her and her partner. It has to be. But nothing makes sense! After all we went through, how can she kill innocents?

She chuckles with a frosted, dead look in her eyes. "Look at you. You figured it out, huh?" She starts to clap. "Bravo!"

"I—I don't get it." My words quake out of me. "We don't kill innocent people. We save them. We help them. How…how could you do this?"

"Mmm." She twists her mouth and pouts. "I'm sorry, but we aren't all superheroes like you and your boyfriend, killing the *bad* people." She rolls her eyes, then stares at me with sinister intent. "Not all of us are *sooo* perfect," she snarls. "I hated them, you know. All those beautiful, perfect girls walking around the world like their lives were untouchable."

She inhales deep, then releases, as though attempting to collect herself.

"Perfect families. Perfect boyfriends. Perfect jobs. Nothing out of place. Until they met me, that is." She grins, and all the hairs on my body stand up.

I have never seen her this way. So callous and broken. Is that what she became? I feel sorry for her in this instant. She was hurting, and no one truly saw it.

"What did you do?" I whisper.

"Well, I'd meet them. Become their friend, then I'd drug them and let my friend have a little fun." Her lips thin into a calculating sneer. "See, some of them didn't actually die. Some were sent away to a much more horrifying place." Unblinking, she glares. "You know, the kind you and I know very well."

"Oh my God!" I clutch my mouth with a hand. "You were working with the trafficking ring?"

"Yes." Her grin widens. "See, initially, he was gonna take me, but I couldn't let that happen, so we became friends. Once he found out about what I was doing to the girls, we came up with a business arrangement. Of sorts." She shrugs a shoulder. "He gets some of the girls to expand his business, and the others, I let him test drive before I got to have my fun. Because no life is perfect, Kayla. You should know that more than anyone."

"I'm…" I pant. "I'm so sorry." Large tears roll down my eyes. "I'm so sorry I never truly saw your pain, how much more you needed from us. I'm sorry we all failed you," I weep.

"Shut up, shut up, shut up!" She drives the barrel of the gun into my temple. "There's nothing wrong with me!" Her features contort into something demonic. "*They're* the ones who were deluding themselves into believing a perfect life exists. They thought the rules of the world didn't apply to them. I set them straight. They should thank me. Because now they know too."

Unable to help myself, I continue to sob, while Sophia clutches on to me, crying too.

"And…and the star? Was that you or your partner?"

"All my idea." Her face radiates like she's proud. "Mommy used to call me her little star. Look how that turned out." Her gaze narrows. "She never wanted me after she found out what a whore I was. Never forgave me. None of them did. Even my twelve-year-old brother looked at me with disgust. Wouldn't talk to me when I'd go to his school and try. Laughed at me with his friends, whispered about me while they all stared from the playground." Her nostrils flare. "So I showed them who I truly was. And that moment right before they died, when their eyes connected with mine as I sank the blade into them for that final time, that was when they truly saw me."

"This…this isn't you." Pain seeps out of me in waves, unable to comprehend how she could do this, how far she's fallen.

She keeps her hand fastened around my hair as she pins her nose to mine. "This *is* me! And soon, you'll see that too."

"And…and where's the doctor? Is he here? Is he watching us?"

Her laugh sends another cold shudder down my body. With a sigh, she rises to full height.

"Oh, the doctor won't be joining us I'm afraid."

"Did you kill him?"

"No." Her eyes dance maniacally. "But sweet Dr. Collins is no longer with us." A wrinkle appears between her eyes in mock sadness.

"I—I don't understand. I thought he…he was working with you."

Her laughter echoes. "I lied, you idiot! I'm such a good actress, aren't I?"

She clears her throat and tilts her chin up.

"He was so nice to me. He was helping me. How? How could he?" she sniffles dramatically, repeating the words she said when she told A and me the doctor was the one who hurt her.

"Who?" I can't seem to breathe, the question barely falling from my lips. "Who killed him, Cammie?"

"I did." But the voice that answers is no longer hers.

And when I see the man who starts toward me, my heart stops beating.

"Wh-what… No." Tears spill over. "It can't be you."

Prince smirks wryly. "Hey, Kayla. You're not looking so well."

Spine-chilling fear engulfs me.

"H-how… Why?" My head spins, black and yellow dots flashing before my eyes.

"Why?" he mocks before he crushes his teeth and bares them.

With a quick rush, he's in front of me, a hand tightening around my throat. The dots grow until I'm craving my next breath.

Sophia screams, and my hand reaches for hers and squeezes. I can't let them hurt her. Not Sophia.

"Your friends took my father from me," he says. "And for that, you'll be the first to pay."

"Your…your father?" I manage to choke out as he squeezes, his eyes filled with more rage than I've ever seen on his once-kind face.

"Agnelo Bianchi. You may remember him." His mouth curls up for only a second. "I was just getting to know him after I found out I was his kid. My whore mother kept it from me until I found out and confronted her. So I located him and told him who I was. And instead of turning me away, he welcomed me into his inner circle." Boiling with fury, he flays me with a stormy gaze. "He taught me how to be a man, wanted me to run his club after he retired. But then the *fucking* Cavaleris stepped in and took him from me! But I made him a promise that I'd continue his legacy, and I have. Now his name will live on forever."

A sneer stays frozen on his smug face right before he lets me go and gets back up.

"Don't worry, though. I made him another promise after he died, that when I found you, I'd sell you to the vilest piece of shit I could find. And I found just the right home for you and that little girl." He gives Sophia a look that sends nausea into my gut. "He's gonna love her."

He chuckles, and Cammie joins him.

"And when I'm through here, I'll come for Eriu too. Cute thing like her would sell for a lot of money."

"No! Don't you touch her!" I scream.

Sophia's unending sobs cause my own to come in floods. She holds on to me through it while I grasp my fingers around hers, not knowing if anyone will save us in time.

Forty-One

ADRIEL

I find her car, yet I don't see her, and all the blood leaves my body.

Without a second thought, I rush across the street, and the instant I peer in through the door left ajar, I hear voices coming from inside on the left.

A child cries, and I know immediately it's Sophia.

Fuck!

If they hurt her or my little wolf, there'll be hell to pay. No one will be able to stop me from unleashing my fury on every single person involved.

More voices ring through, clearer now. I register Cammie's laugh. At first, I don't understand why she'd be laughing. Not until she's telling Kayla how she lied… Lied about the doctor being the murderer. And in that instant, all the muscles in my body tense.

She's involved?

My teeth snap. She lied to Kayla? I'm…I'm gonna kill her.

The more I listen, the angrier I seem to get. But once I hear another voice, that punk from college, I want to rush in there and gut them both. I never fucking liked him. Now I know why.

Who am I kidding? I hated the bastard because he wanted to fuck the one woman who belongs to me. By the sound of it, though, he had much more sinister plans.

Glancing around the perimeter of the house, I realize I have to surprise them. Gotta shoot them from the outside. If I can take him out quick, I can kill Cammie and save the girls. No way can I storm inside and think one of them wouldn't shoot Kayla or Sophia. I have to be smart about this. Think before I act.

Silently jogging around the house, I creep down under a window, the one slightly opened, no curtain to hide what's happening inside.

Hand on my weapon, I observe Prince and Cammie standing before a frightened Sophia and Kayla, her hands bound in front of her.

My fingers curl until my knuckles go white, hating that I'm not inside saving her, saving Sophia. This is killing me!

There's no way I can wait anymore. I don't know if they're gonna keep them alive for long. They could do just about anything.

Prince holds a Glock in his grasp, while Cammie seems to be without one. She must have one too. There's no way she's not armed. We underestimated her. All Kayla wanted to do was help that girl, but she was playing us.

It all really hits me then. They were the ones who broke into Kayla's place and did all that to her.

My breathing ravages from my lungs like I'm possessed. Flashes of Kayla right after I found her appear before me.

My sight grows hazy.

The pulse in my neck beats in my ears.

They won't make it out of this house.

Prince strides back and forth, telling her how much he'll enjoy selling her and Sophia to someone who's gonna hurt them. That no one is coming for them.

A grin wraps around my lips. I can't wait to see the smug look on his face when I prove him wrong.

This time when he darts toward her, I ready my gun.

And for that split second when he turns toward my direction, I don't hesitate.

Pop.

A bullet fires from the open part of the window and sinks right into his stomach.

Cammie screams in surprise.

Sophia sobs.

While Kayla… Her eyes sink into mine in utter relief.

I drag the window all the way up and jump inside.

"You son of a…" Cammie whips out her own gun, and I fire.

Sophia hides her face in Kayla's shoulder just as Cammie collapses to the floor, blood spilling from her upper arm.

She gasps, inching to sit up, but I kneel and push my fingers into her wound until she cries out.

"How does it feel?" I dig deeper into her flesh. "To know you've lost? To know you'll die like every one of your victims?"

A small, dry laugh puffs out of her. "I ruined them all. Didn't… didn't lose."

"How about now?" I straighten and put a bullet into her stomach, letting her bleed out in pain, not giving her the mercy of a quick death. She deserves worse.

Kayla pants, her vision overtaken by tears. But I must end this before I get them out of here.

"I'm coming, babe. I promise."

She nods, trying to reassure a scared Sophia, and my heart hammers with a single look into her eyes, because she has me. She owns me. I'd rip my own heart to make her smile again.

When I near Prince, I find that he's still alive. But that's about to change. Aiming my weapon, I fire a single shot into his groin, his scream trapped inside these walls forever.

Lifting my foot, I dig the heel of my shoe into his wound. "Like father, like son." I scowl. "Can't say you'll be buried with him, I'm afraid."

Not that there's a grave for any of the Bianchis.

"Winning…" He huffs a laugh as he tries to catch his breath. "Looks different…f-for everyone."

Before I can grasp what he's saying, a shot rings out, coming straight at Kayla.

Sophia screams as Kayla's body falls backward, blood leaking from her stomach.

Looking down, I find the gun slipping from his grasp just as the last few seconds of his life disappear.

"No!" I run toward Kayla and fall to my knees.

That shellshocked look in her eyes has me lost in fear. With a pocketknife, I cut through the zip ties binding her wrists and rip off my shirt to put pressure on her wound.

When her blood soaks through it, agony like I've never known hits me in every cell of my body.

"No, no!" I shout. "Don't fucking leave me!"

I fight for breaths that never come, my eyes burning with a raw kind of pain until a tear trips down my face. More come in its wake.

I realize in this moment as I gather her up in my arms that I've never cried before, not since I was a small child still seeking the comfort and love of the world. But I never felt an ounce of it, not until this woman, and I can't let her go. I won't.

"Un-Uncle A," Sophia sobs, almost unable to get the words out. "Is she o-okay?"

The fresh flood of tears in her eyes causes more of mine to surface. I don't know how or why she called me her uncle, nor do I have a chance to ask. Because my focus is on getting Kayla to a hospital. Her pulse still beats, but it's weak.

As I grab Sophia's hand, her eyes widen when I register a rush of footsteps behind me.

"Daddy!" she screams, dropping my hand immediately and charging for her father.

"Princess!" His emotions wrack within him.

As soon as she jumps into his arms, our eyes lock, and he gives me one solemn nod. And I do something I never thought I would: I return it.

I ignore my other two brothers, my half sister, and all the others standing there as I hurry out the door with a dying Kayla in my arms.

"Wait!" Michael calls out with Sophia still in his embrace. "We have our own hospital. Take her there."

"I can drive," Raph offers, slapping my shoulder with his palm.

I don't shake it off. This is about more than my hate for them. This is about Kayla.

"Fine."

Together, we race into his SUV, while he does over a hundred to save her life.

And mine.

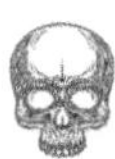

Everyone's gathered in the hospital while the docs operate on

Kayla. The bullet is out, we were told, but she needed a transfusion for all the blood she lost. No one knows yet if she'll be okay.

My mother keeps her worried attention on me, while Elsie is huddled with Jade and Kayla's crying parents, who don't understand why someone who lived through what Kayla did would do something like this. They have no idea what Cammie truly did. How many women she killed. And they won't. The news will never catch wind of the Midnight Murderer's real identity. Cammie will not get fame in her death. Nor will Jade's center get bad press because of this. It was the one thing we all agreed on— me, my brothers, and the Cavaleris, who are all also here.

I pace like a madman, waiting for her to wake up. To call me A just one more time.

"Fuck!" I whisper-shout just as I feel a hand on my back.

Pivoting, I find Michael there.

"I'm sorry." His stern expression doesn't make it seem as though he is, nor why he's apologizing. "She clearly means a lot to you. I'm sorry this happened. That she's here."

"Should've been me. If I wasn't at a fucking meeting, I would've been here!" I dig a fist into my forehead.

"I get it. Won't feed you bullshit to make you feel better, because if Elsie was in the hospital, I'd feel the same way."

I don't respond. There's nothing to say. I don't know what the hell to say to any of them. I don't even want to be here with them, but I also don't want to be alone.

"The ring…" He glances behind his shoulder at Sophia, who's in Raph's arms, her pout breaking whatever's left of my heart. "The ring you gave her. It had a tracker, didn't it?"

I shrug. "Maybe."

He chuckles wryly. "Not mad about it. It's how you found her, and I'm grateful for that. No matter what. Understand?"

"I didn't do it for you."

"Doesn't matter who you did it for. Matters that you did it." He smiles at his daughter, who catches his eye.

It's beautiful, his love for her. At least some in this family know what it means to be a parent.

"She likes you," he tells me.

"I like her too." Peering at her, I ask, "How is she processing everything?"

I can't imagine what that's doing to her—seeing the murders, being kidnapped.

"Not the first time she was taken or saw someone die." His expression stiffens. "I'm failing her, yet it's the only kinda life she knows."

Neither of us say anything else, both looking at Sophia. When she sees me studying her, those big brown eyes of hers pop wide. Without hesitation, she jumps out of Raph's arms and straight into mine. And thanks to Kayla, I know just how to hold her.

"Thanks again for saving me and Kayla." She curls both of her thin arms around my neck, her gaze full of affection that I've only recently grown to understand or feel or want.

Never having people who care for you, then having someone who does… It's funny how you realize how lost you were without it.

I cup her face. "You don't have to thank me for that. I'll always come and save you."

"I know." She kisses my cheek. "Kayla is gonna be okay. You'll see! I made a special wish with Santa and told him that this year all I want is for Kayla to be okay, and he's super magical, so he will make my wish come true. I just know it!"

I nod, pain lodged in my throat. "I think you're right; she will be okay."

Michael leaves us to settle on one of the empty chairs beside his mother, while I continue to focus on my niece, who's the only family member I actually like.

"So…" I ask her, narrowing my eyes. "Why did you call me your uncle back in the house?"

She rolls her eyes. "That's 'cause you are."

"And how do you know that?" I tilt up a curious chin.

She cups her hands around her mouth and lowers it to my ear. "Don't tell anyone I told you, but a few days ago, when Grandma was super sad, I heard her talking to Mommy."

I jerk back and narrow an amused stare. "You mean you were snooping."

"Of course not." She snickers, her face upturning like I said the most ridiculous thing even as her lips jerk. "I was there to gather information about why Grandma was sad," she clarifies rather cleverly. "So I could cheer her up. Obviously. It just so *happens* I heard some stuff."

I chuckle. "Mm-hmm. Go on."

"So, Grandma was telling Mommy how sad she was that she had to give you away." Her brows furrow, and she lays her hand against my cheek. "I'm sorry that happened to you." Her eyes grow sad, and my heart beats faster.

I don't say a word. I can't. Incapable of forming a sound. Because her words mean more to me than her young soul realizes. I place my hand on top of hers as she continues.

"She said she didn't want to give you away, but her mommy made her the day you were born. She said her mommy didn't give her a choice, and that she would send Grandma away and would take both you and Uncle Raph away too."

What? Her mother?

But that still doesn't excuse her never looking for me. She had time and money. She could've found me. She chose to close her eyes and forget.

Sophia sighs. "She cried a lot and said she had a picture of you in her wallet so that she never forgets you. She said she loved you. A lot."

I scoff. "I don't know about that." Those words slip out of me gruffly.

"I'm sorry you're sad. But I'm happy you're my uncle." She places her head on my shoulder. "You're really nice."

I laugh under my breath. "Wait until you actually get to know me."

She giggles.

"Wait a minute, though." My brows furrow as I glance back at her. "How did you even know she was talking about me?"

"Oh, that's easy." She waves off with another roll of her eyes. "She said you had very green eyes like Grandpa Patrick. And when I saw you at the park, you had green eyes too. So I figured…" She shrugs. "It had to be you. Then I asked my mom and she told me who you were, and I knew I was right."

"You're kinda smart."

"Yeah." She drops her head back on my shoulder. "You told me that already."

"I did, didn't I?" I chuckle, recalling that day when I called her insightful and she asked what it meant.

Just then, the doctor walks out in yellow scrubs, removing his cap, and I'm in front of him in an instant.

Keeping Sophia in my arms, I grab his wrist. "Tell me."

Forty-Two

KAYLA

A flash of light zaps in and out of my vision, and there's a groaning sound that I think is coming from me.

With my lashes flickering, I gaze through the slits of my eyes at the blaring lightbulb staring down.

My brain's foggy, and I can't make out where I am. Shivering, I attempt to sit up, my vision adjusting to the white walls I'm trapped in.

"Hello?" I whisper, but my voice comes out all croaky and screechy.

Blinking a few times, I find wires coming out of my arm.

A hospital. That's where I am. But why? I close my eyes and think to the last thing I remember. The call from Cammie… Prince.

"Oh, God…"

She shot me? Did he? I don't remember exactly, but I remember everything else.

"Sophia!"

I startle at the thought of her being gone. Where is she? She can't be gone!

I remember A. He came for us. He had to have gotten us both out. When I try to move this time, my stomach aches.

"Shit," I mutter, and as I do, a door opens, and that's when I see him.

My mouth moves of its own accord, picking up into a smile. Am I dreaming? Is A really here?

"You're awake." His brows snap, and he hurries to the edge of the bed, settling there. "Hey, baby bird."

His sharp intake of breath stops my heart from beating. His knuckles brush down my face as he bores that heavenly gaze into mine.

"Don't you ever scare me like that again."

I let out a small, weeping laugh, placing my hand in his. And I hold it, my soul trembling from the overpowering emotions.

"You mean you missed me?" I tease.

Instead of answering with words, he drags his mouth to mine and kisses me so slowly, so tenderly, the backs of my eyes sting.

"I can't live without you," he whispers, the heat of his breath making me feel more alive. "Does that answer your question?"

With one hand curled around the back of his neck, I hold him to me and cry because I can't live without him either. Somehow, this man has become so much more. I'd give him anything, give up anything, to be in his life for the rest of mine.

"Are you in any pain?" He pulls back and gives me a once-over.

I shake my head even as I grimace.

"Liar." He grabs the call button and presses it.

"What are you doing?"

"Getting you more meds." He gets to his feet and paces,

grabbing the back of his head. "I can't believe you went into that house without me." He grinds his jaw. "Kayla…why would you do that? Do you know how crazy I was when I saw your car outside?"

With a sigh, I pat the spot on the bed beside me. "Come sit with me."

Roughing out an exhale, he returns to me, and instead of simply sitting there, he lies beside me and gently moves my head across his chest.

"I thought she was in danger, A. I couldn't just leave her there."

"That fucking bitch," he growls. "I swear, Kayla, if I could kill them both all over again, I'd have much less mercy. But I couldn't afford to do what I wanted to them, not with you and Sophia in danger."

"How is Sophia? I was just thinking about her."

"She's fine." He kisses my temple. "Keeps asking about you. She told me she asked Santa to make you better."

"Aww, seriously?" Moisture builds in my eyes.

For a moment, I imagine it. A little Sophia of our own. But us as parents? That's not our path. It can't be. We're not cut out for that life, too bruised and broken to parent anyone.

A man in a white coat struts in, with a nurse not much older than me behind him. He scratches the salt-and-pepper hair behind his ear.

"Ms. Jenkins, we are all happy you're awake. How are you feeling?"

"Alive," I laugh even as it hurts to.

"That is always a good sign." He clears his throat uncomfortably, and that's when I know something else is wrong.

A notices the shift in his demeanor, his eyes bouncing between the doc and me. "What is it? What do you need to tell us?"

"Well…" He glances down at me. "Are you comfortable with

me discussing things with your boyfriend present?"

"Yes. Whatever it is, he can be here for it."

"Alright." He nods. "Your surgery went well. We did get the bullet out. However, because of where the bullet hit, I'm afraid that your…"

"Please, just say it," I tell him. "Trust me, nothing can scare me at this point."

He stares with kind brown eyes. "I'm afraid you won't be able to have kids of your own because of some internal damage the bullet caused."

Something heavy and cold and all-consuming hits me all at once.

"Oh." I force a tendril of a smile. "I see."

Anguish creeps up my throat until it becomes hard to mask these emotions I didn't think I'd feel. Because I didn't want them. I didn't want kids. I said that over and over again. But why?! Why is my heart ripping in two?

"We have a counselor on staff who will speak to you. If there's anything I can help with, any other questions, just let the nurses know."

"Mm-hmm." I widen that smile, widen it until my face splits, until he thinks I've gone insane.

Or maybe he can see right through me.

A squeezes me closer to him, because he knows. He always does.

"I'll leave you both to it. You should be able to go home tomorrow night, assuming you're not in major pain."

"Great! Thanks. Can't wait to get out of here." My tone goes all shrill.

I need him to leave!

His expression tenses as he turns with the nurse and they both leave us.

As soon as they do, this heavy, blistering swell of my feelings hits me like a tsunami and I sob against Adriel's chest.

"I'm so sorry," he whispers, holding me tight.

I don't even care if I can barely breathe. Because I'm dying on the inside.

"I didn't want them." I wipe briskly under my eye as I look back at him. "I told you I didn't want kids, so why the hell am I crying?" I laugh through the roar of my tears.

"It was taken from you. That's why." He cradles my face in his tender palms. "It was taken and you lost the choice, and I'm so fucking sorry, baby."

He's never called me that before.

It only makes me weep harder, and I do just that.

"We can have them if you want." He kisses the top of my head. "We can have kids. We can find a way."

Blinking back, I say, "But you don't want kids."

"I want whatever you want, little wolf. So if you want a baby, then we'll figure it out."

"We?"

"Yeah." The back of his hand glides softly across my jaw. "It'll always be we now."

My chin quivers, not knowing how I'll survive this pain. So much has been taken from me. But when I feel his embrace, I realize that through the hell of my despair, I've found more than I ever thought possible.

I found love.

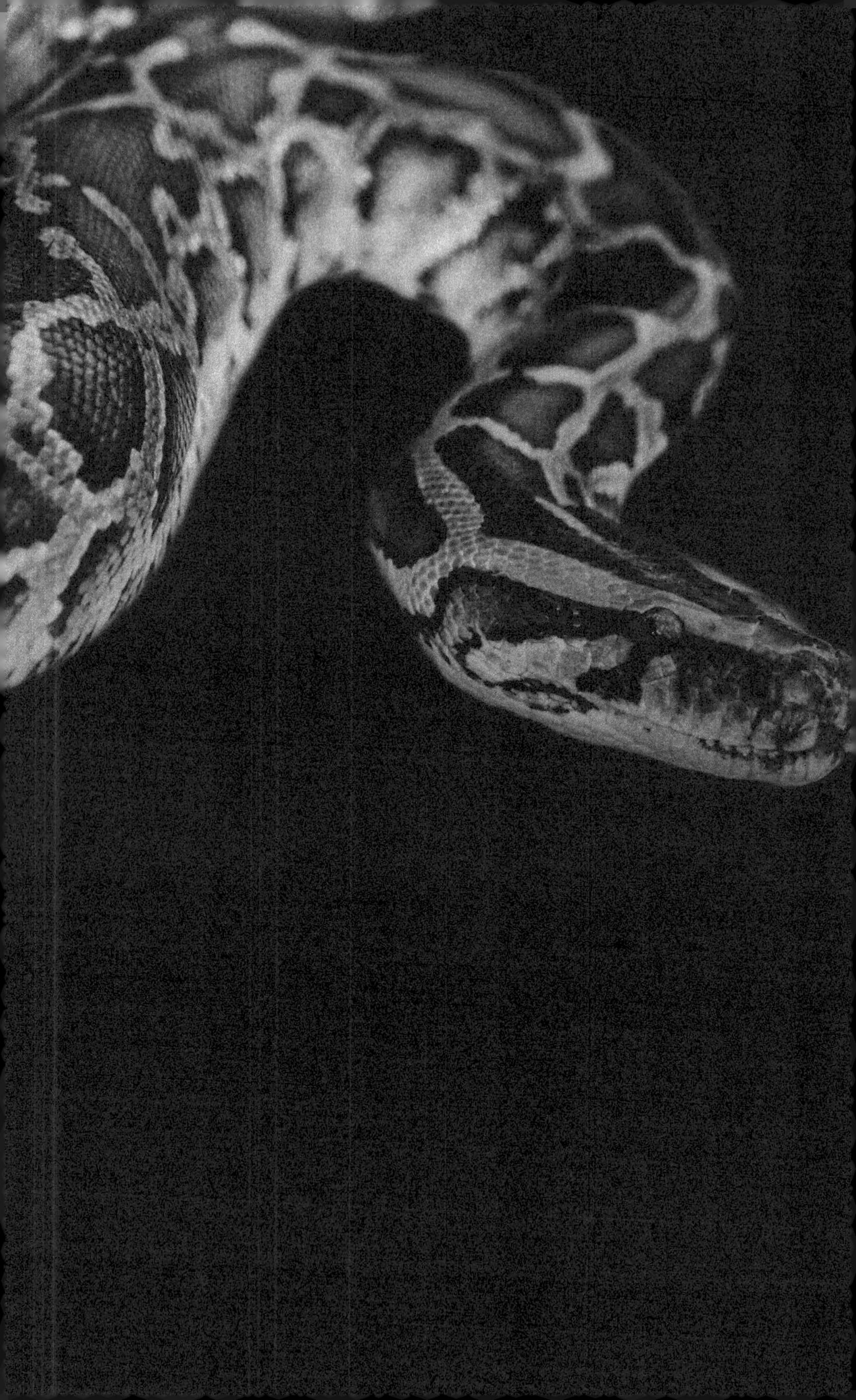

Forty-Three

ADRIEL
ONE MONTH LATER

Kissing across her forehead, I tuck her into my bed. Well, technically, our bed since she's moved in with me now.

Never thought I'd enjoy sharing my space with another person. The thought of it would have been laughable back then.

But now? I don't know what I'd do if she ever left me.

Watching her smile sets my whole heart on fire. It's funny how much I can't live without those smiles now that I have them. Now that I've *felt* them. She's changed so much of who I was, even while those parts of me still remain and always will.

But with Kayla, I've evolved into a man I never saw myself becoming. To touch, to kiss, to make love to her… I never dreamed of such things. I was simply a man looking in, never experiencing the things others always took for granted.

Now all I want is to hold her, to kiss her, to watch her smile that way she does for as long as my heart still beats.

But there's still so much I'm simply not capable of. No matter how badly I try to force it, I can't say those words… The three words I so desperately want to say. Because I feel them. I think I do, at least.

But how do I truly know? How do I make myself say those words? I don't know what it means to be loved or to love. I've never had that before.

Staring at her, knowing she's safe from Prince and his thugs, makes me sleep better at night. After he was killed, Iseult was able to hack his phone and computers, tying his friend Tim to the trafficking. The same guy who danced with Kayla that night I watched her as Chris, wanting to rip the bastard to shreds.

Now he is, though. Burned in my furnace, but not before he talked and told us where to find the rest of the crew who worked for Prince. They were all over Boston, and the Quinns were able to take care of every last one of them until not one remained.

All the victims who were still in Boston, caged and waiting to be shipped off overseas, were saved too. And the others, the ones already smuggled? We were too late. None of us were able to find them. And it fucking kills me.

"Have a good nap, baby." I stroke her lips with my knuckles, and she reaches her hand to grab my wrist.

"You sure you can't join me?"

"Soon. I promise." I pull her hand to my mouth and kiss the tips of her fingers. "I have a little work to do."

Not that kind of work. The blood, it had to stop for now. She's still recovering, but doing so well.

And the fact that she can't have kids? Yeah, it still hurts her, but she's managing the best she can. Elsie and Jade help a lot, and she's wanting to find a new therapist once she's a little more healed. As for me, therapy isn't something I'm seeking. Kayla is all I need.

"A?" Her smile is liquid gold. Priceless.

"Yes, baby?" I want to crawl into bed with her and never leave.

Her smile expands. "I love you."

My sharp intake of breath causes her eyes to widen.

My pulse quickens.

I don't know what the hell to do or say, awestruck at those words. She may not realize it, but that was the very first time anyone has ever said that to me. And something inside me grows until it suffocates me.

"Are you okay?" Her brows knit and concern fits her face.

She just told me she loves me, and I look like I'm about to die. It makes me feel like the biggest asshole in the world.

Unsure what else to do, I slip into bed with her and tuck her head on my chest. "More than okay." I drop a kiss to the top of her head. "I'm sorry I'm so fucked up. I wish I wasn't."

"Hey." She places a hand against my cheek. "Don't do that." Forcing herself on her elbow, she kisses me once. "You're perfect."

"I'm not, Kayla. Nothing about me has ever been perfect."

When she tries to say something else, I place a finger across her lips to silence her.

"Let me get this out."

"Okay," she whispers.

"I've never had anyone say that to me before. Not until you."

When she looks sad, it breaks me, but I continue, knowing she deserves to hear this.

"I don't know what love is. I've never been shown love. I don't know what it looks like or feels like." I talk past the thickness stitching up my throat. "All I know is when I'm near you, I forget how to breathe. So tell me, little wolf, is that what love feels like?"

Her bottom lip quivers, and she curls her arms against me. "Yes, Adriel, that's exactly what it feels like."

With a deep exhale, I hold her closer, filled with this sense of completeness I can't explain.

"I love you," she says, staring up, tears storming into her eyes. "I love you so much, Adriel. And I don't care if you never say it back. Because I *feel* it, your love for me, and that alone is enough."

"Kayla…" I slant my forehead to hers, clasping her nape in my large hand. "Fuck, baby, you deserve to hear it."

"I do hear it. Every time you touch me. Every time you do something that makes my heart beat faster. I hear it. I know you love me, and that is always going to be enough."

I slap my eyes closed and quell this aching in my chest, because I don't feel like I'm enough.

Holding her for a while, I stare up at the ceiling while her eyes start to flutter. And I vow to try, to be a better person and a better man, every single day until I can be enough for her.

She moans as she sinks into me, and once she's completely asleep, I kiss her forehead and gently lower her onto the pillow.

Turning off the lights, I close the door and return to the den.

I have products I need to test in the basement. As I start to head in that direction, there's a knock on the door.

Unsure who it could be, I reach inside my pocket and check the security cams. My chest expands at the sight of two people I haven't seen since the day Kayla was in the hospital.

Fernanda and Patrick are standing there, hushed tones between them. I can't say I have spoken to anyone from my family since Kayla was released.

Family.

I chuckle to myself. What a funny concept. Can't say that

defines them.

Kayla's parents have stopped by to check on her, and so have her friends. My mother and brothers have called to check on her too, but I've never talked to them about anything that mattered. Never had any desire to.

Whatever rivalry I had with them has died, and in its place is indifference. Except Sophia, because I adore that kid. Though I don't see her either. Wonder if she asks about me.

Straightening my spine, I move toward the door and open it, startling my mother.

"Hi there, son." Patrick catches himself and clears his throat. "I mean Adriel." His thick Irish accent is on full display.

"What can I do for you both?"

Neither of them misses my sharp tone.

"Well…" My mother smiles tightly. "We were hoping to maybe speak with you. We've wanted to come for a while, but we didn't want to intrude on Kayla's recovery. But I couldn't wait anymore."

I stare up at the ceiling for a moment before hitting her with a glare. "I'm not here to make you feel better about what you did. So, whatever you have to say to me, tell your shrink or your priest. Not interested."

I attempt to shut the door in their faces, but Patrick's hand whips out and holds it in place. His face hardens as I hold his stare, both of us hard-pressed and unrelenting.

"Now, you listen," he says. "I know you have been through a lot, and I'm willing to let some of your aggression pass toward me, but not your mother."

I laugh dryly. "She'll get respect when she earns it."

When he tries to say something else, she stops him, grabbing his arm. "It's okay."

Patrick grinds his jaw. My mouth curves, finding his anger

commendable.

"She left me," I tell him. "I have every fucking reason to hate her. She told me you didn't know. Is that right?"

He nods. "I may not have, but I'm not innocent in this. We aren't trying to deny our fault in what happened to you, but all I want is a few moments of your time. We both do. And if you don't want anything to do with us or this family after that, then that's fine. We will hate it, but we'll accept it. Right, Fernanda?"

He glances at her, and even as her face falls, she nods, tears coating the rims of her lower lashes.

Blowing a breath, I say, "Fine, but let's go into my office so we don't wake Kayla."

"Aye." Patrick curls an arm around my mother as they follow me inside, and I lock the door once they enter.

I don't know what any of us will get out of this, but I can tell they won't leave us alone until they get to talk.

My mother appears near distraught as we walk into my office. She doesn't deserve my time nor my sympathy, but at least she has one of them.

"You have five minutes," I tell her. "Please…"

Gesturing toward the black leather sofa, I take my seat across from them at my desk. She lowers first before Patrick sinks beside her, taking her hand in his. My eyes catch it before my gaze darts up.

Popping a brow, I cross my arms over my chest. "So, what do you need to tell me, *Mother*?"

Patrick grunts under his breath at my tone. Too fucking bad. He can leave. Or better yet, they can both fuck right off.

"That's okay, Pat." She nods at him with a quick glance. "I deserve that. He has every right." Her eyes go to mine. "You have every right to hate me. But I can't live with myself if I don't at least tell you the whole truth, my mistakes and all. And believe me…" She huffs. "I have a laundry list of them."

"No kidding." I grin.

She ignores my mockery and starts weaving her tale.

"When I was in high school, I met your father, and we became inseparable."

She peers back at him, and I can see it there in her eyes, the love they share.

"We wanted to be together, but you see, our families—especially mine—were not fond of us as a couple. They were traditional, so they wanted me to marry an Italian man. When I was seventeen, about a year after Pat and I started dating, my mother found out, and she planned an arranged marriage behind my back. Promised me to a man a bit older. Once I was eighteen, I was to marry him." She bites her bottom lip.

"If it's too hard, you can stop, sweetheart." Patrick's hold of her hand strengthens.

"No." She raises her chin. "I need to do this." With a quick exhale, she goes on. "My mother told me about her plans to marry me off as soon as the marriage was set. Told me to leave Pat and stop this foolishness before I got him killed. I told Pat about it, and he didn't care. Neither did I. We continued to be together until my marriage." Her voice grows shaky. "He tried to urge his family to stop it, to help us be together, but they too refused. His father couldn't be involved in a war with the Italians."

She sniffles, and my father rounds an arm around her and holds her to him.

"I found out I was pregnant shortly before I was to marry Giancarlo." Her eyes fasten. "I didn't love Giancarlo. He was cruel. I saw evidence of it even before the marriage. I knew of him and his horrible family, so I made plans to run away in hopes that

Pat would meet me and we could start a life with our child."

She pinches her temple and shakes her head before staring back at me.

"But my mother found out. Told me if I didn't go through with the wedding and pretend that my baby was Gian's, I'd be called a whore around town and no one would ever marry me." Her eyes grow with fresh tears. "She told me that I'd bring shame to the family and she'd send me away to a nunnery to have the baby before they took my child away. I didn't know," she cries. "I didn't know I was having twins until I gave birth. They didn't tell us back then."

Pain seeps from her voice, and I hate that for a moment I feel anything for this woman, even sympathy.

"I know it's probably hard for you to understand," she continues. "But having the label of a whore in my circle was like a death sentence. But worse than that, I couldn't be sent away and have my child taken from me. So I married Gian, and I hated every damn moment with that horrible, cruel man." She chokes on a sob. "He found out about my relationship with Pat, but he still believed I was a virgin and that it was just a childhood crush. Or so I thought."

She claps a palm around her mouth for a second, her resolve crumbling the more she talks. "My mother was there with me at delivery when you were born. You had those beautiful green eyes…" She smiles brokenly. "Just like your father's. While your brother had my dark eyes. Like Gian's. And I knew in that moment Gian would know you and your brother were Pat's."

"So you just gave me away?" I chuckle.

"No!" She shakes her head. "I begged my mother to help me get a divorce, to let me run away somewhere Gian couldn't find me. But she simply laughed cruelly, right before she slapped me while I held you and your brother in my arms. And I knew right then and there she was gonna do something terrible. But I didn't expect that."

I sit up straighter. I know this part. Sophia told me her mother was involved, but hearing my mother's words, her voice… It adds another layer to it.

"She told me I was at fault for my actions. That I made my bed and now I had to lie in it. That if we were going to make Gian believe I was a virgin, I had to give you away."

"Is she still alive? Your mother?"

"Why?" Pat asks. "You're gonna kill an old lady?"

"With a fucking smile on my face." I smirk coldly.

My mother sighs. "No, she passed away a long time ago."

"Hope it hurt."

She nods bitterly. "It did."

That brings some level of satisfaction.

"I lay in that hospital, holding you tightly as I wailed for her not to do this. To help me. To help us. But she told me I had two options: keep one or lose two. She left me for a bit to use the phone. While she was gone, a kind nurse who heard everything took that picture of us. The one from my wallet. I begged for her help, but she couldn't cross my family or Gian's."

My throat locks with a silent growl, wondering how the hell people could decide the fate of a single person just like that.

"When my mother returned, she told me to say goodbye. I held on to you so tight," she snivels. "I couldn't let you go! I begged and pleaded, but she took you right out of my arms as I fought her, clawed at her arm. But she pushed me off and ran out of the room and I never saw you again."

With both hands, she clasps my father's shirt and cries.

"I…I," she wails. "I didn't even get to name you!"

"Did that asshole ever find out Raph wasn't his?"

She nods as her attention returns to me. "The bastard did a DNA test soon after he was born, and that's when he found out. Once he did, he lived to make that boy suffer. He hated him. Beat him constantly. Made him feel worthless. Raph had no idea why his own father hated him so much." Her shoulders slump. "I wanted to tell them all the truth, but Gian threatened that if I told anyone I had a baby by another man, he'd kill Raph and me. I believed him."

With a deep sigh, she comes to a stand, letting go of Patrick's hand.

Watching her, I'm unsure of what she's doing until she comes nearer. Skittishly, her hand extends toward my face, and tentatively, as though in slow motion, she places her palm against my cheek.

My skin tingles, starved for the love of a mother I never had. I should push her away, should tell her to stop, but I can't seem to want to. Her touch fills the void of that once-broken little boy who'd cry for his mother and wonder why she never came.

"I know I could've done more." Her mouth thins. "I could've looked for you. I could've checked to make sure you had a good life, and I didn't. I deserve every bit of your hate. I could lie and say it was because I was afraid of Gian, but truthfully, my boy, I was afraid of this very thing. That I destroyed your life. That you weren't better off."

Fresh tears pummel into her weary gaze.

"What those nuns did to you, I wish I could take your place. My—" She wails. "My sweet boy." Her fingers stroke my stubble. "Can I… Can I just hug you once? Please?"

My chest cinches so tightly, I can barely fucking breathe.

"Please, Adriel. I… I beg you."

Before I can change my mind, I nod, rising to my feet, and she throws her arms around my middle and weeps against my chest.

Behind her, my father's own emotions grow and a smile full of his own turmoil flicks across his face.

Somehow, my arms make it around her, and that only makes her cry harder.

We remain this way for minutes that pass us slowly. Yet I don't know how to process any of this. My need to keep her and this whole family at a distance has been my priority. The rage I once felt for them was my only purpose in life. But now, I don't know what I want.

Can I let it all go? Is there a path for redemption?

"Where does this leave us?" Her words echo with her anguish.

"I don't know, but I won't try to kill you anymore, so you're welcome."

She laughs, Patrick joining her.

"That's a start," he adds.

She looks up at me, her palm clasped around my face once again. "I love you, Adriel. It feels just like yesterday when she took you from me. I'm still the same woman mourning the loss of her son, someone she wanted and loved with every fiber of her being. And for all my faults and my mistakes, I am so truly sorry."

Pain lodges in the back of my throat. Her admission of love, it's foreign and tasteless, yet it does something to me.

"I know nothing will undo what has been done to you, but all I have to give are my words and my actions going forward."

My father comes to stand beside her. "It makes me sick to know what those animals did to you." His jaw flexes. "And if I could, I'd kill them. I'm sorry too, son. You need to know we're all here now, and for what it's worth, you have a family." He grips my shoulder. "And we want to know you. If you'll let us."

"I don't know if I'm there yet," I tell them honestly. "I don't know if I ever will be."

She purses her lips. "I understand. Our door will always be open whatever you decide."

"That's right." Patrick squeezes my shoulder before dropping his hand to his side. "And I'll have you know Sophia has not stopped talking about you. She keeps asking when you'll come around to see her."

That has me grinning.

"She wanted me to give you something." Mom reaches into her handbag to retrieve a square envelope.

Curiously, I take it. "What is it?"

Tearing it open, I find a birthday invitation.

"She's turning seven and requested that we personally invite you and Kayla."

Chuckling, I find the date a month from now, and on the back of it, in a child's handwriting, it says, *You better come, Uncle A!*

Stuffing it back inside the envelope, I say, "Tell her thank you and I'll think about it."

"We will," my mother says. "Thank you for giving us the time to talk to you. If there's anything either of you ever need, please call."

"Mm-hmm."

I start for the door, needing time to process everything, needing to talk to Kayla. Having her to talk to now, it helps.

Silently, I lead them out back to where they came from.

As my mother shuffles out the door, she gives me one final, lingering look. "No matter what they took from you, you've still managed to turn out to be an amazing person."

I snicker. "You have no idea who I am."

"Maybe not." She shrugs. "But you never hesitated to save Sophia. You just did it. And bad people don't do that."

Before I can rebut, she grabs my father's hand, and together, they disappear into their car and out of my life for good.

Forty-Four

KAYLA
TWO WEEKS LATER

He holds me in his arms before bed like he's done it his whole life. This man is perfect, and the one thing that makes him even more attractive is that he doesn't even see it. But I'll be there to show him just how special he truly is.

It's funny, though, how the man who once asked me if he was holding me right now knows just how to do it.

Staring off at the ceiling, I watch his mind race like it's doing it right in front of me. I know what he's thinking about. What we've spent days talking about. His family. His mother.

It's hard. I get it. There's so much trauma built up, like scar tissue. It's hard to feel past those wounds. But I know he wants to. He's never actually said it, but I know him well enough by now to see it there in his eyes.

Forgiving her, letting all that go, will give him healing, and in the end, that's what matters to me. Maybe we're not meant to heal in our entirety because not everything can be forgotten, but people can learn to live with their trauma and accept it without it weighing them down. It's something I've been learning to do myself.

While I've been healing from my bullet wound, I've been doing some soul-searching of my own. The first step was finding a therapist. And that part has been hard. I know Dr. Collins didn't do anything wrong. He was set up by Cammie, but the entire ordeal has lowered my ability to trust people even more. But I know I need to have someone to talk to—about my past, about the inability to have children. I won't allow the grief to eat away at me. Not anymore.

"Do you think you'll go to Sophia's birthday party?" I gaze up at him, tucking my hand under my chin.

His lips jerk as he catches my eye. "That's what I was just thinking about."

I know.

But I don't tell him that.

"I'm not sure." He roughs a breath. "I want to see her, but I don't know if I'm ready to see all of them and act like we're some fucking family we never were."

I gather his palm in my hand. "Hey, it's okay if you don't want to. You're allowed to say no. But if there's a part of you that wants to, that's okay too, baby."

He kisses my knuckles and his throat bobs. "I'm at peace with it. I don't need them. I have you."

He grasps my hips and flips me on top of his hard body. As soon as he does, when those eyes hold mine, that spot between my thighs aches for him, needing him badly.

It's been so long since he's been inside me, since I've felt that connection between us. Now that the doctor has given me the all-clear, I've wanted to, but he's been the one scared of hurting me.

I rock my hips into his stiff length, biting into my lower lip. "You'll always have me, Adriel."

My lips lower to his and I stroke them, the tip of my tongue lacing past his full, firm lips.

"Kayla…" A growl fountains out from deep in his chest. "We can't."

I drown out the voices in his head with a touch of my mouth to his, and I kiss him slowly, his groaning whispering life into my heart.

His fingers sink into my hair, and he pushes his cock into me, snapping his hand around my waves until my scalp aches with excitement. He wrenches me back with a jerk of his hand, his gaze intense and earth-shattering. And in this moment, I can feel it, the unspoken way in which he loves me.

He may not be capable of giving me those words, but what good are words when you can't feel them? When they're nothing but lies? How many live that life? How many are happy?

But I am. I've never been happier, more fulfilled, than I am with him. So no, I don't need words if he can't give them to me. I'm content having him the way he is.

As for me, I plan on telling him how much I love him as much as I can. Because this beautiful man has never been told he's loved, and it's my job to prove to him that he's worthy of it.

"I love you, Adriel."

His inhale is sharp, eyes poignant just as he presses his forehead to mine.

"I love hearing you say that," he whispers.

"I plan to for the rest of my life."

His brows knit as he stares back at me. "I want to show you

something."

"Oh?" Excitement shoots out from me, wondering what that could be.

He moves me to the side and sits up, lifting his shirt over his head. And at first, I don't see it. Not until my eyes make out something new on his tattoo that wasn't there before.

Emotions ache behind my eyes as my gaze bounces between the new art and him. Carefully, he watches me as I take it all in. Faces of two wolves, embracing until they form a heart. One with green eyes and one with the same color as mine. My chin shakes as I fight not to cry. A black bird flies above them, and beneath, the words say, *In love there's no fear. Not with you. I love you, little wolf.*

"This," I choke on a cry. "This is beautiful."

My arms jump around him, and he holds me close, kissing my temple.

"I'm trying," he says.

"Never had a doubt, stalker." A grin spreads across my face.

He sighs, fisting my hair in his grip, kissing me roughly before nipping my bottom lip. His eyes turn hooded, mouth brushing mine. "I'm gonna fuck you now."

"Promise to make it hurt?"

"No." He shakes his head. "But I promise to make it feel good."

My heart leaps at the emotional tug of his voice, and when he smashes his lips to mine, I no longer care how he does it, because all I want is him.

His expert hands guide the clothes off my body, the strap of my tank top lowering, his mouth following the path until his lips lock around my nipple, sucking and flicking while his other hand tugs off my shorts. I'm bare and slick, craving this man with a passion so deep, I bathe in the fragility and strength of a love like ours.

His palms cup both of my breasts as he takes his time, causing my eyes to roll. It's then that his lips move south, kissing down my abdomen, opening my thighs until his mouth closes around my clit. He sucks it tighter, while two fingers slowly slip inside me and curve. Hitting my G-spot, he drives deeper with every stroke, my nails clawing his shoulder blades as I cry and beg for release.

"Oh God, yes, don't stop…"

My toes curl as he continues to take me ruthlessly, his eyes on mine, daring me to look away. I know he likes it when our gazes lock, the connection in that moment bringing us to a whole other level. He pounds his fingers into me until I gasp a moan, unable to stop the tidal wave about to rush over me. And when his teeth graze around my throbbing clit, I scream out his name and his alone, because he owns me until my very last breath.

He doesn't give me reprieve. Grabbing my hips, he positions me on top of him, his hard length nudging inside me as my hands land on his shoulders.

"Ride my cock, baby. Show me how good you can take it."

Without his eyes leaving mine, I slowly lower myself onto him, my mouth parting with a desperate cry as he gives me every thick inch of him.

"Fuuuck!" He palms my ass and without warning slams the rest of himself inside me until my body's trembling. "Sorry, babe." He smirks. "Just couldn't help myself."

With a groan, I press my chest to his and kiss him while he rolls my hair around his wrist. His hips bow into me with abandon, and he's the one who's fucking me.

But I don't mind. I like it when he takes control. I want him to.

His teeth sink into my jaw until I'm climbing once more, the release ebbing through me. He's taking it easy on me with my injury, and I know it's because he worries about me. It's that love for me that shines through everything he does. And it only makes me love him more.

We lose ourselves in one another, free to be ourselves. No masks between us any longer. Not literally, and certainly not figuratively.

He flips me beneath him, his hand fastening around my throat as he drives deeper, harder, kissing me, nipping my lips, sucking my tongue into his mouth.

My nails score up his back, my ankles hooking into his behind as I pull him in even deeper. When he wrenches back to stare down at me, I find untethered affection within his gaze. It unearths me.

His knuckles feather down my face as he fucks me slower, yet with more passion than I've ever felt.

"I never thought I'd have this." His thumb strokes my jaw. "But somehow I found forever here in your eyes."

Those words send my emotions into chaos. Because when I was least expecting it, I found forever in his too.

His lips find mine again in the heat of our desire, in the wake of the binding of our souls as one. And together, we reach the precipice. No longer alone. No longer hungry or starved for love nor affection. Because we have it now. We have it and we've earned it, and no one will ever take it away.

When we come down from the high, my arms clasp around him and I cozy up my face into his chest, feeling the weight of his heartbeats thumping as quickly as mine.

His arms drape around me, tighter and tighter, and a grin widens on my face.

"I think I finally figured out how to hold you right." His warm breath across my ear has me sighing.

"You always did, Adriel. Even when you didn't think so."

He growls, snapping his palm around my nape, and pulls me in for a languid kiss.

This right here is what I once always dreamed of. But with him, I somehow found it, and I know I'll always have it. I'll always have him.

Nothing can break us, because together, we'll break them instead.

Forty-Five

ADRIEL
TWO WEEKS LATER

"**C**ome on, we can't be late," I call out from the bedroom while she finishes getting ready in our master bath. "She's gonna have my head if we're late."

Kayla laughs. "Well, she can be a bit temperamental. Wonder who she got that from."

The door opens as she grins at me, wearing a pair of tight jeans and an off-the-shoulder red top that does nothing but make me wanna throw her on the floor and fuck her until we're both too filthy to go anywhere.

But I promised my niece I'd be there for her birthday when we spoke a week ago, and I'm not a man who breaks the heart of the women he cares about.

It was a difficult decision, whether to go or not, but in the end, I decided we had to. Especially being that Sophia herself called me and demanded I attend. Or else. Whatever *else* she had planned, I didn't want to know. Going was the only seemingly smart option.

"You're not supposed to look this breathtaking for a kid's birthday party." My arm weaves around her hips and I tug her to me, kissing the tip of her nose.

"And you're not supposed to look…" Her eyes dance down my chest, a simple black t-shirt on. She rolls her eyes. "You literally could wear a bag and still look hot."

"Hot, huh?" My face practically splits from the happiness she brings me.

"That's right." She tosses her arms over both of my shoulders. "My boyfriend is crazy hot. Have a problem with that?"

"Not at all. But I'm pretty sure my wife is the only hot one in this relationship."

Her brow curves. "I can live with that."

Then it hits her.

"Your wife? I thought we were okay with proper labels these days." She squints in this adorable way that has every part of me warm and fuzzy like a damn teddy bear that I'm not.

I chuckle as I reach into my pocket.

She watches breathlessly, her chest rising. Retrieving a small box I've been saving for a few weeks now, I drop to my knees right before this woman I'm insane about.

"Well…" I stare up at her. "Wife would be a proper label…if you said yes."

The box opens, and her mouth parts when she sees a red diamond staring back at her. Large enough to know she's loved, yet small enough not to overwhelm her hand.

"Wha-what is this?"

"Just me, asking you to marry him." I crack a smirk. "I know

I'm not someone you'd choose if you'd never gone through what you did."

When she tries to argue, I shake my head.

"Let me finish."

Her eyes shimmer, and she nods.

"I don't know how to do hearts and flowers," I confess. "Or how to love like others do. But what I *can* do is put you first. Let you be who you want to be. Take care of you and kill for you and let you kill when you want to. I just want a life with you, Kayla, whatever the hell that looks like."

Emotions spread across her features, and tears in her eyes overflow.

"It probably sounds insane that someone like me could want something like this," I say. "But I can't live in a world where you aren't my wife. You've been my baby bird from the moment I saw you, and I want to fly with you, wherever you'll take me. So marry me, Kayla Jenkins. Be mine. 'Cause I'm already yours."

She lets out a sob and drops to the floor throwing her whole body around me. "Of course I'll marry you. Whenever, wherever. I want you."

I release a weighty sigh and cup the back of her head. "I'm your home now, little wolf. And you're mine."

"Always." She kisses me, sinking those heavenly eyes into mine.

And for a man who's been so used to hell, heaven feels too good right now.

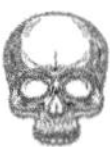

"Yay, it's Kadriel!" Sophia rushes through the foyer and straight into my arms.

I lift her in the air as Kayla laughs.

"Who is Kadriel?" I ask, completely confused.

"You know…" My niece rolls her eyes. "Kayla and Adriel together? Kadriel?"

"Oh." I nod, slowly scratching my temple as I stare at my fiancée.

Shit, that sounds too good.

Michael and Elsie stroll toward us hand in hand. Elsie approaches first, smiling at us.

"Thank you for coming, guys." Her stare holds mine for a moment before she hugs Kayla. And when she sees that ring, her eyes explode. "I'm sorry, are you two…"

Kayla looks down at her hand. "Oh, this old thing?"

Then she's nodding, and Elsie is squealing with excitement.

"Oh my God!" Her eyes water over. "I'm so happy right now! This is amazing news. Right, babe?"

She glances back at Michael, who nods, tentatively approaching me.

"Congratulations." His hand reaches for me.

I stare at it, not sure if I should extend the same gesture. I can't just pretend that we're all okay. That it isn't strange for me to be here with them. Like I'm part of all this.

Sophia snickers. "Would you two shake hands already?"

Michael laughs, and I do too.

"Fine. Fine," I say giving him my palm, and he slaps his hand into it.

"See? We can all be friends now. Right, Daddy?" She narrows her gaze.

"Whatever you want, princess," he tells her. "It's your birthday."

"Good!" She slants her chin. "I think it should be my birthday every day, then. So I can make the laws around here."

"Oh, really?" I ask. "And what laws would you create?"

With Michael beside me and the ladies behind us, we start toward the noise coming from the rest of the guests.

"Well, for starters…" Sophia considers. "I'd make everyone get along."

Michael shifts uncomfortably.

"I'd also make it a rule that everyone must eat ice cream for breakfast."

"Wow." I look up at her. "Sounds like you'd be a great president one day."

"I think so too."

As soon as we step into the large family room, everyone quiets, like someone has muted the volume. So many faces here: the Cavaleri brothers and their significant others, my parents, even Kayla's parents.

Fuck. I just wanna run, but instead, I reach for Kayla's hand and hold it like a lifeline.

"Hey!" Gio breaks the silence and jumps to his feet. "Look, it's the newest member of the family, and his much-better-looking other half!"

"Fiancée now!" Elsie intercedes.

"Shit!" Gio exclaims, and everyone else congratulates us and cheers.

"I'm sorry," I whisper into Sophia's ear while Kayla squeezes my palm and lets go to hug her parents. "I didn't mean for the engagement to take over your birthday party."

"Eh," Sophia says. "I don't mind. I'm happy." She hugs me tighter. "This just means I get to be your flower girl, and I don't know if you heard, but I really love being the flower girl."

I chuckle. "Wouldn't have picked anyone else."

"Duh! I'm, like, your niece. You have no choice."

"Don't make me change my mind," I tease.

She giggles. "I love you, Uncle A."

"Ditto, kid."

She places her head on my shoulder just as Raph steps up to us.

"Congratulations. Happy for you both."

I stare at him, kind of happy I didn't kill him. I let my rage win then. I don't want it to anymore. I give him my hand, and he takes it without hesitation.

"Appreciate it."

Now that I'm here, I've wanted to ask him something for a while, and it feels like we're in a good place for me to do that.

"By the way…" I whisper. "How did you escape that bomb I set in your car?"

He chuckles dryly. "Michael had all the vehicles strapped with some high-tech bomb detection device he purchased through his lawyer from some underground tech company called Apt—"

"Avenue?" I snicker. "No fucking way."

"You know it?"

"Yeah." I grin. "I run it."

His amused laughter increases. "You're telling me your own device saved me?"

"Apparently." My head shakes. "I've gotta be careful who I sell to."

"Damn." He slaps my back. "Thank you."

I feel a bit better, here with them. The hate I've felt for so long has closed its chapter, and in its place is a new one with blank pages. I have the power now. I can write whatever I want in it, and I choose to write this.

KAYLA

Together, with all the people who matter most, we watch Sophia blow out all seven candles on her cake. Adriel's arm is secured around me where it belongs. I crave this man, want him and need him on a level even I don't comprehend. Maybe it's unhealthy. Maybe it's wrong to want someone this much, but I don't care. I've been so lost in this world for so long; now I have someone keeping me steady.

I lay my head on his arm as everyone claps for Sophia. She's the light of this family, and seeing the way Elsie is with her makes my heart twinge. I've never felt it before, not in the other times I saw them together. But now? It hurts. And I hate it.

"You okay?" he whispers down to me, as though sensing my pain.

And when our eyes connect, I shake my head. Because I refuse to lie.

He kisses my temple, knowing exactly why I'm hurting. Though I'm unsure if I could even mother a child in the first place, I hate that I'll never know. Hate that one more thing has been stolen from me, ripped from my body like the rest of me was.

"I'm right here. You're not alone anymore," he reminds me.

And in his arms, I know I'm not. I know that no matter what I go through, he'll always be there.

Reaching into his pocket, he retrieves his phone, staring at the screen for a few moments, concentrating deeply on something he's reading.

"What is it?" I ask him, curiously peeking at the screen to find out what has him so enthralled.

He grinds his jaw for a moment as he looks at me. And without saying a word, he shifts the phone so that I can see what's on it.

My pulse races as I see it: a man with brown hair and even darker eyes, the smirk on his mugshot so vile I want to reach inside and rip the skin off his face.

Everything in me wants to see him suffer, feel him take his last painful breath.

"What is this?" I murmur, even as everyone else around us happily enjoys the pieces of cake now lying across the large dining table.

"You know what it is. The question is, are you still in?"

We haven't discussed this at all. Not the murders, not the future when it comes to that part of our life, but I never intended to stop.

"I want to keep going." My lips curl at one side. "I want us to do it together."

He brushes my jaw with his knuckles and his eyes turn hooded. "Then let's go hunting, little wolf."

And so we do.

Forty-Six

KAYLA
ONE YEAR LATER

Our wedding is a month away, and I can't believe it's almost here. Who would've thought that two people like us would ever have what we do?

And sure, I'd be lying if I said things were perfect. Because this isn't some fairy tale. This is real life.

Adriel has been getting a little closer with his family. We see them more often now, but he's still reserved—except with Sophia, of course. The man is insane for that child.

He still struggles with everything he's been through, however. And who would blame him? Trauma isn't an imaginary thing we can brush aside for prettier, shiner things. But we're managing as best we can.

Though Adriel won't attempt therapy, I have. I found someone new. Someone I trust. Someone I can be completely open and honest with, and there's something beautiful about that.

I still go to school, still pursuing my dream of becoming an oncologist, while also working for Helping Hand. Assisting Jade with finding the girls work, prepping them for job interviews, that's something I do for me. It gives me purpose. Like I'm really doing good.

Leilani, one of the girls from Helping Hand, peeks at me from behind her shoulder, assessing herself in the long mirror in her room at the center. Her long black hair's up in a ponytail, a pantsuit on, something she's never worn before.

"Are you sure about this?" she asks with a grimace.

"Absolutely! You look amazing and professional."

She's only twenty and came to us a year ago after her mother sold her to a trafficker for drugs. When she was rescued by authorities, they brought her here. She was hesitant at first, not trusting a soul. Until I met her. We hit it off right away. And now she's about to go to an interview for a job as a cashier at a bank.

"You're smart, capable. I know you'll do amazing."

"And if I don't get it?" She fidgets with her sleeves, eyes downcast.

"Then you don't get it." I shrug. "There's always the next one."

She sighs. "You're right. Thank you for the suit."

"It was my pleasure."

My phone rings, and when I see Adriel's name, I can't help the way my heart beats.

"Hey, fiancé."

"Hey, baby. I'm here. Ready for lunch?"

"Sure! Give me a minute."

"Take your time." His voice oozes with that deep rasp that has me intoxicated already.

Hanging up, I look back at Leilani. "Please let me know how it goes. I'm just a phone call away if you need me."

She sucks in a big breath. "I'll be fine. I'll text you after."

"Okay." I get to my feet, giving her one last reassuring grin.

Then I'm out the door and in the elevator, taking it to the main floor. As soon as I cross past the exit and onto the street, I see him in his black SUV, rolling down the window.

Excitedly, I start toward him, and as I do, something catches the corner of eye. A large cardboard box just sitting at the corner of the building.

That's strange. Really strange.

My heart hammers, and I don't know why, but for some strange reason, I feel it calling to me.

I know how that sounds. Crazy Kayla. But what if it's a bomb?

Before I can even make it to it, Adriel is beside me. "Are you okay?"

"I don't know…" I mutter, staring at the container. "The box. It's just sitting there. Isn't that weird?"

He squeezes my hand. "Let me go see what's inside. Wait here."

"I'm coming with you." No way will I just stand around, and he knows me well enough by now to know that.

He gives me a harsh look, but I return it.

He rolls his eyes and shakes his head in frustration. "You're infuriating."

I let out a laugh.

Together, we head toward it, but the closer we get, the more fearful I become. My throat thickens, the air around stirring like it knows something I don't.

Whatever's inside that box is dangerous.

With my heart in my throat, anxiety ebbing through my veins, we make it that one final step until…

"Oh my God," Adriel coughs out. "What the…"

My trembling hand meets my mouth as I stare at a sleeping baby wrapped in a simple, thick white blanket, a paper there beside him.

I don't even know if it's a boy. But something tells me it is.

Snapping out of my shock, I reach in and pick up the child, who looks only days old, if I had to guess. An ache lumps in my throat as I stare at him, small mouth moving while in deep sleep, not bothered by anything in the world.

"We have to get him inside and have Jade call someone," I whisper, afraid to wake him.

But maybe we can keep him.

The thought is insane, of course, but when his tiny fist grabs a chunk of my hair and doesn't let go, my heart only wants him that much more.

Adriel senses my emotions, gathering me close to him.

"He is awfully cute." He chuckles under his breath.

"Do we even know it's a he?" I ask.

"I have no idea." The deep, raspy sway of his voice has me wondering what having a child with him would be like.

Could we even do that? Could we do the things we do? Kill and be parents through it all?

We both continue to watch this little person while I hold him protectively.

Won't let the monsters get you, I promise.

Adriel gathers the paper left abandoned in the box. "Let's go in and see if Jade knows who may have left him here."

"Okay." I hold the baby closer.

I've come to terms with not having a child. Closed that chapter of my life. There was nothing there but pain.

We considered adopting, but I didn't want to. I wanted to have one of my own. But now, with this little one in my arms, I wonder if that chapter is really closed.

We make it into the elevator, and while we ride up, A opens the folded piece of paper and reads it.

His name is Jameson. He was loved for two whole days. but I couldn't keep him. So love him for me. Love him like his mother did. Because he deserves that.

—N

He folds the note back up and connects his eyes to mine while my heart breaks, eyes misting at the pain this woman must've felt at giving up her own child. What it took to be that selfless.

As the doors open, we stride out together and straight to Jade's office. She's gonna call Child Protective Services, and they're gonna take him. We'll never see him again.

I fight the pain building behind in my throat. But the longer his hand stays clasped around the thick strands of my hair, the harder it gets. He hasn't relented, like he's fighting to stay with me just as hard as I am to keep him.

Tears stream down my face at the thought of letting go of this child I only just met. It makes no sense. Yet it also does.

"Kayla…" Adriel grabs my forearm, halting me. "You want him, don't you?"

I nod, my chin trembling. "Is that stupid? I mean, assuming we even can. He could have a family. A father out there who wants him. They could say we aren't qualified to adopt him. But…but I wanna try."

Blinking back the tears, I stare at the baby once more, knowing deep down that he's meant to be ours.

"Kayla?" Jade walks out of her office, only a few feet in front of us. "Whose baby is that?" Her attention travels between us.

"We found him in a box outside," Adriel explains, handing her the note.

She reads it quickly. "Oh my God. I don't think it's anyone from here." Her brows stich as she looks fondly at the child. "Come inside my office. We'll call social services and figure this out."

We head into her office, and I settle on the sofa.

"My goodness," Jade gushes. "He really is holding on tightly to you."

"He is, isn't he?" I smile sadly, knowing our time together is limited.

"You look good with a baby in your arms," she tells me, affection fastened to her features.

"Do you think they'd let us adopt him?" Adriel asks, completely taking me aback.

Jade's eyes widen. "Well, the head person at the agency is a good friend, and assuming no one claims him, I don't see why you guys couldn't be first on the list. You did find him." She grins.

He nods, his eyes gleaming as he looks at me.

"Are you sure?" I ask my fiancé.

His hands reach out for the baby, and slowly, I unclench the boy's fist from my hair and hand him to Adriel.

Staring down at him, Adriel looks lost, yet also like he's found something that means much more than he's ever known.

"I'm sure." His mouth twitches. "With everything I've been through, the way I was left at the hands of people who never knew how to love, I want his life to be different. I want him to have more." He gazes at me and smiles. "And I think we can be the people who give him that. So, what do you think, baby bird? Want to make this life of ours even crazier?"

I take his hand and hold it tightly. "I do. I want all my crazy days with you."

ADRIEL
SIX MONTHS LATER

Holding my son, Jameson, in my arms while Kayla makes us lunch, I wonder what the hell happened to the man I once was. The one who didn't know how to love or how to touch another human being. Yet, over the time I've been with Kayla and now our boy, I don't know how else to describe what I feel except love. They've been my purpose, my redemption. A calling in life I never knew I needed.

And for all the bad days I've endured, I've had many good ones. Those days are the ones I hold on to.

After we took Jameson home the night we found him, we fostered him for a couple of months until we were able to officially adopt him.

Jameson Quinn.

Though I'm still working on the dynamics of my relationship with my family, I chose to take a step in the right direction and change my last name to that of my father. I'm building my relationship with my parents, brick by brick. Though it's not easy, we're getting there.

They often babysit at their place while Kayla and I go on our dates—and usually, by dates, I mean slaughtering someone and watching his body burn in our furnace. Some things never change, I guess. I don't think they ever will.

My company is still very active, too. I even had Michael update his tech with a retina scanner. He did like this little addition, considering how easy it was for me to penetrate his system.

Staring at my wife while she carries over two plates with

roasted potatoes and cheeseburgers she made, I wonder who I'd be if I'd never met her. How dreary and dead my life would really still be. Living in hate. Now all I have is love.

I place our son in the bassinet beside me while he coos, and I take the plates from her, lowering them on the table.

Scooping her up, I place her on my lap. "Thanks for this."

My lips land softly on the corner of hers.

"It's just lunch." Her mouth slants up and she holds my face in her palm.

"I don't mean the food, Kayla. I mean all of this. Our life. You. This boy. Everything. You don't know how truly lost I was before you came along."

"I do know." Her thumb brushes the stubble across my jaw. "Because I was lost too."

The deeper I stare at my wife, the harder my heart beats and the more I want to say the words I've never said out loud.

"What is it?" she asks, stealing all my breaths away.

"I just wanted to tell you…"

"Yeah?"

"I wanted to tell you that I love you, little wolf."

"Wh-what?" She chokes up, tears forming in her eyes like raindrops. "Can…can you say that again?" she whispers on a cry.

It breaks my heart to know how desperately she needed to hear those words. And from now on, I plan on telling her how much I love her for the rest of my life.

"I love you, baby. I'll love you until my heart no longer beats, and even after that, because what I feel for you is stronger than anything I've ever known."

She sighs. And tenderly, her lips fall to mine, and she kisses me passionately and with promises of a future that is now ours.

Rising to my feet, I carry her out onto the sofa, strip off her clothes along with mine, and show her just how much I love her with my body the way I love her with my heart.

KAYLA
NINE YEARS LATER

"Tell me about the first time you were taken," my therapist asks.

Nowadays, that question doesn't scare me anymore. If anything, answering it is freeing. It's how I know my trauma doesn't control me anymore. The memories of those days don't make me cry or scream.

I still recoil when I remember certain details. But I accept them. I don't want to run from them like I once did. I embrace my trauma like a long-lost child who needs my comfort.

Looking straight at Dr. Stein's kind eyes, I tell her about that day. I recall every vivid detail that still rings true in my head: the way my friends screamed, the blood, the gunfire. It's all there, living in my head when I choose to play it.

She listens like she always does, recalling those days something

I'm used to by now.

I've come a long way since then. And sure, life hasn't been easy. There were dark days for both Adriel and me, days we thought we'd never wake from. But we have always been stronger together. And with Jameson, things have only become better.

He taught the both of us what it meant to nurture and love. He guided us out of those darkened days when our hurt was great enough to suffocate us. We loved him more than either of us ever knew we were capable of.

But after we brought him home, we decided that was it for us. Too much of a good thing scared us both, I think. How much good could people like us get before things went wrong? Before the beautiful turned to ugly? So we never adopted another child, and we're completely fine with that.

Rising to my feet, I start to head home, my session coming to an end.

"Same time next week?" I grin.

"I'll be here. Great work." She smiles proudly.

I've been with her all these years. Dr. Stein knows everything about me. Well, almost everything. There are still things only Adriel and I will know.

Getting in my car, I head back to my family, done with work already. Adriel and I have a date planned tonight. We can definitely use it.

I can't wait to run home to take a long shower and get ready for a fun night with my husband.

It's going to be the most fun we've had in a while.

ADRIEL

"I'm way too old for a babysitter." Jameson crosses his arms, his green eyes almost the same color as mine.

I laugh at that. What are the chances of us adopting a child who'd have something so similar to me? But his eye color began to change when he was an infant, and the green stayed.

"Well, it's a good thing I'm your grandpa and not your babysitter." My father glances at me, hiding a grin, finding Jameson's sulking incredibly enjoyable.

Mom shakes her head from beside him. "We can do whatever you want, honey. Order some pizza, watch a movie."

"I guess that sounds okay." He shrugs.

"My goodness, what happened to my sweet grandson who would run to me when he was five and beg me to read to him?"

"I'm old now, Grandma." He smiles. Finally, we got a smile.

My father pops his eyes. "If you're old, what does that make me?"

"I don't think it would be very polite of me to answer that." Jameson peeks up at me with amusement, and I shake my head, suppressing the laugh daring to rise.

Our son has definitely been going through his preteen phase a lot earlier than we had hoped.

"Get your little knucklehead self over here!" My father gets up and grabs him off the sofa and flips him upside down while Jameson laughs and Mom gasps.

"You need to be careful with your back, Pat," she tsks.

"Don't you worry, love. I've still got it."

He winks at her, and she rolls her eyes at me.

Things between us have improved throughout the years. It started slowly, and with every brick we added, the foundation became stronger until the past was left there, where it could die.

My parents have been great with watching Jameson when we

needed them, and I liked having to get to know them both.

I hear the front door open at my parents' place and instantly know it's my wife. That single word still causes my heart to rustle and my blood to warm. Because that woman has been my endgame since the moment we met. Now she's saving lives, an oncologist like she once dreamed of.

As soon as she steps into the den and our eyes connect, my pulse quickens.

Hi, babe, I mouth, and her lips spread into a wide grin.

"Hi, Mom!" Jameson instantly jumps to his feet and wraps his arms around her, turning into the once-small child who'd crawl into our bed when he had a nightmare.

"Hey, sweetheart. How was your day?" She kisses his forehead.

"It was okay. Kinda bummed you guys are leaving."

She cups his face and lifts it up to meet her eyes. "Tomorrow, I promise we'll do something just us three. You get to pick. Okay?"

"Really?"

She nods. "Right, Dad?" Her gaze mounts to mine.

"That's right, buddy."

Satisfied, he rushes back to my parents.

My feet move of their own accord until I'm beside her, my arm curling around her back. I draw her temple to my lips and kiss her there.

"I love you, beautiful," I whisper.

"Don't say that with your parents present," she breathes hoarsely while Jameson turns on the TV.

"All I said was that you're beautiful." My palm lands on her ass, and I squeeze through the tight red dress she's wearing.

She went to our penthouse in the city to get changed first before she got here. It was closer than going to our house, the same one I lived in when I first met her. It's where we all live now.

"Maybe don't sound like that when you say it," she scolds quietly as my mother glances at us curiously.

"Maybe I should've said how badly I want to bend you over that sofa and fuck you raw until your pussy's dripping on the floor with my cum. How does that sound, Dr. Quinn?"

"Jesus Christ…" She shuffles uncomfortably.

I chuckle, leaving a kiss on the beating pulse beneath her neck.

"Well, we should get out of here," I tell my parents. "We'll pick him up first thing tomorrow morning."

Mom waves a hand in the air and scoffs. "Take your time. Enjoy each other. We'll be here."

"I'll definitely be enjoying you," I rasp against the shell of her ear.

"Okay, and on that note…" Her voice goes all high and croaky, making me laugh again.

"Yeah, we'll be going now. My wife is getting hungry, aren't you?"

Her cheeks go pink. "Yep. Starving."

She grins awkwardly while my parents knowingly laugh, causing her face to grow redder. Grabbing my hand, she practically drags me out of there.

"Better behave," I warn Jameson, who rolls his eyes.

"Always do, Dad."

"Good boy."

Mom waves right before we disappear down into the foyer and out the door.

As soon as we are inside my car, I grab her jaw and kiss her, my hand sliding up her dress, finding her bare. "I'm gonna enjoy tearing up this pussy after we're done."

She nips my bottom lip so hard she almost draws blood. Her eyes turn hooded, a darkness there I've always enjoyed.

"Can't wait."

We arrive at a lounge on the Upper West Side, my wife sitting at the bar, long legs crossed as she chats up a man. With a glass of water in hand, I watch her flirting, her long, manicured fingers coyly touching the top of his hand while I think of ways to kill him.

She starts to get up, her lips spreading into a smile, and he grabs her hand. She flinches, but fights it. When they pass me, her eyes connect with mine before they leave together.

I drop a one-hundred-dollar bill on the table and walk out behind them, following them close enough just in case he tries something. But he's not paying attention. Too drunk and sloppy to know what's about to happen.

He doesn't have a car, but I do, and Kayla has the keys.

He almost trips on his feet, but she steadies him. He's going to want to call a cab for them so he can take her back to his place.

But see, we have better plans.

Bale Tucker has no idea the hell that awaits him.

"My car is right here," Kayla tells him, and I hear everything from my earpiece.

"You…you sure you wanna drive?" he grumbles.

"Of course. I haven't had much to drink."

In fact, she hasn't drunk at all. She makes me proud. The way she handles herself every time we do this.

I made sure all the cameras in the lounge and the surrounding area stopped working. Whoops. Malfunctions are a bitch, aren't they?

It has been a couple of months since the last time we had a date like this. And shit, it makes my cock hard seeing her hungry for what's about to happen.

Things got a little complicated after Jameson, but thanks to my parents helping us and sometimes my brothers, we've managed to continue the work we started to do together many years ago. Of course, they have no idea the things we actually do on our dates. And they'll never know.

Bale gets into my SUV, and the instant Kayla closes her door, I hop into the back.

"Hey, who—who are—"

As soon as those words leave him, I plunge the syringe full of sleeping meds right into the side of his neck.

She grins at me from the rearview mirror. "Wanna drive?"

"No, little wolf." I lean back into my seat. "This is all you."

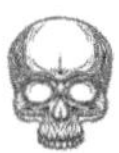

"Wakey, wakey, fucker."

The edge of my knife glides down his now-bare torso, his hands and feet unbound just the way we like it.

"Wha—who…who are you two?" His words die in his throat as his pupils dilate, the remnants of the alcohol vanished, replaced by pure adrenaline.

His wild eyes jump between Kayla and me, a blowtorch in her grasp. Kayla flips a switch, and the fire comes to life before his eyes. He trembles as she leans in, her face upturned with excitement.

"We're your worst nightmare." She glances back at me and laughs. "You can call us Kadriel."

I chuckle. Haven't heard that one in a while. Sophia is older now and has abandoned adorable nicknames for boys, much to the disappointment of my brother. He still sees her as his little girl. Who can blame him? I see her the same way I once did when I'd watch her play soccer, stealing my heart in the way she did.

It's unfortunate, though, that the boys that surround her don't quite know how insane her family truly is. Pretty sure they don't want to find out, either.

"Please!" the man begs. "Please let me go. Whatever I did, I'm sorry."

"Now, why would you think you did anything wrong, Bale?" She nears the torch to his face, and he recoils. "Is it your guilt talking?"

"No!" He shakes his head. "You're crazy! I—I didn't do anything to anyone."

Kayla straightens herself and peers at me from behind her shoulder. "Turn it on."

With my cell already in hand, I let the video play, letting him see it.

"No!" a woman screams. "Please, please, no!"

As soon as his eyes zero in on her, terror fills his face.

"Recognize it?" I spit between clenched teeth.

"H-h-how?"

With my anger boiling, a humorless chuckle rumbles out. "That's one thing about the dark web. You should be careful who you show your videos to."

I witness the instant he finally understands.

"That's right. I'm DarkDevil65."

My nostrils flare, my hand tightening around the phone as the woman continues to scream, begging him for mercy until he stabs her, over and over until her eyes are lifeless. It was easy to track him after that. It's how we find them now.

The world is a sick place, and we both have made it our mission to continue to do what we can to fix that.

His eyes narrow, a snarl now replacing that innocent act he was pulling. "You can't hurt me. I can just get up and walk out of here."

His laugh is just a front. He's scared.

"Go ahead." Kayla steps back on the plastic tarp beneath us.

Our basement is about to look like a bloodbath, but we've always enjoyed cleaning it up together.

He starts to get to his feet, and I hand her the knife while she passes me the torch. It's then he jumps all the way up and rushes for the door.

We both stand there with our arms crossed, watching the man struggle to open it, but it's already been locked.

With his chest rising in quick succession, he slowly faces us. But we're already right in front of him.

"Burn in hell, Bale." Kayla sinks her knife in his gut over and over until he's barely clinging to life.

But before he dies, I turn the torch on and hand it to her. I come to stand behind her, my hands rolling up and down her hips as she nears the flame to his eye. She's going to torture him before he burns in our furnace. It's the least we can do for all the women he's killed.

His strangling scream is the last thing we hear, both of his eyes burnt, as I grab the torch from her hand and shut it off, pitching it to the floor.

Her breaths turn erratic as I fling her around and capture her lips with mine. Desperately pushing her body up against the wall, my hands in her hair, I kiss her, needing her right here.

She groans, her hands yanking up my dress shirt, quickly undoing the buttons while I work her zipper down, lowering the dress off her body until it pools at her feet.

Wrenching back, I stare at my wife, the absolute definition of perfection. My fingertips glide over a pebbled nipple.

"I'll never know why you chose me, but I'll always be grateful that you have."

Her palm clasps my face, emotions writhing in her gaze. "Loving you was never a choice, Adriel. My heart knew who you were even before I did."

"Kayla, fuck…" I slant my forehead to hers. "You're everything, baby bird."

My fingers trace down her hip until they're slipping inside her warm and wet cunt. She bites her lower lip, brows knitting as I twist her long hair around my wrist and yank her head back.

Her panting grows as I play with her clit, rolling my thumb over it, wanting inside her.

"Promise to make it hurt?" she whispers, an unsatiated need in her eyes that I'm about to erase.

Gradually, I thrust two fingers inside her to my first knuckle, her pussy already wet and willing.

"Yes." I brush my lips with hers. "And I promise to love you through every moment of it."

And when she cries out my name, I keep that promise until we're both sweaty, spent, and completely insane for one another.

Until our very last breath.

Thanks for Reading!

Thank you for reading *SAVAGE WOUNDS*!

Up next is the Quinn family. This will be a brand-new series in the same world! Book 1 is titled *RUTHLESS SAVAGE* (*Savage Kings* Series #1)! It's an age gap bodyguard romance between Devlin & Eriu!

Playlist

- "Never Forget" by Kendra Dantes
- "It's a Long Way Down" by Katie Garfield
- "And So It Begins" by Klergy
- "Looking Glass" by Roses & Revolutions
- "Bad Behavior" by Klergy feat. Erin McCarley
- "How Villains Are Made" by Madalen Duke
- "No Rest for the Wicked" by Klergy
- "Animal" by MILCK
- "No F.E.A.R." by Madalen Duke
- "Who Do You Want" by Ex Habit
- "You Belong to Me" by Cat Pierce
- "Monster" by MILCK
- "Walking on the Ceiling" by Class of 88
- "Hostage" by Billie Eilish
- "Rescue My Heart" by Liz Longley
- "Dream" by Bishop Briggs
- "One Wrong Move" by Power-Haus feat. Klergy and Lloren
- "Fight for Survival" by Klergy
- "When the Party's Over" by Billie Eilish
- "Certain Things" by James Arthur feat. Chasing Grace
- "Worthy of Love" by Luca Fogale
- "You Say" by Lauren Daigle
- "Addicted to Love" by Skylar Grey
- "I Know Your Secrets" by Katie Garfield

- "As We Fall" by Klergy feat. Katie Garfield
- "Magic" by Kelly Clarkson
- "Be the One" by James Arthur
- "I Guess I'm in Love" by Clinton Kane
- "Without Fear" by Dermot Kennedy
- "Morally Gray – Nation Haven Edition" by April Jai feat. Nation Haven
- "Happiness Is a Butterfly" by Lana Del Rey
- "Nothing Breaks Like a Heart" by Mark Ronson feat. Miley Cyrus

Fragile Hearts Series

1. *Fragile Scars*
2. *Fragile Lies*
3. *Fragile Truths*
4. *Fragile Pieces*

Cavaleri Brothers Series

1. *The Devil's Deal*
2. *The Devil's Pawn*
3. *The Devil's Secret*
4. *The Devil's Den*
5. *The Devil's Demise*

Messina Crime Family Series

1. *Sinful Vows*
2. *Cruel Lies*
3. *Twisted Promises*
4. *Savage Wounds*

Savage Kings Series

1. *Ruthless Savage* (Coming May 2nd, 2024)

2. *Brutal Savage* (Release TBA)
3. *Wicked Savage* (Release TBA)
4. *Filthy Savage* (Release TBA)

Standalone

1. *Shattered Secrets*

For Lilian, a love of writing began with a love of books. From *Goosebumps* to romance novels with sexy men on the cover, she loved them all. It's no surprise that at the age of eight she started writing poetry and lyrics and hasn't stopped writing since.

She was born in Azerbaijan, and currently resides in Long Island, N.Y. with her husband, three kids, and a dog named Gatorade. Even though she has a law degree, she isn't currently practicing. When she isn't writing or reading, Lilian is baking or cooking up a storm. And once the kids are in bed, there's usually a glass of red in her hand. Can't just survive on coffee alone!

Lilian would love to connect with you!
Email: lilanharrisauthor@gmail.com
Website: www.lilanharris.com
Newsletter: https://bit.ly/LilianHarrisNewsletter
Signed Paperbacks: https://bit.ly/LHSignedPB
Facebook: www.facebook.com/LilianHarrisBooks
Reader Group: www.facebook.com/groups/lilianslovlies
Instagram: www.instagram.com/lilianharrisauthor
TikTok: www.tiktok.com/@lilianharrisauthor
Twitter: www.twitter.com/authorlilian
Goodreads: https://bit.ly/LilianHarrisGR
Amazon: www.amazon.com/author/lilianharris

www.ingramcontent.com/pod-product-compliance
Lightning Source LLC
Chambersburg PA
CBHW071751310726
48976CB00001BA/89